Prague Tales

Prague Tales

Jan Neruda

Translated by Michael Henry Heim
Introduction by Ivan Klíma

Chatto & Windus
LONDON

This edition first published 1993
1 3 5 7 9 10 8 6 4 2

First published in Czech as *Povídky malostranské* in 1878

English translation copyright © Michael Henry Heim 1993
Introduction copyright © Ivan Klíma 1993

The publishers gratefully acknowledge
the financial assistance of the
Central and East European Publishing Project.

First published in the United Kingdom in 1993 by
Chatto & Windus Limited
Random House, 20 Vauxhall Bridge Road, London SW1V 2SA

Random House Australia (Pty) Limited
20 Alfred Street, Milsons Point, Sydney,
New South Wales 2061, Australia

Random House New Zealand Limited
18 Poland Road, Glenfield
Auckland 10, New Zealand

Random House South Africa (Pty) Limited
PO Box 337, Bergvlei, South Africa

Random House UK Limited Reg. No. 954009

A CIP catalogue record for this book
is available from the British Library

ISBN 0 7011 4483 1

Printed in Great Britain by
Mackays of Chatham PLC, Chatham, Kent

Contents

Contents

Introduction

I happened to be in London in August 1968 at the time of the Soviet invasion – that is, I was in my favourite foreign city and a country I greatly admire – yet I decided not to stay. I remember justifying my decision to return to Prague with a comment that must have sounded absurd: most of London's street names have no associations for me.

It was not absurd to me. We visit any number of cities in our lives. We have walked through thousands of streets, seen all kinds of sights. We are inveterate tourists. Yet home is still the place where the streets and buildings have more to say to us than the eye of any foreigner can perceive.

Neruda Street is not only the most beautiful street in Prague; it has every reason to bear our author's name. The entire district of Malá Strana – indeed, all Prague, or, rather, its shape and history in the not so distant past, the spirit of the place – comes down to us largely through Neruda's words and images.

Not that the images are necessarily positive. Having returned to Prague after the invasion, I was often called in for questioning by the police. The first time I went bearing the opening sentence of Neruda's *Police Tableaux* in mind: 'Above the rear of Prague's Bartholomew Street Police Headquarters, a run-down, destitute, gloomy place . . .' A century after Neruda's death, Police Headquarters is still in the same run-down, gloomy street, and that first time – and many times thereafter – I found a peculiar sort of comfort in the idea that the premises have retained something of the old Austrian monarchy, that is, of the days of Neruda.

Why is it that while in the twentieth century we Czechs have enriched world literature with a number of major talents, so little is heard and known of our nineteenth-century writers?

Czech literature evolved from its medieval origins along the same lines as most European literatures, and by the seventeenth century it had given the world a true genius in the person of John Amos Comenius, author of *Labyrinth of the World and Paradise of the Heart* and one of the most important European philosophers of education. However, political developments during and after the Thirty Years' War caused a sharp break in the evolution of the Czech state and Czech culture. Comenius died in exile, a fate he shared with a large number of the intellectuals and noblemen of the time. For the next hundred and fifty years the centre of Czech political, social and therefore cultural life shifted from Prague to Vienna, and the Czech Lands underwent a gradual process of Germanisation. The Czech element declined, above all in urban areas, and Czech was reduced to a language of the countryside.

Paradoxically, the revival of Czech national and linguistic awareness came about under the influence of German philosophy, and in particular of Johann Gottfried Herder's late eighteenth-century theory of the nation as the most natural social construct and of language as the natural manifestation of a nation's genius. The first generation of national reformers consisted chiefly of scholars. They sought to reinvigorate the language, compile grammars and dictionaries, and translate certain world classics into Czech. The second generation, which dates from the beginning of the nineteenth century, included writers whose goal was to use the newly revived language as a vehicle for their own works. In fact, however, they were more patriotic dilettantes than creative artists. They came mainly from provincial, plebeian backgrounds, the first in their families to receive an education. Moreover, they were still very few in number, as was the audience they could expect to read their texts.

Who wished to read Czech at the time? Who, indeed, was able to? Apart from a handful of enthusiastic teachers, priests and remnants of the Czech nobility, the Czech reading public consisted more often than not of the simplest of countryfolk interested in such popular reading materials as calendar texts, morally uplifting tales and comedies or farces. Any poetry they might have read bore the stamp of folklore or the broadside. In other words, it was a time of less than gifted writers and less than demanding readers, the latter holding back the former rather than spurring them on to creative heights.

Naturally enough, literature gave rise to literary criticism, but the critics, coming from the same narrow circle as the writers, wrote with the impassioned dilettantism of the literature they set out to judge. Enthralled by the mere fact that a writer used Czech – especially to translate such great works as *Paradise Lost* or the plays of Aristophanes and Shakespeare – they tended to be fulsome in their praise. The critics, then, did as little as the readers to encourage the development of talent and genuine works of literature. When the first true poet appeared among them, they not only failed to appreciate him; they thoroughly lambasted him. Thus, at a time when Goethe, Balzac, Stendhal, Dickens, Shelley and Gogol were all active – that is, two hundred years after Shakespeare, one hundred years after Swift – Czech critics were celebrating run-of-the-mill authors of the lowest of popular genres.

Yet the first two generations of the Czech reformers did make certain inroads. First, they managed to bring the all but moribund Czech language back to life, enrich it with a number of classics of world literature, and thereby make at least an indirect statement about what constitutes a truly creative work. They also succeeded in making part of Czech society aware of what it means to be Czech and in greatly increasing the numbers of those willing to speak and think in Czech and therefore read and study the language.

One of the major tools of this consciousness-raising process was the press, the sole mass medium of the day (if a circulation of several thousand can be called a 'mass' medium). The reformers attached particular importance to it, hoping it would both propagate the ideas they so fervently advocated and educate a public they – only too rightly – found backward, stagnating on the periphery of Europe. Given that the Czechs had no state of their own and that Parliament met in Vienna (where the political life of the empire was to all intents and purposes concentrated), the press represented the only tribune where writers, poets and politicians might formulate their views, objectives and demands.

Thus, the mid-nineteenth century – to be more precise the early 1860s, when the political situation became more liberal – saw the rise of a series of political, cultural, literary and 'family' periodicals, and most recognised literati considered it their patriotic duty to contribute to them. This was the time that established the Czech tradition of viewing writers and even poets as more than literary personalities, as political personalities, creators of national policy, potential leaders. That this tradition has continued into the twentieth century is clear from the life and works of perhaps the greatest Czech writer of the century, Karel Čapek, and from the fact that at the very end of the century a writer, Václav Havel, has been deemed worthy of serving as head of state.

One did not stick one's neck out in early nineteenth-century Czech society. For proof we have only to look at the tragic ends of Neruda's immediate predecessors. Karel Hynek Mácha, a Romantic poet who bears comparison with Europe's finest, died at the age of twenty-six, unrecognised, misunderstood, alone. Karel Havlíček Borovský spent his last years in exile, abandoned and all but forgotten, returning home only to die; he was thirty-five. Božena Němcová died at the age of forty-two, ostracised by 'high society' and reduced to such poverty that literary historians have speculated that the cause of death was sheer exhaustion.

Jan Neruda, who was born in 1834, belonged to the next generation, and his fate and the fate of his kind was less dramatic, less tragic. His father was an ex-serviceman and a remarried widower. Neruda recalled late in life, with characteristic sarcasm,

> Father *had to* remarry because his first marriage failed to produce anything, as we say, particularly distinctive . . . He may have carried about a marshal's cane in his pack, I don't know, but he certainly never took it out. For having helped to defeat Napoleon at Leipzig and occupy France as far as Lyon (yes, really!) he was granted the position of porter or supplier at various barracks,

which position rewarded the honest man so richly
that my resourceful mother had to work here and
there as a servant to keep them solvent.

Like most Czech writers of the time, therefore, he was
of humble origin, but unlike them (with the exception
of Mácha) he was born in Prague. What is more, he
was born in the magnificent, quintessentially Prague-
like part of the city, Malá Strana (literally, the Small
Side), amid the stately mansions of the aristocracy and
the solid dwellings of the craftsmen, tradesmen and
army of officials without which the administration of
both Bohemia and its capital was unthinkable. He
grew up in what is now Neruda Street. Because it
climbs from Malá Strana Square to the Castle, it was
the route Czech kings took to their coronations and
the scene of numerous processions. Neruda was thus
a true product of the city, a Prague patriot, and he
immortalised his beloved Malá Strana and its denizens
in his finest work.

Poor though his family was, Neruda received a
decent education – in Prague's German schools. Moreover, he received his first experience as a journalist on
the German paper *Tagesbote aus Böhmen*. Ironically,
Neruda's generation of writers, which set itself the
goal of freeing not only Czech literature but Czech
society in general of its German yoke, found its main
inspiration in the stalwarts of *Junges Deutschland*, the
Young Germany movement: Heinrich Heine, Ludwig

Börne, Karl Gutzkow and Jean Paul were the favour-
ites.

Still, at the age of thirteen he began attending lec-
tures on the Czech language ('We sat there piously, as
if in church; we were in rapture, in bliss') and went
on to the finest Czech-language educational institution
of its day, the Akademické grammar school, a centre
of legendary teachers and – as the future soon proved
– no less legendary pupils. Only then did he start
writing his first poems and critical articles. There he
started writing his first poems and articles.

Later he studied law at his father's request, then
abandoned it in favour of philosophy. Although he
was unable to complete his studies for want of funds,
philosophy may not entirely have suited his active
nature. In any case, after trying to find a niche for
himself first as an official, then as a teacher, he turned
to the *Tagesbote* and was soon able to earn a living as
a Czech journalist.

Because he made his entry into Czech belles-lettres
with a volume of poetry (bearing the gloomy title of
Cemetery Flowers and the contents to match) and
because he subsequently published a long pamphlet
in verse and four more collections of poetry (a fifth
appearing posthumously), Neruda – an outstanding
writer of feuilletons and fiction – was known and
celebrated primarily as a poet. But remnants of the
Romantic tradition also played their part: the Roman-
tics placed poetry above all forms of literature and a
halo above the poet's head. Even the most

accomplished prose writer could mount Parnassus only as a poet.

One way of understanding a work of art is to seek out the sources that inspired it, and they in turn are connected with the creator's personality, traumas, interests, fate.

Working years ago on a study of Karel Čapek, who used Neruda as a model, I compared Čapek's life with what might seem the incomparably different lives of two writers roughly contemporary to him: Franz Kafka and Jaroslav Hašek. The only link I could find, in fact, was that none of them had a lifelong companion, none had a family life. Most of Kafka's works were stimulated by this lack; it sent Hašek from one Prague pub to the next or on endless walking tours through the countryside; it was one of the reasons why Čapek bound his life so tightly to that of the First Czechoslovak Republic.

Neruda's fate was quite similar, but while the causes of the other writers' lonely existence are not difficult to pinpoint (Kafka's fear of women compounded by the anxiety that marriage would prevent him from writing, Čapek's illness and Hašek's preference for male camaraderie), Neruda's bachelor existence, which weighed particularly heavily on him towards the end of his life, has no obvious explanation. There were a number of women in his life, and although he had what might be called two tragic loves (the first and possibly greatest love of his life was the well-known Czech novelist Karolina Světlá, who eventually refused to violate convention and leave a husband she did not love; the second died before Neruda could propose marriage), the others seemed to stymie him. After the age of forty he began to blame a series of illnesses for ageing him physically and psychically before his time. The only discernible motive for his solitude was a rather clinging relationship with his mother, whom he loved dearly and celebrated in some of his finest verse.

Be that as it may, there can be no doubt that he filled the lacuna in his emotional life with a love for the Czech people as a whole. He more or less said as much in a speech thanking friends for their kind words on the occasion of his fiftieth birthday:

> We often lament having no friends or too few. Why this lament? It is completely gratuitous. We need no other friends than work and a love for our country. Work is an honest friend: honour her and she will never leave you. Likewise our love of country: there can be no nation so low that such a love cannot raise it up to victory. Thus the Czech nation, a nation of honest, tireless labour, will emerge victorious.

Here we find the values Neruda stood for: honest work, the concept of the nation, the basic principles of liberal democracy (for which he fought all his life), and finally the ideal of a socially just society (which led him over and over to bring the socially disadvan-

taged and their problems to the attention of his readers, but which he never allowed to erupt into the
revolutionary rabble-rousing or sink into the senti-
mental pathos of so many of his contemporaries).

For Neruda as for his time, however, the concept
of the nation took priority. He served it with his work,
and parts of his journalistic and even poetic output are
marked by this bias. Not, however, the pinnacle of
his fictional output, the stories translated here as *Prague
Tales*.

Even though the tales are pure fiction, Neruda was
first and foremost a journalist or, to be more precise,
a practitioner of the very distinctive journalistic genre
known as the feuilleton. The feuilleton consists of a
short sketch reflecting everyday experiences and everyday concerns. It had its origins in France early in
the nineteenth century, but soon enjoyed enormous
popularity throughout Europe. Neruda cultivated it
with great tenacity, developing it, refining it, expanding its thematic boundaries. He used the feuilleton as
a vehicle for parliamentary reports, for book, theatre,
music and art reviews, for travel notes, feature stories,
miniature portraits of the famous and of vagabonds,
servant girls, draymen, beggars and pub crawlers, for
gossip columns, polemics and essays on current events
or the latest scientific advances.

Over the years he cultivated the persona of a
detached observer bringing together the most dispar-
ate of elements, their only link being his commentary,

the fact that he deemed them worthy of interest. The result was a fascinating collage still admirable for its diversity, caustic *aperçus* and unexpected juxtapositions. And because his goal was to instruct as well as entertain, he demonstrated a range of knowledge far beyond the journalistic norm. A series of feuilletons on the ballet, for example, includes scores of references to the history of dance from the classical period to the present, though here too aphoristic irony figures prominently. But he remains most effective and most lively for us in those passages where he is least literary, where he describes his native city and the people and mores of his time, giving free rein to his keen eye and wit.

Sharp observation and precise formulation were obsessions with Neruda, obsessions of which he was well aware. 'As my father lay dying,' he wrote in a letter to his first fiancée,

> I lay in a bed next to him, sleeping perhaps a bit too soundly for a son. At one point I awoke and saw he was nearing the end. I bent over him; he could scarcely breathe. I thought my heart would burst; my throat was so dry and tight I feared I would choke. Yet I kept studying how a man dies. You could never be happy with a devil like me.

What Neruda presents as a cynical confession is in fact proof of a writer's obsession – the desire to know and communicate or, rather, to know everything so as to communicate with the greatest degree of precision.

Journalism promotes stereotypes, and Neruda, who at certain points in his career published up to five feuilletons a week, was not beyond adopting a pose or stance that his readers enjoyed and had come to expect of him but that went against his principles, feelings or character.[1] This may explain why, as he grew older and more isolated, suffering not only debilitating physical ailments (at forty he had surgery for a malignant tumour) but deep depressions as well, he tried to maintain a smile in his articles no matter how biting or bitter their criticism. But it also shows how strong he was and how devoted to his work, his mission. (On the day he died, 22 August 1891, he wrote to an editor apologising for being late with an article – he was 'feeling poorly' – and only hours before his death he was fretting over what to give the editor in its stead.)

Neruda was without a doubt one of the major figures in nineteenth-century Czech society. He had an opinion on all its most basic issues, an opinion eagerly awaited by the reading public. Altogether he published 2,260 feuilletons, about ten thousand manuscript pages. They make up the largest segment of his collected works, which number forty-one ample volumes. Given the broad sweep of subject matter covered by the feuilletons, their diversity of genre is not surprising. It ranges from the essay or critical piece to reportage and the short story. The border between certain of the feuilletons included in his *Prague Tableaux* and certain of the *Prague Tales* is not easily established, nor indeed does it need establishing. Suffice it to say that by the mid-1870s, when *Prague Tales* appeared, Neruda was both the leading Czech 'political columnist' and a greatly admired poet. He had reached the age when writers are at the peak of their creative powers, yet his mother's death and the subsequent self-imposed isolation caused him great distress, and he felt the need to return to the halcyon days of his childhood – a time when everything lay open before him, when the most minor episodes could be construed as events and every chance encounter with the people and things of Malá Strana gave rise to fresh insights – and to write a book dealing with them, a book that turned out to be his only unified work.

Altogether, the *Prague Tales* represent the culmination of Neruda's experience as a writer – the experience of a keen observer of people and the details of everyday life, the experience of a poet and journalist who knows how to smile, but who also suffers with those who suffer around him; indeed the *Prague Tales* tower over all Czech fiction that came before them.

Journalism taught Neruda stylistic diversity and the value of a punch line, but it also made him realise that the best way to reach his readers was not by haranguing and preaching but by telling a story. And that is what he does. If he shows a preference for the first-person narrator, he does so to give his stories a greater sense of authenticity. In any case, his narrator is nearly always an onlooker merely recording what he sees. Moreover, the incidents he records are invariably anecdotal, that is, they provide only a short-term account of what are in fact long-term, deeply rooted problems. Thus, he tells of two men who sit year after year at the same table, linked only by their eerie silence, of a young woman betrayed by practical jokers or a young man betrayed by his pregnant beloved, of a shop-keeper and a beggar who battle against the prejudices of their conservative milieu. The tension between the apparently anecdotal nature of the stories and the undeniably tragic nature of the lives underlying them is one of the mainstays of Neruda's narrative art.

Realism was the prevailing school in Czech literature at the time, and for all his stylisation Neruda remains a Realist. What is new in *Prague Tales* is, on the one hand, its urban setting and, on the other, its author's refusal to impose a message, a moral. Critics were so perplexed that they responded with silence; readers were immediately taken with the work, and it has since been reprinted scores of times. To this day it is one of the most popular – and most read – works of Czech literature.

During my first visit to London, I sought out the places I knew from my beloved Dickens, and when I found the street where Mr Pickwick lived I felt – if only for the moment – at home. Read Neruda and visit Malá Strana in Prague and you too will feel at home.

Ivan Klíma

A Week in a Quiet House

1   In Night Clothes

We have the feeling we are in a completely enclosed space surrounded by sheer darkness. There is not the slightest chink to let in the night. The dark is so profound that if we imagined for an instant we saw something bright before our eyes, it would be nothing but the red nimbus of our thoughts.

When the senses are strained, they distinguish even the most minute signs of life. Our sense of smell informs us that the room is imbued with a grease-laden atmosphere, a jumble of effluvia: in the forefront we discern the odour of fir or pine wood, then tallow and lard, and lastly dried plums, cumin, brandy, garlic and the like. The tick of a clock strikes our ears – an old wall clock, most likely, with a long pendulum tipped by a thin and doubtless slightly twisted brass disc, for the pendulum occasionally falters in its monotonous recital and the disc gives a feeble quiver. But as even the faltering recurs at fixed intervals, it too forms part of the monotony.

Meanwhile, we hear sleepers breathing. We know there is more than one of them, because the sounds of their breathing intermingle, never quite falling together, one dying down while the other grows in intensity, one faltering like the pendulum of the clock while the other wheezes on. Then, from a different quarter, comes a sudden deep, stentorian breath, as if marking a new chapter of sleep.

Now the clock too takes a sudden whirring breath, and the pendulum seems to move more softly. One of the sleepers stirs, rustling the blanket; the wooden frame of his bed gives a creak.

The clock whirs again – once, twice, in quick succession – its voice rich and metallic. It is followed immediately – once, twice – by a dark-timbred cuckoo. The sleeper stirs again. From the sound of it he is sitting up in bed, removing the blanket. Now a foot grazes the edge of the bed; it swishes into a slipper; now both slippers are on. The figure stands and takes a few cautious steps. Then it stops, one hand groping along a wooden surface. Something rattles. A box of matches, no doubt.

A match scrapes several times; several puffs of phosphorescent smoke flare up. Then comes the sound of a stick splintering and the figure muttering. The scraping resumes, and at last a flame erupts and throws its light across a nightgown. Just as the flame seems ready to flicker, a bony old hand holds it up to a glass vessel of water and oil with a black wick floating on the surface in a cork. The wick lights up like a tiny star;

the match falls to the floor. The star suddenly grows larger, showing an elderly woman yawning and rubbing her sleep-filled eyes.

She is standing by a table next to a darkly varnished wood partition that divides the room in two. Since the light from the lamp does not reach beyond the partition, we see only a part of the room, but our sense of smell has not deceived us: we are in a grocery. The room clearly serves as both living quarters and shop. And as grocer's shops go it is stocked rather well, sacks of staples lining the floor, boxes and baskets stacked along the walls, and braids and clusters hanging from the ceiling.

The woman shivered in the chill of the night. She picked up the lamp and set it down on the counter next to some jars of fresh and clarified butter just below the scales and the strings of garlic and onions. Then she sat at the counter, drawing her knees to her chin, opened a drawer and took out a box containing threads, a tiny pair of scissors and miscellaneous scraps of material. She removed it all and delved to the bottom of the box, where some papers and books lay buried. Passing over the papers, which were covered with figures, she opened one of the books. It was a dream book, the 'great' dream book. Soon she was utterly absorbed in turning pages. She stopped and read a bit, gave a yawn, but went on reading.

All that could be heard from the other side of the partition now was the even breathing of a single sleeper; the second, awakened either by the noise or the glimmer of light, was stirring in his bed.

'What's going on there?' a wheezy old-man's voice suddenly grumbled.

The woman made no reply.

'Anything wrong, woman?'

'No, no. Stay in bed,' the woman answered with a yawn. 'I'm just cold.'

'Then what are you doing in there?'

'I had a dream about my poor dead father. I'd have forgotten it by morning. It was beautiful. Like nothing I've ever dreamed before. Lord, it's cold – and June, too!' She went back to her reading with a shake of the head.

There was a moment of silence.

'What time is it?' asked the voice from behind the partition.

'Past two.'

The breathing of the third sleeper was becoming less regular, the loud talk having disturbed his slumber.

'Come back to bed, will you, and let's go to sleep! All you can think of is your lottery!'

'Really, now! A person can't get a minute's peace here. Leave me alone and go to sleep.'

The breathing behind the partition ended in a mighty sigh: the sleeper in the third bed was now awake.

'That no-good son of mine stays out till midnight,' the old man went on, 'and two hours later I'm woken up by the lottery! What a life!'

4

'Leave me alone, will you? I work my fingers to the bone, and what do I get for it? Your lip, that's what. Well, how about trying it on your son for a change? I'm sick and tired of it all.'

'You try if you're so smart!' the man retorted. 'You try talking sense into that layabout.'

'What is it this time, Dad?' asked a young man's voice.

'Quiet! Not a word out of you, you layabout!'

'But I don't see – '

'There's nothing to see, you layabout!'

'But – '

'That's enough out of you, you hear?'

'Oh, he'll go on for ever,' said the woman, yawning again. 'Some son we've got there! A real comfort.'

'Son? He's no son! Stealing the best years of our lives!'

'Stealing in my sleep?'

'Not another word, you smart alec!'

'A real handful!'

'A real hooligan.'

'Layabout!'

The young man, still in bed, started whistling 'O Matylda!'

'Listen to that, will you! Making fun of us to boot!'

'God will send His wrath upon him,' said the woman, writing the numbers 16, 23 and 8 in chalk on the partition. 'We'll live to see it too, and then we can die in peace.' She put away the box, blew out the light and trudged back to bed. 'He'll rue the day, all right, but it will be too late . . . Will you stop it!'

The young man stopped whistling.

'You'll do anything to bring us back! Dig up our graves with a pin! With a pin, I tell you!'

'Forget your pins, woman, and go to sleep. I need my rest.'

'It's all my fault, of course. What have I done to deserve this, O Lord?'

'You'll be the end of me, the two of you!'

'Like father like son.'

'People are at their worst in the dead of night,' the young man observed.

'What's that?'

'Who knows? He's always got a wisecrack up his sleeve.'

'Let's tip the wardrobe over on him or throw him out – yes, throw him out on the spot!'

'Will *you* stop it now! This is hell on earth!'

The old man muttered something; the old woman muttered something back. The young man lay silent.

The muttering and sputtering went on for a time, then gradually died down. The old woman fell asleep; the old man twisted and turned a bit, then fell asleep as well. The young man intoned 'O Matylda' again, this time in a soft bumblebee hum, but fell asleep before reaching the end.

The pendulum swished on through the grease-laden air. There was no other sound but the breathing of the three sleepers. Their breaths intermingled, yet the sounds never quite fell together.

II   Most of the House Begins To Stir

The June sun had cast its rays on the courtyard for quite some time before the inhabitants began to stir. Despite the din of heavy carts reaching the courtyard through the passageway and over the roofs from the street, the first steps still reverberated as loudly as in a vault. One by one, as if each were waiting for her predecessor to disappear, a number of women emerged from the flats, bareheaded and dishevelled or with shawls drawn low over foreheads to shield sleepy eyes from the sun. Bedraggled servants all, they wore loosely fastened dresses and floppy, down-at-heel shoes, and carried jugs that were either empty or newly filled with milk.

Gradually things grew livelier. White curtains vanished from windows; a window opened here and there. Figures appeared, looking up at the sky and Petřín Hill and turning back to comment on the lovely day to other members of the household. People greeted one another on stairways and balconies with a 'Good morning'.

A tall man with a blotchy red face and unruly grey hair appeared in the first-floor window of the front part of the house near the street. Resting his weight on the window ledge, he leaned out so far that his shirt opened to reveal a powerful chest still wrapped in flannel despite the June sun. He glanced over at the window next door, but found its curtains drawn. Then he leaned back and said into the room, 'It's not yet seven.'

At that moment, however, the neighbouring window flew wide open, and another man, equally tall though younger, came into view. He had black hair carefully combed in a decent, sober manner that suggested it varied not an iota from one day to the next. His face was round and clean-shaven, yet some-how lacking in expression; his body was swathed in an elegant grey dressing gown. He was polishing the lenses of a pair of gold-rimmed spectacles with a yellow silk handkerchief. He breathed on the lenses one last time and wiped the mist away. Putting the glasses on, he turned in our direction. Behind the lenses his face, previously so expressionless, took on a more definite character, as is often the case with short-sighted people. It was a kindly face, the eyes shining with a cheery, affable glow, though there could be no doubt that the face had been looking out at the world for a good deal longer than forty years. And were we to look closely, we could be practically certain it was the face of a bachelor. The faces of priests and bachelors are recognisable even in mechan-ical reproductions.

The bachelor made himself comfortable in the window seat, which had a snow-white, exquisitely embroidered cushion. He gazed up at the blue sky and glanced over at the brilliant green of Petřín Hill, the jubilant morning mirrored in his face. 'The beauty of it!' he murmured. 'I really must get up earlier.'

All at once his eye fell on a second-floor window in the rear part of the house. Though shut, the window was clear and transparent, and he caught a glimpse of a woman's dress. The bachelor's smile brightened. 'Of course,' he murmured again, 'Josefinka is up and about in the kitchen.'

His right hand moved slightly, causing a ray of bright light to stream from the large gem on one of its fingers and bringing his attention back to his own person. He twisted the ring until the gem was firmly ensconced above the knuckle, gave his fine shirt cuffs a quick tug, and gazed with evident satisfaction at his plump, alabaster hands. 'There's no harm in their getting a bit of sun,' he murmured. 'It's perfectly healthy.' And he raised his right hand to his nose as if wishing to convince himself of his health by smelling it.

A door on the opposite balcony opened, and out came a pretty girl of eighteen or so. She was morning personified. Her figure was graceful and slender. The dark, thick curls cascading down her neck were caught up in a simple velvet ribbon. Her face was a perfect oval with bright blue, guileless eyes, rosy cheeks, a silken complexion and tiny dark-red lips – the whole giving a most charming impression, if not quite excluding the suspicion that certain features were less than classically regular. Yet where was the slight irregularity to be found? Surely not in the dainty, exquisite ears, ears made to be kissed, though adorned by only small, modest silver earrings. Apart from the earrings she wore no jewellery. True, a thin black band hung round her white neck, but whatever pendant may have hung from it lay hidden between her budding breasts. Her dress – bright, with narrow stripes – was fastened high at the neck; its simplicity of cut and colour had a charm all its own.

She was carrying a brown jug with a tin lid.

'Good morning, Josefinka!' a sonorous tenor voice called out.

'Good morning, Doctor!' Josefina replied, looking over at the window with an amiable smile.

'What have you got in the jug?'

'Beef broth. From yesterday. I'm taking it to Miss Žanýnka. She's not well.'

'Žanýnka? Can't say I'm surprised. It must be like a dungeon down there. From one year to the next she never so much as opens a window, and then there's that horrible dog. Barking and howling the whole night again. Time to call in the dog catcher.'

'How can you say such thing!' Josefina exclaimed. 'She'd go mad with grief!'

'What's wrong with her, anyway?'

'Age,' Josefina replied sadly on her way to the winding staircase.

'A kind soul, that Josefinka,' the Doctor said to himself, fixing his glance on the first landing and then, once she had passed it, on the entrance from the stairs into the courtyard.

Josefina crossed the courtyard, went up to one of the doors and tried to open it. It was locked. She rattled the handle and knocked on the door, but there was no sign of movement within.

'Rap on the window,' the Doctor advised from above.

'That won't help,' came a voice at the steps that led into the courtyard from the street. 'You've got to pound, not rap, and Josefinka here hasn't got it in her. Wait, let me have a go.' And in two bounds a twenty-year-old youth was down the steps and at Josefina's side. He was wearing a light grey summer suit, and his bare head was a mass of black ringlets; he had well-defined features and a lively eye.

'Yes, please do, Mr Bavor,' Josefina begged.

'First let's see what's under the lid,' the young man teased, reaching out in Josefina's direction.

'Hm!' said the Doctor from his station on high, but calmed down when he saw the girl dodge the young man lithely.

'I'll do my own knocking, then.'

But the young man was already standing by the window, drumming at it with his fingers. The only response was a shrill bark, after which all was quiet again. They waited a while, but when no further sign of life was forthcoming the young man moved over to the other window and pounded on the frame with all his might. This time the dog's bark was long and loud, but tapering off to a piercing wail.

'She'll be furious with us.'

'Never mind,' said the young man, banging again. Then he leaned his ear against the window frame and listened carefully. All he could hear was the dog whimpering.

Meanwhile, the racket had roused the entire house. The tall man with the blotchy red face looked out again, this time accompanied by the heads of two women, one middle-aged, the other young. The tall figure of Josefina's mother emerged on the balcony across the way; hobbling after her came the hunchbacked form of Josefina's ailing elder sister. Immediately below them stood a group of three people: a balding man, half-clothed, a woman about his age, also half-clothed, and a girl of nineteen or twenty, her body covered only by a petticoat and a carelessly draped shawl, her hair in curl papers.

There were also two plainly dressed women hurrying down the steps from the street.

'You stay in the taproom, Márinka!' the smaller of them, an agile figure, called back into the passageway. 'And don't let anybody in!'

In the other, taller woman we recognise our nocturnal interpreter of dreams from the previous chapter. Perhaps her crisp, white bonnet becomes her; perhaps all people look and are milder by the light of day. In any case, her whole appearance now seems perfectly pleasant.

'What's going on here, Václav?' she said to the young man.

'Miss Žanýnka seems to have died on us. I'll try knocking one last time.'

He pounded with all his might.

'It's no use, Mr Bavor,' the Doctor called out. 'You'll have to go for a locksmith. Quickly! I'll be right down.'

Young Bavor immediately disappeared.

Questions and answers resounded from all sides, everyone talking at once, though in subdued tones. The Doctor had barely appeared in the courtyard in his walking clothes and told the petrified Josefina she could put her jug down when young Bavor returned with an apprentice locksmith.

The lock was soon removed and the door no longer barred their way, yet for a moment they stood motionless. Finally Václav pulled himself together, stepped in bravely, and was followed at once by the Doctor, while the women crowded into the doorway.

The large room was dark and gloomy. The windows opening on to the courtyard and Petřín Hill were thickly curtained and let in only the dimmest trace of light. The air was stale, all must and mould. The ceiling was hung with large, black, dust-laden cobwebs, the grey walls with dark paintings wreathed by ancient, grimy, artificial flowers. There was no lack of implements, but they were all extremely old and outmoded and showed no sign of having been used for years. On the bed they saw two piteous, emaciated hands, a desiccated, hairless head sticking out from under a dirty yellow coverlet, and a pair of faded eyes staring glassily upwards. An ugly, shaggy old dog bounded from the headboard to the foot, barking desperately at the intruders.

'Quiet, Azor!' Václav said under his breath, as if afraid to inhale the air.

'She must be dead,' the Doctor said gravely, 'or the dog wouldn't be howling.'

'Yes, she's gone to meet her Maker all right,' Mrs Bavor stammered, a large tear running down her cheek, 'and may God forgive her her sins and us our iniquities. Pray for us, Mother of God!'

'When a wedding follows fast on a funeral,' the small innkeeper's wife said to a still petrified Josefina, 'the bride will have a happy marriage.'

From a deathly white Josefina flushed bright red, then grew pale again. She turned and withdrew without a word.

'The first thing to do is get the dog out of the way,' the Doctor said, moving back a few paces. 'We don't want it to bite anyone. It might have the dead woman's germs on its teeth.'

'That won't take long,' said Václav, advancing towards the corpse's frenzied guardian.

Even though the dog knew all the faces surrounding it, it grew more and more frantic. Barking vociferously, it bounded back to the head of the bed as Václav approached it with soothing words. He reached out to the coverlet with his left hand and just as the dog sprang to seize it he grabbed the animal with his right hand and hoisted it into the air. It struggled furiously, but Václav held it fast.

'Where shall I put him?' he asked. 'Mother, give me the key to our woodshed. I'll stick him in a box for the time being.' And off he went with the howling dog.

'So the poor old dog lady's dead, is she?' came a gravelly voice from the doorway. In the speaker we recognise the bald-headed man we saw on the balcony. His hairless pate is covered by a frayed and faded top hat, its shape testifying to the many years it has been out of style. The thin fair hair on his temples is combed horizontally towards his eyes. His cheeks consist of great folds of skin – as is so often the case with corpulent people who lose weight – each of them like a sack emptied after a journey. He has square shoulders, but a sunken chest and arms that dangle helplessly.

'Yes, she is.'

'Then into the chapel with her, and fast. We don't want a corpse in the house. Next thing you know we'll be paying for everything.'

'There's no need to worry,' said the Doctor, who had been rummaging through a box full of papers, to his landlord. 'The dear departed will take care of everything herself. She's clearly made all the necessary arrangements and was going through her papers only yesterday. Under this greasy wig here I found a document indicating she belonged to the Society of St Haštal and a booklet from the Strahov Benevolent

Society. So there's money for the funeral. She even has a requiem paid for.'

'And all on a pension of eighty guilders a year,' Mrs Bavor said, full of admiration. 'My son used to write out the dog lady's quarterly receipts.' It was clear the people used 'dog' as an objective epithet rather than a slur.

'She'll be getting about fifty guilders,' said the inn-keeper's wife, 'which means a fine pall for the coffin and a gilded tombstone.'

'What else did you find among her papers?' Václav asked, coming back into the room.

'Nothing important,' the Doctor answered, looking through them again. 'Private letters, by the looks of them. Dating back several decades.'

'Let me have them for a while, will you? It might be interesting to see what an old maid thought worth keeping. I'll take them up to the roof with me and read them there. Today's Monday, and what with the washing and the pea soup – somehow they always go together – the only place you can breathe around here is on the roof. A novelist needs to read everything, and I want to be a novelist. Besides, I've got time on my hands.' He turned to the landlord. 'I'm not due back at the office until Thursday, isn't that right?'

'Just make sure you don't lose any of them. I want them all back as they were.'

'But who's going to make the arrangements?' asked the landlord. 'Shouldn't you take charge, Doctor? *Denn diese Leute kennen's nicht.*'

16

'If my son didn't work in your office, I'd give you "don't know how",' Mrs Bavor muttered to herself.

'I suppose I'll have to,' the Doctor replied affably. 'Let's see. There's the Civil Registry and the Church Registry and the local rectory . . . But you go for the coroner, Mr Bavor, and bring the death certificate to my office as soon as he signs it.'

Václav hurried off obediently.

'And the two of us,' Mrs Bavor nodded in the direction of the innkeeper's wife, 'will wash the body and lay it out.'

'That's very good of you,' said the Doctor. 'I'll be off now.'

'I'll go with you.'

The men withdrew.

'A penny for your thoughts, Mrs Bavor.'

'Just thinking about the world.'

'What about that dream you had? You were going to tell me about it.'

'Yes, right. It was a beautiful dream! I dreamed that my poor dead father – he's been gone these twenty years, may he rest in peace – came to see me. Mother died before him, and he visited her grave every day till the day he followed her. He had an easy death. They loved each other like children. I remember watching them cry over us. It was during the French wars, when things were hard and they couldn't feed us . . .'

'What was his name?'

'Nepomuk, after the saint. Anyway, all of a sudden

there he was, standing in front of me, downstairs in the shop. Before I could ask him how he got there – he was white as a ghost – he gave me this armful of buns, big ones, twenty-three of them (twenty-three means luck) and said, "Time to go, I've been called up." Army recruitment, number eight, good times ahead. Then he turned and left.'

'Sixty-one. If he turned, that is.'

'Right. I'd completely forgotten. That makes sixty-one, twenty-three and eight.'

'Let's put the whole fifty guilders on them. It was such a lifelike dream. What do you say?'

'I don't see why not.'

'Think of what we'll win! And then your Václav and my Márinka – the pair they'll make!'

III   At Home with the Landlord

The time has come for me to give a clearer idea of my setting and characters. As for the latter, I trust that each will emerge as the week progresses; about the former, however, I hasten to point out that it is one of the quietest houses in Prague's ever so quiet Malá Strana, or Small Side. And while its construction is distinctive, it is not unique along the steep slope that is Spur Street. It extends back relatively far from Spur Street, which its simple façade faces; its rear windows look out over the deep cul-de-sac of St John's Lane.

The slope makes the rear section, though two storeys above the ground floor, lower than the front section, which has only one; moreover, the two sections are joined not by buildings but by the windowless walls of the neighbouring houses rising up between them.

The front section looks out over the grocer's on the left and the inn on the right. There is no staircase to the upper storeys off the passageway leading from the street; the only way to reach them is to take the steps leading down to the courtyard, turn right, follow the short balcony to a winding staircase, climb to another short balcony and proceed to a small corridor. This floor, from the street to the courtyard, consists of a single flat occupied by a retired agricultural official and his wife and daughter. Josef Loukota, the man whom everyone calls 'the Doctor' and who is in fact no medical doctor or even doctor of law but merely a clerk, sublets a room from them and must pass through the kitchen to reach his quarters.

The winding staircase continues on to the roof.

The steps leading down to the courtyard are flanked on the right and left by woodsheds. The courtyard itself exhibits a marked slope. The rear section of the ground floor contains the dwelling, quite familiar to us by now, of the late Miss Žanýnka. Next to it are the stairs to the cellar, and next to them the winding staircase to the first and second floors – both of which have long balconies – and to the roof.

The top flat is occupied by Josefina, her ailing elder sister and their mother, the widow of an estate steward. It too covers an entire – though rather more modest – floor, and its windows look out both on the courtyard and on Petřín Hill.

The flat on the floor below is occupied by the landlord and his family, of whom we caught a fleeting glance on the balcony. Let us now pay them a formal visit.

Passing through the kitchen, where we run into old Mrs Bavor again, now slaving away at the washtub (she is the family maid), we enter the outer room. The furnishings are quite simple and old-fashioned: to the left a bed spread with a knitted coverlet, to the right a linen chest and large wardrobe; here and there a chair or two; in the middle of the room a round table covered with a faded, slightly tattered cloth; in one window a sewing table, in the other an armchair and footstool; on the wall between the windows a large mirror and nothing at all on the other walls, which are painted green. The linen chest and mirror frame are covered with dust, though that does not matter, since it is the next room that is considered the sitting room (which is why Mrs Bavor calls the outer room the 'ante-posh-room'). The next room – the 'posh room' itself – boasts several coloured lithographs on the walls as well as a piano, a couch, a table surrounded by six or so chairs with white loose covers, and another bed. The bed is made up, and a young girl – the landlord's younger daughter – is lounging on it. The third room is her parents' bedroom.

The landlord's wife is sitting at one of the windows

in the outer room; her elder daughter is sitting at the other. Although it is nearly eleven, mother is still not fully dressed, daughter is in her petticoat.

The lady of the house has very sharp features; her face has a pinched look about it and tapers off to a pointed chin. She is wearing spectacles and sewing away diligently at a piece of coarse material. The black marks stamped on the fabric show it to be military wear. The young lady, to be blunt, is a blonde of the most insipid variety. Her face bears a certain resemblance to her mother's, though the features are somewhat softer, and even with her pointed chin she retains some of the charm of youth. Her eyes are light blue, her hair less than luxuriant, though it is still in curlers at the moment. We can now see she is well into her twenties.

There is a sewing basket in the window and some fine white linen on the chair next to the young lady. The ball of red thread lying on the linen suggests that she had either begun or at least considered beginning some embroidery work. The small table, which wobbles every time something moves, is bare but for an inkstand, an album of keepsake verses, and an old newspaper with a blank sheet of stationery on it. There is an exercise book filled with German verses lying open on the windowsill. Clearly the young lady wishes to spirit a bit of poetry on to the blank sheet, but her pen does not appear so willing: she is testing it on the margins of the newspaper, having given up on other expedients, as attested by the black ink stains on her lips.

Her mother lifts her eyes, glances over at her and shakes her head. 'It's time you got to work. Do you hear?'

'Don't worry, I will.'

'You noticed how Loukota stood and stared at you in the kitchen? It's his morning prayer.'

'He can stare as much as he likes,' said Matylda in a harsh voice.

'Though I must say I prefer him to the lieutenant.'

'Well, I don't.'

'He's younger and perfectly decent. We've known him for years. He must have plenty of money stashed away.'

'How can you be so dull, Mother?'

'How can you be so dizzy?'

'You treat me like a towel to wipe your hands on. Let me do things my own way, will you?'

'But I do!' she said, laying her sewing aside and going into the kitchen. 'Anything to keep you from losing your temper!'

But the young lady was not about to lose her temper. She calmly placed the exercise book before her, dipped the pen yet again, and started inscribing letter after letter on the blank sheet. She worked slowly and laboriously. At last the first line was complete, then, after a fitting lapse, the second, the third, until after a half-hour of drudgery an entire stanza glittered on the paper. It read, mistakes and all, as follows:

> *Roszen verwelken Mirthe bricht*
> *Aber wahrer Freundschaft nicht;*
> *Wahrer Freundschaft soll nicht brechen*
> *Bis man einst von mir wird sprechen:*
>> *Sie ist nicht mer.*

That is:

> Roses fade and myrtle snaps
> But true friendship never naps;
> Friendship true shall never fade
> Till of me these words are said:
>> She is no more.

The quatrain was in Gothic script, the dramatic finale in Roman. She gazed upon her creation with great satisfaction and read it through twice aloud, the second time rendering the last line with special pathos. Then she began to sign her name. She had finished the *M* and was starting in on the *a* when the pen gave out for want of nourishment. She dipped it again, but the moment she set it to the paper a great round blot appeared beside the *a*. She quickly lifted the page and removed the blot with a flick of the tongue.

Having thus taken the blot in her stride, she saw no reason to copy the text from scratch. As she held the sheet of paper up to the light, waiting for the wet spot to be wet no longer, her mother scurried back into the room.

'The Bauer women are on their way and you're not dressed yet!' she cried from the doorway. 'Put some clothes on, will you!'

'What do those bores want with us?' Matylda asked, pouting as she slid the unsigned poem under the blotter. She stood up and went over to the bed, where a white housecoat was lying.

In the meantime Matylda's mother had snatched up her sewing and tossed it through the doorway into the second room. 'Don't get up, Valinka,' she commanded, shutting the door again. 'We have company.'

By then inquisitive women's voices were coming from the kitchen. Matylda ran to her chair and grabbed the ball of red thread; her mother raced to the window and started rummaging in her sewing basket.

There was a knock on the door.

'Who is it?' the lady of the house called out.

The door opened to reveal two women seeming to hold back for the sake of propriety.

'Why, Mrs Bauer! Matylda, look who's here!'

'What a pleasant surprise!' cried the dutiful daughter, clapping her hands for joy, then warmly embracing the younger of the two. 'You're a fine one, Marie, staying away for so long!'

'We just thought we'd say hello, Frau von Eber,' the older woman explained. 'We were on our way up to our uncle the canon, and Marie kept on at me – she insisted on seeing dear Matylda. Why don't you visit us any more? It's easy to see who values whose company. We're always the ones to call. But today we've only got a moment. And as I said to Marie, we don't want to inconvenience anyone, it being washing day . . .'

'Heavens!' cried Mrs Eber. 'What's a little scrubbing in the kitchen? You *will* stay, won't you? Look at them, still hugging! They do so love each other! Don't smother your friend, Matylda.'

She sat the women near the window. The older of the two very elegantly dressed women was fifty or so, the younger about thirty. Despite a polite smile, her spare features, so like her mother's, bore the imprint of great lassitude. The only thing that betrayed a trace of life was a sardonic look in her eyes, which wandered inquisitively from object to object.

A conversation ensued, now in German, now in Czech, as the spirit moved them.

'I just hope you haven't any draughts,' said Mrs Bauer. 'My teeth do trouble me so when I catch cold. It was the fine weather today that brought us out. The weather is beautiful, wouldn't you say, Matylda dear?'

'Oh, yes. Ever so.'

'Ever so, ever so,' Miss Marie agreed.

'You've been sewing today, Mrs Eber?' Mrs Bauer inquired, picking up a strip of material from the floor. 'But isn't this the cloth uniforms are made from?'

'Why, yes, it is,' Mrs Bauer was forced to admit. 'Our servant, poor thing, does a bit of piecework on the side, and I try and help her on washing days. I feel so sorry for her. What she goes through for only fifty kreutzers a week! They work their fingers to the bone, those people.'

'So they do, poor souls.'

'And what's that you're doing, Matylda?' asked Miss Marie. 'Embroidering linen? Show me the monogram. MK? That's right, I'd heard you were getting married. Are congratulations in order? It's Lieutenant Kořínek, isn't it? I met him once at my uncle's. Do you love him?'

Without even blushing – for with a friend there was no need – she answered, 'Yes, I've made up my mind. Why wait? What for? He's a good man; he loves me. I've no desire to be an old maid.'

'I can't quite remember him,' Miss Marie said innocently, fingering the pages of the album. 'He's fair, isn't he? Or is he grey?'

'Kořínek's not old,' Matylda said, this time with a slight blush, 'but he told me he lived under very unhealthy conditions in Štýrský Hradec and slept with his head against a damp wall. He's not old at all!'

'So he's just making believe, the rascal. You never know with those men.'

'Yes, he's a sly one. Yesterday I had to laugh. I was scolding him for smoking so much and asked him why he did it. He told me he was getting his lips in training for when he starts kissing in earnest. *Der ist witzig!*'

Miss Marie tittered innocently to show she shared her friend's view of the lieutenant's wit. 'But if he's so hale and hearty, why did he leave his regiment for the Quartermasters' Corps?'

'They wanted to post him to Dalmatia, so he applied to leave the regiment on the grounds that his memory was failing him . . .'

' . . . and he'd never find his way home from such a distance, the poor fellow!'

'Every man has his faults,' Matylda inserted promptly, 'but Kořínek has money. His father made a fortune in the French wars.'

'So I've heard,' Miss Marie replied. 'Buying up broken legs or something – though we girls don't understand these things.' Then she picked up the album and said, 'What a beautiful poem he's written to you!' and read it half aloud.

The text, again with all its orthographical vagaries, read:

> *Dein treues Herz und Tugend Pracht*
> *Hat mich in dich verlibt gemacht,*
> *Mein Herz ist dir von mir gegeben*
> *Vergissmeinnicht in Todt und Leben*

> W. Korzineck,
> Oberlieutenant

That is:

> Your heart so virtuous and true
> Has made me fall in love with you,
> My heart is yours to my last breath
> Forget-me-not in life and death.

> V. Kořínek
> Lieutenant

'Why didn't he write out his name? What is it? Wolfgang? Walter?'

'It's Václav, actually, but he doesn't like it. He says that every time he sees a church procession he feels like being rebaptised.'

'You have a whole exercise book of his poems.'

'He lent it to me.'

'I see, so you can copy them out for yourself. How nice of him . . . Mama, shouldn't we be on our way?'

The two mothers had been going on about domestic matters. 'You're quite right. Time to go. A pity we shan't see Herr von Eber, though he's at the office, of course. Now where's my little angel Valinka? Isn't she at home?'

'Oh yes, but still in bed. I leave her there all morning. They say it's good for the voice. She's going to be a singer, you know. Everyone just marvels at her. She's a positive demon for music: each time she plays the piano she leaves it fairly smoking!'

'Well, I must go and hug my little angel. I couldn't possibly leave without a kiss!' And going up to the adjoining room she added, 'She's just next door, isn't she?'

'But the bed isn't made yet,' Mrs Eber objected.

'Really, Mrs Eber, I thought we were friends! Our house is just like this.'

Since by then she was standing in the doorway, Mrs Eber had no choice but to follow her. Mrs Bauer immediately noticed the pile of military sewing on the floor, and a faint smile grazed her thin face, though

28

she made not a sound and walked briskly over to the bed.

'Leave me alone!' Valinka protested, fending off her embrace. 'Let me be!'

'Where are your manners, child?' her mother scolded. 'Whatever has come over you? Oh, by the way, Frau von Bauer, we're having a little concert here on Thursday evening. Do come. Matylda, make sure that dear Marie agrees to come on Thursday.'

'Of course we'll come,' Mrs Bauer promised graciously. 'We'll be glad to come and admire our little angel.'

The second room – the drawing room – was as large as the kitchen and the anteroom put together and therefore boasted two windows facing the courtyard. The young ladies went up to one of them, hand in hand, just in time to see young Bavor leaving Žanýnka's flat clutching a wad of letters in his hand and hurrying to the first winding staircase.

'Who is that?' Miss Marie asked.

'That's our "starling". He's the son of our cleaning woman, the grocer's wife, and terribly full of himself. You should see the way he flings his coat over his arm.'

'Is Starling his name?'

'No, Bavor. But we call him starling. One day our pet starling flew away, and Papa thought he saw him on the roof. But all he found when he climbed up there was a corner of Bavor's coat. Bavor studies on the roof. There he goes now. See him?'

'So he's a student?'

'No, he works in Papa's office. But Papa says he'll never get anywhere and the best thing he could do is jump off Charles Bridge like St John Nepomuk.'

'Girls, girls! Time to say goodbye,' Mrs Bauer called out. 'We really must be going.'

The young ladies flung their arms around each other. It was a long time before the last embraces had been exchanged and the visitors had been politely escorted through the rooms and to the stairs.

Mrs Eber and Matylda stayed out on the balcony.

'Did you hear how afraid she was of catching cold, Matylda?' Mrs Eber asked when Mrs and Miss Bauer had passed into the courtyard from the stairs. 'Well, I don't think she has a tooth of her own.'

'I'm certain of it. The maid washes her teeth with the dishes!'

Mrs Bauer turned in the entrance and gave one last affable farewell wave. Miss Marie sent Miss Matylda a few more rippling kisses. Then they disappeared into the dark passageway leading to the street.

'God only knows how many times Matylda has started marking linen,' said Miss Marie, smoothing her cape, 'and how many times she's had to tear the stitches out.'

'What do you think about Kořínek, though? Didn't Uncle once mention him to you?'

'Hm, yes,' said Miss Marie, stepping energetically into the street.

IV   A Lyrical Monologue

And there was morning and there was evening, the first day. Now that it is evening, the scene of our story resembles that of the old Russian song: 'a moon in the heavens and moonlight in the hut'. The full moon sailing through the firmament is so brilliant that the stars surrounding it have faded and resume their timid twinkle only a world away. Proudly it spreads its cloak of light over the earth, blanketing the river waters and the riverbanks, the sweeping countryside and sprawling town, trailing it through squares and streets, anywhere it can find space, and when it chances to find an open window it tosses in the hem of its golden garment.

Thus it entered the Doctor's wide-open window and blithely took over his tidy, tastefully appointed, indeed, elegant little 'chamber'. It sprinkled the flowers in the planter by the window until they seemed coated with silver rime; it lay on the white bed, making it whiter still; it sat in the comfortable arm-chair, lit up each of the utensils on the writing desk, even stretched out to cover the entire length of the carpet. And so it remained well into the night.

Finally, however, the latch clicked, the door creaked drowsily and the Doctor entered. He placed his walking stick in the stand at the door, hung his straw hat on it and rubbed his hands.

'Well, well!' he muttered. 'Company! Welcome, Friend Moon. Didn't we meet at Whitsun? Everything

going well at home, I trust? And . . . Damn this knee!'
His voice suddenly rose, and as he bent over and
rubbed the knee, his face, now in full moonlight,
looked half annoyed, half amused.

He rose and took off his coat, and by the time he
had opened the wardrobe to hang it up, he was muttering again, though this time the words had a tune to
them: 'Doctor Bartolo . . . Doctor Bartolo . . .
Doctor Bartolololo . . . lolo . . . lo . . . Was that an
E or an F? Definitely an F. Bartololo . . . lolo . . .
lolo . . .'

Meanwhile he had taken his grey dressing gown from
the stand, put it on, tied the red silk cord around his
waist, and started loloing his way to the open window.

'Josefinka is probably asleep by now. Sweet dreams,
my pet! And a charming little kitten she is too. So
kind-hearted.' He bent over and rubbed his knee again
– not cursing this time – and was soon back at the
window.

'Quite a large flat they've got there, bigger than
they need. We'll keep it, maybe add a few pieces of
furniture. Her mother and poor ailing Katuška are
perfectly welcome; they're good souls. And they've
no one. Except that Bavarian cousin, of course, who'll
be the best man. What's a wedding without a best
man, eh, kitty? We'll do everything quietly.
Bartolololo . . . Why can't I get that doctor from
Seville out of my mind? Bartolo . . . Bartolo . . . I'm
young enough, in good shape, fine shape; I'm no *peri-
culum in Morea*; I needn't fear "I'll never be as hand-

some as I am now"'! It will be a new life, I'll be happy, and being happy takes years off a man.'

He stared up at the round moon.

'I wonder if my kitty's dreaming. No, never. I'm sure she sleeps like a baby. If only I could whisper something sweet for her to dream.'

He turned, took a guitar from the wall above the planter and, going back to the window, strummed some trial chords. The muffled howl of a dog rose up from the courtyard.

'Oh, Azor has managed to scratch his way out,' said the Doctor, leaning out of the window. 'Quiet, Azor! There's a good dog!'

The dog made no response.

'No point in working him up, poor thing,' the Doctor said to himself, and he hung the guitar back on the wall, shut the window and pulled the curtain over it. Then he went up to his desk and, having lit the candle, sat down. When alone, the Doctor always talked to himself half aloud, and he now carried on where he had left off.

'I'm old enough to have a head on my shoulders. At my age this sort of thing must be handled with alacrity, though not without a bit of poetry. The plan is sound enough . . . Oh, drat this knee! I must have given it a nasty knock!' He opened his dressing gown and inspected his tan trousers. There was a rip in the right knee.

'They're new, too!' he lamented. 'That's what one gets for being thoughtful! They were standing on the left side of the passageway (Václav and Márinka – who else?), so I moved to the right and walked straight into the mangle. Damn that Václav! I really must put an end to our friendship. He's nothing but a clerk, and there's no future in that. It's a pity. There's no denying the boy is bright and deserves to finish his studies, but he hasn't the means. And I must put an end to his versifying. There's certainly no future in that. He's chosen the office; he must stick to it. When he asks for my opinion, I'll tell him to chuck everything else. Everything else a waste of time.'

He took a fat notebook out of the desk and leafed through it, stopping at the first bookmark.

'My plan is ready,' he said, continuing his conversation with himself. 'It needs some poems, and as I can't write them myself I'll use what I have to hand. If I didn't use these, I'd find others. Josefinka will never know, nor will he. He'll chuck them all on my advice. Tomorrow I'll send her the first of them, anonymously for the time being, but she'll be sure to guess. This one!'

And he read the following:

> Thou art a mountain landscape fair
> When fresh and young, in early spring!
> Thy hair the wood's enchanted night,
> Thine eye the nimble rapids bright,
> Thy lips are buds, they cheeks ripe fruit,
> Thy voice the night'ngale's song doth sing –

Thou art the world, sky, tree, earth, root,
Thou art a mountain landscape fair.

Now stormy, now serene,
Thou art a mountain landscape fair
By poets only seen.

Oh, tell me if my tender air
To tender feelings moves thee
Or if like mountain landscapes bare
Thou art stone that reproves me.

'Listen to him! You'd think he was just down from the mountains, and I know for a fact he's never laid eyes on a mountain landscape. "The wood's enchanted night", "the nimble rapids bright" – not bad, though "Thy voice the night'ngale's song doth sing" is laying it on a bit thick. I have an idea! I'll underline the *only* in "By poets only seen" to make it clear I'm the only one who loves her. A poem can really turn a girl's head. Then, in a week, my next attack, maybe even signed. Here's a good one.' And he read:

Thy raven hair, thy dusky hue
Have turned my noon to night's dismay;
Thy vibrant voice, thine eyes sky-blue,
Have turned my night to burning day!

O swarthy sun! Pray tell
If thou wilt luminate my nights
My nightmares to dispel.

> O pitch-black moon! Pray tell
> If thou wilt chaperon my days
> My passion for to quell.

'He knows what he's doing, heh heh! He could have any girl he wants! I wonder if he wasn't after a Jewess, though. Josefinka isn't so dark as all that. Never mind. She'll never notice. All that matters is she's like the sun and it sounds nice. Yes, this will do the trick. She'll be dazzled.

'But if she proves a particularly hard nut to crack, I'll need a third poem, something merciless.' And after flipping through some pages, he came to:

> I'd put a bullet through my heart,
> I'd waver not a minute,
> Were I not sure that when I died
> They'd find you buried in it.

> I'd bear excruciating pain,
> I'd hail the regions nether,
> Were I not sure that we are one
> And must endure together.

'There's something spellbinding about the idea of shooting oneself. What girl could resist it? We'll give Josefinka that third dose no matter what. Just to make sure . . . Now why am I so sleepy all of a sudden? To bed, yes, straight to bed.' And with a big yawn he began to undress.

'The best part of all is where he says, "We are one

and must endure together"',' he muttered to himself as he took off his clothes, folding them with pedantic care on the armchair, then transferring them to the chair beside the bed. 'It means he's got her locked in his heart and if he shoots himself he'll hit her as well. How could he miss? Heh, heh. She's right there . . . We are one . . . It's warm tonight. I don't need anything on my feet.' He pulled off his shoes and socks, turned back the covers, blew out the candle and lay down.

Settled into bed, he heaved a contented sigh.

'Bartolo . . . lolo . . . We are one . . . and must . . . and . . .' and he was asleep.

Suddenly Azor let out a howl in the courtyard below, and a moment later he scratched on Žanýnka's door. As though unable to contain his grief, yet fearful of wakening the tenants, he went on howling mutedly through the night.

v   Bachelorhood is Bliss (an Old Saying)

The name of the official in whose flat the Doctor has a rented room is Lakmus. He has lived in Prague for only about three years and took over his subtenant from his predecessor.

Soon after he moved into our quiet house, the tenants learned that the family had a considerable nest egg and received a handsome pension, and they therefore held the Lakmuses in great esteem. They did not have much to do with them, however. Mrs Lakmus, the head of the household, was not particularly sociable. Civil as she was (she gladly gave the landlord the rent in advance when he requested it, she lent the neighbours flour or butter from her stocks when they happened to run out, she acknowledged their greetings and even greeted them first), she never entered into conversations with them. Not that she was a woman of few words; indeed, periodical proof of her rhetorical prowess rang out through the windows and throughout the house.

Although in her forties, Mrs Lakmus was bursting with energy. Her buxom figure was still fresh, her lively face was free of wrinkles, her eyes had a cheerful glint to them – in short, she was the picture of the gay widow, yet her daughter had long been of marriageable age. Miss Klára, who was twenty and then some, was not at all like her mother. She lacked her engaging rotundity; indeed, she was tall and thin as a reed. On the other hand, her clear blue eyes went well with her thick blonde hair, and her rather elongated cheeks still bore traces of the wholesome countryside. Miss Klára was even less sociable than her mother, and Miss Matylda, the landlord's daughter, had long since given up hope of making friends with her.

Of Mr Lakmus the neighbours saw little except at the window. His leg was very bad and required constant care. Hardly more than once a month or two he would hobble out of the house; otherwise he spent his time surveying the street or reclining on the sofa wrapped in flannel and moist cloths. People said he drank a great deal of wine, and his acne-ridden face did nothing to deny the rumour.

It was getting on for noon of the second day of our story when Mr Lakmus laboriously raised himself from the chair at the window looking out on to the street: having spent the morning hours in that position, he was now ready to shift to the sofa. Once there, he sat down again, lifted his leg on to the cushions and gazed with an impatient sigh at the large, loudly ticking, glass-covered clock, which, like all the furnishings, was less than new but had a feel of solidity about it. The hands indicated a few minutes before twelve. His eyes slipped from the clock to Klára, who was sewing away diligently at the other window.

'So you're not even giving me my soup today?' he said with a peevish smile, as if he meant to remind rather than reprimand.

Just as Miss Klára raised her head, however, the door opened and in stepped Mrs Lakmus bearing a steaming cup on a plate. Mr Lakmus's face lit up at once.

'Go into the kitchen, Klárinka,' Mrs Lakmus ordered, 'and get things ready for the pudding. Do a good job of it or the Doctor will laugh at you.'

Klárinka did as she was told.

'I've made you wine soup today, dear,' Mrs Lakmus said affectionately, placing the plate in front of her husband. 'You must be tired of beef broth.'

39

Mr Lakmus raised his head and gave his spouse a somewhat wary look, as though leery of her frugality. Yet he was clearly accustomed to submission, because, abandoning his suspicions, he immediately began to sip the delicacy she had offered him.

Mrs Lakmus picked up a chair and placed it at the table beside her husband's sofa. She sat, resting her arms on the table and her eyes on her husband's face. 'Tell me, darling, what are we to do with Klárinka?'

'To do with her?' he said, continuing to sip his broth. 'Why do we need to do anything?'

'The girl's head over heels in love and with Loukota!'

'Well, she hasn't said a thing to me.'

'Why should she! But she's open with me; she's told me everything. Last night I had to drag her out of the kitchen. Apparently she heard the Doctor saying such beautiful things she was transfixed. The girl's in love, I tell you, and I say we should act on it.'

Mr Lakmus wiped away the beads of sweat which the strong soup had brought out on his forehead and, after a moment of thought, observed, 'He's too old for her.'

'Old! You were no spring chicken when I married you!'

Mr Lakmus vouchsafed no reply.

'He's well preserved and in fine fettle. He doesn't look old and in the end he isn't so old as all that. Better someone we know than the first flash Harry who comes her way, especially as she's been impossible lately. Besides, he's got several thousand guilders put away – more than enough to keep a wife. Why shouldn't we give her to him? Well? What do you say? Don't just sit there!'

'But do we know,' Mr Lakmus ventured to inquire, 'do we know if he wants her?'

'Well, of course we can't force her on him,' Mrs Lakmus said crossly. 'A fine thing that would be. I'll have a talk with him. Klára's a good-looking girl; he always has a smile for her. She keeps his room neat as a pin, and he's so fond of order. I think he's sweet on her too, only he lacks self-confidence because he's . . . well, not so young as he used to be. I'm sure that's the case, but I can handle it.' She nodded contentedly, then suddenly cocked her head towards the door. 'What did I tell you?' she said after listening for a moment. 'He's come home early, unusually early. First he stopped in the kitchen for a few words with Klárinka; now he's in his room. I'm off to the kitchen to settle the matter on the spot!'

Mrs Lakmus found Klára standing at the kitchen table mixing dough in a bowl. She took her daughter's head in her hands and looked her in the eye. 'You're as red as a rose,' she said gently, 'and trembling all over. Don't worry, Klára. Mother will take care of everything.'

She glanced into the small mirror on the wall, pulled down her cap, rolled down her sleeves and marched up to the Doctor's door. She knocked. There was no response. She knocked again, this time with greater resolve.

The Doctor had had a hard day at the office. He was distracted, nearly distraught; he felt unsettled, smiling one minute, sad the next. He was in the throes of that poetic mood which, as anyone who has experienced it knows, makes tending to one's daily routine quite impossible. A vague notion starts creeping like a caterpillar through the brain, tickling and scraping, exciting first one nerve, then another, then a third, until the entire nervous system is aroused. There is nothing one can do about it; one must give up one's work, devote all one's attention to the notion in question until it settles down at last and slowly spins a cocoon for itself. And if the sun of fantasy is warm enough, the cocoon will burst and into the world a butterfly poem will flutter.

Resplendent in its 'mountain landscape' hues, the butterfly had fluttered about until the early morning hours, when the Doctor finally set it down in ink on a sheet of pink paper, slipped it into an envelope, sealed it with scented wax, and entrusted it to the municipal postal authorities. The poetic frenzy did not come upon him until later, but then – as often happens with mature passion – it so overpowered him that he could not bring himself to stay at the office.

He wended his way home slowly. Entering the courtyard, he failed to steal his long-since customary glance at Josefina's windows; indeed, when at last he stumbled into the Lakmuses' kitchen he felt he had escaped a danger of sorts. He heaved a sigh of relief, his blood started circulating more freely, and he spoke to Klára in a pleasant, ringing voice he had never used with her before. He did not linger, however; he went straight to his room.

No sooner had he closed the door than his head sank to his chest. He slipped off the right sleeve of his coat without thinking, then paused, lost in reverie. The next thing he knew he was at the window, wondering whether the letter he had posted that morning had been delivered, that is, whether Josefina had received it or not. Afraid of being seen, he moved three steps back from the window and peered at the opposite balcony through the space between the curtain and the window frame. All at once he gave a start: the postman had come into sight. Just as he jumped even farther back, however, he heard a knock on the door.

'Come in,' he managed to utter, blushing crimson like a rose.

The door opened upon Mrs Lakmus.

Making a frantic grab at his empty sleeve, he twisted and turned and forced a smile to his lips.

'I hope I'm not intruding, Doctor,' she said, closing the door after her.

'Not at all, dear lady,' the Doctor stammered, finally catching his floppy sleeve. 'You are more than welcome.'

'You're home so early today, Doctor. You're not ill, are you?'

'Ill, dear lady?' he asked fatuously, still in very much of a muddle.

'Well, I declare!' she said, going up to him and putting her hand on his forehead. 'Something really must be the matter. You're as flushed as a girl.'

'I've been running, dear lady. I always run. I mean . . .'

'Would you like a compress?'

'Oh no, no. There's nothing wrong. Nothing at all. If you'd just have a seat, dear lady, while I . . .'

The Doctor led her to the armchair, and once she was seated he sat in the chair opposite her.

'You keep calling me "dear lady" as though I were actually dear to you,' she said with a smile so coquettish that at any other time the Doctor would have been dumbfounded by it. 'Well, if I weren't a married woman – and so very fond of my husband – who can tell . . . As it is, though, I'll have to leave you to the young ladies.'

The Doctor smiled feebly by way of response, for he could find no words.

'Don't you think it's a wonderful thing when a person has someone he can call "my dear"?'

'Why, yes . . . I suppose . . . I mean, when two hearts are as one . . . Especially in spring . . .'

'Listen to you, Doctor! Aren't you the rogue! Though who could wonder at your thinking of such things? A man like you in his prime – the picture of health, a model of frugality . . .'

The Doctor was on tenterhooks. Mrs Lakmus

seemed to know all about his secret love, the poem, Josefina. But her final words gave him courage. 'I must say I pride myself on caring for both my person and my assets.'

'Yes, of course,' said Mrs Lakmus by way of commendation. 'You can choose a young bride.'

'Well, I shouldn't consider anything else,' the Doctor said, now cautious again. 'One wouldn't want someone too set in her ways, someone one couldn't make over. No, I could consider only a young girl, a good, obedient, gentle creature, ready to adapt to her husband.'

'Yes, of course,' Mrs Lakmus agreed, 'no one else would do. Now tell me, and I want you to be frank, quite frank, as frank as you'd be if you were, say, speaking to the mother of your intended' – at this point she grasped the Doctor's hand and gazed deep into his eyes – 'tell me, have you decided on a prospect?'

'If it's out, it's out. Why deny it?' the Doctor replied in all candour. 'Yes, I have.'

'Just as I told my husband!' cried Mrs Lakmus, clapping her hands with glee.

'Your husband? Why should – '

'And you know what he said? He said, "Do we know if he wants her?" Imagine that!'

'Well, why shouldn't I?'

'I knew it! I just knew it! Aren't you the rogue! Going behind her mother's back! Keeping it from her mother!'

'From her mother? Nobody knows a thing about it. *She* doesn't even know.'

'*She* may not know for sure, but a mother sees all! The girl's been so miserable, so distraught. She talks about you day and night, even in her dreams. I was young once, but I've never seen anything like it.'

The Doctor's mouth fell open in amazement. His eyes showed a combination of bewilderment, embarrassment and vanity.

'It's all for the best,' Mrs Lakmus went on. 'At first I was against taking on a subtenant, but now I'm glad. Klára will be so happy!'

'Miss Klára . . . ?' the Doctor cried out, leaping out of his chair.

'Don't worry, I tell you. She's madly in love. And there's another thing: we mustn't tarry with the wedding. You live with us; people might talk. What's the point of waiting, anyway? We know you; you know us. You can see we want for nothing. Everyone stands to profit from the match.'

'But if I remember correctly,' the Doctor started stammering again as he paced the room with long strides, 'Miss Klára was seeing a certain official . . .'

'She was indeed, but no longer. He married. A miller's widow. Do you think she misses him? Heaven forbid! All she thinks about is you. She was afraid you'd hold it against her, but I said, "The Doctor doesn't want a girl who's never been kissed." Besides, you know the saying: One suitor's no suitor.'

The Doctor was at a loss how to respond, but Mrs

Lakmus gave him no opportunity. 'It's decided, then: the wedding will take place without delay. Your papers are in order, aren't they? You're so orderly.'

The Doctor shook his head, which Mrs Lakmus took in her own way. 'Well then, take care of them immediately. You're good at that, aren't you? Oh, and you'll dine with us, of course.'

'No, no!' the Doctor managed to utter. 'Please. Here.'

'Bashful, eh?' the blissful mother-in-law said, smiling. 'Oh well, Klára won't be able to eat a bite when I tell her the good news.'

'No! I beg you! I implore you! Don't tell her anything! Anything at all!'

Mrs Lakmus found it all highly amusing. 'If there hadn't been somebody with a bit of sense around here,' she said, 'I wonder how you'd have managed. Just tend to those papers, Doctor. Is there anything you need?'

'No.'

'Then I'll be off, Doctor.'

'Good day, madame.'

For a long time the Doctor stood in the middle of the room as if frozen to the spot, but at last he took a deep breath and gave his head a shake. 'A fine kettle of fish!' he grumbled. 'I'll tend to my papers, all right, but not for your daughter. Your would-be career as my mother-in-law is at an end! There's no help for it now: things must proceed apace. The second poem will go out tomorrow, the third the day after, and the

47

day after that – no, that's Friday, God forbid. So the proposal will be the day after tomorrow, Thursday afternoon. We'll have to find another place to live, of course. Heavens! Imagine coming and going here after that and – '

The door opened before he could finish, and in came Mrs Lakmus and the maidservant bearing supper. 'I've taken out the silver service, Doctor,' she said, placing it on the table. 'Why hide it?' Then she went over to him, laid a hand on his shoulder, and whispered loudly, 'I've told her everything!'

VI   A Manuscript and a Storm Cloud

This chapter begins at the moment the preceding chapter ended; that is, with the return of Mr Eber, the landlord, from his office. Mrs Eber, who was in the kitchen laying the fire, was quite taken aback at her husband's entrance. He did not normally come home until three, and here he was just after twelve – and looking exceedingly strange.

From his threadbare top hat – he had pulled it down to his thick, prickly eyebrows, thus casting shadows in the folds of his once plump cheeks – everything about him seemed transformed. His hair, neatly combed as a rule, protruded straight out from under the hat; his eyes, normally empty, were clearly straining to say something; his tightly shut mouth raised his chin higher than usual; his sunken chest rose slightly higher as well; and his right hand clutched a long scroll of paper, holding it almost parallel to the ground, while his left hand swung back and forth like a puppet's when the puppeteer does not know quite what to do with it.

Seeing him thus, Mrs Eber was immediately overcome by a premonition that lengthened her sharp features. 'They haven't dismissed you, have they?' she asked in a voice suddenly hoarse.

Mr Eber's head jerked slightly, a sign that he found the question highly offensive. 'Fetch Mrs Bavor immediately!' he said gravely.

At another time Mrs Eber would hardly have stood for so backhanded an answer, but her husband's altered appearance made such an impression on her that it suppressed her naturally sour nature. 'Here she comes now,' she said, catching sight of Mrs Bavor entering the courtyard through the window.

Mr Eber entered the anteroom and paused, halfway, at the table, staring down at it because he had to look somewhere. His hat still on his head, the scroll still in his hand, he seemed primed for something he would not and could not avoid.

After gazing at her father for a moment in amazement, Miss Matylda burst into roaring laughter. 'You look like a puffed-up pigeon!'

Although he scarcely stirred, Mr Eber made it clear he was highly displeased.

But just then the door opened and in came Mrs Eber

with Mrs Bavor. 'Here she is,' said Mrs Eber. 'Now you can tell her what it is you want of her.'

Mr Eber half turned towards her, but lowered his eyes. Then his mouth opened and out came the following in a solemn monotone: 'I am sorry, Mrs Bavor, but there is nothing for it: the matter is out of my hands. Your son is in grave danger. That's right, danger. He is frivolous, he is careless, he is – everything! And this time he's gone too far. He has had the audacity to write a piece about the office with something shameful concerning each of us, yes, our much esteemed Director included! What is more, he wrote it in the office itself and kept it in his drawer, not even taking the trouble to turn the key when he went off on holiday. Well, it was found and glanced at, but as it is in Czech and our Director knows that I have the best Czech in the office, he has asked me to report on it. I am told it contains some highly scurrilous passages. I don't know, of course, I haven't read it yet, but you may expect the worst. I feel duty-bound to tell you all this because as his mother you must be prepared for anything. But I now must ask my wife to bring me a wash basin and a pitcher of fresh water, to bar all visitors unless they should be from the office, indeed, to refrain from serving dinner until such time as I request it. Good day, Mrs Bavor.'

Mrs Bavor was as pale as a ghost; her lips quivered, her eyes burned. 'But Mr Eber,' she all but wailed, 'have mercy on us, for the love of God. We're so poor – '

Mr Eber cut her off with an imperious wave of the hand. 'I have neither the power nor the responsibility to intercede on your behalf. It is too late; all is lost. Duty is duty; justice shall be done. What would happen if mere striplings were allowed to . . . But I've no time to go into that now.' And with a few short, constrained steps he disappeared into the next room.

Having shut the door behind him, he looked carefully to the left and to the right and only then removed his hat and went up to the desk, where he laid down the scroll with great care, as if fearing it might break.

Usually he changed into casual wear at home; today he adjusted his office clothes ceremoniously before the mirror. Then he looked over his pens, dusted the blotter, and moved the chair forward and back before finally sitting down. He picked up the scroll, raising his eyebrows to the very top of his forehead, and began to unroll it, carefully following every turn of the paper.

VII   Fragments from the Notes of a Scrivener

What can I do now that I've finished my work? I mustn't hand it in till tomorrow. I was raked over the coals for my first assignment; they said I must have made a slapdash job of it: it couldn't be right if I'd got through it so fast.

So I'll write sketches of office life, the day-to-day

routine; I'll be the photographer and biographer of my colleagues and their superiors, a purveyor of bureaucratic bagatelles and penmen's poetry. An English satirist once made a travelogue of a journey he took round his own writing desk, but I will venture farther: I will call at each of the neighbouring desks; I will range throughout the empire of our much esteemed Director, describing both the lay of the land and its people. But will they provide me with material for satire? And why not! Only the perfectly rational man and the perfectly mindless man fall outside its range, the latter causing it to weep, the former forcing it to take an empyrean stance and argue sullenly that in the face of eternity everything we do is ridiculous.

Though I'll not want empyrean philosophy for that dandy of a junior clerk, no, only the pocket mirror he so dearly loves to ogle. He's a friendly sort: on the first day I asked who that 'fine-looking' gentleman was and he overheard me. As to the others – how earnestly they scribble, how busy they keep themselves! Those heads, those faces, those eyes! All regulation-perfect. Whom could they belong to but clerks? 'Mental labours' tax them but little, yet their owners never dream of going beyond the office: they clearly do not care whether they push papers or pull ploughs. One step at a time and moderation in all things. Perhaps this herd of mental dobbins hides a Trojan horse: wood on the outside, Greeks within. Let's open them and see!

But I note that our Department Head is indulging

in a short respite: reading the newspaper. Now he sets it aside . . .

The look he gives me when I ask him if I can have a glance at it! He says not a word, yet I turn bright red, and by the time I reach my desk there are tears of shame in my eyes. Blind though I am, I feel the jaws of all and sundry drop at the show of such audacity in a probationer.

If only I were back in school with a hopeful outlook on everything – and nothing. Here I feel my outlook narrowing, and I've no idea, none, how high I can rise.

On the first day they tested my style by asking me to write about what I feel when looking at a locomotive. I hitched my locomotive to a Pegasus and sped off boldly to the realm of human progress. The Director shook his head and pronounced me an odd bird.

I haven't had a decent conversation here yet, and it's rumoured they're calling me the 'Firebrand'. I'm in for a hard time, I can see that. Oh, to be back at school! But that's wishful thinking.

The air in this place! Prometheus' clay supposedly smelled of human flesh; these humans smell of clay, and a dry, brittle clay at that.

What awful people! They've barely reached the stage I was at when I threw stones at birds and dragged rats around by the leg. I remember reading *Robinson Crusoe* before I had enough German to know that *Insel* means 'island', and still I liked it; these people harbour all manner of misconceptions about the world, and like it still. Ideas for them are a state monopoly, like salt and tobacco. No, I was wrong to hope for a Trojan horse among them: they're wood through and through, inside and out.

Yesterday I told them that Parisian ladies wear Brazilian monkey feathers, the day before that the coach the Archbishop uses on formal occasions is modelled after the coach used by Elijah the prophet; tomorrow I'll clip a curl from Azor's tail and tell them it comes from the hair Isis tore from her head when Osiris lay dead before her.

They think me ever so learned and enjoy chatting with me, but they don't dare make a sound in the presence of our Department Head, unless he cracks a joke, of course, in which case everyone in the room performs a gymnastic feat of hilarity. The moment he steps out, however, every face broadens, every back straightens, all hell breaks loose. It's part of the routine; indeed, if he fails to make his regular exit, out come their watches.

My reputation as a scholar is growing. I managed to decipher a Serb memorandum in the Cyrillic alphabet; they were stunned. The head of the Fifth Department gave me a pat on the back as he passed my desk. 'One never knows what will come in handy,' he said, 'but stick to what's practical.' This from a man who prides himself on his reputation as a writer and has apparently even published a book. On 'pedepannology', I believe: a practical guide to foot rags.

I'll never see anything like it again!

While visiting our department to look at some file or other, the Director deigned to climb a ladder, and as he stepped down, his foot landed squarely on Mr Hlaváček's. Too respectful to tell the much esteemed Director he was crushing his toes, the old ass looked like nothing so much as a latter-day Laocoön, his face racked with pain yet never losing the academic smile of a petty official. At last the Director sensed someone indecorously close to him and was about to turn on the offender when he realised that what he was standing on was not in fact a bundle of files but merely a humble human foot.

'I beg your pardon,' he said with a benign smile.

Mr Hlaváček's only response was to hobble back to his desk, smiling in torment, a moving exemplar of noble compliancy.

Moreover, his colleagues clearly envied him: one never knew when it might turn to his advantage.

Our much esteemed Director has seen fit to inquire whether I have any sisters. I understand exactly what the old bachelor has in mind, and he will soon learn how dearly he will pay for the information. For I know, sir, where you render homage to love: the dandy of the junior clerks has told me. He also says your mistress is a beauty. But what if she's proportion-

55

ately more beautiful to me as I am younger than you? Or, if not to me, then perhaps to the clerk who regards himself as the reincarnation of Narcissus. Something is bound to happen!

Our much esteemed Director summoned us to his office today. A semicircle of department heads stood awaiting us small fry. They went on talking in hushed tones, while we, having made our formal bows to the Director's back, stood motionless.

The Director sat writing, and for a long time took no notice of us. Beside me stood another example of probationary misery, a fairly decent, human-looking instance of same. I whispered a joke in his ear; I can't remember what it was, but it must have been bad, because he didn't even smile. I was so annoyed I told it again, tickling him for good measure. That did the trick: he sputtered like a rocket, whereupon everyone froze, shushed us from all sides, and our much esteemed Director rose.

Rose, took up his station, and spake:

'I have called you here today to inform you that the style of your documents has disgraced our office in higher circles. Some of you plod like elephants, others wriggle like tadpoles; it is years since I have read a judicious – that is, moderately long and well-conceived – sentence from any of you; indeed, I never have. Either you continue to write after you have ceased to think or your every thought immediately goes bad and loses all stature and weight. Furthermore, your German is abominable, and I can tell you why: because you constantly babble amongst yourselves in Czech. By the power vested in me as Director, therefore, I hereby forbid you to speak so much as a word of Czech in this office, and as your friend and superior I counsel you to speak only German outside the office as well and to improve your written style by means of assiduous reading. Now back to work, gentlemen, and remember: no one will be promoted without style.'

The office is in an uproar, each clerk diligently scrounging for scraps from the German kitchen. Anybody with a year of a German journal like *Bohemia* at home is *eo ipso* a somebody.

All Czech conversation has ceased, unless perhaps two old friends, each of whom can be certain the other won't inform on him, exchange a few words in the corridor or at the far end of the filing department. They remind me of secret snuff-takers.

I speak Czech long and loudly. My colleagues avoid me like the plague.

Here the first act of today's office comedy comes to an end. Exit – like Molière's *malade imaginaire* at the end of the first act – our Department Head.

Entr'acte!

Discussion at the desk to my right:

'Friday at last. Potato dumplings tonight. My wife's melt in your mouth.'

'So you don't eat meat on Friday?'

'Of course we do. Half a pound per meal, as usual. What else is there? We keep major fasts only, and then we have fish. Every once in a while a piece of fish is good for you.'

'Well, I like wild boar with my dumplings or a cutlet fried in bread crumbs. Children – but you have no children – children need flour with every meal. Last year my sister-in-law sent us gobs of snails. My wife cooked them up for us.'

'I can see eating wild duck on fast days: ducks live in water. But snails live in grass.'

'Well, snails used to live in water, or so I've heard; besides, the way they creep along they might just as well be swimming, and they're as quiet as fish, so what's the difference? Strange how they eat no meat. You'd think they knew they were meant for fast days.'

Discussion at the desk to my left:

'The Director is right. They're crazy, those Czech fanatics! We never should have listened to them. No, German's what we need. How can we write without it? Of course if you want to teach your children a little French . . .'

'It can't hurt!'

'My daughter wouldn't speak Czech in the street for anything. If I forget myself and say so much as a word, she turns bright red and cries, "Daddy, how could you!" '

'Yes, yes. Quite right.'

'I read in the paper the other day they're trying to invent a universal language. Daft, isn't it?'

'God won't allow it!'

'It won't be necessary if everybody learns German.'

'True!'

Suddenly the nearest to the door issues an urgent 'Psst!' and everyone scurries back to his desk.

Enter our Department Head, his waistcoat unbuttoned.

'I've been putting on so much weight I may burst,' he says. 'I'd better see a doctor – or a midwife.'

Gymnastic feat of hilarity.

Where there is poverty of the spirit, there is material poverty as well. And so here. I marvel at how deceptive the surfaces of their lives are and how miserable they are underneath.

About two-thirds of them deposit their wages with a Jew, who on the first of the month doles out to them whatever sum he chooses. On the first they pay the old woman who comes to the office selling rolls, and starting the next day they buy on credit again. I've never heard them inviting one another to their homes; they must be ashamed of them.

Which explains a great deal.

Today I received notification from our much esteemed Director to the effect that I must have my rather long hair cut. That will be the day!

I have an ally. At my prompting the dandy of the junior clerks has started signing his name Wenzl *Narcissus* Walter. When a document thus embellished fell into the hands of our much esteemed Director, he admonished him to abandon such tomfoolery and work harder, as he had a noisome reputation for idleness. A *Narcissus poeticus* with a *noisome* reputation – I ask you!

Well, I know what aspect of the dandy's reputation so concerns the Director: a path beneath a certain row of windows.

Trusting that Mr Eber would not give me away, I have told a fib to be granted a leave of absence. I said my grandmother was on her deathbed and I was her heir. The Department Head, while granting me the leave, made it clear in no uncertain terms that a junior clerk should not have a grandmother.

VIII   At the Funeral

It is about noon of the third day, Wednesday, and the house is preparing to accompany Žanýnka's corpse on its final journey.

In the shadowy courtyard stands a simple but rather handsome coffin painted a glossy black and fitted with four gilded bear claws. It rests on a bier covered with black cloth. The lid has a gilded cross surrounded by a wreath of green myrtle with a wide white ribbon hanging down. Lengthwise the bier is decorated with rectangular black tablets about two feet high and embossed in silver with the funeral society's insignia.

Apart from Mr Lakmus, who is observing the goings-on from his upper window, and Josefina's ailing sister, who is standing on a footstool and peering over the second-floor railing, our acquaintances from the house are gathered in the courtyard below, all in their Sunday best. Here and there we can make out the faces of men and women quite unknown to us. It doesn't take much wit to recognise in them – with their serious, stony, somewhat strained expressions – the late Žanýnka's relatives. There is also a throng of women and children milling about the courtyard and up the steps.

Now the priest and his sexton and ministrants arrive, and the prayers begin. Mrs Bavor and the innkeeper's wife are standing together at the door to Žanýnka's flat. The very first words of the monotonous funeral recitative so move Mrs Bavor that her eyes fill with tears and her chin flushes and trembles with emotion. The innkeeper's wife looks on impassively, and paying no heed to her neighbour's tears she suddenly leans over and begins a conversation.

'Pouring in like Jews to an auction! Much they cared about her when she was alive! Now they come running for the inheritance. And why in God's name did they lock up the place? Why did they put the coffin in the courtyard? Afraid we'd steal? Did they give you anything of hers for services rendered?'

'Not a pin!' Mrs Bavor whispered in a quivering voice.

'And they won't, either!'

'Well, I'm not asking. What I did I did out of Christian charity, God rest her soul.'

The prayers said, the coffin sprinkled, a black-clad 'brother' removed the funeral society's tablets, and the servers picked up the coffin and carried it through the passageway and out into the street.

There were several cabs standing behind the hearse. Žanýnka's relatives climbed into the first few, Mr and Mrs Eber and Miss Matylda, Josefina and her mother into the next two, and Mrs Lakmus and Miss Klára into the last. Mrs Lakmus called out to the Doctor to come and join them, and as there was room for yet another person she looked down to see who was still without a place.

She saw the innkeeper's wife, Mrs Bavor and her son Václav standing together.

'Ladies!' she called. 'Won't one of you ride with us?'

They started off together in the direction of the cab, the innkeeper's wife looking askance at Mrs Bavor. They arrived at the cab simultaneously and began vying for a foothold on the step. Finally the innkeeper's wife could tolerate the situation no longer. 'I am the wife of a *burgher* of Prague!' she said bitingly and stepped into the cab.

Mrs Bavor was left standing in the street, completely taken aback. Václav, who had seen and heard everything, went up to her and said in a voice straining to keep firm, 'We'll walk together, Mother. Somebody has to follow the hearse. We'll find a cab at the city gates if we decide to go on to the cemetery.'

Since hearing Mr Eber's bad news of the day before, Mrs Bavor had not so much as spoken to her son. Even now she had trouble bringing herself to address him, but after a moment or two she managed to say, 'Yes, of course we'll go to the cemetery. But I don't care to be driven. Be prepared to take the footpath all the way to Košíře if you want to come with me. I did the poor woman many a good deed when she was alive and attended her after her death. Surely I can sacrifice a few more steps out of Christian charity!'

'Then take my arm,' said Václav gently, proffering it.

'I refuse to be squired like a lady! I'm not accustomed to it.'

'That's not what I meant. I just want to help you. It's a long way and you're worn out as it is. Here, take my arm, Mother. Do!' He took her arm and drew it into his.

The hearse set off. Václav and his mother were the only ones following it. Václav walked as proudly as if he had a princess on his arm, and Mrs Bavor felt on top of the world, as if she alone had arranged the entire funeral for poor Žanýnka.

IX   Further Proof of the Pudding

The summer evening 'chitchat hour' is approaching. The day is still bright, but of a brightness that seems gradually, prudently moving towards sleep. People have ceased working, but the desire for evening talk and relaxation has not yet come upon them.

The Doctor was seated at his writing table, his face pensive. He was meditating on a matter of some weight and had resolved to take an important step. He kept shifting his inkwell from place to place, changing his nibs from one fine ivory holder to another, examining their flexible points. At last he opened a drawer and removed half a package of fine paper. He selected a single sheet, held it before him in the air for a moment, then parted his lips, let out a loud 'Yes!' from deep in his breast, and folded the sheet neatly, lengthwise, in two.

This in itself was clearly an important step, one that cost him some effort, for he immediately rose and started pacing the room to regain his calm. His pacing took a curious form: he seemed almost to be reeling – two steps forward, one back – his head either sinking to his chest or lurching up with each new show of courage.

'Yes,' he sighed again from deep within. 'If it must be – and it must – then let it be as soon as possible. Unless I hurry, I'll be in her clutches for good. She won't let go and neither will Klára – good girl that she is. No, I've made up my mind. I can't stay on here. Everything must be resolved within a few days. Tomorrow I'll deliver the third poem to Josefina in person. I'll strike up a conversation with her, give her the poem to read, watch my kitten's every tremor – and we'll settle things one, two, three. But I'll write the petition today, at once. I'm in the mood.'

He wrapped the dressing gown tightly round him and tied the cord, as though wishing to keep out the cold. Then he sat down again, resolutely, at the desk, dipped his pen, waved it a few times over the sheet of paper, and lowered it carefully. A large, beautifully turned M appeared in black. He proceeded immediately to the next letter and the next, and soon they were tumbling briskly one after the other. He wrote as follows:

'Most Esteemed Magistrate of the Royal City of Prague:

The undersigned hereby begs to inform you that he intends to enter into the state of matrimony with Miss . . .'

He looked long and hard at the paper and shook his head. 'These glasses are utterly useless! It's getting dark. Time to close the windows and light the lamp.'

Just then he heard a rap at the door and, grabbing a blank sheet of paper and dropping it over the letter, he uttered a feeble, 'Come in.'

In came Václav.

'I'm not disturbing you, am I, Doctor?' he asked, and closed the door.

'Not at all,' the Doctor muttered, still hoarse with

alarm. 'Do come in. Actually I was about to do some writing, but take a seat. What brings you here?' He asked more out of habit than curiosity, because the mist of embarrassment covering his eyes prevented him from focusing clearly on Václav, to say nothing of the scroll of paper he was holding.

Václav sat down. 'I've brought you something to calm overwrought nerves. Not much of a yarn, perhaps, but it won't make you yawn. The idea is simple, maybe even a bit thin, but the way I handle it is original: I loathe the current forms and themes. Let me know what you think. It's my first attempt at fiction.'

He placed the scroll on the Doctor's desk. His youth showed in his every movement.

'Always joking,' said the Doctor with a smile. 'Well, you're young. And how are things with you?'

'Not very good, and likely to get worse. They're giving me the sack at the office. They came upon some notes I made for a satire of our esteemed Director. Mr Eber's reviewing my case.'

'That was careless of you, poor boy,' said the Doctor, clasping his hands. 'What do you intend to do?'

'What do I intend to do? Why, nothing! Or, rather, I intend to become a writer.'

'Really, now!'

'It would have come to this sooner or later, and I think I'm ready for it. Or do you feel I haven't the talent?'

'A major writer wants a major talent, and minor writers don't do the nation any good – they underscore our spiritual inadequacy, weaken our ability to think, and send us abroad when we feel the need for more substantial fare. No one has the right to enter literature without fresh, new ideas. We've got too many dexterous drudges as it is.'

'You're right, Doctor, and it's because you hold such advanced views on the matter that I have unbounded faith in you. I feel as you do and judge myself by your standards. Leaving aside the business of "major" and "minor", I can state boldly and without hesitation that I grasp the grandeur of the goal, and anyone aware of the problems and daring enough to proceed does so with a certain justification and must make some progress at least. I don't wish to fill gaps in our literature; I refuse to copy worn models. My standards will be those of European literature; my writing will be modern, that is, "veracious". I'll take my characters from life, describe life as it is, unadorned; I'll say exactly what I think, what I feel. How can I fail?'

'Hm. Have you any money?'

'You mean, have I anything on me? Only about two guilders. But I'm afraid I can't quite – '

'No, no. I mean, have you any capital?'

'Why, you know I . . .'

'Well then, you can fail very easily. If you had the capital to see you through, to pay for the publication of each and every one of those fine upstanding works you long to write, you might win some recognition within ten years or so, enough to attract a publisher other than yourself. As it is, you'll never get anywhere. You'll bring out your first new and independent masterpiece on credit, and it will sell so poorly you'll never bring out another. You'll be hauled over the coals, first for being independent, which neither small families nor small nations can endure, then for telling the truth, which means having a go at their smug little world. The more malicious among them will say you've no talent or brains, the more benign that you're mad. And no one will give you a review.'

'What do I care for reviews?'

'You can't do without them at first. People trust what they read. What the press won't endorse, they ignore. Besides, critics will praise other writers just to spite you, and as their reputations grow yours will stagnate. You'll be so bitter you'll either start writing madly or stop writing altogether. And all the while you'll have to feed yourself. So you'll give in and take on hackwork, which will also put you off writing. You'll do as little as you can and go sour or lazy. Either way you're finished, and there's no starting over.'

'It can't be that bad! I know I'll get results as soon as I give a reading. Have you looked at the poems I gave you, Doctor?'

'I have.'

'And what do you think?'

'Well, they read well. Some of the lyrical pieces are

nice. But I ask you, what good is lyricism to us? Have you thought of burning them?'

Václav sprang out of his chair, bringing the Doctor to his feet as well. There was a short silence, during which the latter stood leaning on the desk with his hand and the former went up to the window and pressed his forehead against the pane.

'Are you going to the wedding on Sunday, Doctor?' Václav asked in a voice still uneasy.

'Wedding? What wedding?'

'What wedding? Josefinka told me you were to be the witness. I'm the best man.'

'But who's getting married?'

'You really don't know, do you! Josefinka's marrying Bavorák, the engineer.'

Everything went dark before the Doctor's eyes and he fell back heavily into the armchair, his head whirling.

'Are you all right?' Václav cried, dashing across the room and bending over him. 'Is something the matter?'

He received no answer beyond a repeated rattle that told him help was urgently needed. 'Mrs Lakmus! Miss Klára!' he cried, dashing to the door. 'Bring some water and a lamp! Quickly! The Doctor's had an attack of some kind.' Then he rushed back to the Doctor, undid his tie and loosened his dressing gown.

Mrs Lakmus ran in with a lighted lamp and with Klára close on her heels. 'Water!' Václav shouted. 'And be quick about it!'

But by then the Doctor's eyes had opened and he heard Václav's words. 'No, no. No water,' he managed to say. 'I'm better now. It's the heat, that's all. It happens sometimes in summer.'

'Run and fetch some raspberry juice,' Mrs Lakmus ordered. 'We've got everything on hand. Run along now, Klára.'

Miss Klára scurried off.

'Yes, you're better now,' said Václav, 'but you did give me a fright. It wasn't all that hot today. Anyway, you're all right and in good hands, so I'll be going. Goodbye, Doctor. Goodbye, Mrs Lakmus.'

'Goodbye,' said the Doctor, forcing a smile. 'And remember, what I said to you before was meant well.'

'I'm certain it was and I'm grateful to you for it. Goodbye!'

As he left, Miss Klára came in carrying a tray with the juice and a powder. The Doctor resisted, but in the end had to swallow the refreshing draught.

'Drink it down,' Mrs Lakmus said. 'I must take care of my son-in-law, mustn't I? We'll sit with you for an hour or so. I've been meaning to drop in with Klára anyway. You're such babies, the two of you, so timid and shy. Why, if it hadn't been for me, you'd never have got together . . . Oh dear, now look what I've done! I was so frightened I put the lamp down on your writing paper!'

As she picked up the lamp, the topmost sheet slipped away, revealing the letter. The Doctor, mortified, could think of nothing to say.

Mrs Lakmus's face lit up like the sun. 'Splendid! Splendid!' she said. 'Look, Klárinka! The application for the marriage licence! You see? He had just come to your name! Oh, do give Klára the pleasure of watching you fill in her name! Here's your pen. Please!'

The Doctor sat frozen to the spot.

'Don't be shy, now,' she said, dipping his pen in the inkwell and placing it in his hand. 'Come and watch, Klárinka!'

Suddenly the Doctor was pierced by a bolt of determination. He gripped the pen, pulled the chair forward with a scrape, lowered the point to the paper and wrote 'Klára Lakmus'.

Mrs Lakmus clasped her hands in joy. 'Now seal it with a kiss. Go on, it's perfectly respectable. Don't be shy, you silly man!'

x   In a Moment of Agitation

The moon sails over Petřín Hill, clear and radiant, flooding its wooded slope in misty light, giving us a dreamy, poetic view, as if we were gazing down through limpid sea waters upon a sunken forest. Many an eye wanders or lies at anchor there, deep in thought or feverish agitation.

Josefina looks out upon the shimmering hill from a second-floor window at the rear of the house, her husband-to-be by her side. The bright moonlight enables us to make out the young man's fine lineaments: the oval face framed in a thick, fair beard, the eyes shining with vital energy. Josefina stares silently into the flood of light, while her fiancé, his right arm around her waist, keeps turning to her, pressing her lightly, ever so lightly to himself, as if afraid to dust the bloom from so perfect a moment.

Now he leans over and grazes the girl's locks with his lips. She gazes into his eyes and, taking his hand, presses it to her mouth. Then, releasing it, she reaches out to the beautiful thick bunch of myrtle on the windowsill.

'How old would your sister have been?' she asked in a solemn voice.

'In the flower of her youth. Your age.'

'Your mother doesn't know how happy she made me by sending me myrtle for the wedding. And from so far.'

'Where I come from they believe that if you take myrtle from the hands of the dead and preserve it in the ground until a wedding, it will bring good fortune. Ever since I took the sprig from my sister in her coffin and planted it in the ground, Mother has prayed over it daily, watered it with her tears. Mother is so kind.'

'Like you,' the girl breathed and pressed even closer.

The two fell silent again, gazing into the glimmering air as if it were a dream of their future.

'You're unusually quiet today,' the girl whispered at last.

'True feeling has no tongue. I'm so happy, so blissful I shall never find words to express my bliss. Don't
you feel the same?'

'I don't know what I feel. I'm different from my
old self; my head's in the clouds. If I didn't think the
spell would last, I'd want to die while it was still with
me.'

'So the Doctor could weep over your grave and sing
his ditties,' her fiancé teased. 'No, but what I do
think,' he went on in his natural voice, 'is that no one
truly in love could write like that. I never could, no
matter what, but I suspect the Doctor is playing a
game with you.'

'No, he's not. He's a good man.'

'You're awfully quick to take his part. Own up!
You're thrilled with those poems.'

'Well . . .'

'There, you see? I knew it! You women are all alike.
You all need your sweets, your delicacies on the side.
Tell me, what have I done to deserve this?'

'Karel!' she cried out in horror, staring him in the
face as if she no longer recognised him.

'Well, it's true!' the young man continued in a rage.
'If you hadn't been so two-faced in your dealings with
him and me both, he would never have dared.'

Pushing her away slightly, he withdrew his right
arm from around her waist and let it fall to his side.
His left hand remained in hers, but their hands were
lifeless now and both of them stared silently into space.
Thus they stood, scarcely breathing, until suddenly

Karel felt a burning tear on his hand. He pressed her to his breast with a shudder; she broke into sobs.

'Forgive me, Josefinka!' he begged. 'Forgive me!'

The girl moaned.

'Don't cry! Please don't cry! Shout, yell, but don't cry! I was wrong. You're incapable of deceit. I know. Your love is as true as mine.'

'You didn't love me when you pushed me away like that!'

'That was a bad moment. I had no idea I could be so jealous! It was as if I'd renounced my love. I must have been mad! I forgot how young and beautiful you are and that any girl with a healthy body, any girl who isn't downright ugly or deformed – '

A rustling noise made the lovers turn abruptly. Katuška, Josefina's ailing sister, had been in the room behind them the whole time, but so quiet that they had forgotten her. At Karel's last words she pulled herself up, but before she could go more than a few steps she collapsed in a nearby armchair, weeping convulsively.

'Katuška! Oh, dear! Katuška, darling!' Josefina grieved.

Their hearts pounding, the lovers stood beside the poor sobbing girl. Tears welled up in their eyes; their lips quivered, but they dared not tender a word of consolation.

XI   A First Attempt at Fiction –
Begging the Reader's Indulgence

Dr Josef Loukota felt strange the following morning when he awoke to the kiss of the radiant sun. His head was awhirl, his brain about to burst, his nerves throbbing feverishly. Bizarre figures raced through his imagination; Josefina, Bavorák, Klára, Mrs Lakmus and Václav flitted here and there, interspersed with people he had never seen before and even animals.

Then the first clear, coherent thought crossed his mind: he recalled he was engaged to be married. It sent shivers down his spine and brought him bolt upright in bed. His gaze fell on the bedside table and a pile of papers covered with writing. By now the good Doctor was wide awake and remembered having turned – in agitation and insomnia – to the 'yarn' Václav had brought him to read.

I have no intention of giving a circumstantial description of the Doctor's nervous condition, my readers being sufficiently percipient to fill in the details on the basis of his character and the events. By way of assistance, however, I feel bound to reproduce here his reading material. Then the reader will have all the evidence at hand and be able to make sense of even the Doctor's elaborate dream.

Here it is.

On Certain Domestic Animals
A Semi-Official Idyll by Václav Bavor
From the Diary of Mr Ondrej Dílec, p. 17

going to pay that foreman less, you bet I am! How
much does plaster cost anyway, and he can't be
paying his masons that much. I'd never have started
if I'd known how much he'd charge. No, I'm calling
it off. It would pay in the end, I know, but all she
has is that little tavern, which brings in practically
nothing, and there's her boy and mine and who can
tell how many more to come. When you marry a
widow you have to think of the future, but my house
is big enough for now and there'll be plenty of time
later, so I'm going to tell him to stop. I didn't sleep
a wink the whole night, and it's all her fault, trying
to force my hand with that pipsqueak of a student.
Well, it won't work. She should know better at her
age. So he has an education, so he ends up a doctor
or teacher or editor. If I hadn't given her a six-month
lease, I'd kick her out – he wouldn't marry her then.
She knows it too; she just wants to make me jealous.
Well, I'll do her one better – a landlord can always
find a way; in fact, I've got an idea already. I'll stop
you from turning away when I walk through the
courtyard, from tra-la-la-ing so you don't need to
say 'Good morning'. And I'll put my plan into

A Week in a Quiet House

A Private Letter from Jan Střepeníčko, Probationer Clerk, Municipal Court, to Josef Píščík, Junior Clerk, Same

Dear Friend and Honoured Patron,

I beg your forgiveness for burdening you with the following request, but you have been so kind as to offer me the support of your influence and experience in my career. I also beg your forgiveness for failing to present my request to you in person, but, as you are certainly aware, our department heads look askance at probationer clerks who run from one office to the next instead of keeping to their desks.

So as not to detain you unnecessarily, I shall proceed to the matter at hand. The head clerk has given me the task of filing yesterday's memoranda with the cases to which they pertain. I believe he considers it a kind of test, and as a neophyte I am greatly puzzled by one document. Allow me to acquaint you with its contents.

A Prague landlord by the name of Ondřej Dílec (house number 1213–I) has charged an innkeeper's widow by the name of Helenka Veleb with maintaining, for purposes other than trade, a large number of chickens, capons and cocks, which last consistently wake the tenants of said house by crowing at an unreasonably early hour. The plaintiff asks that the defendant should be forbidden to keep poultry.

Such is the contents of the document for which I have been unable to locate a file. I would have sent

77

it to Your Excellency for your personal perusal, but, as you are well aware, official papers may not be removed from the premises.

I beg you to favour me with a reply, no matter how brief, and hope you will not take offence if I ask you to send it *sealed*.

Yours most sincerely,
Jan Střepeníčko

Official Memorandum N.C. *13211* to Edvard Jungmann, Doctor of Medicine

The Executive Board hereby informs you that on the 4th of August next you are to appear at the Town Hall, Room 35, thence to proceed with an official assigned you to house number 1213–I and there to inspect a matter pertaining to the Department of Public Health.

Veřej, Councillor at the Municipal Court

Prague, 2 August 1858

A Private Letter from the Innkeeper's Widow Helenka Veleb to Her Sister,
Alojsie Trousil, a Teacher's Wife Living in Chrudim

Dear Sister,

Greetings and many kisses from both me and little Toníček, who asks you to send him a present. Ask your husband whether he remembers the Kalhotkas' youngest son, Jeník. Well, he's grown up now and a student, and he wants to be a teacher too. He may

remember him because Jeník used to go home for
the holidays. I'd quite forgotten him myself, and you
wouldn't recognise him, he's so big and strong. He'd
been taking meals with us for two months before he
could pay, because – like so many students, at least
the ones who amount to something – he hadn't a
penny to his name. But he's finished his studies now
and sends greetings to you and your husband. He's
always cheerful and so outspoken he makes me
laugh. He wrote some poems for me – your husband
is a teacher, so you know poetry – the worst fiddle-
de-dee, about how I'm like the starry night and I
don't know what else. I nearly burst my sides
laughing. But then he went and had them published
in a magazine, all pretty, and there, above it all, in
bold print it said '**To Her**', *her* being *me*.

Tell your husband to stop teasing me: it's none of
his business whether I marry again. Still, I'm too
young to live single and my boy needs a father and
there's lots of good fish in the sea. My landlord
would be only too glad to have me, but he's a boor
and I haven't got the kind of money he's after, only
enough to live on, so he went and lodged a complaint
with the municipal court, said I kept so many
roosters that they woke up his tenants with their cock-
a-doodle-dooing. Well, these two gentlemen came
to see me, and I really had to laugh when they kept
asking to see my flock of poultry and all I could
produce was those few specimens I keep for myself
and my guests. The landlord will have a fit when he

finds out, but it serves him right and he's nothing to me. By the way, he's no spring chicken either.

I'm sending you the little hat for Fanynka. I've trimmed it with cherries instead of roses – I hope you don't find it too loud. And could you tell me how much you pay for clarified butter? It may be cheaper if you send it than if I buy it in Prague. I apologise for all the jabber, but I've no one to talk to and am outgoing by nature.

Your faithful sister,
Helenka

P.S. Have to run.

Page Four of the Senate Minutes for 15 August

approved the agenda set forth by Councillor Veřej insofar as only matters of substance require the Senate's attention, whereupon the Senate proceeded to Item Seven.

Councillor Veřej reported on the complaint lodged by Mr Ondřej Dílec, proprietor of house number 1213–I, against Mrs Helenka Veleb, innkeeper, of the same. Mr Dílec alleges that said innkeeper keeps a flock of poultry, the matutinal crowing of which disturbs other tenants' repose. Councillor Veřej then read the report made by a Senate commission consisting of Messrs Edvard Jungmann, Doctor of Medicine, and Josef Píščík, Junior Clerk of the Municipal Court, according to which the above-mentioned commission made a thorough

investigation at the site of the complaint and found
that the defendant kept only two chickens, one
cockerel and one capon, and those only for such of
her guests as should desire to partake of fowl flesh.

The presiding magistrate recommended that no
action should be taken in view of the fact that the
number of fowls in question is so small and that an
innkeeper cannot be expected to keep deceased
poultry.

Councillor Veřej added that as Plaintiff Dílec is
somewhat hard of hearing the cock's crow should
not overly inconvenience him. He then moved that
the complaint be dropped.

The motion was carried unanimously, whereupon

*A Private Letter from the Innkeeper's Widow Helenka
Veleb to Her Sister,
Alojsie Trousil, a Teacher's Wife Living in Chrudim*

Dear Sister,

Greetings and many kisses from both me and little
Toníček, though I'm very cross with you, going on
like an old woman when you're younger than me and
– even if you are married to a teacher – haven't got an
ounce more sense than me, so stop acting like you
have. Besides, who knows what you'd do if you
were a widow. I don't like Dílec, I don't want Dílec,
and I won't let you force him on me. Would you
want a man who insults you? What's it to him if I'm
fat or I'm skinny? What does he mean he could make

'three cadets' out of me? If he doesn't like my looks, he can find someone else to pester. And why did he go to court if he was so taken with me? Which reminds me, he lost his case and can't look me in the eye any more, and I'm gong to get even with him. It's all set. A certain young man – all right, it's Kalhotka again, but don't think I go running after students, though it would be nobody's business if I did, I do as I please, and that's that, besides which, he's a better man than you think – anyway, Kalhotka remembered that keeping pigs in Prague is forbidden by law, and Dílec has two of them running around the garden all day long. Toníček plays with them, but that's not the point; the point is, we've lodged a complaint and Dílec is going to blow his top. Well, let him. I wish things didn't upset you so, and I'm sorry you find the hat loud. Tell it to pipe down, why don't you? Sorry. You know me: I say the first thing that comes into my head. But then we're sisters, aren't we?

Your faithful sister,
Helenka

P.S. Have to run.

A Confidential Memorandum from the Mayor of the Royal Capital of Prague to Councillor Veřej of the Municipal Court

Dear Councillor,
I am writing you this letter as I shall not be seeing you again today and will be at my villa all day

tomorrow and am therefore unable to broach a certain matter with you in person. The matter in question is a complaint lodged by a Helenka Veleb against an Ondřej Dílec, proprietor of house number 1213–I, in which the former accuses the latter of keeping swine in the city in contravention of the law. The case has now come *ad manus inclittisimi præsidii* for the second time and from Advocate Zajíček, who, as you are aware, may be counted amongst the prime opponents of the current municipal administration. The previous hearing of the case, my sources inform me, was less than thorough: the investigation, carried out by a municipal official and the District Medical Officer, revealed that Mr Dílec 'keeps only two sucking pigs and for his own needs', and no action was taken. It was not fitting for you, my dear Councillor, to rule upon so grave a matter *brevi manu*, on your own, without consulting the Senate. For there can be no doubt that sucking pigs are members of the swine family, and keeping members of the swine family in Prague is strictly forbidden. Moreover, presently, in autumn, when the *cholera morbus* commonly makes its appearance, we could suffer serious consequences from the affair, as Advocate Zajíček will be quick to point out. In the interest of both propriety and security, therefore, I must ask you to order the case reopened and reexamined immediately, to have it debated in the Senate in my presence, and to word your resolution in such a manner as to ensure *ex senatu concluso* that

the offending stock be removed from the premises
within eight days.

Prague, on this the 17th day of September 1858

*A Private Letter from the Student Teacher Jan Kalhotka
to his Friend
Emil Blažíček, an Assistant Teacher in Písek*

Dear Emil,

In nomine domini I bring you glad tidings: I have been
posted as an assistant teacher to Hradec Králové,
fortress, metropolis and home to a fine Gymnasium.
So off I fly to groom future generations of my fellow
countrymen and labour like you in the 'fields of our
nation' (which quotation you may have read
somewhere before). I look forward eagerly to my
noble calling, my new walk in life, especially as
Hradec Králové is known for its pretty girls and I am
an ardent admirer of same. I have fantastic luck with
the ladies, by the way: I only need to fall in love and
the rest takes care of itself. I haven't had a penny to
my name these past few months (it happens now and
again), yet I've been living like a king – or a
contented innkeeper. Picture a young widow with an
inn (from my home town to boot) and a young
blade in his prime. All I can say is that for a time I
lived quite cheaply, quite cheaply indeed. But things
have taken a bad turn for my widow: her landlord
proposed marriage, she refused him because of me,
and now he's given her notice and she's at her wits'

end. Since I have a heart of gold (and have come up with a few guilders), I've stopped seeing her. I shouldn't want to stand in the way of her happiness. Women are resourceful, particularly widows. She'll manage. She's not such an ill match for the landlord in the end. They'll make a fine couple. I can see them now, munching their Sunday kidneys and salad in perfect harmony. Believe me, I never pulled the wool over her eyes, and had I been indifferent to her I'd not have written you so much about her. But what can I do? It's over.

Let me end with the hope that things are going equally well for you.

Yours,
Jan

Extract from the Vice-Regent's Decision in the Matter of Mr Ondřej
Dílec, Proprietor of House Number 1213–I, Re His Appeal of the
Magistrate's Earlier Decision

cannot attach any significance to the arguments advanced above, given that the keeping of swine in Prague is expressly forbidden by law, and the circumstance that His Honour the Mayor keeps two horses which produce more dung and inconvenience has nothing to do with the case.

Mr Ondřej Dílec is herewith fined five Austrian guilders and ordered to have his pigs slaughtered or

removed from Prague. Official measures shall be
taken should he fail to comply within three days.

Prague, on this the 14th day of October 1848

A Private Letter from the Innkeeper's Widow Helenka
Veleb to Her Sister,
Alojsie Trousil, a Teacher's Wife Living in Chrudim

Dear Sister,

You're right. You see? I admit it. It comes from
having a teacher for a husband, while I'm as much a
fool as my dearly departed. But you can stop
throwing Kalhotka in my face: it's all over, he's
made a run for it. Of course that's how they were in
his family – Mother never could stand them. It
wasn't my fault; he just talked and talked and you
know what we women are like and what a soft heart
I have. You were right about Dílec too, and now I
don't know how to win him back. He's quite dried
up. I can tell it's bothering him, but he's got a hard
head and thinks – well, who knows what he thinks:
he's a landlord, after all, though he's got no debts and
is basically a good man. I was playing with his boy
the other day, a sweet little tyke with big blue eyes
and cheeks made to be pinched (he's only six months
younger than Toníček and they play together all the
time now), and Dílec happened to come home, and I
pretended I didn't see him and kissed the boy, and he
just stood there speechless. And that day he didn't
send for the boy as he usually does. Thanks for the

butter. It wasn't that cheap in the end – I could have
found it for the same price in the market here – but the
quality is good. St Catherine's Day is still five weeks
off and I'll take Dílec the rent tomorrow, but I must
say I'm a little ashamed: he's been very nice and
hasn't pressed me a bit. Toníček sends you kisses
galore and hopes you'll send him a present, and I add
my kisses to you and your husband and remain, as
always,

Your faithful sister,
Helenka

P.S. Have to run.

The Diary of Ondřej Dílec, Page 31

can't remember so joyful a Christmas. Helenka is a
fine housekeeper and a fine cook and she loves me
dearly; besides, she's not half so hard-headed as I
thought: she does everything I tell her – she's almost
better than my poor first wife, may she rest in peace –
and I don't believe for a minute she ever really loved
that student fellow. They're so funny, women: they'll
love a man – and do everything they can to get his
goat. But if she stays like she is now (and she will, I
can tell), well, then she'll have no regrets. I'll make a
good father to her boy and leave them well provided
for even if I pass away from one day to the next. In
the spring I'll whitewash the house and turn the
garden into a restaurant with a band. Nothing goes
right when a man has empty hands, but now things

are really looking up. And now I may have some respite from those lawsuits. Two gentlemen came to see me today – in connection with the appeal I'd sent to Vienna, they said. At first I just stood there with my mouth wide open – I'd forgotten all about it. Apparently Vienna is calling for a thorough reinvestigation, though how they'll manage I don't know: I ate the last piece of evidence for breakfast this morning. Helenka couldn't stop laughing (she's got a big supply of lard in the kitchen), but I can't help wondering who would have won if things had taken

XII   Five Minutes After the Recital

Her thin, childlike soprano having squeaked its way into the stratosphere, Miss Valinka closed her music and her accompanist tossed off a few final chords. An artfully studied smile and seemly bow made it clear the recital was over.

'What a pleasure! A true artist! You're a lucky man, Mr Eber!'

Mrs Bauer was ecstatic, ceasing to applaud only as she rose from her chair and threw her arms around Valinka in unfeigned rapture. The others leaped up after her – they were some twenty in number and had been sitting in two rows here in the reception room – and showered Valinka with kisses until she hardly had the breath to call out, 'But Mama . . . My hair!'

Mr Eber had stood motionless near the window throughout the performance, swallowing his emotion, now shutting, now opening his eyes. 'We must give her lessons for two more years,' he pronounced with a quaver, 'then let the chips fall where they may. True, she'll be only fourteen at the time and people may wonder, but little matter: talent will out. Would you believe, Mrs Bauer, that after only twenty French lessons she can carry on quite a decent conversation with her tutor?'

'Is it possible?' Mrs Bauer cried, clasping her hands in amazement. 'Is it true, Valinka?'

'*Oui, madame,*' Valinka stammered by way of proof.

'There, you see! I couldn't believe my ears either. Of course it helps to have good teachers. Her singing master is particularly fine. He has an excellent method and attends to every detail. He even puts his thumb in her mouth if she opens it the wrong way. Still, I can't keep her in Prague.'

'No, that would be a sin!' Mrs Bauer agreed and sat down again beside her daughter.

Miss Marie, who sat with her friend's fiancé, Lieutenant Kořínek, at her left elbow, had removed her gloves so as to applaud with suitable vigour. Mr Kořínek – a man of feeble constitution and sickly mien though with a fixed, almost petrified smile about his toothless mouth – applauded with her.

'It's so hot in here,' said the young lady demurely, her task accomplished, though her neighbour was still exerting himself, 'and we girls are so weak. The child has a beautiful voice, don't you think?'

'Oh, I do!' the lieutenant agreed. 'The C at the end was particularly fine.'

'But it was only an F, wasn't it?'

'No, no. It was a C. There was another one earlier. It's always C when it's that high.'

Miss Marie made a long face and asked, perhaps merely to make conversation, 'So you're musical, are you?'

'Me? No, they tell me I had no talent for music. But my brother could play anything you put in front of him; he never let a note get past him.'

'I had a brother like that too,' the young lady said with a sigh. 'Died young, poor boy. A fine tenor. From high C, as you observed just now, to low A. I assure you, low A.'

'That must have been beautiful!'

'Then you do love music?'

'Yes, of course.'

'And you go to the opera often?'

'Me? Oh, no. It costs so much, and a man has only two ears, after all. Once I did hear an opera I liked. Now what was it called? How annoying! Well, anyway, I liked it. I don't usually; I'm too much the soldier: it bothers me to see a husky chap playing the violin when he could be beating a drum. And I don't much care for sopranos doing their circumflexes or whatever you call them.'

At this point Miss Marie turned rather abruptly to her mother.

'Well, how's the conversation going?' that lady inquired in a whisper.

'Fine. I don't believe he'd recognise a match if you showed it to him head down.'

'Well, what of it?'

'True, true,' she whispered back and turned again to her neighbour. 'It's wonderful of them to give their child lessons, don't you think? Especially when you consider how little they have for themselves. They're up to their eyes in debt. We've got capital in this house, and I keep telling Mother to be careful. She's so tender-hearted.'

Mr Kořínek was clearly taken aback by her remarks and was about to make inquiries, but at that moment a flurry of activity announced that the guests were starting to depart. Miss Marie and her mother stood as well.

'We've such a way to go and all alone,' Miss Marie lamented to the lieutenant. 'Friends are few and far between and gallant friends a rarity.'

'Perhaps I might . . .' the lieutenant began with a chivalrous smile.

'Oh, how kind of you! Mother, Mr Kořínek has offered to see us home.'

'But it's so far! I know! Mr Kořínek will stay for supper. Yes, excellent. We'll have a marvellous time!'

Mrs Eber was taking leave of her guests one by one, and Miss Matylda, forced to abandon Mr Kořínek for a time to help her, was distributing kisses when suddenly mother whispered something into daughter's ear and the latter went up to the gallant lieutenant and said in a low voice, 'You *will* stay, won't you? Mama has asked me to invite you to take some ham with us.'

'I . . . I'm afraid I . . .'

'Oh, Matylda dear!' Miss Marie cried, rushing up to her friend and embracing her warmly. 'What a wonderful party! A pity it couldn't have gone on a bit longer. But now Mr Kořínek has promised to see us home, all the way home. No need to fear. Ta-ta, angel! Just one more kiss! There! Your humble servant.'

Miss Matylda stiffened and grew pale.

'What's the matter, dear?' Mrs Eber asked. 'Say goodbye to Miss Marie.' But then she spied the lieutenant preparing to leave with the Bauer women and let out an involuntary gasp.

'Ta-ta, angel!' Marie repeated, waving and sailing off towards the door.

Miss Matylda stood frozen to the spot.

XIII   After the Draw

Mrs Bavor sat at the counter taking her ease, for on Friday afternoons there was not much, aside from a few late customers, to keep one busy even in a grocer's shop. Václav was rarely at home and her husband was off in the city on business, so she had spread out her dream books and figures in front of her and was having a fine time, yawning occasionally, true, but content, her face radiant, her eyes shining softly through the lenses of her spectacles.

Suddenly she glanced up, sensing a presence at the threshold. It was the innkeeper's wife. Mrs Bavor pretended not to notice and went on with her figures. The scene at the late Žanýnka's funeral was doubtless still casting its shadow.

The innkeeper's wife entered the room with the greeting 'Praised be the name of the Lord.'

'Now and for ever more,' Mrs Bavor responded without looking up.

'So we've won, have we?' said the innkeeper's wife, going straight to the point.

'*We*?' Mrs Bavor retorted coldly. 'Nothing to speak of.'

'Then it's true what my customer told me: you entered the line again, the way you had it at first, and you hit the jackpot.' Each word was pointed, probing.

'Right. I always do well when I listen to what the old head tells me.'

'Well, don't I get a share of it?'

'I don't see why you should.'

'That's not fair!'

Mrs Bavor turned white as the wall but still did not look up. 'Did you contribute anything towards my line?' she said slowly, icily. 'No, you advised me to change numbers, you put your money on the new ones, they won a double, you get half, and that's that.'

Strained as Mrs Bavor's reserve was, it did not fail to make an impression. 'Well, we needn't quarrel,' said the innkeeper's wife in an equally strained attempt at reconciliation. 'I just want God's will to be done. Which reminds me, there's something I've been meaning to talk to you about. Your Václav and my Márinka, they seem to get on together . . .'

'There's no rush. They're young. Why push them? Besides, I've got my pride. My son is the son of a grocer; what he does with himself he'll do on his own!'

'Well, I hope you don't think I'm forcing myself on you. My daughter is the daughter of a burgher, and no one can take that from her.'

'But will it put food on the table?' Mrs Bauer jeered and took off her spectacles.

'Honour is honour,' the innkeeper's wife retorted, 'and you've either got it or you haven't. I go where I please, I'm accepted everywhere, but once a lumberjack, always a lumberjack, no matter how you dress him. Which is all I have to say on the matter. Good day!' And she fairly flew out of the shop.

'Your most humble servant,' Mrs Bavor called after her, only now raising her head.

She looked out of the window for a while. Gradually her cheeks regained their hue, her eyes their lustre. 'You'll be back!' she said aloud, clearly pleased with herself for having mastered her emotions. Then she put her spectacles back on and turned again to her dream books and figures. For Mrs Bavor played the lottery body and soul. She was that most sublime variety of player who cares only for the art of the thing and as such enjoyed the highest reputation in the neighbourhood. But the work of true adepts is never done; they must devote their every free moment to maintaining supremacy.

No one would believe the amount of preparation required to enter a lottery confident of victory. One cannot compute the winning number with cool reason; nor can one expect it to appear in a flash – unless by a chance so remote that no serious player would bother with it. A good number is no mere mathematical quantity, nor yet a disembodied vision; it derives neither from the mind nor from the imagination. I would rather liken it to a flower or still more to a crystal, which needs time to take shape and good, firm soil to develop in. And for the lottery ticket that soil is the human heart. Yes, the heart is the wining number's native soil, and just as the human heart is intimately conjoined with the universe as a whole – the farthest star exerting its magnetic force upon it – so is the winning number. Moreover, by its very nature it is the indisputable province of the female sex, and whenever a man meddles in such matters he immediately goes astray, sinking, drowning in a mire of rationality and computation.

Of all this – though she would have been unable to word it as eloquently as we – Mrs Bavor was perfectly aware. She cultivated figures as a gardener cultivates flowers: far be it from her to indulge in the chance 'tear-off' games that hung from shop walls or in convoluted calculations; no, the basis for her far-reaching operations was the dream book or, to be specific, the Kammerlicht edition of same.

Tradition has lent the very name a mystical ring, and it is enhanced by the celebrated work's full sub-title, which reads: *Explanations of the Impressions Left Upon Various and Sundry Natures by Dreams as Inter-preted According to Tribe, and of the Numbers To Be Staked in Lotteries in Conformity with the Meanings of Said Dreams*. The introduction cites a number of ancient sages – Aristotle and Hector's wife, the Severi and Virgil's mother, Jacob's ladder and the pharaoh's cattle, the dreams of the Three Magi in the east and of Nebuchadnezzar in Babylon – all in a style as limpid as that of the above-cited title, a style impenetrable to mere reason but eminently cogent to the heart.

The accurate interpretation of dreams is the basis for playing the lottery, and the goal of the Kammerlicht is to provide that interpretation. Not every dream lends itself to interpretation, however. Some months have few lucky days, but they are well known to the experi-enced practitioner, being 'impressions noted by the ancient stargazers and confirmed by the supreme ruler of the planets'. Yet not even a lucky day yields forth its pearl immediately, for – as only the uninitiated fail to comprehend – there are eight 'tribes' of dreams and of the eight only the fifth is genuine. The first thing one must do when interpreting dreams for purposes of the lottery, therefore, is to exclude all dreams eman-ating directly from the evil spirit (tribe eight) as well as those granted to the virtuous as direct revelations (tribe seven). Dreams having their roots 'implanted in disease' – fevers of the blood or brain, water in the liver or lungs – are of no significance. The fifth tribe appears only to those 'who have partaken of little or no food before retiring and are of a healthy and tranquil disposition withal'. True adepts must therefore adjust their lives to the procreation of dreams, and Mrs Bavor adjusted hers accordingly.

To the dream thus elicited the Kammerlicht provides the necessary numerical interpretation. (True, there are other varieties of dream book, some of which are even illustrated, but while each has its good points, the Kammerlicht towers over dream books as the Sněžka towers over the peaks of the Krkonoše.) The numbers it supplies do not yet guarantee success, but will be used once, at the next draw, to test the waters, so to speak. If they win, well and good; if not, no matter: lottery receipts are never discarded. Lottery dreamers divide the night into four periods of three hours each. (The first begins at seven o'clock in the evening, which testifies to roots in antiquity.) The period in which the dream occurs tells them when they can hope to see it come true, whether within the week or by the third draw or in three months or three years or, yes, as many as twelve. Now you see why maintaining a carefully tended collection of lottery receipts is so important.

But do not imagine we have thus exhausted the aids available to the lottery player. True, Mrs Bavor paid no heed to such inane schemes as cutting out ninety numbers and dropping them into a glass with a large garden spider to draw them into its web: she was too prudent for that. But she did keep a linen bag with ninety marbles in it, and not a day would pass but what she would draw three marbles with her right hand and three with her left, carefully entering the numbers thus obtained in a special list with the designation 'me'. She also had her husband and son and a number of other people close to her draw numbers and she recorded them all with the proper name against every line. Winning numbers she entered in another list, and a crucial list it was: it may be impossible to devise a law to predict when numbers will recur, but going over one's lists at regular intervals one begins to feel a tug at certain lines, the tug of inspiration.

Then at last comes the day when the dream of the proper time and tribe is ripe for fulfilment, when both right hand and left draw the same numbers and inspiration tugs, so one places one's money on them, for one can be absolutely certain of winning. Mrs Bavor, having followed these precepts, was so confident that she had held her ground, refused to change her line – and hit the jackpot.

I have pointed out that the work of true adepts is never done and that they must devote their every free moment to maintaining supremacy. Mrs Bavor did not intend to retire merely because she had now hit the jackpot. She needed the lottery: it whetted her spirit, comforted her heart. That is why we found her hard at work.

She was still writing, rewriting and comparing figures when Václav came home. He nodded his greeting
and paused in front of the counter. She nodded back
without stopping work, but then picked up her linen
marble bag, gave it a shake and handed it to him.

'You haven't drawn your numbers yet,' she said.
'Right hand first. By the way, have you heard you
were dismissed from your post today?' Her voice was
perfectly even.

'What?' Václav cried, scowling up at her, non-
plussed by her calm.

'One of them is the same as mine. Strange, I keep
drawing that thirty . . . Yes, Mr Eber was here to
give you the message. And what's this I hear about
the hairdresser yesterday? That giddy Eber girl came
round at noon spouting thanks and some tale about
how you'd done her a great service.'

'It was nothing, really. Her sister had a recital yesterday, and the man who came to do her hair tripped in
the dark hallway and got stuck behind the mangle. I
ran over and pulled him out, that's all. Márinka happened to be there, and . . .'

'Well, I'll thank you to keep away from Márinka in
future. No, no questions. I say so, that's why. I don't
like her mother; she's not to be trusted.' Her voice was
more agitated now as she entered his numbers. 'There!
And now your left hand. That Eber girl has been turning up here an awful lot lately. She told me to apologise for her, for not inviting you yesterday. She was
ashamed, she said. (Ashamed! Her!) Her mother

forgot and they were very upset about it. Well, I know what they're after. They're drowning in debt and that awful chatterbox has gone and told them . . . Oh, that's right. You don't know. I hit the jackpot today.'

'The jackpot!' Václav cried.

'Yes, I broke the bank. We're in for several thousand at least.'

'I don't believe it!' he shouted, clapping his hands.

'Has your mother ever lied to you?'

Václav leaped over the counter and started hugging and kissing her.

'Oh, get away with you, crazy boy!' she said, giving him a push. 'Must you always lose your head? It was bound to happen eventually, I knew it was. Now you can go back to your studies.'

Václav's eyes suddenly sparkled. He jumped up and grabbed a bunch of keys from the wall.

'And where might you be off to?'

'The roof.'

'To do what, if I may ask?'

'Map out my future!'

XIV   A Happy Family

Mr Eber paced back and forth, still in early-morning attire (trousers without braces, chest uncovered, hair sticking out wildly in all directions), his angular features and wrinkled face showing acute distress, his arms swinging aimlessly.

His wife, who was also only half dressed, stood at the chest of drawers with a duster in her hand, and while she made a pretence of using it, her every movement showed she shared his discomfort.

A third person, the cause of this discomfort, was seated at the table. An insider could have sized up the situation in a flash. The face of the individual in question bore definite traces of the nation whose only member to have returned capital it had once acquired was, to our knowledge, a biblical figure named Judas. Moreover, the individual in question was clearly at home in the Eber household, for he would expose his bald pate, edged only by thin grey strands, then hide it again with a shabby hat; he drummed on the table and spat unceremoniously on the floor. A sense of conscious supremacy radiated from his eyes, an undeniably brazen smile twisted his lips.

Suddenly he gave a twitch, leaned against the table, and rose.

'I've been throwing my money away on you,' he said in a resonant voice. 'Now I must think of myself. You won't get another penny out of me.'

Mrs Eber turned to him and, forcing a smile to her lips, said, 'Just fifty guilders more, Mr Menke. We'll be grateful for your aid. You'll see.'

' "Grateful", you say?' the Jew sneered. 'I'd be grateful too if somebody gave me fifty guilders.'

'But we're still worth something, Mr Menke. We've got our house and – '

'Your house! Prague is full of houses, full of land-lords too. But you know who the real landlord is here. Though what good does your tenant list do me? I get no percentage from it. No, if I haven't got my interest by Tuesday, I'm going straight to the president!' He started for the door.

'But Mr Menke – '

'No. I've got my children to think of. I can't deprive myself of an income. Good day!' And off he went, leaving the door wide open.

Mr Eber flapped his arms and pursed his lips as though about to say something; Mrs Eber marched over to the door and slammed it shut.

The door to the other room, partly ajar until then, now opened fully to reveal Miss Matylda in her petti-coat, yawning and peering about listlessly. 'I don't know why you even talk to such people,' she remarked. 'I'd have thrown him out.'

Mr Eber was combing his hair in front of the mirror. Stung by his daughter's words, he turned to her and snapped, 'Quiet! You don't understand.'

'I certainly don't,' she replied, perfectly unper-turbed, and, going over to the window, yawned a contented yawn into the beautiful morning.

Mrs Eber made a show of holding her tongue, brushing the dust from the chest of drawers with such zeal that the wood all but sighed. The silence went on for some time, during which Mr Eber dressed and his spouse flew about the room, picking things up and setting them down again. Knowing that the situation could not long continue thus, Mr Eber took it upon himself to break the silence.

'Bring me my coffee, dear,' he said as calmly as he could. 'You know I have to leave for the office soon.'

'It's not warm yet,' she answered dryly, opening the large wardrobe.

'What do you mean warm? You're not giving me yesterday's coffee, are you? I mean, really!'

'And why not? Do you bring in so much that we can afford to cook all day? Earn your fresh coffee!'

Miss Matylda had turned away from the window and sat down, her hands in her lap, her eyes moving back and forth between her father and mother. She was clearly enjoying herself.

Mr Eber knew his wife well and, not wishing to start a row just then, took a different tack. 'What are we having for dinner today?' he asked, as though never having inquired about breakfast.

'Dumplings with horseradish sauce,' came the biting reply.

Mr Eber could not stand dumplings with horseradish sauce. Sensing the intention behind the choice, he felt a certain gall.

'And why that damned concoction today of all days, if I may ask?'

'Because! Because we're washing all day today, and when we wash that's all I cook.' She was searching for something in the wardrobe and, unable to find it, started pulling things down from their hooks and strewing them over the floor.

'So you're washing all day, are you? Well, where am I supposed to go?'

'Wherever you please! Take a walk with your daughter Valinka, for instance. A fine father you are – you haven't been anywhere with her for a year.'

'Anything else I can do for you?' he said hoarsely, now in a towering rage.

'Yes, as a matter of fact. You can go to the corner and beg!' Still unable to locate what she was after, she stepped into the wardrobe. 'With your brains it will soon be all we have left. Don't be surprised if I poison myself, even if it means swallowing glass. And just when Matylda and I should be encouraging the Bavor boy to take an interest in her, you go and throw him out of the office! Playing the big fish in the pond when in fact – '

She did not finish her sentence. Mr Eber, no longer able to control his fury, shoved her to the back of the wardrobe, slammed the door and turned the key.

Miss Matylda clapped her hands in glee.

There was such a din, such a vigorous banging that the wardrobe shook. Mr Eber seized a glass and shattered it against the wardrobe doors. Miss Matylda clapped again.

The clamour within increased. Mr Eber threw on his coat, grabbed his hat, then paused.

Noting his irresolution, Miss Matylda called out, 'No, leave her there! It will teach her a lesson!'

'You're right,' he agreed. 'Don't let her out till I'm down in the street. Well, I'm off.'

And off he was. But at that moment Matylda had an idea. She rushed to the wardrobe, unlocked it, and said to her mother as she burst forth, deathly pale, 'Quick or he'll get away!' Not that Mrs Eber needed the encouragement. She fairly flew to the door, her daughter hard at her heels, not wishing to miss a trick.

Grabbing a broom in the kitchen, she charged on to the balcony. Mr Eber was just squeezing past the servant, who was scrubbing the steps. 'Dump your bucket on him!' Mrs Eber shouted. 'Get him good and wet!'

Mr Eber quickened his pace to a perilous speed. He had reached the courtyard when the broom whisked past his ear. Seeing it had missed its mark, Mrs Eber tore the bonnet from her head and flung it after her fleeing master. 'Murderer! Thief!' Her shriek rang out through the house. 'If you look foolish now, think how you'd look without all that flannel, you wretch! A fine husband he makes! Three hundred guilders a year, and he calls himself a gentleman! A pox on *gentlemen*! Don't you come home for a week, you hear?'

But Mr Eber did not hear the good advice, having disappeared into the passageway.

The whole spectacle was over so quickly that the tenants, rushing to their windows, saw nothing but Miss Matylda, who had looked on from the doorway, enfolding her mother in a joyful embrace.

xv   The Week Draws to a Close

Although Josefina's wedding took place early on Sunday morning, the courtyard and passageway were full of curious neighbours, and a considerable crowd had gathered before the house as well. Having followed everything with rapt attention, they concluded it was a 'pale affair'.

They did not thereby imply that things were too plain, because Josefina's bridegroom had spared nothing (his bride had a lovely silk gown, and there were plenty of coaches), yet the neighbours were right. The familiar faces taking part in the ceremony were unwontedly pale, as though some awful catastrophe awaited them before they set off. No one gave a thought to the bride's deathly pallor, because, as the saying goes, 'pale bride, jolly wife', but she was followed by a bridegroom pale with emotion and by Miss Klára, the bridesmaid, who never had much colour. Moreover, as luck would have it, the others lacked colour as well. Even the round cheeks of the witness, the Doctor, noticeably lacked their usual glow. Only Václav, the best man, laughed and joked as always. But everyone knew he held nothing sacred.

Later in the day the Doctor stood in front of the house, pulling on his gloves and peering down the passageway from time to time as though waiting for somebody. Suddenly the door to the shop opened and out came Václav, fully dressed.

'Out for a stroll, Doctor?'

'Yes. To Stromovka.'

'By yourself?'

'Yes. I mean, Mrs Lakmus is going, too.'

'I see. With Miss Klára. She looked nice today.' The Doctor cast a quick glance down the street. 'And where might you be off to, Václav?'

'To Šárka.'

'Not alone, I imagine. Márinka, perhaps?'

'No, *not* with Márinka, actually,' said Václav with a smile. 'With the Ebers.'

A chorus of feminine voices came echoing through the passageway. The Lakmus ladies and the Ebers had just entered it from the courtyard.

'The Ebers?' the Doctor asked, surprised. 'Surely you've no intention of . . . Really, now, really!'

'Don't worry, Doctor, don't worry. I know what I'm doing. I'm only avenging our sex. Aren't you, Doctor?'

The Doctor looked down in embarrassment. He opened his mouth as if to reply, but closed it without a word. He cleared his throat and then said, 'Quiet, they're coming!'

Mr Ryšánek and Mr Schlegel

I

It would be laughable for me to doubt that any of my readers should be unfamiliar with Malá Strana's foremost restaurant, that is, Steinitz's – the one in the first house past the Bridge Tower on the left, at the corner of Bridge and Bath streets, the house with the large windows and wide glass door – the only restaurant daring to occupy this most public of streets and opening directly on to the thoroughfare (the others are all in side streets or have inside entrances or are at least sheltered by an arcade with true Malá Strana modesty). That is why your Malá Strana native, son of those hushed, subdued streets full of poetic nooks and crannies, does not frequent Steinitz's. It is frequented by functionaries, professors and officers swept into Malá Strana by fate, soon to be blown away again, as well as by a small number of pensioners and an occasional rich, old landlord who has long since entrusted his livelihood to others – that is all. Half bureaucratic, half aristocratic.

Even years ago, when I was still a schoolboy, the

clientele was of a similarly exclusive character, yet there was a slight difference. To be brief, it was the Olympus of Malá Strana, the meeting place of the local gods. According to well-established historical fact, gods arise from their peoples. Jehovah was a sullen god, cruel and vengeful, vicious and blood-thirsty like the Hebrew nation as a whole. The Hellenic gods were witty and elegant, handsome and gay – Greeks, in a word. As for our Slav gods – I'm sorry, but we Slavs lack the ingenuity to build great states or create distinctive gods, our one-time divinities (the best efforts of folklorists like Erben and Kostomarov notwithstanding) remaining a motley crew, all mist and uncertainty. One day I may write an article – a witty one, of course – about the God/man parallel, but all I need say at this point is that the gods who gathered at Steinitz's were indubitably our local gods. Malá Strana – both houses and people – has something quiet, dignified, behind-the-times, one might even say drowsy about it, and the gentlemen in question shared all its qualities, including the drowsiness. To be sure, they were the same mix of officials, soldiers, pro-fessors and pensioners as today's clientele, but at that time officials and officers were not shuffled from one country to the next and a father could put a son through his studies in Prague, ease him into a good position, and use his connections to keep him there. Whenever a group of the Steinitz regulars went outside for a chat, they were greeted by each and every passer-by. Everyone knew them.

For us schoolboys the Steinitz Olympus was all the more Olympian in that it included all our old teachers. Old! Why even qualify them as such? I knew them all and I could tell: not one of them had ever been young or, rather, they had looked the same as children – only a bit smaller, perhaps.

I can see them all before me as if it were now. First, a Privy Councillor at the Court of Appeal. Long, lean and respected by all. He was still active at the time, but I could never quite picture what his job entailed. When we came out of school at ten in the morning, he was only just leaving his Carmelite Street house, wending his solemn way to Čarda's, the wine tavern. When we went rampaging along the Marian Ramparts on our Thursday-afternoon holidays, we found him strolling in the park. But by five he was always at Steinitz's. I made up my mind to work hard and become a Privy Councillor too, but later I somehow forgot about it.

Then there was the one-eyed count. Now, Malá Strana was never short on counts, but the one-eyed count was the only Steinitz regular, at least in those days. He was tall and bony, had a rosy red complexion and closely cropped white hair, and wore a black patch over his left eye. He would stand in front of Steinitz's for two hours at a stretch, and I gave him a wide berth if I had to go past. Nature gives aristocrats a profile that is known as noble and makes them similar to birds of prey. The count reminded me of nothing so much as the hawk that alighted on the dome of St

Nicholas's daily at noon with merciless regularity and a pigeon in its claws, which it would maul with such ferocity that the feathers fluttered down to the square. If I gave the count a wide berth, it was because I vaguely feared he would peck at my head.

Then there was the fat army doctor who, though far from doddering, had long since retired. Rumour had it that once, when a highly placed personage made some comment or other on a tour of Prague's hospitals, our doctor told the highly placed personage that he didn't know what he was talking about. For this he lost his post but won our love, because we regarded him as a flaming revolutionary. He was also friendly and garrulous. Whenever he met a boy he liked – the boy might also be a girl – he would stroke his cheek and say, 'Give your father my regards', even though he did not know the man.

Then – but no! All the old men grew still older and then died. Why raise them from their graves? I recall with pride the moments I spent among them, the feeling of independence, manhood, even majesty I experienced the first time I entered Steinitz's as a university student and sat free of fear amid my former teachers. True, they did not pay me much heed, those lofty creatures; they ignored me, in fact. Though once in the course of a few weeks the doctor did pause at my table on his way out and say, 'Take it from me, young man, the beer they make nowadays isn't worth drinking.' And giving a contemptuous nod in the direction of the men with whom he had just been sitting, he added, 'No matter what they think.' A regular Brutus, he! I would venture to say that had the occasion arisen he would have told Caesar to his face that he didn't know the first thing about beer.

They ignored me, but I watched them closely. I may be a pale copy, but whatever I have of the sublime I owe to them. Two unforgettable men have remained engraved in my heart above all. Their names are Mr Ryšánek and Mr Schlegel, and they could not stand each other. But here I must beg your indulgence, for I wish to take a new tack.

When you enter Steinitz's from Bridge Street, the first room you pass through, the room with the billiard tables, has three windows on the right overlooking Bath Street. In the recesses of each of the windows is a little table with a horseshoe-shaped bench that seats three: one with his back to the window, the other two at the ends of the horseshoe facing each other or, should they choose to sit with their backs to the window, facing the billiard table, in which case they can watch the players.

Every evening from six to eight the third table was invariably occupied by the universally respected Mr Ryšánek and Mr Schlegel. Their places were always kept for them. The idea that someone might venture to take the seat of a regular guest was something the fine, upstanding citizens of Malá Strana rejected out of hand, because – well, because it was simply unthinkable. The place by the window was always vacant; Mr Ryšánek sat at the end of the horseshoe closer to the entrance, Mr Schlegel opposite him, an arm's length away. They both sat with their backs to the window and hence partly turned away from the table and each other, their eyes on the billiard match; the only time they turned back to the table was when they wanted to take a sip or fill a pipe. For eleven years they had sat thus, day in and day out, and in all those eleven years they had never said a single word to each other, never taken the slightest notice of each other.

Everyone in Malá Strana knew of the bitter hatred they had for each other, their animosity being long-standing and unrelenting. Everyone knew its cause as well – the root of all evil: woman. They had loved the same one. At first she inclined towards Mr Ryšánek, who had a well-established business; then in an unexpected about-face, she fell into the arms of Mr Schlegel, perhaps because Mr Schlegel was nearly ten years younger. And thus she became Mrs Schlegel.

Whether Mrs Schlegel was of a beauty to account for Mr Ryšánek's permanent grief and lifelong celibacy I cannot tell. She had long since passed away, shortly after giving birth. Perhaps the daughter she left behind was in her image. At the time of which I am speaking, Miss Schlegel was approximately twenty-two years old. I knew her because her friend Poldýnka – the captain's daughter, known for stumbling at every twentieth step – lived in the flat above ours. Miss Schlegel was supposed to be a beauty. Perhaps she was – but only to an architect. Everything was in the proper place, the correct proportions; one could see the why and wherefore of it all. Yet for anyone but an architect she was a total disaster. Her face was exquisite, but as immobile as a façade; her eyes sparkled, but for no reason, like a pair of newly washed windows; her mouth, though in the shape of a fine arabesque, opened slowly, like a gate, and either remained ajar or, just as slowly, shut again; and her complexion – well, she always looked freshly whitewashed. Maybe now – if she is still with us – she is not quite so comely, yet has improved in appearance, the way buildings improve with years of weathering.

I apologise to my readers for being unable to tell them how Mr Ryšánek and Mr Schlegel first came together at the table in the third window. It must have been fate herself, accursed fate, wishing to plague their old age. But once fate had set them down at the table, manly pride kept them there: they met a second time in an act of defiance and from then on to prove how steadfast they were – and to keep tongues from wagging. In any case, it had long been clear to everyone at Steinitz's that both viewed it as a question of honour and neither could give way.

They would arrive at about six, one of them a minute earlier one day, the other a minute earlier the next. They would nod politely in all directions, greeting everyone but each other. The waiter took their hats and sticks in summer, their coats and shaggy hats in winter, and hung them on their pegs behind their seats. Thus divested of outer garments, they bobbed their upper torsos as pigeons do – old people have a habit of bending forward before sitting – then each leaned a hand on his corner of the table (Mr Ryšánek the left hand, Mr Schlegel the right) and slowly sat down with his back to the window and his face to the billiard table. When the fat innkeeper came up to them, all smiles and chatter, to offer the first pinch of snuff, he had to tap on his snuffbox anew for each and repeat to each what nice weather they were having; otherwise the second of them would refuse the snuff and ignore the remark. No one had ever managed to have a conversation with the two together. Never did either take the slightest notice of the other: there *was* no other person at the table.

The waiter would serve them their beer. After a while – but never at the same time, because they watched each other like hawks, for all their detachment – they turned to the table, took large, silver-plated meerschaum pipes from their breast pockets, tobacco pouches from their coat pockets, filled their pipes, lit up, and turned back again. Thus they would sit for two hours, drinking three glasses of beer. Then, rising (one of them a minute earlier one day, the other a minute earlier the next), they would put their pipes and their pouches away, bid the waiter help them on with their coats, and, thus prepared, nod farewell to everyone except each other.

I would purposely sit at a nearby table beside the stove, where I had an unobstructed view of them and could look on in comfort without being too conspicuous.

Mr Ryšánek had been a canvas merchant; Mr Schlegel had dealt in hardware. Both had retired wealthy, but their faces still reflected their lifelong occupations: Mr Ryšánek's always reminded me of a red-and-white striped awning, Mr Schlegel's of a much pestled mortar.

Mr Ryšánek was taller, leaner and, as I have mentioned, older. He was often under the weather, ailing, and his lower jaw tended to sag. His grey eyes were aided by lenses in black horn-rimmed frames. He wore a light-coloured wig, and from his not entirely grey eyebrows one could guess he had been fair-haired. His cheeks were sunken and pale, so pale as to make his long nose look red, even crimson. Perhaps that was why it seemed always to have a drop at the end of it, a tear from the very core of his being. As a conscientious biographer, I must point out that Mr Ryšánek was occasionally late in wiping the tear away; that is, it fell into a sympathetic lap.

Mr Schlegel was the stocky type; I don't believe he had a neck. His head had the shape of a bomb, his hair, though still black, was greying. His face, where shaven, was blue-black; where no beard grew, it was pink – a combination of luminous flesh and dark shadow, like the chiaroscuro in a Rembrandt portrait.

I held my two heroes in high esteem; yes, I admired them greatly – sitting there, waging their battle day after day, fierce, unremitting, their weapons venom-drenched silence and the utmost disdain. But the battle remained undecided. Who in the end would plant his foot on the neck of his foe? Mr Schlegel was physically the stronger: everything about him was compact, concentrated, his every utterance a bell tower's clang; Mr Ryšánek was soft-spoken and weak, but he sustained his hatred with equal heroism.

II

And then something happened.

On the Wednesday two weeks after Easter Mr Schlegel came in and sat down as usual – sat down, filled his pipe, and blew out a smoke cloud that might have come from a forge. The innkeeper went up to him at once. He tapped on his snuffbox and offered it to him, but after shutting and shaking it, he looked over to the door and remarked, 'We'll not be seeing Mr Ryšánek today.'

Mr Schlegel stared with stony indifference straight before him.

'We heard it from the doctor,' he went on, running his eyes over Mr Schlegel's face as he turned back from the door. 'He got out of bed this morning as usual, but was suddenly taken with a fever and had to lie down at once. They sent for the doctor immediately, on the spot. Inflammation of the lungs. The doctor's been to see him three times today – an old man, too. But he's in good hands. We can only hope for the best.'

Mr Schlegel gave a grunt without parting his lips. He never said a word or blinked an eye. The innkeeper moved on to the next table.

I peered into Mr Schlegel's face. For a long time it remained immobile except for the mouth, which opened to blow out smoke or allow the pipe to shift a bit. Then an acquaintance came up to him, and as they talked Mr Schlegel laughed aloud several times. I found his laughter repellent.

Mr Schlegel's behaviour was decidedly different that day. At other times he sat nailed to his seat like a sentry to his box, while on that day he was restless, jittery; he even agreed to a game of billiards with Mr Köhler the merchant. He had luck all the way to the double, and I must confess I hoped he would muff the final double each time so Mr Köhler could catch up.

Then he sat down again and smoked and drank. When anyone went up to him, he spoke louder and in longer sentences than usual. Not a single gesture escaped me. I could tell he was pleased and lacked the most common form of commiseration with his rival in his infirmity. I found him repellent.

Several times his glance strayed to the buffet where the doctor was sitting. I was certain he wanted to shake his hand and tell him not to take too many pains with his patient. An evil man, truly evil.

Towards eight the doctor left. He paused at the

third table. 'Good night,' he said. 'I've got to see Ryšánek once more today. One can't be too careful.'

'Good night,' Mr Schlegel replied coldly.

That evening Mr Schlegel drank four glasses of beer and stayed until half past eight.

Days passed, weeks passed. A cold, fitful April gave way to a warm May – we had a fine spring that year. When May is fair, Malá Strana is heaven: Petřín Hill is covered with white blossoms and looks as if milk were bubbling up out of it; all Malá Strana is awash in the scent of lilac.

Mr Ryšánek was well out of danger by then. Spring had soothed him like a salve. I would meet him making his way through the park. He walked slowly, leaning on his stick. Always lean, he was now incomparably leaner, and his lower jaw never shut. One felt like winding a scarf round his chin, closing his dull eyes, and laying him in a coffin. Yet he was slowly recovering.

He did not show up at Steinitz's, however. There Mr Schlegel reigned supreme at the third table.

Then one day in late June – it was the day of St Peter and St Paul – I suddenly beheld them together again, Mr Schlegel once more nailed to his seat and both men positioned with their backs to the window.

Friends and neighbours came and shook hands with Mr Ryšánek, wishing him a warm welcome back. The old man trembled with emotion, smiling and responding graciously. He had grown mild.

Mr Schlegel kept his eyes on the billiard table and smoked his pipe.

Whenever he was left alone, Mr Ryšánek turned his gaze to the buffet, where his doctor was sitting. A grateful soul he was.

Once when Mr Ryšánek was thus engaged, Mr Schlegel's head moved a bit to the side. His glance advanced slowly from the floor past Mr Ryšánek's pointed knees to a hand lying on a corner of the table, all skin and bones, and, after resting on the hand for a moment, resumed its climb, alighting eventually on the sagging jaw and ravaged face, only to dart away immediately. Then the head straightened again.

'Up and about!' cried the innkeeper, emerging from the kitchen or cellar and, spying him for the first time, running over. 'Good to see you looking so well. Thank God you're back!'

'Yes, praise God,' said Mr Ryšánek with a smile. 'I managed to slip away. I'm my old self again.'

'But you're not smoking. Still off tobacco?'

'You know, today's the first day I've felt like smoking. I think I will.'

'Well, well,' said the innkeeper, 'a good sign!' And after giving his snuffbox a tap and offering it first to Mr Ryšánek, then to Mr Schlegel, he withdrew with a polite remark.

Mr Ryšánek took out his pipe and reached into his pocket for his pouch. He shook his head, reached in a second time and a third, and then called over the tiny kitchen boy and said, 'Run over to my place. You

know where I live, don't you? Right. On the corner
here. Tell them to give you my tobacco pouch. It will
be lying on my desk.'

The lad rushed off with a leap.

All at once Mr Schlegel came to life. He slowly
stretched his right hand to his open pouch and pushed
it most of the way to Mr Ryšánek. 'It's Three Kings,
red label, if you'd care for some,' he uttered in his
brusque way, ending in a grunt.

Mr Ryšánek did not reply. Mr Ryšánek did not look
over. His head remained where it was with the stony
indifference of the past eleven years. Yet his hand
shook several times and his jaw shut.

Mr Schlegel's right hand lay on the pouch as if
frozen to it; his eyes were fixed on the ground. From
time to time he would puff on his pipe or clear his
throat.

The kitchen boy returned.

'Thank you,' Mr Ryšánek said to Mr Schlegel without looking at him, 'but as you can see I've got my
own pouch now.' He paused and added, 'I smoke
Three Kings, red label, too,' apparently feeling something more needed to be said. Whereupon he proceeded to fill his pipe, light it and take the first puff.

'How does it taste?' Mr Schlegel growled in a voice
infinitely gruffer than usual.

'Good, praise God.'

'Yes, God be praised,' Mr Schlegel said. The
muscles around his mouth twitched like flashes of

lightning across a dark sky, and he added quickly, 'We were beginning to worry about you.'

For the first time Mr Ryšánek slowly turned his head, and the eyes of the two men met.

And from that time forth Mr Ryšánek and Mr Schlegel spoke together at the third table.

A Beggar Brought to Ruin

I wish to describe a tragic event, but the merry face of Mr Vojtíšek, a face beaming with health and as radiantly red as a Sunday roast basted with fresh butter, shines over the whole thing from the outset. Mr Vojtíšek shaved only on Sundays. By Saturday, when a white beard gleaming like thick cream had sprouted once more on his chin, the face looked even more handsome. I liked his hair, too; not that he had much. It began at his temples beneath a rounded bald spot and was so grey that it had passed the silver stage and seemed to be turning back to gold; moreover, it fluttered gently about his head like silk. (Mr Vojtíšek always carried his cap in hand unless crossing a stretch of particularly harsh sunlight.) I found everything about him pleasing: his blue, innocent eyes, his whole face a round, innocent eye.

Mr Vojtíšek was a beggar. What he had been before that I have no idea, but judging by how well he was known throughout Malá Strana he must have been a beggar for a long time, and judging by his health – he was as strong as an ox – he could have remained one for many years. I have a clue to how old he was at the time. Once I saw him, hobbling his way along St John's Hill, go up to Mr Schimmer the policeman, who was leaning on the railing, sunning himself. Mr Schimmer was the fat policeman, so fat that his grey uniform always looked ready to burst and his head, when seen from behind, resembled – if you'll excuse the comparison – a bunch of greasy sausages. His shiny helmet wobbled as he moved, and when he set off after an apprentice who had shamelessly and in violation of every law in the book decided to cross the street with a lighted pipe in his mouth, he had to grab the headpiece off his head. That would make us children laugh and hop up and down, but as soon as he looked in our direction we would pretend nothing had happened. Mr Schimmer was a German from Šlukov, and if he is still with us – which I hope to God he is – I'll wager he speaks Czech as poorly as he did then. 'And to think I learned it in a year,' he liked to say.

On the day in question Mr Vojtíšek tucked his blue cap under his left arm, thrust his right hand into the pocket of his long grey coat and greeted the yawning Mr Schimmer with the words, 'The Lord be with you!' Mr Schimmer saluted. Mr Vojtíšek, happy, fished out his modest birch-bark snuffbox, slid open the lid by its leather loop and handed it to Mr Schimmer. Mr Schimmer took a pinch of snuff and said, 'You must be getting on. How old are you, anyway?'

Mr Vojtíšek smiled and said, 'Yes, indeed. It's well

nigh eighty years since my father brought me into the world for his greater amusement.'

The attentive reader will doubtless wonder that a beggar like Mr Vojtíšek would dare speak to a policeman in such a familiar tone, as if to a close acquaintance, and that Mr Schimmer was careful not to talk to him as he would to a country bumpkin or anyone clearly his inferior. Besides, remember what it meant to be a policeman in those days. There weren't droves of them as there are now. There was Mr Novák, Mr Schimmer, Mr Kedlický and Mr Weisse, each relieving the other throughout the day on our street patrol. First little Mr Novák from Slabce, who preferred the beat along the shops for the plum brandy, then fat Mr Schimmer from Šlukov, then Mr Kedlický from Vyšehrad, morose but good-natured, and finally Mr Weisse from Rožmitál, tall and with uncommonly long yellow teeth. We knew where each of them came from, how long they had served in the army and how many children they had, and we local children would follow them around whenever we could. They knew each of us, man, woman and child, and could tell my mother where her offspring had strayed. When in 1844 Mr Weisse died fighting a fire in Renthaus, all Spur Street flocked to his funeral.

But Mr Vojtíšek was no common beggar either. He did not cultivate the appearance of one: he was quite clean, at the beginning of the week at least; the scarf round his neck was always neatly knotted; his coat was patched in places, but the colours matched fairly well. He would cover the entire district in the course of a week. Everyone let him in; indeed, as soon as a housewife heard his gentle voice outside her door, she would take him a half-kreutzer. Half a kreutzer was worth quite a bit in those days. He would beg all morning, then stop in at St Nicholas's for eleven-thirty Mass, but he never begged in church or even acknowledged the presence of the squatting beggar women. After Mass he would go off for a meal, knowing where on which day to find a full pot of leftovers. There was something effortless about what he did and the way he did it, something like what prompted Storm to exclaim in a touchingly comic poem: '*Ach, könnt' ich betteln geh'n über die braune Haid'!*'; that is, 'Oh, to go a-begging o'er the broad, brown lea!'

The only person who refused him his half-kreutzer was the innkeeper in our house, Mr Herzl. Mr Herzl was rather long-legged and rather tight-fisted. All he would give him was a sprinkling of tobacco from his pouch, after which – every Saturday – they invariably had the following exchange:

'Times are bad, Mr Vojtíšek, very bad.'

'They are indeed, Mr Herzl, they are indeed. And they won't get any better until the Castle lion swings on the Vyšehrad swing.'

By which he meant the lion on St Vitus's steeple. I must confess that Mr Vojtíšek's prediction made a deep impression on me. For I could not with propriety and as a reasonable young man – I was all of eight at the time – doubt for an instant that said lion was capable of doing what I did on church fair days, that is, crossing the Stone Bridge, walking to Vyšehrad and swinging on the famous twirling swing. Although how it would make things better I never understood.

It was a beautiful day in June. Mr Vojtíšek had come out of St Nicholas's, set his cap on his head to protect it from the sun's rays and was slowly crossing what is now Stephen's Square. He paused at the statue of the Holy Trinity, then sat down on the steps to bask in the resonant plash of the fountain and the warmth of the sun. What could be more pleasant? Evidently he would be dining at a place where they did not gather until after twelve.

No sooner had he settled on the steps than one of the beggar women left her post at the entrance to St Nicholas's and headed in his direction. She was the one known as 'Mother Millions'. Whereas other beggar women promised almsgivers that God would repay them a hundred thousand times, she started at 'millions and millions'. That is why Mrs Hermann, the wife of a church-court official and a regular at Prague's auctions, gave alms to her alone. Mother Millions walked when it suited her and limped when it suited her, and now she was making straight for the statue and Mr Vojtíšek, linen skirts swishing over scrawny shanks, a blue headscarf sliding up and down over her forehead. I always found her face repellent – all tiny, noodlelike wrinkles converging on a pointed nose, thin mouth, and eyes the yellow-green of a cat's.

As soon as she was close enough to address him, she said, 'Praised be the Lord Jesus Christ,' with puckered lips.

Mr Vojtíšek nodded in response.

Mother Millions took a seat at the other end of the steps and sneezed. 'Brr!' she said. 'I don't like the sun. The moment it shines on me I sneeze.'

Mr Vojtíšek made no reply.

Mother Millions pushed back her scarf, revealing the whole of her face. She blinked like a cat in the sun, her eyes closing, then gleaming like two green dots. Her mouth never stopped twitching, and each time it opened it displayed a single tooth, quite black, sticking out of the front upper jaw.

'Mr Vojtíšek, Mr Vojtíšek,' she began again. 'I always say, "If only you would." '

Mr Vojtíšek made no reply, but turned in her direction and stared at her mouth.

'I always say, "Yes, if Mr Vojtíšek had a mind to, he could tell us where the good people are." '

Mr Vojtíšek made no reply.

'Why are you staring at me like that?' Mother Millions asked after a pause. 'What is it about me?'

'That tooth. I was wondering why you have that one tooth.'

'Oh, that tooth,' she sighed, and added, 'You know, when you lose a tooth it means you lose a friend. Well, everyone who wished me well and had my interests at heart – they're all dead and buried, every last one of them. There may be one left, but where is he, the friend our all-merciful God has seen fit to grace my life with? No, I am utterly forsaken!'

Mr Vojtíšek stared straight ahead and made no reply.

Something akin to a smile, to joy, suffused the beggar woman's face, but it was an ugly joy. She pursed her lips again, and her entire face seemed to draw together there.

'Mr Vojtíšek, Mr Vojtíšek. The two of us could still be happy. I've always thought of us together. It's God's will. Everyone likes you, you know all kinds of people, but you're so alone, Mr Vojtíšek. There's no one to look after you. I could move in. I've got a nice feather bed . . .'

While she talked, Mr Vojtíšek slowly rose to his feet. Having reached his full height, he smoothed out the leather peak of his cap and said, 'I'd rather take arsenic.' At which he turned, without so much as a farewell, and set off for Spur Street. A pair of green orbs gleamed after him until he disappeared round the corner.

Mother Millions pulled her scarf down almost to her chin and sat motionless for a long time. Perhaps she had fallen asleep.

All at once strange rumours started making their way through Malá Strana, and the people they reached scratched their heads over them. 'Mr Vojtíšek,' you would hear in the course of a conversation, and then, 'Mr Vojtíšek!'

I soon got to the bottom of it. Mr Vojtíšek wasn't so poor after all, people were saying. Mr Vojtíšek owned two houses across the river in the Old Town, they said. He had been making fools out of all the good people of Malá Strana. And for years!

There was a wave of indignation. The men were especially upset. They were not so much insulted as embarrassed at having been taken in.

'The scoundrel!' said one.

'It's got to be true,' another reasoned. 'Has anyone ever seen him beg on Sundays? You can be sure he's off in one of his mansions feasting on a roast.'

The women wavered. They found Mr Vojtíšek's kind face too sincere.

But the rumours continued: he had two daughters and was bringing them up as ladies; one of them was engaged to a lieutenant and the other was about to go on the stage; they never went out without gloves and took regular carriage rides to Stromovka.

That made up the women's minds for them.

In no more than forty-eight hours the fate of Mr Vojtíšek was reversed. Everyone turned him away with a reference to 'bad times'. Houses that had once left him dinner told him, 'Nothing today' or 'We're poor folk; our pease-pudding's not for the likes of you.' The street urchins danced around him shouting, 'Gentleman! Landlord!'

On Saturday I was standing in front of my house when Mr Vojtíšek came in sight. Mr Herzl was as usual leaning against the stone doorpost in his white apron. Seized by an inexplicable panic, I ran inside and hid behind the heavy door, but I could see Mr Vojtíšek clearly through the space between the hinges.

The cap shook in his hands. His bright smile was gone; his head was bent, his flaxen hair dishevelled. 'Praised be the Lord Jesus Christ,' he said in his normal voice, raising his head. His cheeks were pale, his eyes heavy with sleep.

'Glad to see you,' said Mr Herzl. 'I wonder if you could lend me twenty thousand. Don't worry. It's for a mortgage, a sure thing. I've been wanting to buy the house next door to the Swan here, and . . .'

He did not finish the sentence.

A flood of tears welled forth from Mr Vojtíšek's eyes. 'But . . . but I . . . I've been an honest man all my life!' he sobbed.

Then he staggered across the street and collapsed against the wall at the turn to the Castle, continuing to sob loudly, his head on his knees.

I raced in to my parents, shaking violently. My mother was standing at the window. 'What did Mr Herzl say to him?' she asked.

I stared out at Mr Vojtíšek. He was still weeping. Mother was busy with mid-morning coffee, but every other minute she came up to the window, looked out and shook her head.

At one point she saw Mr Vojtíšek rise up slowly, and she quickly cut a slice of bread, laid it on top of a pot of coffee, and hurried outside. She called to him from the doorstep, she waved, but Mr Vojtíšek merely looked up and said nothing. Then at last he whispered, 'God bless you!' and added, 'I couldn't swallow a thing.'

Mr Vojtíšek never begged in Malá Strana again. Nor could he go from door to door across the river: the people did not know him, the police did not know him. He would sit at the entrance to the Church of the Knights of the Cross near the Clementinum arcade, just opposite the bridge guardhouse. I saw him there every time we crossed the bridge to the Old Town on our Thursday half-holiday to ogle the displays of the Old Town Square booksellers. His cap lying on the ground before him, his head drooping on his breast, his hands clutching a rosary, he took no notice of anyone. Pate, cheeks, hands – none of them shone and blushed as they had only a short time before, and his skin had turned sallow and shrunk into scaly wrinkles. Shall I admit it? Why not? I did not dare go up to him; I skulked along the pillars, tossed my Thursday fortune – a single groschen – into his cap from behind and beat a quick retreat.

Then one day our paths crossed on the bridge. He was being led in the direction of Malá Strana by a policeman. I never saw him again.

It was a frosty February morning and still dark. The window was coated with thick, floral-patterned ice reflecting the orange glow of the stove opposite. A cart rattled past the house; the dogs barked.

'Fetch me two pints of milk,' my mother said, 'and be sure to put on your scarf.'

The dairywoman stood outside by her cart. Behind it was Mr Kedlický, the policeman, a stub of tallow candle burning gently in his square glass lantern.

'Who?' the dairywoman asked, and stopped churning. 'Mr Vojtíšek?' Dairywomen were strictly forbidden to use spoons for making cream, but Mr Kedlický, as I have mentioned, had a kind heart.

'That's right,' he replied. 'We found him round about midnight near the Oujezd barracks and took him straight to the Carmelites' mortuary. He was frozen stiff. All he had on was a ragged coat and trousers, not even a shirt.'

The Tender Heart of Mrs Rus

Josef Velš, merchant, was one of Malá Strana's wealthiest tradesmen. I believe he sold everything that India and Africa ever produced, from scented wood and burnt ivory for boot polish to gold dust, and his shop on the square was packed with customers all day long. Mr Velš himself spent all day every day in the shop except during the hours of High Mass at St Vitus's Cathedral and major ceremonies of the Prague Burgher Corps, for Mr Velš was a sharpshooter (first company, first platoon, third man to the right of Lieutenant Nedoma). Although he had two assistants and two apprentices, he did his best to serve all customers himself, and those he was unable to serve he greeted with a nod and a smile. In fact, Mr Velš smiled perpetually – in the shop, in the street, in church, everywhere: his shop smile had so carved itself into his facial muscles that he could not erase it. He cut a pleasant figure: medium-sized, plump, a small head constantly nodding, and the smile. In the shop he wore a flat cap and merchant's leather apron, in the street a rounded top hat and a long blue coat with gold buttons.

I had a certain fantasy about Mr Velš. I never set foot in his lodgings while he was alive, yet I would always picture him sitting there capless but in his apron before a steaming bowl of soup, his elbow propped on the table, his hand holding a full spoon poised between plate and smile – sitting there like a carving, the spoon suspended for ever in midair. A silly picture, I know.

At the time our story begins, however – the third of May 184– at four in the afternoon – Mr Velš was no longer with us. He lay in his flat above the shop, in his drawing room, in a fine coffin. The coffin was still open, and Mr Velš was still smiling, though lifeless, his eyes closed.

The funeral was to take place at four. The hearse – a tasselled affair – and a company of sharpshooters complete with band were waiting in the square in front of the house, and the drawing room was full of Malá Strana notables. Of course the priest and his assistants would be a bit late: such was the custom at the funeral of any important citizen lest it be rumoured he was being spirited away with undue haste. The room was stuffy. The afternoon sun pouring in reflected from mirror to mirror, and the large wax candles around the catafalque burned brightly and smoked, saturating the sultry air with fumes, the smell of the freshly varnished coffin and perhaps the odour of the corpse as well. Silence reigned; people conversed in whispers. There were no tears shed: Mr Velš left no close relatives, and distant relatives always say, 'If only I could cry, but even though my heart is breaking I have no tears.' 'Yes, that makes it all the worse.'

Then in came Mrs Rus, widow of the Rus who had kept Gráfovská Gardens, where the finest artillery balls were once held. Because it has actually nothing to do with the case, I shall mention only in passing what people said about the manner in which Mrs Rus was widowed. At the time every artillery regiment had its own company of bombardiers, young, dashing, rosy-cheeked lads to a man. Word had it that Mr Rus despised the company for reasons somehow connected with his better half and that they had eventually done him in on account of it. But as I say, it has nothing to do with the case. Mrs Rus had been eating the bread of widowhood and living childless in her Peasant Market house for some twenty-five years, and had anyone thought to inquire what she did with her time, the answer would have had to be that she attended funerals.

Mrs Rus elbowed her way through to the catafalque. Though in her fifties, she was still vigorous and above average in height. A black silk mantilla flowed from her shoulders, and a black bonnet trimmed with bright green ribbons framed her round and forthright countenance. As her brown eyes gazed at the dead man's face, her head began to twitch, her lips to quiver, and great tears welled up in her eyes. She burst into sobs.

Quickly drying her eyes and mouth with a white handkerchief, she looked round at her neighbours to the left and right. To her left stood Mrs Hirt, the candlemaker's wife, praying from a book; to her right a well-dressed young lady she did not recognise. If the lady was, as appeared likely, from Prague, then she must have been from across the river. Mrs Rus addressed her – I need hardly state – in German, for at the time Malá Strana leaned clearly towards the Germans in matters of nationality.

'May the Lord grant him eternal glory,' said Mrs Rus. 'Lying there smiling as if he were alive.' Again she brushed away a torrent of tears. 'He has gone and left us here, gone and left all his wealth as well. Oh, death is a thief, a veritable thief!'

The stranger did not respond.

'I once went to a Jewish funeral,' Mrs Rus went on in a near whisper, 'but I can't say I enjoyed it. They cover all the mirrors, supposedly so they can't see the corpse no matter which way they turn. Our way is better. You can have a fine view of the poor soul from any part of the room. I'd say the coffin was worth a good twenty guilders in silver. Really splendid! But he deserved it. He was such a kind man. You'd think he were still smiling at us in that mirror. Death hasn't changed him, not a whit; it's just – drawn him out a little. He still seems alive, wouldn't you say?'

'I didn't know Mr Velš when he was alive,' the woman replied.

'You didn't? Well, I knew him very well. I knew him before he was married, in fact. His wife too, may she rest in peace. I can see her as though it were yesterday, crying her eyes out on the day of her wedding. Imagine crying all day when you've known the man for nine years. Silly, don't you think? Yes, he waited nine years for her, though maybe he should have waited nine times nine. Because she was really something. A terror, I mean. Oh, there was no one smarter, no one prettier, no one who could keep house the way she did – she'd bargain an hour to save a penny, make sure the washerwoman didn't waste a drop of water, keep her servants hungry – but oh, my! Poor Velš had his hands full with her! Two of my maids came to me from them, so I know the whole story. She never gave him a minute's peace. The only reason he was at all decent, they said, was that he was scared of her, and the only reason he didn't answer her back, they said, was that it made her furious. You know, she was what we call a romantic – she wanted the world to feel sorry for her. She would constantly complain that he tortured her. If he'd poisoned her out of spite, she'd have been thrilled; ditto if he'd hanged himself: think how the world would have pitied her.'

Mrs Rus turned to have another look at the stranger beside her, but she was gone. In her ardour Mrs Rus had failed to notice that the woman's face had grown redder and redder and that she had moved off in the middle of her observations. She was now engaged in conversation at the other end of the room with the lean Mr Uhmühl, an official at the District Treasury and a relative of Mr Velš's.

Once more Mrs Rus gazed upon the dead man's

mute visage, and once more her lips began to quiver, her eyes to gush tears.

'Poor soul,' she said in a loud voice to Mrs Hirt, the candlemaker's wife, 'though he's got plenty to atone for, and atone he shall. Because he wasn't exactly what you'd call honest, was he? I mean, he could have married poor little Tonda. She bore his child, after all . . .'

'Did that woman ride in on a broomstick?' a loud voice wheezed behind her, and a man's bony hand came to rest on her shoulder. Everyone gave a start and turned to watch Mrs Rus and Mr Uhmühl, who placed himself in front of her, stretched out his arm towards the door, and ordered in his wheezy but penetrating voice, 'Out!'

'What's going on in there?' asked a second Mr Uhmühl, the police commissioner for Malá Strana, from the door. He was all skin and bones, like his brother.

'This witch has wormed her way in and is maligning the dead. She has a tongue like a sword.'

'Then give her scabbard a smack!'

'She carries on like that at every funeral,' people called out from all sides.

'She even makes scenes on hallowed ground!'

'Out with her then!' the police commissioner ordered, seizing her by the hand. And off she went, bawling like a baby.

'What a scandal!' the room buzzed. 'And at such a fine funeral!'

'Quiet, now!' the police commissioner ordered in the anteroom. The priest and chaplains had just arrived. Then he escorted her to the stairs. She attempted a word or two, but he ushered her down and out of the house implacably. There he nodded to the guard on duty and said, 'Show this woman home. We won't have her spoiling any more funerals.'

Mrs Rus was as red as a peony and no longer knew what was going on around her.

'A scandal!' resounded through the square. 'And at such a fine funeral!'

The Uhmühl brothers – the sons of Mr Uhmel, a municipal clerk, and grandsons of Mr Uměl, a dyer – were, as you will have observed, extremely uncompromising gentlemen. Moreover, Mrs Rus had earned the wrath of the entire district – nay, the entire world, for as a native of Malá Strana I consider it a world unto itself.

Next day Mrs Rus was summoned to the Bridge Street Police Station.

Things were always lively there. In summer, when they went about their business with the windows wide open, they could be heard up and down the street. And that was a time when they didn't pull their punches, and there were none of these fancy new regulations about police behaviour. The well-known Malá Strana revolutionary, Josef the Harpist, used to station himself beneath the windows, and when one of us young lads passed by he would wink, jerk his thumb up at them, and say with a placid smile, 'Yapping away.' I'm sure he meant nothing disrespectful by it and was simply using the most colourful expression he could find.

In any case, at noon on 4 May in the year 184–, Mrs Rus stood before the uncompromising police commissioner in her black mantilla and green-ribboned bonnet, her spirit broken, her eyes on the ground, her lips sealed. And when at the end of his uncompromising tirade the commissioner said, 'You shall never attend another funeral as long as you live. You may go', she went. Of course in those days the commissioner had the power to prohibit people from dying, let alone attending funerals.

After she had left the office, the commissioner turned to a subordinate and said with a smile, 'She can't help it. She's like a saw: she cuts everything and everyone to pieces.'

'She should be forced to contribute to the deaf and dumb,' said the subordinate, and after a good, loud laugh they were both in excellent spirits again.

It was a long time before Mrs Rus recovered hers. But eventually she found a way. About six months later she moved out of her house and rented a flat next to the Oujezd Gate. Every funeral must pass through the gate, and whenever one does, there stands the good Mrs Rus, weeping her heart out.

Evening Chitchat

A beautiful, warm June night, the stars barely glimmering, the moon shining gaily, the air all silver radiance.

But the moon is at its gayest over the roofs of Spur Street, and especially, I feel, over the roofs of two neighbouring houses: the Two Suns and the Deep Cellar. Curious roofs they are, a hop, skip and jump from each other, all nooks and gutters. The roof of the Two Suns with its double gables on both the street and courtyard sides – a 'saddle roof', as it is called – is especially unusual. A broad gutter, cut in two by a passageway connecting the attics, runs between the crests. The passageway is covered by a small roof of oval tiles, making a hundred grooved stripes along the surface. Two large dormer windows look on to the broad central gutter, which bisects the house much as a well-combed parting bisects the head of a Prague dandy.

All at once a mouse squeak comes from the direction of the windows.

There it is again.

At the same time the head and shoulders of a man

appear in the window facing the courtyard. With a graceful leap he is outside, standing in the gutter. He is about twenty and has a lean, swarthy face, black curls, and down on his upper lip; he is wearing a fez and carrying a clay pipe with a long black stem. Grey jacket, grey waistcoat, grey trousers – may I introduce Jan Hovora, student of philosophy.

'Here I squeak and squeak,' he grumbled, 'and our nocturnal retreat is still empty.' He went over to the chimney, which had half a sheet of paper pasted on it, and shaded his eyes to read it.

'Someone's been here and replaced the sheet I . . . No, it's *my* paper. But . . .' He looked closer and clapped a hand to his forehead. 'So that's it. The sun's gobbled up my poem. Quite a delicacy. Did the same to a Petöfi poem a while back. Poor Kupka, now he'll have to go unsung on the eve of his name day. It was a good idea, too – straight from St Anthony!' He tore the paper off the chimney, made a ball of it and tossed it over the roof. Then he sat down, filled his pipe, lit it and, stretching out on the warm tiles, braced his feet against the gutter.

Suddenly another mouse squeak resounded. Hovora responded in kind without turning his head, and another young man leaped out into the gutter – smaller, pale, fair-haired and sporting the blue cap of the 1848 Students' Legion, a tight-fitting jacket, and trousers of a light canvas material. He had a lit cigar in his mouth.

'Greetings to you, Hovora,' he intoned.

143

'And the same to you, Kupka.'

'What have you been up to?' asked the budding engineer as he stretched out slowly next to Hovora.

'Me? I've supped on potatoes and groats and am waiting to be sick. How about you?'

'I supped like the Lord in Heaven.'

'And what does the Lord in Heaven have for supper?'

'Nothing.'

'I see. Tell me, why are you squirming like that?'

'I'm trying to get my boots off. Couldn't we have a bootjack in our salon? Or is that too much to ask?'

'A bootjack's not just a thing; it's a member of the family.' Hovora turned his head lazily in Kupka's direction. 'Tell me, what kind of cigar is that you're smoking? That ordinary stuff? Or is it you that's ordinary?'

'You know, I like our salon, and its beautiful ceiling.'

'And cheap rent.'

'The higher the flat, the lower the rent. God has the highest flat of all, and He doesn't pay a penny.'

'The fact that your saint's day is coming up seems to have made you rather pious.'

'Roofs, O roofs! My one and only love!' Kupka declaimed, waving his cigar in the air. 'I'd be envious of chimney sweeps if they hadn't such a black outlook on human existence.'

Their conversation continued freely, easily and in hushed tones. For some reason people unwittingly lower their voices in dense forests, in the wilderness and on mountaintops.

'A glorious night!' Kupka went on, in raptures. 'Utter silence! No! The weirs on the river, the nightingales on Petřín Hill – don't they sound ecstatic?'

'Yes, and in three days' time St Vitus's Day will be past and with it the nightingale's song. It's so beautiful. I wouldn't live in the Old Town for love or money.'

'Nor would I. Not a bird for miles around. If they didn't bring home a leg of goose from the Coal Market now and again, they wouldn't know what a bird looks like.'

'Only the two of you?' a sonorous baritone called out from the dormer.

'Novomlýnský! Greetings!' Kupka and Hovora sang out.

Novomlýnský, who was past thirty, crawled unhurriedly into the gutter on all fours, joint by joint, so to speak.

'Damnation!' he shouted, slowly straightening his back. 'This is not for me. I'm not used to it.' Novomlýnský was of above average height and rather corpulent. He had a swarthy complexion, a smooth, round face, smiling blue eyes and a luxuriant moustache. His coat was black, his trousers light, and he too wore a fez.

'Besides, I can't loll about on the tiles like you – not in this coat I can't. Sit up and act human.'

Kupka and Hovora did as they were told. The

earlier, somewhat forced serenity in their faces had given way to bright smiles, and they regarded Novomlýnský with obvious affection. Clearly he ruled the roost here not merely by virtue of his years. He sat down opposite them, on the slope of the other roof, and lit his cigar.

'Well, what were you up to, lads?'

'I was praising Malá Strana,' Hovora replied.

'And I was gazing at the moon,' said Kupka, 'that dead man with a heart that lives . . .'

'Nowadays everyone gazes at the moon,' said Novomlýnský with a grin. 'What you need is a job like mine, in an office, with figures.' His ringing voice had nothing hushed or subdued about it: Novomlýnský would have thundered forth every bit as unaffectedly in dense forests or the wilderness or on mountaintops. 'Now tell me, what's new? Is it true that Jäkl nearly drowned at Emperor's Mill yesterday?' He laughed heartily.

'Quite true,' Hovora nodded with a smile. 'He swims like a millstone. I was right next to him when he slipped. Oh, the grunts and bubbles! We had a hard time pulling him out, didn't we, Kupka? And when I asked him what he thought about when he was under, he said he just had to laugh. That's what all those grunts were.'

All three of them laughed too, Novomlýnský like a bell.

'And what was the fuss this morning at the professor's house? You were there, Hovora, weren't you?'

'It was quite racy, actually,' said Hovora, pursing his lips. 'The professor's wife came across a letter buried in his desk, a letter from an admirer, full of passion and fire. Well, it turns out to have been a letter she'd written to him twenty years ago, and today she found it – unopened! You can imagine how hurt she was.'

'A one-act comedy,' said Novomlýnský, laughing again. He stretched his legs and called out to Kupka, who had wandered off to the end of the gutter and was bending over and peering into the courtyard. Kupka returned, clearly satisfied with the results of his reconnaissance mission. 'Where the devil do you keep sneaking off to? What were you staring at? You'll fall off one day.'

'What was I staring at? The bookbinder. He's been reading the life of Hus every evening now for twenty years, and it never fails to bring tears to his eyes. I just wondered if he was crying yet. He isn't.'

'What nonsense! I should think you'd have eyes for something other than bookbinders.' He snapped his fingers. 'You haven't by any chance seen the new nurse at the potter's across the way, have you? A real beauty! She won't last.'

'Novomlýnský is like a good housewife,' said Hovora with a straight face. 'His biggest problem is finding the right girl.'

'It's worse than you think. It robs him of his sleep. He has to be up at five in the morning – the pretty

147

girls go out early for water. They don't want to be seen with their pails.'

'That's enough out of you. The reason I'm up early is I don't need much sleep. Besides' – and here Novomlýnský tapped his cigar against a tile and started speaking with great nostalgia – 'I'm a man with a past. I was an incredible dandy at one time. I'd go through eight pairs of gloves in a season. I still have a way with the ladies. Can I help looking the way I do? Little do you know! I wish you could see me sweet talking them. I'm a real terror. But now,' he went on more briskly, 'have you got anything to keep us amused this evening? Whose turn is it to come up with something?'

'Jäkl's.'

'Then he won't come,' said Novomlýnský with utter confidence. 'A group of us had a supper arrangement once: a different person would pay the bill each night. Well, whoever's turn it was invariably stayed away.' At that moment his eye lit on the other roof. 'The drowned man!' he cried in a terrified voice, and Kupka and Hovora whirled round immediately.

What they saw was a third fez sticking up over the rim of the roof, with Jäkl's broad, red face and radiant smile just below it.

'Hurry up! Hurry up!' his aerial companions called out to him.

More and more of him appeared over the roof: first his shoulders, next his chest, then his stomach.

'There's no end to him,' Novomlýnský muttered. 'He could come out in instalments.'

A long right leg swung over the rim and was followed by a left one, but suddenly both slipped and Jäkl came tumbling down with a terrible racket, collapsing in the gutter at his friends' feet.

The friends burst into gales of laughter; indeed, the whole roof seemed to be laughing and the moon in the sky with it. Jäkl – lying on his belly and kicking the gutter with his shoes – laughed hardest of all. It took several good prods and a friendly kick or two before he managed to pull himself together. He then rose slowly to a majestic six-foot, brushing down his summer suit, which was of an indeterminate yellow hue. 'Didn't miss a trick!' he said proudly, sitting down next to Novomlýnský.

'But have you found something to keep us busy tonight?'

Jäkl slipped his arms between his knees, rocked back and forth for a moment, and said, 'Well, I thought each of us might tell the others our earliest memory, the very first thing in our lives we still – '

'I knew you'd come up with something stupid,' Novomlýnský broke in. 'Really! A man with a legal education, on his way to a doctorate . . .'

'Look, you're no genius either,' Jäkl retorted in a huff.

'Who, me? I beg your pardon! My mother carried me for sixteen months. I talked from the day I was born. I went to Latin school for twenty-four years, and every word I said earned my father twenty kreutzers.'

'Look, maybe it's not such a stupid idea,' said

Hovora, knocking out his pipe. 'Let's give it a try. I suppose you've got yours all ready, Jäkl?'

'Me?' said Jäkl, still rocking gently. 'Of course I have. I remember an incident from when I was barely two. Father was away and Mother had to run across the street for something, so she left me on my own. (We had no maid.) To keep me from feeling lonely, she'd brought in the goose she was fattening, and I was so scared of being by myself that I gave the goose a convulsive hug round the neck. The goose gaggled in terror, I began to bawl – a nice vignette, don't you think?'

'Exquisite,' Novomlýnský mumbled.

A momentary silence of meditation descended upon the gutter. Three times Hovora set fresh matches to his newly refilled pipe, but each time it failed to catch. Finally he got it going and said, 'It's just come to me! I was with my father at the Ursuline Convent and the nuns took me on their laps and kissed me.'

'Even better than the goose,' Novomlýnský mumbled again. 'Got anything to top that, Kupka?'

Kupka smiled. 'My grandfather was the sexton at Rakovník. He was terribly old, and one day he rang his own death knell: he chimed the church bells, went home, climbed into bed and died. They took me to see him (he was laid out by then – I remember the white stockings) so I could kiss his big toe. I don't know what the superstition was. Then I played for a while near the carpenter who was making the coffin and happened to be a boarder in the house.'

'It's going famously,' said Jäkl, delighted. 'Now Novomlýnský.'

Novomlýnský sat scowling in silence for a long time, but finally opened his mouth. 'I . . . well, I haven't got a first memory or, rather, I have two, but I don't know which precedes the other. I remember that when we were moving from the New Castle Steps down to the Elephants, I refused to leave the house until they carried my cradle out after me. And I remember – well, once I said a bad word to my sister, an extremely bad word, and my mother washed out my mouth with soap and made me stand next to the back leg of the piano. You know, a child's an interesting creature: the comic miniature of a grown-up, but so indifferent to the consequences of his acts that you can't help believing in guardian angels. My first prayer book was in German, but I didn't know a word of German at the time, and for an entire year I prayed the "Prayer for Pregnant Women" – *"Gebet für schwangere Frauen"* – and nothing whatever happened!'

Jäkl fell to kicking the gutter again.

'Know what I like about Jäkl?' said Novomlýnský, looking on fondly. 'You tell a joke, and he immediately registers the effect it has on him.'

'What makes you think I was laughing at your joke?' Jäkl protested. 'No, I've just had the silliest idea. The ancient Romans had children too, didn't they?'

'It would seem so.'

'Well, maybe they didn't sound like Cicero; maybe they talked baby talk. Think of how *"Hannibal ante portas"* would come out in baby Latin: *Hannibo ante potas!* Good God! *Hannibo ante potas!*'

The kicking was almost frenzied by then. Everything and everybody laughed with him: his friends, the roof – even the moon and the stars seemed to be chuckling at the thought of '*Hannibo ante potas*'.

'Jäkl's in fine form today,' Hovora observed.

'Indeed,' Kupka agreed. 'I wonder why.'

By then Jäkl had regained his calm. He sat up, looking straight into Kupka's eyes. 'Well, why not tell you? I need to get it off my chest. You see, I'm in love. Well, not any more actually. But I'm getting married. Well, not quite. I don't really know how to put it.'

'Pretty?' Kupka inquired immediately.

'You don't think he'd do his best friends the injustice of marrying a dog, do you?' said Hovora.

'Getting married, eh? Well, I've got nothing against family life; it's henpecked husbands I can't take.' That was Novomlýnský, of course. 'Money?'

'Who said anything about money? Or dowries, for that matter. Come a few dry years and it all goes down the drain in drink.'

'So young and yet so noble!'

'But who is she?' the other two asked in unison.

'Lizinka.'

'Lizinka who?'

'Perálek. Her father's the tailor in Hay Scales Street. Know her?'

'Of course I do,' said Hovora. 'He's got three

daughters. The eldest, Marie – well, I can't stand the sight of her. I yawn the moment I see her. Then Lizinka. And then Karla, the skinny one.'

'So skinny she has to lick her teeth to get her mouth shut,' said Kupka. 'Yet she was the first to marry.'

Novomlýnský, knowledgeable in such matters, raised a finger and said, 'Mark my words: the ugliest of three is always first.'

'Talk, talk, talk!' Jäkl grumbled. 'How can I get a word in if you keep babbling on?'

'Lizinka *is* pretty.'

'She certainly is.'

'How long have you been in love?'

'Let's see,' said Jäkl with a glint of irony in his eye. 'Eighteen years by now. She was just starting school; I was a year ahead of her. It was love at first sight – and for ever! She was a beautiful girl: a rose of a face, long, flaxen braids. I remember a green silk hat perched on her head, a yellow-green cape flowing from her shoulders, a school bag with a little white poodle embroidered on blue – oh, that poodle! I didn't leave her in much doubt about the feelings she'd aroused in me, because I soon plucked up my courage and pelted her with snowballs – it was winter – and when she started to run I caught up with her and snatched the hat from her head. From that day on she smiled at me, understood me. I didn't venture to speak to her, of course, but I went on throwing snowballs.

'About two years later I was tutoring one of the younger boys, and since he lived at the end of Hay

Scales Street I passed the Peráleks' every day. Lizinka
would stand in front of the house, and with her head
and shoulders bare she was even more beautiful. I
couldn't help blushing the moment those innocent,
clear, blue eyes sparkled at me. We got to know each
other better and better. One day she was eating a
sandwich and I plucked up my courage again and
asked for a bite. "Here," she said, breaking off a piece.
To provoke her, I said, "More." She replied with a
charming laugh. "Then there'd be none left for me,
and I'm hungry." I left in a daze, waving my piece of
bread at Lizinka as I went. Unfortunately, the parents
of the boy I was tutoring soon found a substitute for
me on the absurd pretext that the two of us spent all
our time together playing.

'For the next fifteen years Lizinka and I scarcely saw
each other. Then, last May Day – it was a Sunday – I
decided to go to the country, to Šárka. I don't know
why. Every city gate could have been walled up for a
year for all I cared. It must have been magnetism of
the heart. Anyway, who was sitting at Čistecký's but
Perálek, his wife, and Marie and Lizinka. A rose in
bloom! Shoulders as shapely as a sentence of Goethe's,
eyes pure and innocent as a child's. I fell as quickly as
a man as I had done eighteen years earlier as a boy.

'The men at the table where I was sitting happened
to be going on about Perálek.

' "He always points to his skull when he talks, the
idiot. It's to show he's thinking."

' "And I hear he slaps those girls of his when they're not asked to dance."

'I stood up. Poor Lizinka! There was a group of young people dancing nearby. You know I don't like to dance myself. I'm too lanky to be graceful, but graceful or not . . .

'What's the name of that retired captain? Vítek, that's it. Well, Vítek was at the Peráleks' table, chatting away with Marie. He and I know each other, so I went up to him and greeted the Peráleks as well. Lizinka smiled, then blushed. I asked her to dance. With a glance at her mother she promised me a quadrille; she said she didn't do circle dances, which was fine with me.

'We danced the quadrille without exchanging more than a few words, but then we strolled along the brook and found our tongues. I asked her whether she remembered me. She answered with her innocent eyes. Suddenly I was a child again: I talked about snowballs and poodles and sandwiches. She felt the same way I did, I could tell. And, well, then I walked them home. Lizinka was a little drained by the walk, so I gave her my arm. "Ah, to be young again!" said Vítek, the old goat. When you're in love, even innocent remarks can seem offensive.

'A few days later I had a letter from Lizinka requesting me in somewhat questionable German to meet her at three that afternoon at St Nicholas's. I trembled with bliss. From the church we walked to Valdštejn Gardens, where we vowed eternal love. I promised to finish my studies by August and make her mine within two years. Then she took me to see her parents. I could see that Mr Perálek was a decent man, Mrs Perálek a good mother. I still didn't care much for Marie, though; I didn't like the way she looked at me.

'Almost immediately after that – about four weeks ago – Lizinka left for Klatovy to look after an aunt who had been taken seriously ill. And yesterday I had a visit from my friend Bureš, the medical student. "You know Lizinka Perálek, don't you?" he asked, and when I told him I did he said, "Well, she had a baby boy today in my ward." '

Jäkl's friends had been listening attentively, but when he came to this point it was as though he had never said a word, and they turned to the dormer window with a start.

'Then at noon old Captain Vítek came and asked after her health and whether she'd had a boy or a girl.'

'The housemaids are eavesdropping,' Novomlýnský whispered. 'I can hear them giggling.' He was on his feet in an instant and disappeared with amazing agility into the dormer. Kupka and Hovora bounded after him.

The man in the moon stretched down from on high and cocked an ear. He thought he heard a slight, girlish cry followed by a smacking of lips.

Perhaps Jäkl heard something similar. At any rate, he slipped his long arms back between his knees and, rocking gently, muttered, 'Night-time theft calls for particularly harsh punishment.'

Doctor Spoiler

They didn't always call him that. It began only after a certain incident, but an incident so bizarre that it got into the papers. His real name was Heribert, and his Christian name was something out of the ordinary, though I can't quite remember what. Mr Heribert was a physician or, to be more exact, held the degree of Medical Doctor, but he had never treated anyone or anything. He would have been the first to confess that from the time he made the rounds of the clinics as a student not a single patient had passed through his hands. Or, rather, he would have been the first to confess it had he ever spoken to anybody. But he was a most peculiar man.

Dr Heribert was the son of Dr Heribert, a once much-loved Malá Strana physician. His mother died young, and Dr Heribert, Sr, died shortly before Dr Heribert, Jr, received his degree, leaving him with a small two-storeyed house in Oujezd Street and perhaps some money as well, though not much. Dr Heribert, Jr, lived in the house himself. The two small shops on the ground floor and the front upstairs flat earned him a certain income. He himself lived upstairs

in the flat facing the courtyard, his rooms having their
own staircase, which was uncovered, though closed
off by a wooden lattice at the lower end. What the flat
looked like inside I do not know; I do know he led a
simple life. I know because one of the two shops
was a grocer's and the grocer's wife looked after the
doctor's rooms for him, and her son Josífek and I were
friends (though we parted company a long time ago,
when he became coachman to the Archbishop and
grew cocky). It was from Josífek I learned that Dr
Heribert made his own breakfast, went to a cheap
eating house in the Old Town for dinner, and somehow made do for supper.

Dr Heribert the Younger could have enjoyed the
good will of all Malá Strana, had he so desired – the
ailing transferred their faith to him after his father's
death – but he failed to hear out those who came to
him, rich or poor, and gradually their faith subsided.
Indeed, they began to consider him a 'coddled student'
and eventually even sneered, 'Him? A doctor! Why, I
wouldn't trust him with my cat!'

None of which seemed to bother him particularly.
He appeared completely oblivious to people. He never
greeted anyone or returned greetings. Walking
through the streets, he gave the impression of a withered leaf being battered by a gale. He was quite small
– only about a metre and a half by the new metric
scale – and he steered his gaunt little figure in such a
way as to ensure that it was always at least two steps
removed from all other humans. Hence the wind-

battered effect. His eyes were blue and as timid as those of a kicked dog. His face was framed by a light-brown beard so bushy as to be socially unacceptable. In winter he wore a grey miller's coat, pulling a cloth cap down over his eyes and sinking his head into the astrakhan collar; in summer a light, grey-checked suit or a still lighter linen one, his head wobbling precariously as if on too thin a stalk. In summer he would be out at four in the morning, strolling along the Marian Ramparts or sitting with a book on a secluded bench. Occasionally a good-natured Malá Strana neighbour came up and started a conversation, whereupon Dr Heribert would stand, slam his book shut and depart without a word. With time people left him completely alone. Indeed, things came to such a pass that, though scarcely forty, he inspired nary a thought in Malá Strana's spinsters.

And then came the incident, the one I said got into the papers. It is that incident I wish to tell you about.

It was a lovely June day, the kind that makes one feel a smile of perfect contentment has spread across heaven and earth and the faces of all humankind. And late in the afternoon of that day a magnificent funeral procession was wending its way to the Oujezd Gate. The funeral was for Mr Schepeler, a councillor to the District Treasury (or Estates Treasury, as it was called then), and God forgive us for saying so, but it certainly seemed that the smile of contentment extended to the funeral as well. (The face of the dead man was concealed, of course, our customs not being those of the south, where corpses are carried to the grave in open coffins, that they might – one last time before slipping into the pit – be warmed by the light of the sun.) Yes, despite the show of propriety, a certain general contentment could not be denied; it had in fact penetrated the mourners' very bones: The day is so lovely, let's make the best of it.

Most content of all perhaps were the chancellery clerks carrying the councillor's bier. For two days they had been in a state, flying from office to office; now they walked proud and aloof beneath their burden, each one convinced that the eyes of the world were upon him and that the world was whispering, 'There go the clerks from the Estates Treasury!' Also content was tall Dr Link, who, after treating the late lamented councillor for an illness lasting only a week, had received a fee of twenty ducats from the patient's widow (which fact had already made the rounds of Malá Strana) and who now walked with his head slightly bowed, as though in meditation. Then there was Ostrohradský the harness-maker, the councillor's neighbour and closest relative. True, his uncle had paid scant attention to him during his lifetime, but knowing he was in for a legacy of 5,000 guilders he remarked to Kejřík the brewer several times in the course of the procession, 'He had a good heart.' Ostrohradský walked directly behind the coffin with plump Mr Kejřík – the best and most faithful friend of the deceased, and the picture of health – at his side. They were followed by Messrs Kdojek, Mužík and

Homann, also councillors at the District Treasury, but of a lower rank than the late Mr Schepeler. They too appeared most content. And much as it pains us we must also note that even Mrs Marie Schepeler, sitting by herself in the first carriage, was not immune to the general feeling of contentment, though, alas, in her case it did not derive from the June weather. The good lady was of course a woman, and being for three full days the object of deep sympathy to so many people was nothing if not gratifying. Then, too, the mourning weeds were most becoming to her figure, and the black veil showed her somewhat pallid face to good advantage.

The only one who took the councillor's death to heart and experienced deep grief was Mr Kejřík the brewer, a bachelor and – as I have noted – the deceased's best and most faithful friend. The young widow had made it clear to him on the previous day that she expected her just reward for having been faithful to her husband as long as he was alive. When Mr Ostrohradský turned to him with his first 'He had a good heart', Mr Kejřík replied, 'He couldn't have had, or it would have kept him going longer.' And from then on he made no reply whatever.

At length the procession reached the Oujezd Gate. In those days it was not nearly so easy to negotiate as it is today: it twisted and turned along heavy ramparts and through two dark tunnels, a fitting introduction to the cemetery on the other side.

The hearse had arrived before the procession and

was waiting at the gate. The priests turned, the clerks set the bier down slowly, and the sprinkling began. Then the coachmen pulled out the movable baseboard and the young men lifted the coffin to place it in the carriage. And then it happened! Either there was an overabundance of zeal on one side or both sides were equally clumsy, but all at once the narrow end of the coffin slid to the ground and the lid sprang off and fell with a crash. The corpse remained in the coffin, true, but it slid down a bit and bent its knees and one arm flew up over the side.

The general dismay was followed by a silence so perfect one could hear one's neighbour's watch ticking in his pocket. Everyone's eyes were fixed on the dead councillor's motionless face. And who should be standing next to the coffin but Dr Heribert. He had just passed through the gate on his way home from a walk and was steering a path for himself through the crowd when he was forced to pause behind the priests. Now his grey coat stood out against the dead man's black shroud.

It lasted only a moment. Heribert seized the dangling hand, perhaps with the intention of placing it back in the coffin. But he held on to it, fingering it uneasily and peering into the corpse's face. Then he reached out and opened its right eye.

'What is the meaning of this?' Ostrohradský bellowed suddenly. 'Why don't they do something? How long are we going to stand here?'

Several of the young men made as if to move.

'Wait!' cried tiny Heribert in a voice amazingly rich and sonorous. 'This man is not dead!'

'Nonsense!' Dr Link roared in reply. 'You must be out of your mind!'

'Where are the police?' Ostrohradský interjected.

All faces showed great consternation. Only Kejřík the brewer had the presence of mind to go up to the calm and collected Heribert and ask, 'What do you mean when you say he's not dead?'

'I mean he's in rigor. Have him taken indoors and we'll try to revive him.'

'This is arrant lunacy!' shouted Dr Link. 'If he isn't dead, then . . .'

'Who is this man?' Ostrohradský demanded.

'A doctor, supposedly.'

'Dr Spoiler!' the harness-maker yelled, suddenly alarmed at the thought of the 5,000 guilders. 'Police!'

'Dr Spoiler!' councillors Kdojek and Mužik repeated, but by then Schepeler's devoted friend Mr Kejřík and several of the young men were carrying the coffin into the nearby Lime Kiln Inn.

Suddenly the street was all din and hubbub – the hearse turning, the carriages turning, Councillor Kdojek calling out, 'Let's go, let's go! We'll find out the details later.' No one knew what to do.

'Glad to see you, commissioner!' Ostrohradský called out to the police officer coming up to him. 'The most dreadful, unlawful farce has been going on here: corpses violated in broad daylight, before half of Prague!'

Ostrohradský followed the commissioner into the Lime Kiln. Dr Link was nowhere to be seen. In a few moments Ostrohradský came out with the commissioner in tow.

'Move along, please,' said the commissioner. 'Nobody is allowed inside. Dr Heribert claims he can bring the councillor round.'

Mrs Schepeler was about to climb down from her carriage when she fainted dead away. Joy can kill at times. Mr Kejřík came rushing out of the inn to the carriage, where the ladies were tending the swooning widow. 'Take her home,' he advised. 'She'll revive faster there.' Then he turned, leaped into a cab and flew off on an errand for Dr Heribert.

The carriages dispersed, the mourners departed, but the throng at the Oujezd Gate persisted, and a police detail had to be posted to keep order. The most curious gossip began to circulate. Some were quick to criticise Dr Link and spread slander about him; others made fun of Heribert. Now and then Mr Kejřík appeared, scurrying about or telling someone, his face radiant, 'There's every hope!' or 'I've felt his pulse myself!' or 'That doctor can do wonders!' until at last he cried in rapture, 'He's breathing!' and hurled himself into a waiting cab to take the joyful news to Mrs Schepeler.

Late that evening – it was getting on for ten – a covered stretcher emerged from the Lime Kiln. Dr Heribert and Mr Kejřík walked on one side of it, the commissioner on the other. But there was not a single inn throughout Malá Strana that was not full to overflowing until well after midnight. The sole topic of conversation was Dr Heribert and the councillor's resurrection, and feverish conversation it was too.

'He knows more than all those Latin books put together!'

'All you have to do is look at him. Besides, his father was a fine doctor – the finest. Like father, like son.'

'Then why doesn't he practise? He'd be as rich as a court councillor.'

'He's got all the money he needs, I suppose.'

'And why do they call him Spoiler?'

'Spoiler? First time I hear of it.'

'I've heard it a hundred times today.'

Two months later Mr Schepeler was back at the office. 'I've got the Lord God in heaven and Dr Heribert on earth,' he would say. And 'That Kejřík's a jewel!'

All Prague was talking about Dr Heribert. Newspapers reported the incident worldwide. Malá Strana was proud. People said the oddest things: that barons, counts and princes had tried to engage Heribert as their personal physician, that a certain reigning king of Italy had named an unprecedented sum. The most insistent offers came from people whose death would have given large numbers great joy. But Dr Heribert was like one walled off from the world. Rumour had it that Mrs Schepeler had taken him a sack full of ducats and he had not only refused to admit her but even doused her with water from the balcony.

Once more it was plain that he was oblivious to people. They greeted him, but he never greeted them back. Once more he steered his way through the streets, his frail, almost transparent little head shaking timorously, like a piece of fluff. He never saw a patient, yet people kept calling him Dr Spoiler. The name seemed preordained.

I haven't seen him for more than ten years now; I don't even know if he's alive. His little Oujezd house still stands intact. I must find out.

The Water Sprite

He always walked hat in hand, in cold snap or heat wave, his only concession being to hold the low, rounded, wide-brimmed topper above his head like a parasol. His grey hair was smoothed down over his skull and drawn together behind in a pigtail pressed and bound so tightly that it never so much as jiggled. (It was one of the last of its kind in Prague – there could have been no more than two or three left.) His green, gold-buttoned frock coat made up for its short front with long tails, which flapped all the way to his emaciated calves. A white waistcoat covered his hollow chest; then came black trousers, reaching only to his knees, and a pair of gleaming silver buckles, then snow-white stockings reaching to another two silver buckles, and finally a pair of large shuffly shoes. Whether he ever changed the shoes I cannot tell, but the leather of which they were made always looked as though it had come from the roof of a tumbledown cab.

The withered, pointed face of Mr Rybář – for that was his name – shone with an eternal smile. He was a strange sight, walking through the streets. He would pause every twenty paces and look to the right and to the left, as though his thoughts, instead of travelling inside him, maintained a respectful distance, keeping him amused and forcing him to turn and smile at them, the pranksters. To greet people he would simply raise the forefinger of his right hand and give a soft whistle. The same soft whistle also preceded everything he said, and he usually began with a 'djah', which implied acquiescence.

Mr Rybář lived on the lower left-hand side of Deep Lane and had a fine view of Petřín Hill. Whenever he spied strangers turning right in the direction of the Castle District, he would follow them, and when they stopped at the observation point and admired the beauties of our city, he would stand beside them, raise his finger, and whistle. 'Djah, but the sea! Why don't we live by the sea?' Then he would follow them into the Castle, and when they admired the gem-studded walls of St Wenceslas's Chapel he would whistle a second time and say, 'What do you expect? Here in Bohemia when a shepherd throws a stone after his herd, the stone is likely to be worth more than the sheep!' And more he did not say.

On account of his name, his green coat, and 'But the sea!' we called him the 'water sprite',[1] but everyone, young and old, held him in great esteem. Mr Rybář was a retired court official from the Turnov region now living in Prague with a relative of his, a young woman married to a low-ranking civil servant by whom she had two or three children. People said he was fabulously wealthy, not in banknotes but in gems; they said his room contained a tall black cabinet filled with square black boxes, large boxes, each of which was divided by white pasteboard into further compartments, and in each compartment, on a bed of cotton wool, a gem lay gleaming. They claimed to have seen them with their own eyes. They said he had found and collected them all on Mount Goatherd. We children used to say that when the Šajvls mopped their floor – Šajvl was the name of Mr Rybář's young relatives – they sprinkled it first with fine sugar instead of sand, and on Saturday, cleaning day, we envied the Šajvl children no end. One day I was sitting near Mr Rybář above the moat to the left of Bruska Gate – he would go there every fine day for an hour or so to sit on the grass and puff on his short pipe – when two strapping students happened by. One of them spluttered and said, 'Look at him! Smoking Mama's wadded jacket!' From that time forth I considered 'smoking Mama's wadded jacket' a luxury that only the well-heeled could afford.

And so our water sprite – but no, we shan't call him that; we're no longer children, are we? – and so Mr Rybář could often be seen walking along the Bruska Ramparts. If he happened to meet any of the canons, who also took their constitutionals there, he would stop and exchange a few friendly words with them. Once – I loved to listen to what grown-ups had to say – once I heard him prattling away with two canons who were sitting on a bench. He was standing.

They were talking about '*Frankreich*', France, and something called 'liberty', and all at once Mr Rybář raised his finger, whistled, and said, 'Djah, I side with Rosenau. Rosenau says, "Liberty is like rich food and strong wine: the strong natures accustomed to them thrive and grow even stronger on them, but they deplete, inebriate and destroy the weak." ' And so saying he waved his hat and went his way.

The taller of the two canons, a fat man, said, 'Why does he keep going on about that Rosenau?'

'He must be a writer,' said the shorter of the two canons, who was also fat. 'He can only be a writer.'

But the sentence remained in my mind as the pinnacle of human wisdom, and of Rosenau and Rybář I had an equally exalted impression. Making my way through a number of books years later as an adolescent, I discovered that Mr Rybář had indeed quoted his source verbatim, the only difference being that the statement in question came not from Rosenau but from a certain Rousseau. Clearly Dame Fortune had misled him with a frivolous printer's error.

Not that he fell in my esteem for that. No, he was a worthy, an inestimably worthy man.

It was a sunny day in August, about three in the afternoon. People strolling along Spur Street suddenly stopped, people lolling in front of their houses called in haste to those inside, customers came running out of shops, and they all stood and stared at Mr Rybář marching down the hill.

'Off to flaunt his riches, he is,' said Mr Herzl, tapster at the Two Suns.

'Well, what do you know!' Mr Vitouš, the corner shopkeeper, declared. 'Things must be bad if he's got to sell!'

(Much as it pains me, I must point out that Mr Vitouš did not enjoy the best of reputations in the neighbourhood. He was said to have teetered on the brink of bankruptcy, and to this day his decent Malá Strana neighbours look upon 'the bankrupt' as a species apart from the rest of humanity.)

Meanwhile, Mr Rybář went his quiet way, though a shade more quickly than usual. Under his left arm he held one of the square black boxes that were the subject of so much speculation. He clutched it so tightly that the hat he carried in the same hand was all but glued to his leg. In the other hand he carried a walking stick with a flat ivory knob, a sign he was paying a visit, for at no other time did he use one. He answered all greetings with a wave of the stick and a whistle much louder than usual.

At the bottom of Spur Street he crossed St Nicholas's Square, turned into Žamberecký House and climbed to the third floor, where Mr Mühlwenzel, the teacher of mathematics and natural science and therefore a man unusually well-educated for the time, had his flat. The visit did not last long.

Mr Mühlwenzel was in a good mood. His powerful, stocky body had just enjoyed the benefit of an afternoon nap. The long grey hair wreathing his bald spot stuck out comfortably in all directions, and his intelligent, blue and ever kindly eyes shone brightly. His cheeks, ruddy by nature, were positively glowing. Broad and benevolent, they were also quite liberally strewn with pockmarks, which provided the professor with pretexts for endless jokes. 'That's life,' he would say. 'When a girl with a dimple in her cheek gives a smile, people say she's charming; when I smile, people say I'm a fright. Yet I've got a hundred dimples.'

He showed Mr Rybář to the sofa and said, 'What can I do for you?'

Mr Rybář laid his box on the table and removed the lid. The stones glittered in a riot of colour. 'I was just . . . I mean . . . Well, how much would you say they're worth?' He sat down and leaned his chin on the knob of the walking stick.

Mr Mühlwenzel took a long look at the stones. Then he picked up one of the darker ones, weighed it in his hand and held it up to the light. 'This is moldavite,' he said.

'What?'

'Moldavite.'

'Djah, moldavite.' Mr Rybář whistled. His face made it fairly clear that he had just heard the word for the first time in his life.

'It would make a good addition to our school collection. They're quite rare. We'd be willing to buy it.'

'You would, would you? And how much do you think . . . ?'

'We could give you three guilders for it, in twenties. What do you say?'

'Three guilders!' Mr Rybář exclaimed with a thin whistle, his chin first rising, then falling back to the knob of his stick. 'And what about the rest?' he managed after a pause in a constrained whisper.

'Chalcedony, jasper, amethyst, smoke quartz – nothing special.'

A few minutes later Mr Rybář was back at the corner of Spur Street, trudging slowly up the hill. It was the first time his neighbours had seen him with his hat on his head. He had pulled the broad brim down low over his eyes and was dragging his stick in such a way that the tip scraped against the paving stones. He paid no heed to anyone and did not whistle once. Nor did he turn his head. Clearly his thoughts were not frolicking about outside him; they were all within, deep within.

He did not leave the house again that day – not for the ramparts, not for the gate. And a lovely day it was.

It was nearly midnight. The heavens were as blue as at the break of day; the moon shone at its proudest, its most bewitching; the stars glimmered like white sparks. Petřín Hill lay shrouded in a glorious silver mist; a flood of silver overlay the whole of Prague.

The cheerful light poured into Mr Rybář's room through both wide-open windows. He stood at one of them, motionless as a statue. The loud, steady thunder of the Vltava's weirs rose up from the distance. Did the old man hear it?

He gave a sudden start. 'No sea!' he whispered, his lips quivering. 'Why have we no sea?'

Perhaps his grief surged within him like a raging sea.

'Oh, well,' he said with a twitch, tearing himself from the window. His gaze fell upon the boxes lying open on the floor. He slowly bent, picked up the nearest of them and removed a handful of stones. 'Pebbles!' he muttered, flinging them through the open window. 'Mere pebbles!'

There was a crash and the splintering of glass. Mr Rybář was so distracted he had forgotten about the greenhouse down in the garden.

'What in the world are you doing?' cried a pleasant young voice. It could only be coming from the next window.

Startled, Mr Rybář took a step backwards.

The door creaked, and in came Mr Šajvl. Perhaps it was the beauty of the night that had kept him so long at the window, though perhaps he had observed signs of unwonted disquiet in his ageing uncle and heard the continuous bustle in his room; perhaps the old man's sighs were loud enough to have reached him through the night.

'Don't tell me you're throwing all those beautiful stones away.'

The old man twitched again and, staring up at Petřín

Hill, whispered, 'They're worthless, mere pebbles . . .'

'I know they're of no monetary value. I knew that from the start. But they have value of another kind. For you, for us. Think of the time you spent collecting them. Think of what they'll mean for the children, how they'll learn from them when you tell them about – '

'But didn't you think I was rich?' the old man went on in a laboured monotone. 'Why, even I . . .'

'Really, now,' said Mr Šajvl in a firm yet gentle voice, and took the old man's hand. 'Isn't having you with us riches enough? Without you my children would have known no grandfather, my wife would be an orphan. Can't you see how happy we are to have you, what a blessing it is?'

Suddenly the old man turned back to the window. He felt his mouth quiver; he felt an indescribable pressure in his eyes. He gazed into the night, but could make out nothing: everything glittered like diamonds, everything surged like waves to his window, to his eyes – the sea, the sea!

I shall stop here. I can't go on.

How Mr Vorel Broke In His Meerschaum

O n the sixteenth of February in the year one
thousand eight hundred and forty and then
some, Mr Vorel opened a flour shop in the
house known as the Green Angel. '*Du, Poldi, hörst,*'
the captain's wife from the floor above us called out
to her daughter, who was on her way to market and
already out in the street, 'buy the semolina at the new
shop. We'll see what it's like.'

Some of you may be frivolous enough to think that
opening a new flour shop is no great event. All I can
say is, 'You poor innocents!' or I might merely shrug
my shoulders and say nothing at all. In those days a
man from the provinces who had not set foot in
Prague for, say, twenty years could, entering Strahov
Gate and proceeding to Spur Street, find the same
shopkeeper on the same corner, the bakery under its
old sign, the grocery in its original spot. Everything
had its place, and the idea of setting up a flour shop
where there had always been a grocery was so absurd
as to be unthinkable. Shops were handed down from

father to son, and should one or another occasionally
end up in the hands of a newcomer, whether from
Prague or the provinces, the natives would accept him
only grudgingly and provided he conformed to the
time-honoured order of things and did not bewilder
them with innovations. But this Mr Vorel was not
only a complete outsider, he had set up shop in the
Green Angel, where no shop of any kind had existed
within living memory; he had even had the wall of
the ground-floor flat knocked out. It had always had
an arched window where Mrs Staněk sat from dawn
to dusk at her prayer book, a green shade over her
eyes, and everyone passing could see her. Then, three
months earlier, the old widow had been carted off to
Košíře Cemetery, and now . . . What good was the
shop anyway? Spur Street already had a flour shop.
To be sure, it was all the way down at one end, but
what did people want with another? They still had
money in those days and bought most of their supplies
straight from the mill. Mr Vorel may simply have
thought, I'm bound to make a go of it. He may also
have thought, smugly enough, that he was a good-
looking young fellow with round cheeks and dreamy
blue eyes, that he was slim as a maiden and still very
much a bachelor, and that the servant girls would
come running. But who can tell what he thought?

It was barely three months since Mr Vorel had
moved to Spur Street. He had come from somewhere
in the provinces. People knew nothing about him
except that he was the son of a miller. He might have

told them more, and gladly too, but they never asked him. Theirs was the pride of the native; he was an outsider. He spent his evenings in the Yellow House with a jug of beer, sitting all alone at a table near the stove. The rest of the company took no notice of him, barely acknowledging his greetings with a nod. Anyone who came in later than he did stared at him as if he were a total stranger there for the first time; when *he* came in later, they would immediately stop talking.

Not even yesterday had they taken notice of him, and there had been a great celebration: Mr Jarmárka, the postman, had been celebrating his silver wedding anniversary. Admittedly, Mr Jarmárka was still, properly speaking, a bachelor, but 18 February marked twenty-five years from the day when he *nearly* married. His bride had passed away on the eve of the wedding, and Mr Jarmárka had never dreamed of another match. Having thus remained true to his bride, he was very much in earnest about the anniversary. Nor did his neighbours, good people all, see anything peculiar in it: when at the end of the usual drinking session Mr Jarmárka produced three bottles of a fine Mělník vintage, they were nothing if not sincere in their toasts. Yet although the glasses went from hand to hand – the hostess had but two wineglasses in her entire stock – neither found its way to Mr Vorel. And Mr Vorel was smoking a brand-new meerschaum, which he had bought only to be neighbourly.

In any case, on 16 February, at six o'clock in the morning, Mr Vorel had opened his shop in the Green Angel. He had taken care of the finishing touches the previous evening, and everything was spic and span: the flour in the drawers and open sacks shone whiter than the freshly whitewashed wall; the split peas were a brighter yellow than the paint on the surrounding implements. The neighbours peered in as they passed, and one or two of them even took a step back for a better look. But no one ventured inside.

'They'll come,' said Mr Vorel to himself at seven. He was wearing a short grey miller's jacket and white dimity trousers.

'All I need is a first sale,' he said at eight, lighting up his new meerschaum.

At nine he advanced almost to the doorway, peering out to see whether that first sale was not finally on its way, and who should be coming up the street but Poldýnka, the captain's daughter. Poldýnka was a roly-poly little miss, short but sturdy in the shoulders and hips and well into her twenties. She had been rumoured about to be married four or five times, and her pale eyes wore that expression of indifference or, rather, lethargy that creeps into the eyes of women left on the shelf for too long. She walked with a waddle and – what was even more of a trademark – at intervals she would stumble and grab hold of her skirts, as though she had trodden on them. I thought of her gait as an epic poem divided into regular cantos of an equal number of lines and feet. And it was on

Miss Poldýnka that the flour merchant's gaze now alighted.

The young lady came up to the shop with basket in hand and looked at it as though surprised. She then stumbled over the step and found herself in the doorway. She did not quite enter, however, and quickly raised her handkerchief to her nose: for want of anything better to do Mr Vorel had smoked up quite a storm, and the shop was thick with fumes.

'I humbly kiss your hand, miss,' Mr Vorel said eagerly. 'How may I serve you?' And he took two steps back to lay his pipe on the counter.

'Two pints of medium-grained barley,' Miss Poldýnka ordered, half turning towards the street.

Mr Vorel leaped into action. He measured out two pints, added nearly half a pint more, and poured it into a paper bag. He had a feeling he should say something else. 'I hope you'll be satisfied, miss,' he stammered. 'There you are. Thank you.'

'How much do I owe you?' Miss Poldýnka inquired, trying to hold her breath, then coughing into her handkerchief.

'Four kreutzers. Thank you very much. I kiss your hand! My first sale and to a pretty young miss. That's a good sign.'

Miss Poldýnka gave him a long, cold stare. A merchant, and an outsider at that! Why, he'd be lucky to get the soap-maker's red-headed girl – what was her name? Anuše. And he presumes to . . . She stalked out with no reply.

Mr Vorel rubbed his hands. Looking back out into the street, his eye fell upon Mr Vojtíšek the beggar. A moment later Mr Vojtíšek stood, blue cap in hand, on the doorstep.

'Here's a kreutzer,' said Mr Vorel philanthropically. 'You may call every Wednesday.' Mr Vojtíšek thanked him with a smile and went his way. Mr Vorel rubbed his hands again and thought, It seems I only have to fix my eyes on a person for him to come into the shop. Oh, I'm bound to make a go of it!

But already Poldýnka the captain's daughter had reached the Deep Cellar and was telling Mrs Kdojek, the councillor's wife, 'He puffs so much on that pipe the flour's bound to taste smoked.' And when her barley soup was served at noon, Miss Poldýnka stated in no uncertain terms, 'It reeks of tobacco smoke', and laid down her spoon.

By evening the neighbours were all telling one another how everything in Mr Vorel's shop was tainted with tobacco – the flour roasted in it, the barley smoked in it. He was 'the smoky flour merchant' now, and his fate was sealed.

Mr Vorel never suspected a thing. He had not done well the first day, true, or the second or the third. But things would pick up in time. By the end of the week he had not taken in two guilders. Still, it was only the first week . . .

Yet on it went: none of the local people gave him their custom; only a few country folk wandered in now and then. He had but one regular visitor: Mr

Vojtíšek. Mr Vorel's comfort was his meerschaum. The more miserable he became, the greater the wreaths of smoke that rolled from his lips. His cheeks grew pale, his forehead furrowed, but the meerschaum grew redder by the day and fairly shone with opulence. The Spur Street policeman cast venomous glances into the den of the inveterate smoker. If only he would step into the street with that pipe in his mouth! Just once! One of them in particular, little Mr Novák, would have given a great deal to knock the lighted pipe from Mr Vorel's mouth, though they all shared instinctively the neighbourhood's distaste for the outsider. And Mr Vorel just sat there miserable, never budging from behind the counter.

The shop declined, deteriorated. Within four or five months Mr Vorel began to receive visits from suspicious characters, Jews. After each visit he half closed the glass door of the shop. The neighbours said in no uncertain terms that Malá Strana was about to witness a bankruptcy. 'When a man sinks to calling in the Jews . . .'

By St Havel's day word was out that Mr Vorel would be evicted and that the landlord intended to turn the shop back into a flat. And finally, on the day before the eviction, the shop closed for good.

On the following day, however, there was a crowd in front of the shop from nine in the morning till late at night. It seems that when the landlord failed to locate Mr Vorel he had the door of the shop forced open. Out fell a wooden stool, and directly above where the stool had been he found the unfortunate flour merchant hanging from a hook in the ceiling.

At ten o'clock a delegation from the district court arrived and entered the shop through the house. The men took down the suicide with the help of Mr Uhmühl, Malá Strana's commissioner of police, who reached into the pocket of the dead man's jacket and pulled out a pipe. 'Look at this,' he said, holding it up to the light. 'Never have I seen a pipe so expertly broken in!'

The Three Lilies

I must have been out of my mind at the time. I could feel my veins pulse, my blood boil.

It was a warm but dark summer night. That evening the dead, sulphurous air of the past few days had finally congealed into black clouds, which, whipped up by a stormy wind, turned into a raging downpour. The thunder and rain went on for hours.

I sat beneath the wooden arcade of the Three Lilies near Strahov Gate. It is a small inn, which was then much frequented only on Sundays, when cadets and corporals came to dance to the piano in the small room. That day was a Sunday. I sat by myself at a table near the windows. Claps of thunder roared overhead in fast succession, rain hammered the tiled roof just above me, water streamed in hissing torrents to the earth, and the piano within paused only for the briefest of respites before striking up the next dance. Now I would gaze in through an open window at the happy, twirling couples, now out at the dark garden. Whenever a flash of lightning proved particularly vivid, I would see white piles of human bones by the garden wall and at the end of the arcade. There had been a small cemetery here once, and just that week they were digging up the skeletons for reburial. The soil was still in mounds, the graves open.

But I could not stay at my table for more than short intervals. I kept getting up and crossing to the open tavern door to watch the dancers at close quarters. I was drawn to them by a beautiful girl of about eighteen. Though slender, she was shapely and warm with black hair cut short at the neck, a smooth, oval face, bright eyes – a beautiful girl! What attracted me most, however, was the eyes. They were clear as water, inscrutable as the surface of the deep, insatiable. The mere sight of them brought to mind the words: 'Sooner will fire be sated with wood or the sea with water than a bright-eyed woman with men.'

She danced almost continuously, yet she was well aware she had attracted my gaze. When she danced close to the doorway in which I stood, she would fix her eyes on me, and when she whirled off into the room I could see and feel those eyes grazing me at her every turn. I never saw her talk to anyone.

Again I stood there. Our eyes met at once, though she was in the farthest row. The quadrille was almost over, the fifth figure just ending, when another girl came running into the room, out of breath and dripping wet. She elbowed her way straight to Brighteyes. The music for the sixth figure had just begun. The newcomer whispered something to Brighteyes, who nodded without a word. The sixth figure, which she was dancing with a lithe cadet, went on a while longer.

When it came to an end, she glanced again in my direction, then, pulling the outer layer of her dress over her head, disappeared through the main door.

I went back to my place and sat down. The storm was starting up again, and what had gone before seemed a mere whisper now. The wind howled with renewed vigour; thunder and lightning exploded. Yet though I listened in rapture, all my thoughts were with the girl and her marvellous eyes. I could not dream of going home.

About a quarter of an hour later I looked over at the door again. There she stood, smoothing out her dripping dress, drying her hair, assisted by an older woman.

'Why did you go home in this storm?' the woman asked.

'My sister came to fetch me.'

These were the first words I heard her utter. Her voice was silken, soft yet rich.

'Is something the matter?'

'My mother's died.'

A shudder ran through me.

Brighteyes turned and stepped out into the solitude. She stood beside me, her eyes resting upon me. I felt her touch my quivering hand. I seized her hand. It was so soft.

Wordlessly I drew her deeper and deeper into the arcade; willingly she followed.

The storm had now reached its climax. The wind tore past in torrents; heaven and earth bayed and shrieked, claps of thunder detonated just above our heads, and all around us the dead clamoured from their graves.

She pressed against me. I felt her wet dress clinging to my chest, I felt her soft, warm body, her ardent breath – I felt it was my lot to drain the demonic spirit from her.

The St Wenceslas Mass

I was sitting at the foot of the steps leading to the choir loft, scarcely breathing. Through the half-open grille I had a good view of the church, from St John's silver tomb on my right all the way across to the sacristy. It was well past the afternoon benediction, and St Vitus's Cathedral was empty except for my mother – still kneeling devoutly at St John's tomb, lost in prayer – and the old verger making his final rounds. The verger passed within three paces of me, but veered off to the exit beneath the royal oratory, where he turned the lock with a great jangle of keys and tested the handle with a harsh rasp. Then he moved on. My mother rose too – crossing herself – and walked off beside him. The tomb hid them both from me. All I could hear was the echo of their steps and some scraps of conversation until they reappeared on the other side, at the sacristy, and the verger slammed the door shut, jangled the keys in the lock, and gave the handle a grating tug. Then they proceeded to the exit on the right, whence two more iron clankings reached me, and I was alone, locked in the church. A strange feeling came over me, a stream of heat flowing down my back – but it was not unpleasant.

I jumped up in a flash, pulled out my handkerchief and tied it as securely as possible to the grille door, which was otherwise closed only by its handle. Then I ran up the steps to the first landing of the loft, pressed against the wall, and sat down again on a step. I did so out of caution, certain that the church door would open again and a night watch of church dogs would come bounding in. We altar boys had never laid eyes on the church dogs, nor had we ever heard one bark, but we told one another stories about three brindled dogs, huge and fierce, just like the dog of King Wenceslas depicted in the painting behind the main altar. They were said never to bark, a sign of the utmost ferocity.

It was because I knew the dogs were able to open closed doors that I had secured the grille below with my handkerchief. I reasoned that they could not reach me up here in the choir, but in the morning, when the verger took them away again, I could run down and make my getaway. I had made up my mind to spend the night in St Vitus's Cathedral. I had told no one, of course, but it was of the utmost importance to me. The thing is, we boys knew for a fact that every night at the stroke of midnight St Wenceslas celebrated Mass in the chapel bearing his name. To be honest, I was the one responsible for spreading the rumour among my peers. But I had it from a prime, thoroughly reliable source. Mr Havel, the verger (he was called Havel the Turkey for his unusually long and resplendent nose), had spoken of it once to my parents at home, and the odd sidelong glances he gave me as he spoke made it immediately clear to me that he was not happy about my being let in on the secret. I shared it with my two best friends afterwards, and we resolved to have a look at the Mass: St Wenceslas was our hero. I as the chief initiate naturally had priority, so there I sat, the first of the trio, in the lower loft, shut off, isolated from the whole world.

I should not be missed at home, I knew, for I had contrived with the duplicity characteristic of many a gifted nine-year-old to make my mother believe that our aunt in the Old Town had asked me to spend the evening with her. It was taken for granted that I should stay the night but also that I should report for my acolyte's duties at matins. I might eventually give myself away, but what did it matter? I would be able to say I had witnessed St Wenceslas celebrate Mass! I saw myself in the same category as Dame Wimmer, the mother of the Castle District cabinet-maker, who in the time of the cholera saw the Virgin Mary of the Capuchins, saw her with her own eyes, dressed in her golden gown and walking one night through Loreto Square, sprinkling the houses with holy water. People thought the vision meant deliverance from the plague, but when it raged more fiercely than ever in the very houses she had sprinkled, they revised their interpretation, to wit, that she had used the holy water to mark those in the neighbourhood who were to enter her kingdom of heaven.

Almost everyone has, if only for a moment, found himself in an empty church and knows the powerful effect those vast, mute spaces can have upon the spirit. But the impression they make upon children, who have vivid imaginations and expect unusual things to happen, is immeasurably more intense. I waited for a while (the quarter-hour chimed, the half-hour, the strokes of the clock cascading into the church as into a pool of water), but heard not the slightest rustle at the door. Had they chosen that night of all nights to dispense with the guard? Or did they loose the dogs only after dark?

I got up from the step and rose slowly to my full height. Only the pale glow of twilight filtered through the nearest of the large windows. It was late November, past St Catherine's Day, and the days were short. An occasional sound drifted in, echoing loudly, but late in the day a silence, almost mournful, descends upon these parts. From time to time I heard a heavy, solitary step. At one point there were more of them: two men walking past, talking in rough voices. Then an obscure rumble emerged out of the distance: a heavy cart on its way through the Castle entrance. The rumble grew. Clearly the cart was driving through the Castle grounds. It drew closer, grew louder, hoofs clattering, chains clanking, great wheels jolting: a military cart on its way to the St George Barracks. The din was such that the church windows rattled and up in the loft the sparrows twittered uneasily. I heaved a deep sigh of relief at the sound of their piping: the knowledge that I had living creatures with me set my mind at rest.

Not that I felt any anxiety or fear in the solitude of the church. There was no reason to. Though aware of the extraordinary nature of my undertaking, I saw nothing wrong in it. My soul was free of disheartening, dispiriting guilt; on the contrary, I felt uplifted, exalted. A kind of ecstasy had transformed me as it were into a creature unique and sublime; never before had I felt – and, I must confess, never since have I felt – so perfect, so worthy of universal envy. Were a child capable of the foolish complacency of an adult, I might even have gone so far as to bow down to myself. At another time, in another place I might have been afraid of ghosts, but what power could ghosts have in a church! As for the spirits of the saints buried here, I was concerned only with St Wenceslas, and I could cause him nothing but joy, braving, as I had, so much to see him serving God in all his glory. Should he so desire, I was ready to be his altar boy, carefully carrying the metal-bound missal from one side of the altar to the other, making certain the bell gave not one tinkle more than necessary, pulling down the straps of the choir organ, and singing, soaring so high and heavenly that St Wenceslas, moved to tears, would lay both hands upon my head and say, 'What a fine child!'

The loud chimes signalling the hour of five roused me from my reverie. I took my reader out of my satchel, which was still slung over my shoulder, opened it on the balustrade and set to reading, my young eyes adjusting to the gathering dark. But even the faintest noise from outside distracted me, and I would not resume my reading until the outside world was dead silent.

All at once I heard some light, rapid footsteps. They stopped just beneath the window. I was ecstatic, convinced my two friends had come. The special whistle we used rang out. I trembled with joy to know they were thinking of me and had come all this way – they might well be beaten when they got home, poor things! At the same time I trembled with pride to think how they must admire me and wish they could be in my shoes, if only for an hour. No, they wouldn't sleep a wink all night! And how glad I'd have been to have them with me for that hour!

That was Fricek calling, Fricek the cobbler's son. I'd recognise his voice anywhere! I liked him so much, and he'd had such a hard time of it that day, poor boy. Early in the morning at first Mass he had spilled water on the priest's shoes (Fricek always looked about the church rather than at the priest), and in the afternoon the teacher had caught him kissing the headmaster's daughter while passing a note to her (we were all three fond of Anynka and she of us). And that was Kubíček's shout. Kubíček! Hello! I would have liked to shout back or whistle, to make my presence known somehow – but I was in church.

The boys talked in loud voices so that I could hear

them. They even shouted, but all I could catch was a
phrase or two. 'Are you there?' 'Yoo-hoo, are you
there?' 'Are you scared?' I was there and I wasn't
scared. They ran off whenever they saw someone
coming, but they came right back. It was as if I saw
their every movement through the wall. I couldn't
stop smiling. Suddenly there was a rap at the window.
The start it gave me! But it was only a stone they had
tossed. Then another. Immediately thereafter a man's
voice bellowed out nearby. I could hear him giving
them what for and them running away. That time
they did not come back. No, no use waiting.

For the first time I felt a certain anxiety. I stuck the
book back into my satchel, went over to the other
balustrade, and peered down into the church. Everything looked sadder than before, sadder in the
absolute, not because of the dark. I could still make
out individual objects; I knew them so well that I
could have done so had the dark been much thicker.
But it was as if the columns and altars were hung with
the blue cloths used on Good Friday, their long folds
enveloping everything in a single colour or, rather,
lack of colour. Leaning over the balustrade, I saw the
eternal light gleaming just below the royal oratory. It
was held by a miner cast in stone and suspended in
air, a famous caryatid painted in lifelike colours. The
tiny lamp burned with never a flicker, like the calmest
of stars, making the floor below appear divided into
paving stones. I saw the pew directly opposite me in
all its deep-brown lustre and, on the nearest altar, a

gold stripe glowing faintly on the gown of a wooden saint. Try as I might, I was unable to recall how that saint looked in daylight. My eyes turned back to the caryatid. The miner was illuminated from below, his chubby body looking for all the world like a dirty, deformed red ball, his bulging eyes, which we found quite frightening by day, sunk deep in shadow. Just beyond him St John's tomb had faded into the twilight; I could distinguish only a patch of a lighter shade. My eyes turned back to the miner, and I had the sudden impression that he was deliberately holding his head back, laughing duplicitously, and that the redness came from the strain of concealing it. Could he be taking sidelong glances at me? Could I be the butt of his mirth? Overcome with fear, I shut my eyes and began to pray. I felt calmer at once and gave him a stout-hearted glare. His lamp burned peacefully on. The tower clock chimed seven.

Before long I was faced with another unpleasant sensation: I began to shiver with cold. There was a dry frost in the air and the church of course was frigid. My clothes, though decent, were not very warm. Moreover, I felt a sudden pang of hunger. The usual time for my supper had passed, and I had quite forgotten to lay in supplies for my expedition. I resolved to resist it heroically, indeed, to look upon my fast as meet preparation for the blissful midnight event. The cold creeping into my body, however, failed to respond to mere willpower; I needed to walk about and warm up. I paced the loft for a while, then went as far as the lower organ and the stairs behind it leading to the main choir loft above. Thoroughly acquainted with the terrain, I started climbing. The first step creaked and I held my breath, but on I went, climbing slowly and cautiously, as cautiously as we climbed on holy days to ensure that the organ blower should not hear us and turn us back before we found refuge behind the musicians.

Having reached the main choir loft, I advanced one step at a time until I was right at the front. We would venture that far only with great trepidation and stand there in a kind of poetic trance; now I could linger there all alone, unsupervised, unobserved. The tiered seats on either side of the organ rose one above the other like benches in a Roman arena. I took a seat on the lowest one next to the timpani, which had always fascinated us. No one could stop me from playing with them now. I touched the surface of the nearest one, but barely grazed it, as if afraid to brush away the bloom. Then I touched it again, a bit harder, and got a response, though so soft as to be unrecognisable. Yet I felt I had committed a sinful act and gave up the game.

Before me the great psalters loomed black on their stands and on the raised balustrade. I could have touched them too, tried to lift them; had it been day I should probably have yielded to the temptation. We had always found those gigantic tomes mysterious: they were bound in brass; their boards were cracked; their parchment pages, which were turned by means

of wooden sticks, were smudged with dirt at the corners, but each page had gilded and coloured initials,
old-fashioned Gothic script, and black and red notes
on broad staves, notes so large we could see them
clearly even from the highest tier. They must have
been enormously heavy, because the gaunt tenor from
the Castle could not budge them (we boys despised
that string bean of a man); when one of them had to
be moved, the task would fall to the fat ruddy bass,
and even he moaned and groaned. We loved that bass
– his low notes surged through our bodies like a stream
– and whenever there was a procession we kept as
close to him as possible. On major holidays he stood
just in front of where I was standing then. He shared
his music with two other basses, but he was in a
category by himself. The two tenors stood a few steps
away, and little as we cared for tenors in general we
did respect the second, shorter one. He was the one
who played the timpani, and when he picked up his
drumsticks and Mr Rojko, the merchant and landlord
of the Stone Bird, placed his trombone to his lips, we
were in heaven. A bit farther to the left came the boys'
choir and the all-powerful choirmaster. I can still hear
his admonitions before Mass, the rustling of the parts
being passed out, the chiming of the bells. Now the
bell tinkles in the sacristy, the organ launches into the
opening voluntary, shaking the entire church with its
long, deep tones, the choirmaster stretches his neck in
the direction of the main altar, swishes his poised
baton, and suddenly the music bursts forth in all its

glory, a majestic Kyrie soaring to the vaulted ceiling. I heard the choristers, the music, the entire Mass down to a magnificent '*Dona nobis pacem*'. There has never been nor shall there be a Mass so perfect as the one that suffused my being then, the bass ineffably mellifluous, the timpani and trombone entering the flow with ever fresh rejoicing. I cannot tell how long it lasted, though I sensed an occasional chiming from the tower amid its magic chords. Then a sudden bitter cold ran through me again and I jumped to my feet involuntarily.

A silvery, gossamerlike radiance floated over the nave, the glimmer of the stars – and the moon, perhaps, as well – penetrating the countless windows. I mounted the step to the balustrade and peered down into the church. A few deep breaths and my lungs were full of that distinctive combination of incense and mould found in every house of worship. I saw the white marble gleam of the great mausoleum, the glint of a second eternal light opposite it at the main altar, and a tiny pink shimmer here and there along the altar's golden walls. I was still in a state of ecstasy, wondering what St Wenceslas's Mass would be like. The bells would hardly peal for it, because then all the world would hear and it would lose its wondrous mystery. Perhaps the clear sacristy bell would tinkle, the organ would sound, and out would come the procession, bathed in a magical light and advancing augustly from the main altar along the right aisle to the Chapel of St Wenceslas. The order of the procession would be the same as for the Sunday after-noon Mass: I could conceive of no other.

First would come a group of shiny metal lanterns on red poles – borne by angels, of course. Then – but who would be the choir? To my mind the most likely candidates were the figures whose busts lined the upper reaches of the triforium in painted stone: Czech kings and queens of the House of Luxembourg, arch-bishops, canons and the men who built the cathedral, all proceeding two by two. The current canons, how-ever, would be excluded, being deemed unworthy of the honour. Especially Canon Pešina, for Pešina had especially wounded my pride. On one occasion he decided the heavy lantern I was carrying during a service was not quite straight and boxed my ears, and on another, after the sexton had let me climb the bell tower to ring the Joseph bell for the service (it was the first time I was up there on my own, lord of all those fascinating metal giants), I heard Canon Pešina ask the sexton, 'Who was that fool ringing the bell? It sounded like a call to arms!'

While I had no trouble picturing my stone-eyed dignitaries leading the procession, I could provide them with neither torsos nor legs; they remained busts, yet moved as though walking. They would be followed by the archbishops, who were buried in the adjacent Kinský Chapel, by St John's silver angels, and then, crucifix in hand, by the silver St John. Next would come the bones of St Sigmund – just the bones on a red cushion, but the cushion would also move as though walking. Then a group of knights in armour and kings and dukes from local mausoleums, some in resplendent flowing crimson robes, others – including George of Poděbrady – in white marble. And finally, bearing a chalice veiled with a silver fabric, St Wenceslas himself, a tall, youthful, powerful figure. Instead of a biretta he would wear a simple metal helmet, but the coat of mail protecting his body would be covered with a chasuble of gleaming white silk; his auburn hair would be a cascade of curls, his face all compassion and tranquillity. Oddly enough, while I could conjure up his face quite clearly – the large blue eyes, the healthy bloom on the cheeks, the softly flowing beard – it seemed to consist less of flesh and blood than of a serene glow.

My eyes were shut as I envisaged the procession to come. The silence, the late hour and an overwrought imagination had taken their toll: my head nodded, my knees buckled. I quickly recovered, however, and gazed out over the cathedral's expanse. Though mute and lifeless as before, it now had a different effect on me: I felt the entire burden of the hour and of the cold, and suddenly I was overcome by a vague – yet for its vagueness all the more shattering – terror. I did not know what I feared, yet fear I did, and my weak, childlike mind was powerless to resist.

I collapsed on the step in sobs, tears flowing, chest heaving, loud hiccups erupting from my lips. My attempts to suppress the hiccups only increased their intensity, and they echoed through the church, disturbing the silence and fanning my fears. If only I weren't locked in and so utterly alone!

I let out a loud groan – louder perhaps than the hiccups – and in reply, as it were, a twittering of birds broke out above my head. Of course! I was not alone. The sparrows were with me. I knew their refuge well. It was between the beams directly over the tiered seats, where they could be assured asylum even from the mischievous whims of us boys. Any of us could have reached up for them, but none had ever done so.

I made up my mind in a flash and crept up the stairs with bated breath. When I came to the beams, I inhaled deeply and stretched out my hand. Before I knew it, I was holding a sparrow. The startled bird piped shrilly, but I would not let it go. Feeling its warm little heart beating wildly beneath my fingers, I lost all my fear. I was no longer alone, and yes, the awareness of being the stronger creature instilled renewed courage in me.

I decided to hold the sparrow for a while: it would keep my courage up and prevent me from falling asleep. It couldn't be long to midnight now. I would be careful to listen for the chimes. Clasping the hand with the sparrow to my breast, I would stretch out on two steps and face St Wenceslas's Chapel so as to see the light shining for the miraculous Mass at once.

Lying thus, I fixed my eyes upon the chapel window. It was dark grey. I do not know how long I stared at it, but gradually the grey in the window grew lighter and began to turn blue – clear, limpid blue – until at last I thought I was gazing into the bluest of skies. Then the clock began to chime, stroke after stroke, endlessly, without number . . .

I awoke racked with pain from the cold. My whole body felt beaten and bruised; my eyes seemed to be staring into a great, red-hot oven, and my ears rang with hellish whistling and squeals.

Gradually I came to. I was still lying on the steps, my hand clasped to my chest, but my hand was open and empty. The window of St Wenceslas's Chapel was gleaming from within, the choir organ was puffing away, and up soared the matins music I knew so well.

Could this be the St Wenceslas Mass?

I picked myself up slowly, went down the stairs to the window that opened on the lower loft, and peered timidly through the glass.

The priest was celebrating Mass at the altar. The verger serving as his ministrant had just rung the bell for the elevation.

My eyes turned immediately and fearfully to a familiar place among the benches. There, as always, my mother knelt beating her breast, her head bowed. And who should be kneeling next to her but my Old Town aunt.

When my mother raised her head, I saw tears pouring down her face.

Everything was clear. I was mortified and desperately unhappy. My head started aching, spinning as if in a whirlwind. My heart bled with anguish for my mother, who was surely mourning me as lost. I wanted to rush down and fling myself before her, but suddenly my legs gave way, my head slid down the wall, and I collapsed. It was my greatest good fortune that I burst into tears almost simultaneously. At first the tears burned like fire; then they calmed me.

It was still dark and a cold drizzle began to fall as the worshippers left the service. A humble, disheartened hero of the faith stood waiting outside the cathedral entrance, though nobody noticed him, nor did he take notice of them. Yet when at last his old mother came out in the company of his aunt, she suddenly felt two burning lips upon her wrinkled hand.

How It Came to Pass

*That on the Twentieth Day of August
in the Year Eighteen Hundred and Forty-Nine
at Half Past Twelve in the Afternoon
Austria Was Not Overthrown*

O n the twentieth day of August in the year
eighteen hundred and forty-nine, Austria was
to be overthrown, or so the Brotherhood of
the Pistol had resolved. I can't quite recall what crime
Austria had committed this time, but I can state
beyond the shadow of a doubt that the decision was
taken only after deep deliberation and as a last
recourse, a matter agreed upon, confirmed by vow,
and entrusted to the reliable hands of John Žižka of
Trocnov, Procopius the Great, Procopius the Small
and Nicolas of Hus,[1] that is, yours truly, Pepík
Rumpál the pork-butcher's son, Frantík Mastný the
cobbler's son, and Antonín Hochmann, who hailed
from the Rakovník area and was studying at the
expense of his farmer brother. The historical pseudonyms were not allocated at random; they depended
entirely on merit. I was Žižka because I was the swar-
thiest and the most outspoken and because I arrived at

the Brotherhood's very first meeting (which took place in the Rumpáls' attic) with a black patch over my left eye, which caused a sensation. As a result I had to wear the patch to every meeting, and uncomfortable as it was there was nothing I could do about it. The others had equally valid claims to their pseudonyms.

The plot was prepared with truly amazing ingenuity. For an entire year we had turned every excursion into catapult practice. Mastný (a.k.a. Procopius the Small) supplied us with excellent ammunition, and soon we could hit any tree trunk at a hundred paces – provided it was thick enough, that is. But we did not stop there. For the entire year we deposited every kreutzer we could scrape together in the communal Pistol Fund that gave the Brotherhood its name. In the end our savings amounted to eleven guilders. For five we bought a pistol of what the salesman in the Old Town shop called 'Liège design'. We spent a whole meeting admiring it – we met daily once the holidays began – passing it from hand to hand, each confirming that it was genuine Liège. We hadn't fired a shot from it, of course, first, because we had no powder, and second, because the situation was a perilous one and called for great circumspection on our part. We had been very careful not to betray our secret and had therefore refrained from taking on new members. Besides, we were first-year Latin School students; four of us was enough. We could have bought another pistol with the remaining six guilders, thus doubling our armoury, but we reserved the sum for gunpowder, uncertain as we were about how much it would set us back. One pistol was quite sufficient for our purposes. We had another common asset in the form of a porcelain pipe (which Procopius the Small smoked on behalf of all of us at our secret meetings) , and a beautiful pipe it was, tellingly decorated with the chalice, flail and halberd,[2] but without any specific role to play in our undertaking. We also had an electric device made for us from an old two-groschen coin by Procopius the Great's brother, a locksmith's apprentice, but it never worked and we left it behind.

I shall now set forth our plan for all to admire. Ultimate goal: overthrow Austria. First step: take Prague. Modus operandi: seize the citadel and lookout point on the promontory of the Marian Ramparts, thereby capturing the city and, according to our calculations, forestalling all possibility of bombardment. Clever detail: storm the citadel at noon. Given that all attacks on all strongholds have from time immemorial taken place at midnight and that midnight is therefore the time when the guard is sure to be at its most vigilant, our scheme must be considered devilishly cunning.

At noon the citadel was guarded by no more than a handful of soldiers, six or eight at most. One of them was posted just beside the iron gate leading into the courtyard. The gate was always slightly open, and we had noticed that the sentry was very casual in his movements. A second sentry stood watch over the Prague side and the several cannons there. Our intention was to saunter up to the gate – the four of us and someone else (you'll learn who the fifth was by and by) – jump the sentry, kill him, seize his rifle, shoot up the guardroom window with our catapults, charge in and attack the lolling guards, kill them and seize their rifles. Then there was the second sentry. He would most likely surrender, and we'd tie him up and take his rifle. If he didn't surrender, well, that was his affair, but we'd have to kill him. Then we'd push one of the cannons over to the gate, fire the flare waiting there on a pole, and shout down from the ramparts to the citizens of Prague that the revolution had begun. Then the army would attack. Naturally. But they wouldn't be able to scale the walls, because we'd keep opening the gates, firing at them with our cannons, and quickly closing the gates again. And after we'd mowed down the front line, the rest would have to surrender, because by that time they'd be surrounded by the revolutionary forces. Though if they didn't surrender, that was their affair. We'd charge out and join ranks with the citizens of Prague, and the first official move we'd make would be to free all political prisoners still languishing in the Castle. The rest would follow like the night the day. We'd lure the army down to Německý Brod and win our first great victory there. The second would take place on the Moravian Fields, where the spirit of King Otakar cried out for revenge.[3] Then on to Vienna, where we'd overthrow Austria with the help of the Magyars. After which we'd massacre the Magyars. Not bad!

A key role in the early stages of this bloody drama was to be played by the fifth person I have mentioned. He knew nothing about it, however, nor was he to learn of his role until the last moment. He was Pohorák the pedlar. Pohorák was from the other side of White Mountain, near Jeneč, and drove a dog-drawn cart into Prague three times a week with chickens and pigeons for sale. Commander Rumpál-Procopius drew our attention to him when a serious issue came up, namely, the procurement of gunpowder. Getting hold of gunpowder at the time was extremely difficult: only holders of official permits were allowed to purchase it. But Procopius the Great informed us that Pohorák, who was a regular customer of his father's, stocked up on gunpowder for a Jeneč merchant whenever he was in Prague, and when he asked him whether he would be willing to buy some for us – for a handsome consideration – Pohorák agreed.

On 19 August, therefore, Procopius the Great gave Pohorák the sum of six guilders, of which two constituted the royal commission and four covered the cost of the powder. Pohorák promised that the following day he would make haste with his buying and selling and return home via Bruska rather than the Strahov Gate and there deliver the powder to Procopius the Great. At that point he would learn of our great regiment and, unhitching his dog and leaving his cart on the highroad, follow us. We had no doubt whatever that he would follow us. We'd paid him two guilders, hadn't we? And think of the honour! We'd find something for him to do, he could be sure of that. After all, Procopius the Great had told us that Pohorák had told him that once, while working in the fields just after Whitsun last year, he had pulled a hussar from his horse.

'People from that side of White Mountain are the strongest in Bohemia,' said Procopius the Great.

'And that holds all the way to Rakovník,' said Nicholas of Hus, brandishing his mighty fist.

I should point out that I was totally in favour of Pohorák's participation in our cause, and I should imagine the other commanders shared my view. As I have made amply clear, our entire plan centred on the guards at the gate, yet an incident that had taken place about a month earlier had left its mark on us all. We had been playing ball – rather more than four of us, actually – in the moat below the ramparts. Our game, a military game called 'the great shepherd', kept us going for hours at a time. We had a fine rubber ball worth at least forty kreutzers, and we must have been playing well, because a passing grenadier stopped to watch. After standing there a long time, he made himself comfortable on the turf. At one point the ball rolled past him and he stretched out indolently, rolled over on his stomach, and stopped it. He rose slowly to his feet – he seemed to take forever – while we waited to see where his mighty hand would throw the ball. But his mighty hand simply dropped it in his pocket, and his mighty body betook itself indolently up the hill. We surrounded the grenadier, we pleaded with him, we threatened him. All we got for our pains was that first Procopius the Great, then Nicholas of Hus had his ears boxed. We pelted him with stones, but he ran after us, and if the truth be told we ran for our lives.

'You know,' said Jan Žižka of Trocnov later that day, 'we did well not to thrash him. Think of what was at stake. You never know what might have happened. With a plot like ours, I mean. I was just itching to jump him, but then I thought, No, wait, hold on!' Everyone gratefully accepted this explanation of the incident: yes, of course, each of us had been fairly itching to give him a drubbing, barely able to restrain himself.

In early August, when we were getting down to the details, I suddenly asked, 'Does Pohorák's dog bite?'

'It does,' said Procopius the Great. 'Yesterday it tore the skirt of the baker's girl.'

It was highly important that Pohorák's dog should bite.

The morning of the memorable day. The indisputable heavenly chronicle records that it fell on a Monday.

I had watched the dark turn ash-grey, then blue-grey, then clearer and clearer – all in the course of an age or two. And all the while I longed for nothing so much as for the dark to stop growing light, nature to skip over the day altogether. Something of the sort

was bound to happen – I prayed and prayed it would
happen – but my spirit, I confess, was all anguish.

I hadn't slept a wink all night. From time to time I
slipped into a feverish doze, but soon I would be
tossing and turning again, hard put not to moan.

'Is that you sighing?' my mother asked several
times. 'Is something the matter?'

I made believe I was asleep.

My mother got up, lit a candle, and came over to
my bed. I kept my eyes shut. She laid her hand on
my forehead. 'The boy's on fire!' she cried. 'Come
and see, Father. He's not well.'

'Let him be,' my father said. 'He was off gallivant-
ing with those friends of his. They're the devil when
they're together – Frantík and Pepík and that boy from
Rakovník. We'll have to break them up.'

'But they do their lessons together. They learn more
that way.'

I shall be frank. I felt extremely uneasy. I had been
feeling uneasy for days, and the feeling had only
grown as 20 August drew near. Moreover, I had
observed a similar reaction in the other commanders.
At our most recent meetings the discussion had been
more than a bit muddled. In my heart of hearts I
attributed it to a certain fear on their part. Two days
earlier I had got a grip on myself and given a particularly rousing speech, and soon we were conquering
heroes again, full of fire; indeed, never had we spoken
with such resolution. That night I was able to sleep,

though poorly, for I still lacked confidence in my confrères' capacity for valour.

Not for a moment did I admit to myself that *I* might be afraid, but I couldn't help cursing my fate and wondering why so terrible a burden had been placed on my shoulders. I suddenly regarded the overthrow of Austria as a cup full of indescribable gall, and had I felt there was any turning back I should gladly have prayed, 'Lord, let this cup pass from me!' for I knew that my glory would be my Golgotha. Besides, I was bound by oath.

At ten o'clock we were to take up our positions. Pohorák would come at eleven, and at half past twelve the operation would begin.

I left the house at nine.

A fresh summer breeze fanned my temples. The blue sky smiled like Márinka, Procopius the Great's sister, when she had some prank in mind. I might mention in passing that Márinka was my love, and at the thought of her and the admiration she had for my heroic temperament I suddenly felt calmer, my breast swelled, my spirit soared. Indeed, a magical change had come over me by the time I reached the Stags' Moat. I even caught myself skipping twice.

I went through everything in my mind; everything was as it should be. I had two catapults hidden in one pocket and a black eye patch in the other, and I was carrying a school book by way of camouflage. Walking along the Marian Ramparts past detachments of drilling soldiers, I did not so much as tremble. I knew that by the time we were to take the field they would have long since returned to their barracks.

As I was in no rush, I made the rounds of our positions. I walked through the Chotka Gardens, where Nicholas of Hus would take his stand near the highroad leading down to the river; I looked down into Bruska, where Procopius the Small would wait for Pohorák, then run through the hollow to report; I climbed all the way to the citadel and walked along the ramparts to Bruska Gate. Approaching the citadel, I felt my heart pound, but it settled down as I withdrew. The ramparts between the citadel and Bruska Gate have two projecting bastions. The first is on high ground, and at the top there is a flat area with a small, brick-rimmed fish pond surrounded by thick rushes and bushes, the scene of some of our happiest hours. Under one of the bushes we had hidden a pile of large pebbles for our catapults. The second bastion is in a basin. Today it houses the Café Panorama, but at that time it was a tangle of bushes. And just beyond it was Bruska Gate, my post as commander in chief.

I sat down on a bench above the gate and opened my book. A shiver kept running through my body, a chill down my back, but I didn't think it was fear. I was doing quite well, I thought. Perhaps because I hadn't seen any of my comrades in arms, I harboured the pleasant suspicion that they had got cold feet and wouldn't show up. My heart kept urging me to thrust out my chest, but my mind responded superstitiously that a thrust-out chest might summon them. I did not thrust out my chest.

Drums and bugles took turns on the Marian and Belvedere parade grounds. Men and carts passed in and out of the gate just below me. At first I didn't notice them; then superstition started getting the better of me again. If the man at the end of the bridge turns in the direction of Bubeneč, we're in for it; if he turns towards Podbaba, we've nothing to worry about. One, two, three, four, five – everybody was going to Bubeneč!

Suddenly the Belvedere bugles blared out what sounded like a call to arms, and I leaped to my feet. At the same time St Vitus's tower chimed ten, and I turned and saw Nicholas of Hus wending his way towards his post. Stout-hearted he was and noble, a valiant warrior who had sacrificed his holidays for the cause – he could have been at home with his brother for a fortnight – yet I had to admit I was less than happy to see him: now I was *obliged* to make the rounds, do my military duty. I set off, holding the open book before me. I was the only one walking along the ramparts.

When I got to the fish pond, I found Procopius the Great lying in the grass. The moment I saw him I began to take long, heavy steps, as if I had huge, armour-clad legs.

Procopius the Great also had a book in his hand. When he looked up at me, I saw that his eyes were red.

'Everything all right?'

'Everything's fine.'

'Got it?'

'Yes.'

In other words, he had the pistol that had been entrusted to him.

I looked over at the bushes that hid our pebbles. Procopius the Great did the same, attempting a smile. He did not succeed.

Just then a soldier emerged from the citadel. He was wearing a smock and cap and carrying a watering can. He was the orderly. We had quite forgotten to include him in our calculations. Well, that meant one more. He advanced slowly in our direction and, having reached us, set down the watering can. Our hearts were pounding like clocks.

'You young gentlemen wouldn't have a smoke for me, would you now?'

'No, we . . . uh,' I started, but couldn't go on, for how could I tell him that apart from Procopius the Small none of us smoked yet?

'But you must have a couple of kreutzers you could give me for tobacco. I've been here since the rebellion last year' – I gave a start, it was like an electric shock – 'and every day the gentlemen help me with tobacco.'

I took two kreutzers from my pocket and handed them to him. My hand was trembling. The soldier gave a whistle, picked up his watering can, and walked off without so much as a thank you.

I waved goodbye to Procopius the Great and walked

down to the road. I entered Chotka Gardens and went over to Nicholas of Hus, who was sitting on a bench near the lookout point surveying the scene below over his book. Again I took long, heavy steps.

'Everything all right?'

'Everything's fine,' he said with the trace of a smile.

'What about Procopius the Small?'

'At his post and puffing away.'

There he was, down below, perched on the balustrade, dangling his feet and smoking a cigar. It must have cost three kreutzers.

'Tomorrow I start smoking.'

'So do I.'

Another wave and off I went, treading heavily back to my post near the gate. By then the soldiers were returning in their platoons from the parade grounds, which was all well and good. But oddly enough on that day I felt a kind of distaste at the sight of them. They usually excited me. The mere roll of the drum unleashed the most dazzling fantasies in my mind, and even without it I would imagine the whirling, tantalising strains of Turkish music and picture myself on a snorting white steed returning from a victorious battle, behind me my men intoning a jubilant song, around me a cheering throng. I would not move a muscle of my face, only bend my head slightly from time to time. But on that day my fantasies were as flat and bland as yesterday's beer, from which my mother would make a soup I could not stomach. I had no taste for victory, and my tongue seemed coated with clay. When one or another soldier glanced up at me, I immediately turned away.

I gazed down at the landscape. It was tranquil yet festive, as if a rain of the finest gold had fallen on the hills and dales. But it had an oddly elegiac quality about it, and it gave me a chill despite the warmth of the air.

I gazed up at the blue sky. I thought of Márinka again, the dear girl! Though I had the feeling I was actually afraid of her at that moment. Time to move on to something else. Yes, Žižka overpowered a hundred thousand crusaders with a handful of men, and Percival slew a hundred armoured soldiers in an hour, but God only knew what this would be like, there were some things for which history offered no formulas. Flat beer, clay-coated tongue.

No! Impossible! There was no turning back! Stiff upper lip!

More and more people were passing through the gate. I gazed after them mindlessly. Then I caught myself playing the superstitions game again and caught myself cheating: I chose only those people who were wearing country clothes and who could therefore be expected to turn left, that is, in the direction of Podbaba.

I felt a fever coming on and pulled myself up. Even going my rounds again would be better than this! And it was my duty after all.

By the time I had trodden my heavy way over to Procopius (though I could tell it was less heavy than before), the inspecting officer was entering the citadel. We'd have to wait until he came out again, anyway. Procopius the Great looked as pale as a ghost.

'Scared, Pepík, aren't you?' I said with genuine sympathy.

Procopius the Great did not respond. Instead, he placed the forefinger of his right hand under his right eye and pulled on the skin until the eye's red rim appeared – a well-known gesture among Prague youth to express absolute negation.

Why couldn't he come out and say it! Austria could still be . . .

'Eleven!' he shrieked.

The chimes floated down leisurely through the clement air, each stroke quivering for a long time in our ears. I couldn't help looking up to see whether the sound had a visible incarnation. They were powerful, those chimes, tolling for one of the greatest and most ancient of Europe's political entities!

I moved on slowly to the post of Nicholas of Hus and thence to Procopius the Small, whose vigilance seemed in need of a bit of encouragement on the part of the commander in chief. Procopius the Small was still sitting on the balustrade, but he had given up his cigar for the capful of plums in his lap. He was obviously relishing them, carefully removing each stone from his mouth, balancing it on his index finger, pressing his thumb against it, and fire! Off in a flutter and loud lament would go one of the hens passing by on the other side of the road. All but one had run off out of danger, and that one, pitch black, was pecking about incautiously within close range. Procopius the Small was about to take aim at her when his eye lit on me. His trigger finger suddenly shifted direction, and the stone hit me instead of the hen, stinging my chin as painfully as if it had been slashed with a whip. Procopius the Small beamed with delight.

'What do you think you're doing? You're supposed to be keeping watch!'

'But I am. I've got eyes, haven't I? Want some?'

'I'm not hungry. How much were they?'

'Eight kreutzers. Have some.'

'I'll take four for Pepík. And keep those eyes of yours peeled. He could be here any minute now.'

Climbing back up, I felt another stone graze my ear painfully, but I marched on with dignity and never looked round.

It was half past eleven by the time I reached the post of Procopius the Great. He was still lying on the grass.

'I've brought you some plums. From Frantík.'

He pushed my hand away. I plopped them and myself down next to him and stretched out on my back.

A cloudless sky. But when I looked straight up, my eyes clouded over. I saw the air swarming with white, violently threshing worms. Not only my eyes, my entire body filled with worms; my blood first raced, then froze; first one muscle twitched, then another. The heavens rained molten lead.

I turned on my side and faced Procopius.

A quarter to twelve.

'What if . . .' he said, turning to me abruptly, his eyes out on stalks, 'what if Pohorák has betrayed us?'

'He wouldn't do that,' I stammered without conviction. I rose and began to pace, plagued by thoughts of treachery most vile. Then, turning from the bushes to the hollow, I saw Procopius the Small tearing uphill as fast as his legs could carry him.

'Procopius!' I yelled, and thought, Run for it!

By then Procopius the Great was on his feet and Nicholas of Hus, who must have seen Procopius the Small, was speeding in our direction.

'Some grooms drinking brandy down in the market,' Procopius the Small panted, 'they say the police have just picked up a pedlar.'

No one said 'Pohorák', but like birds, when a heavy stone falls in their midst, we scattered in all directions.

I bolted down the hollow, my head pounding. I reached Valdštýn in a flash, but something drew me on. I turned into Hay Scales Street, the pavement fairly rolling under my feet. At St Thomas's I took the arcade along the square, but after the first column I ground to a halt and just managed to flatten myself against the second: the police were taking Pohorák, his cart and his dog to the nearby station. I could tell by his grief-stricken face that he was terribly upset.

A gaping hole would be left in the history of humankind were we not to relate what had happened to Pohorák.

That morning he had entered Prague a bit later than usual; indeed, by pedlar's habit and Prague practice it was very late: seven o'clock. From Strahov Gate he had descended the steep streets at a swift clip, his white dog happy at having no pulling to do and he himself holding the cart back, almost plucking it into the air at regular intervals with his left hand on the shaft.

'Why so late today, Pohorák?' asked the baker in Deep Road, who was sitting in front of his shop in his shirtsleeves enjoying a pipe.

'Had some stops along the way,' said Pohorák with a smile and brought the cart to a halt with a long whoa. He reached into his right-hand pocket, pulled out a small, wicker-covered bottle of cumin brandy and handed it to the baker. 'Have a drink with me, why don't you?'

'Thanks, but I've had my nip for the morning.'

'So have I, but five Lord's Prayers are better than one.'

Pohorák drained the bottle, stuffed it back into his pocket, waved goodbye and rattled on.

The Peasant Market was full by the time he got there. A policeman tried to tell him there was no room for him to set up shop, but he argued with 'the officer' until room was finally found. Sometimes Pohorák brought hares, butter and eggs as well as poultry; on that day he had only chickens and pigeons, both already slaughtered. Poultry was his stock in trade, and he was so imbued with the characteristic – and not particularly pleasant – odour of domestic fowls that it extended several yards around him into the atmosphere.

Pohorák was well past fifty. If my readers have concluded from the account given of him thus far that he was powerfully built, I must unfortunately place a rein on their imaginations. Pohorák was not the type to challenge the local Hercules to a wrestling match. Though slightly above medium height, he was something of a hunchback and more bony than solid. His sunken cheeks were so decorated with pockmarks that a guileless soul might have thought to advise him to have his face repaved. He wore a blue checked coat (though in places – chiefly on the back beneath the collar and on the left shoulder – it looked more like dry, unchecked mud) and filthy brown trousers rolled up high, even if it hadn't rained for weeks. Winter and summer he covered his head with a dark cloth cap, from which his food-vendor's permit protruded.

Pohorák sprinkled some straw in the shade under the cart, and the dog curled up on it. Then he unloaded his wares, spreading them out beside the cart, stood up and looked round. 'Do me a favour, my pretty,' he said to the sixty-year-old woman stallholder next to him, 'and keep an eye on my merchandise. The trip's given me an appetite. I'm just going for some coffee.'

He stepped into a nearby café and drank a cup, then went a few paces farther to the bar, where he downed two tots of brandy and slipped a bottle into his pocket for later. Then he bought two poppy-seed rolls – one for himself and one for the dog – and returned to the cart.

'Right or left?' asked the woman who rented out stools. Pohorák indicated where to put it, gave her a kreutzer and sat down. His hand slid into his left coat pocket and out came a pipe and tobacco pouch. He pulled open the pouch, filled the pipe, and out of his waistcoat pocket came a box of matches. Soon he was puffing away with great relish and looking over his wares.

'I'll charge forty kreutzers for the chickens and twenty for the pigeons,' he muttered to himself between puffs.

Up stepped a stocky brewer. You can always tell a brewer or his wife by the servant who follows them carrying a vat with copper hoops.

'What do you think those chickens are worth?'

'What do I think they're worth?' Pohorák said deliberately, shifting his pipe to the other side of his mouth. 'Their weight in gold is what I think they're worth, but I'll give them to you for forty apiece.'

'You must be out of your mind! How about thirty-two? What do you say? I'll take six.'

But Pohorák stood there shaking his head until the brewer withdrew. Whereupon he sat down and started puffing away again.

'You won't sell a thing at that price,' the woman he had called 'my pretty' said to him. 'The market's full of poultry today.'

'What business is it of yours, you old witch? I'll sell

them at any price I please. You look after your rotten eggs and don't teach Pohorák how to hawk.' Then he took a few guilders out of his pocket and, jingling them in the air, added, 'Even if I don't sell a thing, I'll take a nice little profit home with me.'

The old woman said nothing. Nor did Pohorák, for he was washing his anger down with brandy.

A woman and her maidservant.

'How much are the chickens?'

'Forty kreutzers.'

'Why, that's frightfully dear! Will you take thirty-five?'

Silence.

'Come now, don't be so hard.'

'I can't help it. I've set my price, and that's that.'

'Let's go, ma'am. They look green anyway.'

'Green! Green! *You* look green, you cabbage stalk! My chickens come in all colours!' And picking up a bunch of chickens by the legs, he whirled them in the air and shouted, 'Heigh-ho! Heigh-ho!'

The 'pretties' in the surrounding stalls burst into raucous laughter, while Pohorák fed his fury another snort.

And so it went. The market began to empty, but Pohorák's chickens and pigeons remained. Now and then he looked down at them, as if surprised to see them there, and grumbled, 'Stick to your guns, man. Stick to your guns.'

The brandy had begun to make itself felt.

Up came the sausage man shouting, 'Get 'em while they're hot!'

'Give us one here!'

Pohorák took a sausage and gobbled it down while the sausage man served the neighbouring vendors. The sausage man turned back to Pohorák.

'Three kreutzers for the sausage.'

'What sausage?'

The woman from the next stall: 'The one you ate.'

'Me? A sausage? You must be crazy!'

A quarrel. Pohorák curses; the sausage man brandishes his hook and calls the policeman.

The policeman: 'Did you have a sausage?'

Pohorák glares at him. 'I did.'

'Then pay for it.'

'Yes, yes. I completely forgot. You know how it is, officer. Old age. The old noggin – it ain't what it used to be.'

General laughter.

Pohorák is disconsolate. He sits there lamenting. 'The noggin, the old noggin.' Then he polishes off the brandy and lights his pipe again.

The sun beats down mercilessly. Pohorák feels sick. He looks over at his dog, who is fast asleep in the shade beneath the cart, and slowly collects himself, covers the chickens and pigeons with his kerchief and crawls in next to the dog.

By now even 'Mrs Good Buy', always the final customer of the day, has left with her purchases. Hampers and lids are disappearing, women stallholders clearing away their egg boxes. The policeman makes his rounds, calling, 'Pack up, everybody!'

'Pack up, whoever owns this cart!' He has reached Pohorák's space. A low growl emerges from below. The policeman peers under the cart and sees Pohorák sleeping peacefully, his cap under his head. 'Up with you, Pohorák!' He grabs one foot and shakes it.

At this the dog jumps up and jolts the cart in such a way that a wheel runs over Pohorák's hand. Pohorák goes on sleeping. The policeman smiles.

'Hey, pour a little water on him, will you?' he calls to one of the street cleaners, who have begun their work. Slosh! Half a can of water souses Pohorák's poor head.

Pohorák gives a start, sits up and rubs his eyes.

'Up with you now!'

Pohorák slowly gets to his feet. 'Why do I feel so groggy? I'm too old to slave like this.'

'Well, you come along with me, old boy, and we'll give you a place to rest for a while.'

'Whatever you say.'

And Pohorák grabs hold of the shaft and with deep grief in his heart goes where the policeman takes him.

An agitated meeting in the Rumpál attic. Oaths of mutual and eternal loyalty. A report by Jan Žižka of Trocnov: 'There he stood, as I am standing here! I yearned to help, but could do nothing.' Absent: Nicholas of Hus, who has left for the forests of Rakovník.

Our mortal fears were put to rest at six that evening

when Pohorák, dragging his cart laboriously up the hill, stopped at the Rumpáls' shop and Procopius the Great, his heart pounding, listened at the door connecting the shop and the flat.

'Suddenly I felt sick and they had to help me away. I had a nice little sleep there. I have to spend the night in the Broad Courtyard. The market was miserable today. I hope it's better tomorrow.'

Several days later a brand-new pistol was found, off in a corner near the fountain. No one knew how it had got there, and strange things were bandied about.

Not until four weeks later did Procopius the Great venture to go up to Pohorák as he was pulling his empty cart away from the marketplace and ask, 'What did you do with the six guilders?'

Pohorák stopped.

'What six guilders?'

'You know. The six guilders I gave you to . . . to buy powder with.'

'*You* gave *me* six guilders? You wouldn't be trying to pull an old man's leg, would you now, Pepík my boy? That's a sin, you know, pulling an old man's leg.' And he raised a reproving right forefinger.

Written This Year on All Souls' Day

I cannot tell how many more times she will come to Košíře Cemetery on All Souls' Day – she had trouble walking today; her legs are beginning to fail her – but everything was as it is every year. At about eleven she hoisted her monumentally corpulent body out of the cab, and the coachman lifted out the memorial wreaths, which were wrapped in white cloths, and a five-year-old girl, also warmly wrapped. The little girl had been five for fifteen years now: Miss Mary borrowed a new one each year from her neighbours.

'That's right, my sweet. Look at all the people. And the lights and torches and flowers. Go ahead, don't be afraid. Go on, go wherever you please. I'll be right behind you.'

The child moves forward timidly; Miss Mary follows, urging her on, though not in any particular direction. And so they wander until all at once Miss Mary says 'Wait a moment!' and takes the child by the hand. Leading her in among the graves, she takes a wind- and rain-battered wreath from one of the iron crosses and replaces it with a new one made of red and white artificial flowers. Then she grasps the arm of the cross with her empty hand and starts to pray – kneeling would be too exhausting. At first she fixes her gaze on the grave's withered turf and brown clay, but suddenly she lifts her head, and her broad, pleasant face and large, blue, guileless eyes stare out into the distance. Her eyes grow slowly dim, the corners of her mouth begin to twitch, her praying lips contract and quiver, and great tears gather and overflow. The child gazes up at her in wonder, but the woman sees nothing, hears nothing. Then suddenly, by sheer force of will, she recovers, sighs long and hard, gives the child a sad smile, and says to her in a melancholy whisper, 'Go on now, child. Go ahead. Go where you like. I'll be right behind you.'

Once more they wander up and down, wherever the child's whims take them, until again Miss Mary calls out 'Wait a moment!' and approaches another grave. Here she repeats exactly what she did at the first grave, spending not a minute more at one than at the other, and after wrapping the second weather-beaten wreath in the cloth next to the first she takes her little companion by the hand and says, 'Feeling chilly? Come along, then. You mustn't catch cold. We'll get back in the cab and drive home now. You enjoyed the ride, didn't you?' They walk slowly back to the cab and, once the child and the wreaths are safely inside, Miss Mary too climbs in laboriously.

The carriage groans, and after two or three flicks of the whip the horse goes into action. And so it goes, year in and year out.

Were I still a naïve young writer, I should probably write at this point: 'You may wonder who was lying under those graves.' But I know that no reader ever asks a question. A writer must force his favours upon his readers, and in this instance that is rather difficult. Miss Mary is unsociable and reticent about her life; she has never forced herself upon anyone, not even her closest neighbours. She had only a single friend in childhood and has only one today, the once lovely Miss Luiza, the now faded widow of Mr Nocar, a former treasury official. They will be spending this afternoon together in Mrs Nocar's flat. Miss Mary does not often venture out to Italian Street to see her friend; indeed, she rarely leaves her ground-floor flat at the foot of St John's Hill and then only early on Sunday mornings for Mass at St Nicholas's. She is too corpulent, and walking has long been an effort for her. Her friend saves her the effort and pays her daily visits at home. Their many years of friendship have brought them even closer.

But on this day Miss Mary would find her flat too depressing – it would feel emptier, more solitary than usual – and so off she goes to her friend. Which makes this day a holiday for Mrs Nocar as well. Never does she roast her coffee with such care as on All Souls' Day; never is she so careful to make her *Gugelhupf* cake light and fluffy. Everything about the day has a subdued holiday spirit to it. Neither of them says much, but what they do say, however prosaic, resonates richly. Moreover, a tear may occasionally glisten and hugs are more frequent than on other occasions.

Then at last, after sitting a long time together on the sofa, they come to the point of the annual conversation.

'You know,' says Mrs Nocar, 'the Lord gave us nearly the same fate. Although I had a good and worthy husband, he passed away after only two years, leaving no child to comfort me. From that time on, I have been alone, and I don't know which is worse: never to have known love or to have known and lost it.'

'Well, as you know, I have always been resigned to the will of God,' Miss Mary says solemnly, 'and I learned my fate early. I learned it from a dream. I dreamed when I was twenty that I was at a ball. And you know I'd never been to a ball in my life. Well, there we were, promenading to the music under the bright lights, but for some reason the ballroom was like an enormous garret just under the roof. Suddenly the first couples started dancing down the stairs. Soon only a few of us were left up there. I thought I was the last – I can't recall my partner's face – but when I chanced to look back I saw Death behind us. He was wearing a green velvet cloak, a white-plumed hat, and a sword. I tried to hurry so that we too could escape down the stairs, but the others had vanished by then, my partner included, and all at once Death took me by the hand and carried me off. For a long time I lived in a palace with Death as my husband. He treated me most kindly and loved me, but I found him revolting. We lived in the greatest of luxury – all crystal and gold and velvet – but I was inconsolable. I longed to return to the world, and our messenger, who was a kind of second Death, kept me abreast of what was happening on Earth. I could tell that my desire to leave him caused my husband great pain, and I felt sorry for him. Ever since the dream – and who but God sends us our dreams? – I have known that I can never marry, that my bridegroom is Death. So you see, Luiza, a double death separates my life from the lives of others.'

Whereupon Mrs Nocar weeps (though she has heard the dream time and time again), and her tears serve to heal Miss Mary's ailing soul like drops of cool, fragrant balsam.

It is actually quite surprising that Miss Mary never married. Orphaned at a tender age, she was financially independent and the owner of a decent two-storeyed house at the foot of St John's Hill. Nor was she unattractive, as was evident even now. She was tall in stature, taller than most women, and her blue eyes were nothing less than beautiful. If her face was a bit broad, it was well proportioned and pleasant, but from her youth she had been on the heavy side, which had early earned her the nickname 'Fat Mary'. Her corpulence made her rather sedentary; she never played with the other children, nor was she seen much in society, and her only daily outing was a short stroll along the Marian Ramparts. Yet I cannot say that Malá Strana ever wondered why she had failed to marry. Malá Strana society has its set categories, and as Miss Mary belongs to the category of old maids no one would ever dream it might be otherwise. Though if a woman happens to pose the question, as women will, she replies with a tranquil smile, 'I believe one can serve God even when single. Don't you agree?' And if one asks her friend, Mrs Nocar shrugs her pointed shoulders and says, 'She didn't want to! She had several opportunities – and good ones, believe me. I know of two – fine men both. She just didn't want to!'

As a native of Malá Strana, however, I can state that both men were miscreants, totally worthless. For the men she has in mind were none other than Cibulka the merchant and Rechner the engraver, and no matter where their names might come up they were always referred to as 'those ne'er-do-wells'. Which is not to say they were criminals – no, that would be going too far. But they had nothing to recommend them either: no order, stability or sense. Rechner never picked up a tool before Wednesday, and by noon on Saturday he had laid them down again. He could have made good money, for he was highly skilled (or so said Mr Hermann, a clerk from my mother's home town); he simply had no taste for work. As for Cibulka, he spent more time in the wine shop than in his own. Besides, he slept late every morning and when he did finally appear behind the counter he was groggy and morose. He was rumoured to know French, but he neglected his business and his assistant did as he pleased with him. Cibulka and Rechner were as thick as thieves, and if a noble spark ever ignited in one of them the other most assuredly snuffed it out. In other words, one couldn't imagine two more entertaining drinking companions.

A restless smile played over Rechner's clean-shaven, sharp-featured face as a sunbeam plays over a meadow, and although the high forehead below his shock of slicked back auburn hair was always smooth, his pale, thin lips never quite lost their sneer. His small, wiry body – clad always in yellow, his favourite colour – was in perpetual motion; his shoulders constantly twitched.

His friend Cibulka, clad always in black, was much more sedate – or at least so it appeared. He was thin, like Rechner, but somewhat taller. His small skull culminated in a low, tetragonal forehead, and the slightly protruding, thick dark eyebrows rose above a pair of sparkling eyes. He combed his black hair forward over the temples and his long, velvet-soft moustache down over a sharply chiselled mouth. When he laughed, his teeth gleamed snow white through the moustache. There was something wild, yet good-natured about that face. He would hold back his laughter until it burst out of him, but then he was calm again immediately.

The two of them understood each other perfectly: a wink and they knew everything there was to know. But few sought out their company: their wit was too worldly for honest burghers, too wild; they failed to comprehend it and mistook it for blasphemy. Nor did Cibulka and Rechner set great store by staid Malá Strana society. When evening came on, they found the remote Old Town taverns many times more inviting, and they roamed the city together, visiting even far-off František's three times a week. If long past midnight the streets of Malá Strana rang with merry laughter, you could be sure Rechner and Cibulka were making their way home at last.

They were both about the same age as Miss Mary. They had gone to St Nicholas's parish school with her, but taken scant notice of her, or she of them. They met only in the street, their only exchange a cursory nod.

Then out of the blue Miss Mary received a hand-delivered letter in a meticulous, almost copperplate script. No sooner had she finished reading it than it slipped from her hands to the floor. The letter ran as follows:

My dearest Miss Mary,
You will doubtless be surprised to learn that I, of all people, should be writing to you, and you will perhaps be amazed at what I have to say. Although I have never dared approach you – let me not beat about the bush – I love you! I have loved you for

years. Having probed my innermost being, I am certain that if I am ever to be happy it can be only with you.

Perhaps you will be affronted, Miss Mary, and will reject me; perhaps fallacious reports have soiled my reputation with you as they have with others and you will dismiss me out of hand. Yet I implore you to consider the matter with all due deliberation. I can assure you that in me you will find a husband whose every breath will seek to make you happy.

Once more I beg of you: consider well. I shall expect your answer four weeks from today – not a day before or after.

In the meantime – my apologies!

I remain, with ardent longing,

Your devoted,
Vilém Cibulka

Her mind reeled. Here she was, thirty years old, and suddenly, without a word of warning, her first declaration of love lay at her feet. Yes, her first. She had never even thought of love before, nor had anyone broached the subject with her.

Searing red flashes went off in her brain, her temples throbbed, she could scarcely breathe or put two thoughts together. But amidst it all a clear-cut figure emerged: a new, melancholy Cibulka.

Finally she picked up the letter and, trembling, read it through a second time. How beautiful it was! How tender!

She could not resist: she had to show it to her friend. She handed it to her without a word.

'Well, well, well!' the widow Nocar uttered at last, her face a mixture of wonder and consternation. 'What do you intend to do?'

'I don't know, Luiza.'

'Well, you've got plenty of time to think it over. Now, it's always possible – forgive me for saying so, but you know how men are – that he's only after your money. Though why shouldn't he be in love with you? I'll tell you what: I'll make inquiries about him.'

Miss Mary did not respond.

'Look, Cibulka's a handsome man. He's got eyes like coals, a jet-black moustache, and teeth – well, teeth like sugar. Yes, a fine-looking man.' And she leaned over and gave her silent friend an affectionate hug.

Miss Mary blushed crimson.

A week later Miss Mary found another letter waiting for her when she returned from church. She read it with increasing bewilderment.

Dear Miss Mary,
Do not think ill of me if I venture to write to you. I do so because I intend to marry and need a good manager for my household but have no acquaintances because my occupation leaves me little time for entertainment and the more I look the more clearly I see that you would make me an excellent wife. Do not think ill of me if I say I am a good man and you

will not regret your decision. I have a steady income
and work hard and with God's help we shall want for
nothing. I am thirty-one years old, you know me
and I know you. I know you are well off, there is
nothing wrong with that, it is perfectly all right. I
must assure you that my household cannot do without
a good manager much longer so I ask you not to
keep me waiting more than a fortnight for your kind
reply as I shall have to look elsewhere if it is no. I
am no romantic, I do not know how to use fancy
words, but I do know how to show affection, and I
am, until two weeks hence,

Your devoted and respectful,

Jan Rechner, Engraver

'He has the straightforward style of a simple fellow,'
said Mrs Nocar that afternoon. 'Well, now you've a
choice to make, Mary. What do you intend to do?'

'Intend to do?' Miss Mary repeated as if in a dream.

'Does one of them appeal to you more? Be honest
now. Do you care for either of them? And if so, which
one?'

'Vilém,' Miss Mary whispered with a blush.

If Cibulka was 'Vilém', Rechner was lost. It was
decided that Mrs Nocar, who was more experienced
in such matters, would compose a letter to Rechner
and Miss Mary would copy it in her own hand.

Not a week had passed before Miss Mary was back
at her friend's, a new letter in hand, her face glowing
with joy. The letter read as follows:

Dear Miss Mary,
Do not think ill of me, but it is perfectly all right and
there is nothing I can do about it. Had I known that
my dear friend Cibulka had asked for your hand I
should never have brought the matter up, but he
said not a word and I knew nothing. Now I have told
him everything and withdraw on my own because
he loves you, but please do not laugh at me, that
would be unkind and I can still find my happiness
elsewhere. It is a pity, true, but there is nothing
wrong, and so forget that I am

> Your devoted and respectful,
> Jan Rechner, Engraver

'Well, now you're rid of that dilemma,' said Mrs
Nocar.

'Thank God!' said Miss Mary, and she went home
to a new, sweet solitude. For her thoughts were now
all of the future and so pleasurable that she ran through
them over and over in her mind, thus making each of
them more and more vivid and merging them into a
coherent whole, the vision of a full and beautiful life.

Yet the following day Mrs Nocar found Miss Mary
unwell. She was lying on the sofa, her face pallid, her
eyes red with weeping.

Dismayed, her friend could scarcely bring herself to
ask what had happened. Fresh tears gushed from Miss
Mary's eyes, and she pointed, wordless, to the table.
Mrs Nocar sensed something dreadful, and indeed the
letter proved a serious matter. It read:

My dearest Miss Mary,

My happiness is not to be, then. Gone is my dream.
I press my hand to my head, which reels in pain.

But no – I cannot tread a path paved with the ruined
hopes of my best, my only friend! My wretched
friend, as wretched as I am myself!

You have not yet made your decision, but what
decision can there be? I cannot live in joy, seeing my
Jan in despair. Should you indeed offer me the cup of
life's pleasures, I should be forced to reject it.

I have made up my mind. I renounce my plans.

I have only one request: that you should think of
me kindly and never mock me.

Yours most sincerely,
Vilém Cibulka

'Why, this is ludicrous!' Mrs Nocar cried, breaking
into loud laughter.

Miss Mary threw her an anxious, questioning
glance.

'Of course!' said Mrs Nocar, now deep in thought.
'They're noble souls, both of them. That's clear. But
you've no experience with men, Mary. Noble sentiments don't last. Before you know it, they'll toss them
to the winds and think only of themselves. Just leave
them to their own devices, Mary; they'll work it out
between them. Rechner's a practical sort, but Cibulka
– well, it's plain to see he loves you passionately. He'll
come round.'

Miss Mary's eyes immediately regained their

dreamy look. She believed her friend, and her friend believed what she had said. They were both good, honest souls without an ounce of suspicion in them. They would have been shocked at the idea that the letters might be a tasteless, despicable joke.

'Wait and see,' Mrs Nocar reassured as she took her leave. 'He'll change his mind.'

Miss Mary waited, and her dreams returned. Admittedly, they lacked the blissful bloom of first love, but they had an elegiac air about them and, sad though they were, she found them the more precious for it.

Miss Mary waited, and month flowed into month. Sometimes, taking her constitutional along the Marian Ramparts, she met the two friends, for they were still inseparable. Perhaps she had failed to notice the meetings as long as she was indifferent to them, but now they seemed to occur unusually often.

'They're keeping track of you,' Mrs Nocar said. 'You'll see.'

At first Miss Mary lowered her eyes when she encountered them, but later she grew bold and glanced up. Although they gave her a wide berth, they would greet her respectfully and then look away in sorrow. Did they ever notice the naïve question gazing out of her beautiful eyes? She never noticed – I am certain of it – how carefully they bit their lips.

A year passed. In the meantime Mrs Nocar had started hearing strange reports, reports she was loath to deliver. She had heard that the men were going to the dogs. No one spoke of them as anything but 'ne'er-do-wells'. They would come to a bad end – everybody said so.

Miss Mary was deeply shaken by each such report. Was she to blame? Her friend did not know what to tell her, and womanly modesty kept Miss Mary from making a move on her own. Yet she felt she had committed a crime.

A second, even more distressing year went by, and then Rechner was no more. He died of consumption. Miss Mary was disconsolate. Had the 'practical sort', as Mrs Nocar used to call him, pined away?

Mrs Nocar sighed deeply and said, 'There's your decision for you. Cibulka won't be long now.' Then she kissed the trembling Miss Mary on the forehead.

But Cibulka was not long for this world. Four months later he followed Rechner to the grave. He died of pneumonia.

It is now more than sixteen years that they have lain buried in Košíře Cemetery.

Not for anything in the world would Miss Mary have decided which of the two graves she would visit first. An innocent five-year-old made the decision for her: wherever she toddled, Miss Mary laid the first wreath.

Miss Mary has now adopted yet another grave. People think she has a mania for tending graves of people who mean nothing to her. The third grave belongs to Magdalena Töpfer, and yes, she was a wise woman of whom many tales are told. When Mr Velš, the merchant, was buried and Mrs Töpfer observed

Mrs Hirt, the candle-maker's wife, stepping over a neighbouring grave, she said at once that Mrs Hirt would have a stillborn child. And so it was. When Mrs Töpfer dropped in on the glover's wife and found her scraping carrots, again she said at once that the woman would give birth to a freckled child. And sure enough her Marina has brick-red hair and is a perfect fright for freckles. A wise woman, yes, but . . .

But as I have said, she means nothing to Miss Mary. Now, Mrs Töpfer's grave does lie midway between Cibulka's and Rechner's, but I should be insulting my readers' intelligence were I to expound my opinion of why she chose it or where she herself will one day lie at rest.

Figures

Idyllic Fragments from the Notes of an Apprentice Lawyer

I turned thirty yesterday. I am a different man. Only since yesterday am I a whole being: my blood flows in strict time, my every nerve is of steel, my every thought on the mark. It is miraculous how a man can mature overnight – no, from one moment to the next – and what power there is in the realisation that yes, you're thirty now! I am truly enamoured of my new self; I feel I not only *can* but *shall* do great things. I look upon everything with sublime confidence. Now, yes, now is the time to keep a diary again, fashion a fresh portrait of myself. I know that one day I shall read through these pages with pride, and whosoever reads them after my death will exclaim, 'There was a *man!*'

I am suddenly so different that the day before yesterday seems the distant past, a past I can no longer even grasp. I used to jot down observations almost daily, but reading them now I can make no sense of them whatever. Why on earth did I write like that, I wonder? 'What are ideals for? Why study them? . . .

The cooling sun – oceans of ice . . . I am so forlorn – if not unto death then unto suicide . . . A cloud of imminent disaster, a sense that the world has collapsed . . . Perhaps I have gone astray . . . Before me stands the task of living, but no joy, only sad queries.' Pure claptrap! Morbid emotion! And all for want of a clear goal and a firm will, the result of being bogged down by day-to-day existence and dulling habit. How far above it all I stand now!

First, I'll polish off the Bar examination – and fast. Second, I'll devote myself entirely to my studies. I won't set foot in the office again until the exam is over and done with (though I can't have my chief crossing me off the rolls – I mustn't lose any of my seven-year training period). Third, I'll confine myself to my flat and won't enter a tavern, not even at night. It's a sin, the money I squander daily on cards. No more Sunday promenades along the Moat, no more theatre, nothing. Wait till Františka finds out! Apparently she's told everybody at the Loukotas' that I've been looking the worse for wear.

A splendid idea! I could kiss myself for it! *I'll move to Malá Strana*! Serene, poetic Malá Strana. Nice, quiet neighbours off in their nooks and crannies. Yes, for my new exalted state of mind poetic surroundings are absolutely essential. It will be lovely! A quiet house, an airy flat, a view of dreamy Petřín Hill and a tranquil garden – for it *must* have a garden – work and peace. I can almost feel my chest expanding.

Go to, then! St George is at the door!

Am I mistaken or is Petřín known for its night-ingales?

★

I'm in luck! The flat is nicer than I could have wished and in peaceful Oujezd Street. I shall curl up in my little hideaway like a child, and no one will know where I am, no one!

I liked the two-storeyed house the moment I laid eyes on it. The only disadvantage is that I shall be only a subtenant, but what of it? My landlady-to-be is the wife of a railway guard. I haven't seen the guard himself: he was off somewhere on duty, as he is most of the time. Their first-floor flat is so large they don't need all of it. It has a large room facing the street, a kitchen, and two small rooms in a back wing, the ones I've taken. Three windows look down into the courtyard, and one – in one of the back rooms – overlooks the garden and Petřín Hill. It's a pretty little garden, and the guard's wife says the tenants are welcome to it. I shan't spend any time there – I'll be studying – yet it's nice to have. The house is right at the foot of Petřín Hill, and since the courtyard is below ground level and the garden almost on a level with the first floor, I have what is to all intents and purposes a ground-floor window. The first time I went up to it I heard the song of a skylark coming from Petřín. It was lovely! I asked whether Petřín had nightingales too. It has!

The guard's wife is young, twenty-two or so. And

pretty, in a healthy sort of way. Her features are not classically regular, her chin is a bit too wide, but her cheeks are rosy and velvet and her eyes, though slightly protruding, are as blue as cornflowers. She is nursing a baby, a seven-month-old girl by the name of Kačenka – these people tell you their whole life story at once. Kačenka is a bit funny-looking: she has a head like a ball and her mother's bulging eyes, but with an expression of boundless stupidity. Yet give her a friendly smile and the ball smiles back, the dull eyes sparkle and are suddenly so winning that . . . (I'll finish this later; I can't come up with anything now.) I pat Kačenka's cheek and say, 'A lovely child!' Praising children is always good for winning over mothers. 'And so quiet,' her mother says. 'She hardly ever cries.' Which is good news if I'm going to be studying.

When I told the guard's wife I had a degree in law, she was obviously delighted, and when I told her my name was Krumlovský she exclaimed, 'What a nice name!' These people say whatever is on their mind. We settled on the room and board. She'll be doing washing and cleaning for me and making my breakfast. There's a tavern next door to the right. It looks decent enough. I'll carry in dinner and supper from there. 'When my husband's at home, we bring food in from there too. They have real home cooking.' Fine, I love home cooking. I set no store by spicy restaurant dishes. Give me potato balls and millet pudding and fried noodles any time! Next door to the left there's a cobbler and right above me a tailor. Who could ask for more? I might add that a few doors down is the house where Mácha was born,[1] though I care not a jot for written poetry; the poetry of life is a hundred times more to my liking, and so I mention Mácha only in passing. I have never written poetry myself or, rather, I stopped after my student days. I may even have had some talent. I do remember one quite good poem I wrote then, a ballad with some fine alliteration. I can't recall much more than this bit of alliteration, actually:

> Hark, hark, the hound doth bark
> Responding to the *w*anderer's *w*istful *w*histle.

They laughed at me when I recited my ballad in school, and I defended myself by pointing out the alliteration. They only laughed the more, and from then on they always said 'wandererswistfulwhistle' for 'alliteration'. The fools.

While the guard's wife and I were talking, a man of about forty came into the kitchen smoking a pipe. A neighbour, apparently, as he was not dressed for the street and just stood there leaning against a doorpost, smoking.

'This gentleman is Dr Krumlovský,' she said, emphasising the word 'doctor'.

The man went on smoking. 'Pleased to meet you,' he said, holding out his hand. 'Glad to have you for a neighbour.'

I shook his hand – one must get on with one's neighbours, after all, and they seemed decent people in any case. The man was heavy-set with a ruddy face and blue eyes that were as watery as if swimming in tears. Oh, the candour they radiated! Though in my experience – and I am an excellent judge of people – the candour of watery eyes can also come from drink. Besides, he had a fat upper lip, and all drinkers have fat upper lips.

'Do you play twenty-six?'

I'd have liked to say I was studying and had no time for cards, but there was no point in ruining neighbourly relations from the start. 'Show me the Czech who doesn't,' I said with a polite smile.

'Good. We'll make a day.' (A typical Germanism, I thought, 'make a day'. Czech is cruelly abused in the cities.[2] I must try and correct his mistakes unobtrusively while we chat.) 'We artists like educated people. We can always learn something from them.'

Well, they'll learn plenty from me! But now the time had come for me to say something flattering to them. I wish I knew what the man did. An artist with watery eyes, a ruddy complexion, and fleshy hands – though I bet he has calluses on his fingers. I can't see them, but he must have: he plays the double bass, yes, I'm certain of it, and I'm an excellent judge of people.

'A musician like you must be in great demand.'

'You hear that?' he said, laughing so hard that he moved up and down the doorpost like a rhinoceros scratching itself on a log. 'Me a musician like that lunatic . . .' he went on, motioning back over his shoulder at the middle door in the passage, and his laughter turned to a rasping cough.

'Mr Augusta is a painter,' the guard's wife explained.

Just then a boy of about eight came running up, attracted most likely by the laughter and coughing. He leaned against the painter and stared up at me.

'Is that your son, Mr Augusta?' I asked for want of anything better to say.

'Yes, his name is Pepík. We live in the right wing, the one opposite yours. We can look into each other's windows.'

'Who is that?' asked Pepík, pointing at me. I love the simple, artless speech of children.

'Dr Krumlovský, you little mischief-maker.'

'Is he going to be staying here?'

'Tell me, Pepík,' I said, patting the boy's curls, 'how'd you like a kreutzer?'

The boy held out his hand without a word.

I think I've made a good impression.

★

It's been a hard day! Moving and unpacking and putting things in order – my head is reeling. I haven't moved much in my life, and I can't say I take to it. I hear there are people who actually enjoy moving. Sounds like a disease to me – they must be unstable. Though it does have its poetry, I'll allow that. When an old dwelling starts looking empty and desolate, a mixture of regret and anxiety comes over us and we feel we are leaving a safe harbour for the rolling sea. As for the new place, it looks on us with alien eyes, it has nothing to say to us, it is cold. I felt what I must have felt as a child in an unfamiliar place holding on to my mother's skirts and crying, 'I'm scared!' But tomorrow morning I shall certainly wake up and say, 'What a fine sleep I've had!'

I wonder what time it is. Half past ten. And the house is as quiet as a well. A good image that: 'quiet as a well'. Far better than 'quiet as a churchyard'. Not so hackneyed at least.

I had to laugh at the guard's wife. She marvelled at everything, examining, even fingering it all. There's nothing offensive in such naïve curiosity. She did everything she could to help, starting with making up the bed. She particularly admired the doeskin mattress and the pillow with the doeskin case. When she had finished, she couldn't resist lying down on it so that she could 'feel what it would be like to sleep on', laughing for joy like a squirrel (if squirrels laugh, that is). Next she laid the baby on the bed and laughed again. She has her own special laughter – like a bell tinkling. Then, spreading out my shaggy fox rug by the bed, she had new reason for delight: the baby was frightened by the vixen's head and glassy eyes. 'I'll scare her with it when she's naughty!' These people take great pleasure in small things.

At one point, though, I almost lost my temper. When I arrived with my second load of things, what did I see through the open door but Pepík kneeling on a chair in front of my aquarium with a goldfish in his hand. Just as I lurched forward, I heard a female voice behind me call out, 'For heaven's sake!' but all I could see when I turned was the woman's back retreating into the passage. The guard's wife was standing by the bed holding her sides with laughter.

'That was the painter's wife. She'd just given the bed a try. The landlord's daughter also thought it comfortable.'

She seemed ready to invite the whole house in to try the bed. What do they sleep on anyway, these people? In any case, Pepík mustn't be allowed back without supervision. He might overturn my aquarium. He's a good-looking boy, actually, with his flaxen curls and sloe eyes. He didn't get those eyes from his father; they must come from the mother's side.

I keep listening for a nightingale. No luck. It may be too cold yet. A fine spring we're having! Six weeks into the season and we're still bundled up in winter coats. It may grow colder the closer we come to summer and we'll be forced to wear summer furs. Heh heh, that's a good one: 'summer furs'.

Actually I thought a little cold wouldn't stop a nightingale. I strain my ears. Not a note. Footsteps! A man's steps, heavy, coming closer. A door creaks, the door to our kitchen. A woman's voice, a man's. The guard must be back from his journeys. I quickly blow out the light and lie down. Otherwise she'd

bring him in to try the bed, and a railway guard
coming off duty is likely to be filthy!

★

Civil Law. Currency Regulations. Commercial Law.
Legal Procedure. Patent Law. Decree on Procedures
for the Liquidation of Holdings. Decree on Procedures
in Lease Litigation. Mining Law. Maritime Law.
Criminal Law. Penal Regulations. Law on Procedures
in Undisputed Cases. Municipal Law. Notarial Procedures. Trade Regulations. Publishing Regulations.
Syndication Procedures. Game Law. Tax and
Customs Law.

There! Every morning I will review the list to deter-
mine how much I have yet to cover and see to it that
my industry does not flag. Not that I'm afraid it will:
I'm a new man now. Still, whenever I hit upon good
new resolutions, I will write them down at once and
read them through every day, every day! It's so easy
to forget . . .

A good breakfast. Coffee without chicory, a fluffy
roll. The guard's wife resplendent in a white robe.
Clearly her marriage is a happy one.

'Good coffee, excellent,' I say to win her favour.
'Glad to hear it. I do my best. Can I get you anything
else?' I remember hearing her husband come in last
night. 'Your husband's back, isn't he? Shouldn't you
introduce me?' 'He's gone to the station with his
report. He'll be here for dinner.' And again she laughs.

She's always laughing. 'I'll make your bed now and tidy up a little. I've just given Kačenka her bath. She's asleep. I don't want to disturb you. You might go into the other room.'

I go into the other room and look out of the window into the courtyard. There are flowers in the windows of both floors opposite me, the flowers we Czechs usually put in our windows, naturally. One could compile a special window box *Czech Flora*: sweet basil, whose large, succulent leaves wither when bruised, and which is also called 'jilted maiden'; balsam, scentless but flowering profusely, and usually cultivated from the previous year's seed; that awful pelargonium with its sad, leathery leaves and loud red flowers; eglantine with its serrated leaves; and nutmeg and rosemary, of course. Rosemary the wedding flower, the funeral flower: its scent – love, its evergreen leaves – fidelity, and good for the memory too, I hear. I'll have to buy a few pots. People also drop sprays of it into water.

> Blossom in the brook so clear,
> Will this be my wedding year?

Not mine, for sure. It's too soon for me to marry.

The garden has a nice design to it. Plenty of arbours, one for each family, it seems. She'll probably have mallows growing up the arbours so Pepík can pick the 'cheeses', and she'll plant dill in the beds for dumpling gravy.

'Your rooms are ready,' she says, smiling at me

from the doorway. She has opened the windows in the first room as wide as they go. I'll have to shut them, but I'll wait until she leaves. 'Can I get anything for you?' She is nothing if not accommodating. I really should find something nice to say to her.

Just then an infant's wail floats in from the painter's flat; it is followed by a full-grown, high-pitched soprano.

'So they have a baby too.'

'Yes, a one-year-old. She screams the whole day through.' (I shan't be opening the courtyard windows often.) 'Mrs Augusta's quite a screamer herself. She keeps her bread bin well oiled.' (I shan't be opening the courtyard windows at all. The garden window can stay open all day.)

I observe that the guard's wife does not always use the language of the drawing room. And why should she, simple woman that she is? It would appear, moreover, that Malá Strana has certain expressions of its own. I shall have to keep a list of them. A well-oiled bread bin!

Seeing me writing, the guard's wife says, 'I'm not keeping you from your work, am I?' 'Oh, no,' I say. 'I'm just jotting something down. By the way, who lives above the painter?' 'An old crank, a bachelor. Provazník his name is. Can't say I know what he did for a living. Now he doesn't do a thing, doesn't leave the house. All he does is look out of the window with those vicious, owl-like eyes of his and watch what the neighbours are up to. The least he could do is give the cat's back a pat!' She laughs (and I scribble 'give the cat's back a pat'). 'The front flat on the first floor is where the landlord and his daughter live, and just above them there's an official and his wife, Mr and Mrs Vejrostka. They can't have been married long, because their rings are still yellow. But here I am, going on and on, and my Kačenka may be awake by now.' And laughing, she disappears.

Now I know everything. I run and shut the windows and open my first book.

Nine o'clock. Tuesday. A fine day to start studying.

Like everyone, I begin with Civil Law. I'm sure it will go quite –

'I forgot to ask you,' comes a merry voice from the door, 'how you slept on your first night. Look Kačenka! Say "Good morning" to the gentleman. And curtsy.' (She bends the baby's head slightly.) 'That's it. Catch!' (She pretends to toss the baby to me.) 'Anyone would have a good sleep on a bed like that!' (Now she is at the bed.) 'Try this, why don't you?' (She lays the baby down on the bed.) 'Tell me, you little rascal. How does it feel to be a lady? Some bed, eh?' (She half sits, half reclines next to Kačenka.)

A pretty girl, a charming spectacle, yes, but . . . I stare fixedly at my book.

'Come along, Kačenka. The gentleman has work to do. We mustn't disturb him.' And she laughs her way out again.

Incredibly naïve!

Now then, I'll read each article carefully. I can skip

over the opening decree. There. 'Introduction. On Civil – '

A cat. A white cat. Standing at the door, miaowing away. Where did it come from? Does it belong here? How do you get rid of a cat? Oh, I know. 'Scat!' But what if that only makes it miaow the more?

It's no good. As long as it's here, I can't concentrate. I hate cats. They're nasty and deceitful and they kill mice. They scratch and bite too. And when you're asleep they'll lie on your neck and suffocate you. Resolved: every night before I go to bed, I'll give a 'Scat!' They go mad, too. Just what I need. I must ask the guard's wife – tactfully, of course: it may be the apple of her eye – if she hasn't noticed any tendency towards madness in it.

There it goes again! I open the door a bit and the cat runs out. Enter the guard's wife. Is there anything she can get me? No, nothing. But I opened the door. Because of the cat. Oh, is that all? Laughter.

'Introduction – '

A knock. The painter. He doesn't wish to disturb me, but when my window was open before he noticed a few pictures on the wall and he's curious about them. I have two gouaches by Návratil, one *Stormy Sea*, a dark piece, the other *Sunlit Sea*, a cheerful one. The painter goes up to them. He is in his Sunday best, that is, in a black tail coat, cane and cone-shaped hat. If the hat had a viburnum growing out of it, it would do for a Cossack. He says they must be Návratils. I acquiesce. He says he's never seen Návratils like those before and wonders when we're going to have our game of twenty-six. In due time, I tell him, and he says that with the landlord we could have a threesome or invite a friend of his as well and make it a foursome. He then tells me his wife is terribly ashamed of what happened yesterday, when I surprised her lying on my bed, though it was the guard's wife who told her to try it. I give him a polite smile and tell him I'll reassure her, it's nothing, really. Women! he says. We shake hands and he leaves.

The guard's wife again. It's nearly ten. Wouldn't I like some nice soup or meat from downstairs? Thank you, I never take mid-morning snacks.

'Introduction. On Civil Law. The Concept of Civil Law.'

I am making such progress and am so absorbed in the articles that I am almost sorry when dinner comes. Decent fare, but not very substantial, though it isn't healthy to gorge when one is sitting all day long. Black coffee? No, thank you, not until evening. Round about eight, shall we say? I don't need a thing. Not even a cigar? I never smoke at home.

Excellent! Like a torrent hurling a skiff at so vertiginous a speed that the objects along the shore rush past in a blur, so § after § flashed past my eyes. Or should I say the articles slipped like rosary beads through my fingers. I didn't realise I knew so much or that it would move so fast. I neither hear nor see anything.

The guard's wife must have come in eight or ten times, and I seem to recall her trying to scare the baby two or three times with the foxskin. If she spoke to me, I certainly didn't respond. At least she understands now I mustn't be distracted.

I'm pleased as punch. A hundred and thirty-five articles! Now for some supper, then onward! Who says there's no pleasure in work? My body's fairly trembling with ecstasy.

The roast is a bit tough.

I don't believe it! I completely forgot about her husband!

'Yes, another half-litre, please. And may I speak to your husband now? It's time we got to know each other.' 'He's back at the station. His train leaves at nine.' She smiles. 'I'm a widow again.' I may never get to meet him.

Half past ten. I'm tired. The spirit is willing, but the nerves are weak. Civil Law has 1502 §§; I'll have mastered them all in eight days. Time for a little rest.

I've totted up all the sections in all the laws and discovered by a simple process of division that *in one month at the outside I shall be completely prepared!*

My body's still trembling, my arteries throbbing; I shan't fall asleep for a while, but I'll lie down anyway. I put the lamp and my notebook on my bedside table. I intend to meditate.

Oh, what a fright it gave me! I was just about to

stretch out when I saw it on the bed, lying there, staring up at me with its two tiny upright triangles.

What do I do? If I knew how to scare the creature . . . No, I've no desire to do that. But how do I shoo it away? Shoo! Go on, off with you! It looks at me as if I hadn't said a word. Go on, skedaddle! No, that's for some other animal. Are you going? Are you leaving? Here, puss puss puss! Oh no, she's not even looking at me any more! She's laid down her head and gone to sleep! Now what?

Wild beasts are supposed to be afraid of fire. I hold the lamp up to it, all but touch it. No response. Well, it does screw up its eyes a bit. Rather crossly, I think.

A shoe! I miss, but the beast's off the bed and at the door. I open it a crack and – thank the Lord! It's gone.

Outside the door a voice asks if it can get me anything. No. But I opened the door? 'I was just putting the cat out.' Well, if I should want anything, I've only to ask. She says she doesn't sleep well when she's alone; time goes by so slowly. I don't respond. Muffled laughter.

Heavens! Sheer delight! Tyu tyu tyu tyu, spe tyu tyu! A nightingale! How sweet the song! How magnificent the throat! Divine Philomel, celebrated by a thousand poets! Harbinger of spring, harbinger of love, harbinger of ecstasy!

Tyo tyo tyo tyo tyo tyo tix.

Kootyo kootyo kootyo kootyo.

People are such tyrants. Imagine depriving birds like

these of their liberty! Only when they're free can their song flow freely. Praised be the laws . . .

Tsi tsi tsi tsi tsi tsi tsi tsi tsi tsi.

Kvorror tyu kva pipikvi.

Pure honey! Praised be the laws that protect all feathered songsters.

Kvee kvee kvee kvee kvee.

That's a trifle piercing, actually. Could you try something else?

Chak chak chak chak chak chak . . .

Shut up, will you! It's like a red-hot spike in my brain!

Chak chak chak chak . . . Chak chak chak chak chak chak . . . Chak chak . . .

I'm out of bed. It's driving me crazy. My nerves were on edge to begin with. I know! If I close the door to the second room, I shan't hear it. Chak chak chak. No, it doesn't work. The damned tweet-machine must be right there in the courtyard. Chak chak. A rifle! Oh, for a rifle! If I had a rifle, I'd fire out of the window even if it sent the neighbourhood into convulsions. Why don't they just exterminate the pests?

Chak chak chak chak chak chak . . . Blast it all! My brain is festering. I can't take it any more. If I knew where it was hiding, I'd jump into my clothes and . . .

Chak chak chak . . .

I have a better idea! I drag an old overcoat out of the wardrobe, rip open the lining, gather up the padding and stuff my ears full of it. Go ahead! Squawk all you like!

Chak chak chak . . .

No good. Out comes the padding. I wind a thick scarf over my ears and round my head. Not too helpful either. That fellow could knock his spikes through the wall of a fortress!

A night of pure torture!

★

Ten o'clock, and I'm only just out of bed. My head is killing me. I've no idea when I finally fell asleep. At about three, I imagine. I know I dozed feverishly between two and three, though the nightingale was squawking away. Nightingales don't squawk in the Old Town. I think I've caught a cold. I've got a throbbing pain between the eyes and a tickle in the nose. The sky is black, the air wintry. There are summers when July is like November: cold showers, falling leaves, everybody shivering.

The guard's wife chases me into the other room while she tidies up. She'll leave the windows open again and my cold will get worse. No, thank you. I'll pop in and see the painter instead. I owe it to his wife to settle the matter of the bed. One must be civilised. Besides, he's called on me, and I must return the call. I know what's fit and proper.

I knock. I listen. Nothing. I knock again. Still nothing. I press the handle gingerly. The door opens slightly. I see the whole family gathered. 'Please excuse me . . .' No one pays me any heed. He is sitting at an easel holding his head; she is standing with her head bent over a low linen cupboard with a duster in her hand. Then Pepík looks up at me, sticks out his tongue, and turns away again, glancing from Father to Mother. All I can do is pretend I failed to notice Pepík's prank; he'll stop by himself. A small black puppy sniffs at me, but doesn't bark. It must be too young.

'Please excuse me,' I said in a louder voice.

'Why, Dr Krumlovský! I'm so sorry. I thought you were the maid. It's Dr Krumlovský, darling. Our new neighbour. We're having potato soup today – I could eat it three times a day myself – and we were trying to decide whether to add groats to it. Do sit down.'

I must be as suave as possible.

'I trust I'm not a complete stranger. You and I have met, sir, and your son as well. I've even caught a glimpse of your good lady. Now I wish to introduce myself properly, ma'am. I am Dr Krumlovský.'

The thin, washed-out blonde gives a stiff bow, like a wooden jointed doll suddenly bent in the middle. She wants to say something. 'Mr Augusta here tells me I've rubbed you the wrong way, heh heh. But what's a little tiff between neighbours?'

Again she bends down the middle, this time inviting me to take a seat and asking me how I like my new flat.

'Oh, it's fine, except that last night – and I tell my story.

'Really! A nightingale. I didn't hear it!'

'How could you?' a razor-sharp soprano cuts in. 'You were drunk as a lord.'

'Who, me? Well, maybe a little . . .'

'Is this "a little" too?' she counters, rolling up her sleeve and showing me a series of bruises. 'Here, have a look! And I had plenty of suitors. The men were wild about me. But I went and chose – well, you can see for yourself.' (She speaks with an affected lisp, I notice, though she obviously has no more than a shop-girl's education.)

I don't know quite how to respond, but she is busy dusting again, and I might just as well have disappeared.

'Well, we did have a little incident,' says the painter, attempting a smile. It fails. 'I'd made the rounds of my taverns, six of them, but I never drank more than one glass in each and came straight home afterwards. I'm not very lucky in these matters. I'm a decent sort, but I get a few drinks in me and I'm someone else, and then that chap goes on drinking and gets up to all kinds of nonsense. But he's not me now, is he?' He gives a laboured chuckle.

'It does no harm now and then; it can even be good for you. Luther says . . .' But I suddenly change the subject: I sense a duster is about to be hurled at my head. 'That nightingale last night nearly drove me to distraction.' The dog is worrying my trouser leg. I don't want to kick it, but I'm very uncomfortable.

'You should hear me! I can be pretty funny, can't I,

264

Anna?' Anna says nothing. 'What I mean is, I imitate nightingales. I can lure five or six at a time when I set my mind to it. A regular concert. You'll see.'

If he dares to do anything of the sort, I'll shoot him.

'I thought you were a landscape painter, and now I see you do portraits.' There is a human figure on the easel.

'Saints, nothing but saints. It's the only way I can earn a living. Three robes, red or blue, a bit of flesh, and there you are. Not that it brings in much. I'm a portrait painter actually. I used to have plenty of work. The whole Jewish Town was mine once – though that didn't bring in much either: twenty guilders a Jew – and then a German came and lured them all away. You know what? I've got a St Crispin to do, and you could be my model! You'd be perfect; there's something about you . . .'

I wonder what he means. Is he accusing me of stealing? I change the subject again. This time to Pepík. Yes, I'll win over Pepík.

'Come and say hello to me, Pepík. Come on.'

'What for? You're stupid.'

Papa boxes his ears. I feel my own growing red.

'But that's what Kačenka's mama told my mama today,' he says, bawling away. 'Didn't she, Mama? That there's something stupid about him.'

'Quiet!'

So I'm stupid, am I? 'Come over here, Pepík,' I say. 'Come on.' I feel my voice tightening. The boy approaches, still whimpering, and stands between my knees. How does one play with a child? 'Give me your hand. This one cooks, this one looks; this one boils, this one toils; this one says, "Give me a slice, give me a slice" and that one says, "Not on your life, not on your life!" ' The child does not smile. 'This one's father, this one's mother, here's grandfather and grandmother. This one's . . .' I'm stuck. The child does not react. 'I know what, Pepík. Here's a riddle for you: I'm green, but not grass; I'm bald, but no priest; I'm yellow, but not wax; I've a tail, but don't bark. What am I?' 'I give up.' I want to tell him, but I don't know myself. All I can remember is the riddle. 'Go on,' he says by way of encouragement. 'Tell me something else stupid.' I pretend I haven't heard.

'Well, time for me to get on with my studies. It must be twelve by now.' 'As late as that!' says the painter. 'Our clock must be off by half an hour.' 'No, it's not,' says his wife. 'I set it yesterday with the whisk broom when the tower clock struck.' It's been a great pleasure and I must come and visit them often. She's certain we shall be good neighbours.

I wish I knew why they think me stupid!

In the passage I nod to a woman I take to be the landlord's daughter. Past the first bloom of youth, she is.

'Did she lisp?' the guard's wife asks when I enter. 'She did.' 'Then they're in the money. When they're in dire straits, she talks like the rest of us.' Clearly the guard's wife has a wicked tongue. 'While you were walking along the passageway, Provazník leaned out of his window and watched you.' I look up. I think I see a thin, yellow, waxen face. Do I need anything? Rather irritably: No. Well, could she leave the baby in my room? She has some shopping to do. She won't be gone long, and Kačenka cries so when she's alone. 'But I haven't the faintest idea how to look after a baby!' 'I'll just put her on the bed.' 'But what if she cries?' 'She never cries when she knows somebody's there.' 'Or gets up to some mischief?' 'Poor little Kačenka?' Yes, poor little Kačenka. I'm terribly put out.

Resolved: to exert a moral influence on Pepík.

I've read Burnand's *Happy Thoughts*, but my 'resolutions' are of a different nature. I am not imitating him.

I should never have thought I'd return to my studies today, but I did and I'm satisfied. Satisfied but exhausted. I must go to bed.

The nightingale isn't squawking tonight. Perhaps it's frozen to death. I certainly hope so!

I wish I knew why they think me stupid!

★

First of all, congratulations! I trust you are still willing to accept the advice of an old friend, for I feel it my fraternal duty to give you good counsel if I have good counsel to give.

Most important, prepare for the examination with a cool head. You shall know enough – of that I have no doubt – but a cool head is worth twice as much as all the knowledge in the world. The councillors prefer questions which test the faculty of reason, so if one of them asks, 'Should a client approach you with such and such a case, what would you do?' you may always answer for want of anything better, 'I should ask him for part of my fee in advance.' You may be certain that . . .

The idiot! I hate it when someone constantly has to play the fool and dress everything up in worn-out anecdotes. No wonder they called him Mr Twaddle all through school. Though it's nobody's fault but my own for writing to him about my preparations and adding a polite note to the effect that should he have any advice . . . Well, I need no advice from anyone – least of all him. That is the end of our correspondence!

My cold has developed apace. I've a slight fever running through my bones, and my eyes are pouring. I'm astonished I can still study and haven't lost my appetite. But now to work!

The landlord has been to see me. An odd man, about seventy. His slight build appears even slighter because of a sunken chest and a pair of shoulders that slope so precipitously that he seems to be carrying a bucket of water in each hand. A gaunt, clean-shaven face, lips that have fallen in because teeth have fallen out, a chin in the shape of a kreutzer, a small, turned-up nose and grey hair, but black eyes burning feverishly, thin, wrinkled hands constantly groping in the air, the whole body twitching. When he speaks, it's almost a whisper. One can't be entirely at ease in his presence; one never knows when something might happen.

He's come to ask whether I've notified the police of my change of residence. I've forgotten all about it, of course. Well then, I ought to see to it. The painter has told him about the prospect of the card game, and he's looking forward to it. I bow. He observes I have a cold and opines, 'Many is the man who fails to realise what he has when he has his health.' As I do not find this particularly clever, I respond merely with a smile and a 'True'. Pause. I express the hope that he enjoys good health. Not especially, it appears: he has a pain in his neck and must have it looked after. He gives a cough and sputters all over my shoe. I'm glad he doesn't notice (there would only be pointless apologies) and hide my foot under the chair.

Am I musical? Not very (I took piano lessons as a boy and didn't learn a thing), but I say, 'You'll not find a Czech who isn't something of a musician.' 'Excellent, excellent! We can do some four-hand music. In summer I move my spinet into the garden. It's old now, but decent. We can play there. Excellent!' 'Piano?' I say, realising that a retreat is in order. 'I'm so sorry. I play the violin.' 'Have you got a good instrument?' he asks, looking round the walls. 'I haven't played in ages,' I say, retreating even farther.

'Practical concerns do so intrude.' 'A pity,' he says, rising. He doesn't wish to keep me from my work. He's not the type of landlord who infringes on his tenants' privacy. He does have something on his mind, though. He looks me straight in the eye with a cunning look on his face and asks whether I don't think Bismarck is behind what's going on over there in Spain. I reply that the ways of diplomats are inscrutable. 'True,' he remarks, 'but, as I always say, it takes more men to move a boulder than a match' and, treading squarely on my right foot, adds, 'Kings are never satisfied with what they've got.' I don't object, I merely smile politely, and he takes his leave.

A naïve way of putting things, but valid none the less. Even if these people couch their philosophy in sayings, one must be careful not to underestimate the sayings themselves, for they represent an integral if not particularly broad view of the individual's world. A collection of such 'personal proverbs' would prove extremely valuable.

All things considered I am satisfied with the day. I am going to bed.

The nightingale is squawking, but somewhat farther off. Well, let him. And if the painter lures it back with his imitation, I'll kick up a rumpus – a courteous rumpus, of course, just enough to let him know there are limits to what I will put up with. But I hope he is hurrying home from his taverns. We shouldn't want his Anna to stop lisping.

I have the impression that the guard's wife asked slightly less often today whether there was anything she could do for me – everything finds its place in due time – though I may be wrong: I may have been so absorbed in my studies as not to notice.

★

My cold and my studies. I know nothing of the world; I've withdrawn completely.

Now I'm certain that the guard's wife has been asking less often whether she can do anything for me. Today she said I was a fine person and God would repay me. There was a cobbler's widow, the mother of two, in the kitchen, and when she started bemoaning her lot I gave her a guilder. Somehow I don't think the Lord keeps track of every guilder.

The cat stays out of my rooms now, even when the door is open; it only stands there and miaows. Evidently it doesn't trust me.

I have still to lay eyes on the railway guard. Has he been home at all?

★

Chicory in the coffee! No doubt about it. This is terrible! *Something will have to be done.*

I'm charging to the end of Civil Law with ever greater velocity, like a racehorse approaching the winning post.

*

Chicory again, more than yesterday if I'm not mistaken, and the guard's wife hasn't even once asked what she can do for me. At least I have my peace. Yesterday she brought home another cobbler's widow with children. Because I'm *so* fine a person. Another guilder gone.

Pepík got an awful thrashing today; his screams echoed through the house. I asked the guard's wife what he had done. Nothing, really. He bought some nuts, his father started eating them – 'You wouldn't believe what that man can eat!' – and when Pepík tried to stop him Papa gave him a thrashing. I'm sorry for Pepík. 'For that brat!' He's impossible, she says. Last Good Friday during the Mass of the Presanctified he stole coins from the Kajetán church offertory.

Yes, I *must* set an example to Pepík. As soon as I can find time. He's such a fine-looking lad, and his father's a bad lot, unfit to bring him up.

George Washington was all but impossible as a boy, but George Washington had a wise father. God should endow children with the gift of determining whether their fathers measure up to George Washington's. If they fall short, they should waste less time with their failed fathers and turn elsewhere. (A hint for Mark Twain, who tried to bring up his father by acting like G.W.)

The painter popped across to find out whether I was up to sitting for St Crispin. I replied that the only thing I was up to sitting for was my examination. I am growing firmer.

I have finished Civil Law! Tomorrow – Currency Regulations. I'll sleep soundly tonight!

★

Now I know what Pushkin's calf must have felt when he exclaimed, 'Oh, what an ass am I!' A dreadful moment!

This morning, thinking I had finished Civil Law, I tried to answer a question about it. *I hadn't a clue!*

'Blast it all!' I cried impulsively, clutching my head and feeling the blood drain out of it.

In ran the guard's wife, wanting to know what was wrong.

'I don't know a thing!' I shouted like an idiot.

'My sentiments exactly,' she said and ran back out laughing loudly, the impertinent hussy.

I'm a bit calmer now. I know from former study sessions that this is how it goes. The material needs to mellow for a while.

I wonder whether her outburst is connected to what she said about my being stupid. No, it's more than candour; it's out-and-out cheek!

Two more cobbler's widows, though one was actually married to a tailor. The guard's wife seems intent on luring all the weeping widows on the left bank of the Vltava.

★

A turn-about! A complete and radical turn-about, the like of which I never could have expected. A turn-about in both nature and society.

First: mild, radiant, beautiful days that have whisked away my cold. Second: I've had it with chicory. I've just made myself a cup of real coffee on the spirit stove. From now on I'll make all my own coffee. I've made other changes as well. The guard's wife will bring up only dinner from the tavern; I'll go down there for supper. I want no favours, and her willingness to serve has dried up completely. Fine. It's better this way. Sitting indoors all the time isn't good for one; it dulls the brain, impedes progress. The point is to study for as many hours as one feels the first, all-consuming desire to do so, then relax a bit. I don't imagine the company of good, simple folk will upset my regime. I'll go for daily walks in the garden, too, short ones at least. There have been people strolling there for two days now. I could even get up early in the morning and go there to study. I remember how much I enjoyed studying out of doors when I was at school.

Resolved: to get up early every morning, *very early*.

I've just thrown out another cobbler's widow.

I do like this sort of tavern. It is amusing, yet not overstimulating, and that is precisely what I want at present. One needn't try to shine; one can simply watch and listen. Simple folk they are, yet each his own man, full of common sense. Naturally witty and content with modest wit in others, they laugh heartily at everything. But to go beyond the superficial level one must be a psychologist and probe the individual, and that is one of my talents.

A clean, inviting room, though not particularly well lit. A billiard table in the middle towards the far end, small tables along the walls, and several more tables in the foreground, of which four are occupied. To judge by this evening, most of the clients are regulars; indeed, the company probably remains constant for years. It is clear the moment I enter: all present fall silent and train their eyes on me.

I bow to one and all. White, freshly laid sand crunches beneath my feet. I choose a table where a lone man is sitting. He responds to my greeting with a mute nod. The short, stocky innkeeper appears out of nowhere. 'Ah, Dr Krumlovský! How happy we are you've come down to visit! Tell me, are you satisfied with your meals?' Very much so, I say; in fact, I could make any number of complaints, but one must win people over even at the cost of a fib or two. 'Glad to hear it. My only desire is for my guests to be happy. You gentlemen know each other, I trust?' I look over at the man opposite me. He is staring straight ahead with a fixed, sullen expression. 'Not yet? Why, you're neighbours. He lives just above you. Dr Krumlovský, meet Mr Semper, our tailor.' 'Well, well,' I say and offer him my hand. He responds by raising his head slightly, shifting his gaze to the far end of the table, and producing his hand with as much grace as an elephant might offer its paw. An odd bird! But here's the waiter, ready to take my order. I prefer to be waited on by a man. A waitress always has at least one favourite and sits and whispers with him in a corner. One has to keep knocking for service.

During my meal I see and hear nothing, but when I've finished and have lit my cigar I look round attentively. At the table opposite me there are several gentlemen engaged in lively conversation. To the left of me there are a gentleman, his wife, two young ladies and a portly army lieutenant who is getting on in years. I hear laughter coming from all the tables, especially the table on my left. The younger of the girls is looking at me. Since she has nice teeth and smiling eyes, I see nothing untoward in her interest. Her father has an odd head, all right angles, and a shock of grey hair combed into a tuft; he looks like a square bottle full of beer with froth coming out of the top. His daughters also have bottle heads, but theirs are at least round.

Our table is the only quiet one. 'Tell me, Mr Semper, how is business?' He shifts his weight a little and manages a 'so-so'. Not the loquacious type, I see. 'Have you many journeymen?' 'Two. At home. I contract a lot of work out.' There, a whole sentence! 'And you have a family, I expect.' 'No.' 'So you're a bachelor.' 'No.' Then, with an effort. 'A widow. Three years.' 'You must be lonely with no wife or children.' Another great effort. 'I have a daughter. Seven.' 'You should think of marrying again.' 'Yes.'

The innkeeper comes and sits at our table. 'How nice,' I say. 'Our host is honouring us with a visit.' 'It's my duty. Business demands it. An innkeeper must go from table to table. Guests like it. They think it a great honour.' I am about to laugh at his joke when I look into his eyes, which are blinking without a flicker of intelligence, and realise he must have meant it seriously. He does seem rather dense. But those eyes! Never have I seen such light-green eyes. He has a ruddy face and hair to match; in fact, it matches so well that it seems a tousled continuation of his skin. The moment one looks at him from a distance, the outline of his head begins to waver.

'Nice weather we're having,' I say to keep the conversation going. 'Yes, but when the weather's nice, people go out walking and taverns are empty. I went out for a walk myself this afternoon, but I soon came back. My back got hot from the sun, and whenever my back gets hot from the sun we're in for a storm. Though there was none today.' I bite my lip and say, 'You needn't be put off by a little rain here in town. All you need is an umbrella.' 'Well, I haven't got one.' 'Then you can run home.' 'If I run I'm not walking.' 'Then you can stand under an arcade until the rain stops.' 'If I stand I'm not walking.' Uncommonly dense! He yawns. 'Are you tired?' 'I went to bed early last night, so I'm yawning early tonight.' 'You mean you had no customers?' 'Oh, we had plenty of customers, but the beer was no good. Why stay up for nothing?' A true character!

The lieutenant at the next table is suddenly roused to passion. 'You can take it from me. Not a man in a thousand can tell you how many types of grey' (that is, white horse) 'there are. *Seventeen*! The satin variety is the rarest. You can take it from me. A beautiful specimen! Pinkish-white around the eyes and mouth, light yellow hooves . . .'

Just then a new guest enters. The silence and stares tell me he is a stranger. He takes a seat at one of the back tables. Conversation resumes. The lieutenant points out that 'your grey is born black'. The girl is still looking at me. Does she think I'm a horse?

I've emptied my glass. The innkeeper takes no notice, nor does Ignác the waiter. I give a knock, and Ignác comes running. I find this Ignác interesting. I follow him constantly with my eyes. He is in his forties, wears silver stud earrings, and has a wad of cotton wool coming out of his right ear. He looks a little like Napoleon, but an inordinately stupid Napoleon. His large eyelids blink only at great intervals, as if punctuating his thoughts, though I'll wager he hasn't a thought in his head. After taking up a position somewhere or other, he stands there self-absorbed until a guest knocks and catapults him into action.

The topic of conversation at the table opposite me is now Polish. I note that the participants have adopted a 'witty' way of addressing each other, using animal epithets followed by the words 'nose' or 'ear'. Strange. One of them claims that if you know Czech and German you know Polish, because Polish is merely a mixture of the two. His proof is a mixture of fractured Czech and German.

Yet another new guest enters. A heavy-set man with the torso of a deeply rooted tree stump. A regular by the looks of it, he smiles and sits at our table. 'Another neighbour,' says the innkeeper, bustling over again. 'Dr Krumlovský, meet Mr Klikeš the shoemaker.' Mr Klikeš shakes my hand. 'A handsome lad, as handsome as they come. I'm sure the girls are wild about you.' I'm so embarrassed I may even be blushing slightly. I should like to take it in my stride and, say, flash a smile at the girl at the next table, but I fail. 'Well, anyone's handsomer than you,' the host says with a laugh, 'with those bullet-hole pockmarks all over your face.' 'I see the municipality's been after you to wash the floor again,' said Klikeš, shuffling his feet in the sand. Laughter. 'That's right, Dr Krumlovský. He never does it on his own. And once a year two police-men come and drag him off to the baths. Sometimes it takes three of them, he puts up such a fight.' Loud laughter all around. Klikeš must be the local wag. And he does have a sharp tongue. But there's not a scrap of malice in his rough, pitted face, and his eyes are more frank than crafty. 'He's got to economise,' he adds. 'He needs plenty of the ready. I can't keep up with him when it comes to beer.' And so saying, he drains his glass. 'Now for some supper.' He constantly waves his arms above his head as he speaks. He looks like a tree stump with its root system in the air.

Two young men have had the billiard balls set up in a pyramid and are getting up to play. While seated, they were the same height, but now one turns out to be tiny and the other unseemly tall. I know a fellow who, as long as he sits at a table, is nothing out of the ordinary, but the moment he stands there is no end to his unfolding – or to the laughter it provokes. He considers himself extremely unfortunate.

'Nothing, as usual,' Klikeš grumbles, looking at the bill of fare. 'Goulash, paprika, breaded tripe . . . So that's what you do with your mouldy crumbs!' 'That's enough out of you!' 'Why can't I even have boiled chicken?' 'You'd like one boiled just for you, is that it?' 'But it's simple as can be: take some boiled eggs and set a hen on them, heh heh heh.' 'Yes, well, first take the hair out of your eyes.' Irony: Klikeš is as bald as a church father.

'Psst!' someone beckons from the neighbouring table. 'Karel's catching a flea.' General silence. All heads turn. Suspense. The man called Karel is sitting with his hand thrust into his shirt, his face radiating complacency and self-confidence. He withdraws his hand from his chest, rubs his thumb and forefinger together, and places something on the table. Laughter, applause. The ladies bite their handkerchiefs. 'He catches every one of them,' Klikeš informs me. 'Every one?' 'Every last one. Hey, Ignác! Where's my supper?

And bring my glass back when you come. I haven't finished with it.' Then he turns to me and says, 'I never finish with it.' A joke, apparently. I laugh and say, 'You're a real wag, you are.' Ignác comes in from the kitchen wearing a look of heightened stupidity. 'I'm terribly sorry, Mr Klikeš, but what was it you ordered?' 'I don't believe it! He's forgotten! Have you ever seen anything like it? I ordered . . .' But Klikeš himself has forgotten by now.

The piercing voice of Mama to my left proclaims, 'When a mother has two daughters, she must never dress them alike after the age of twenty or she'll never marry them off.' Which is her way of telling all and sundry that her two similarly dressed daughters are under twenty. Ha!

'You want to be careful around here,' Klikeš tells me, as he gulps down his goulash, 'or they'll add items to your bill. The innkeeper was a soldier once and specialised in removing beers secretly from bills; now he specialises in chalking them up. He's trying to square things with his conscience.' I laugh, of course. I do my best to bring Semper into the conversation, but all I can get out of him is that every morning he goes to the wine shop.

Ignác is now glued to the billiard table, following the action with great interest and clearly favouring the smaller man. Occasionally he gives a leap of excitement; now he is hopping up and down.

Klikeš has finished his supper. He fills and lights his pipe. In the flickering light his face looks like an old blacksmith's. He peers about contentedly as he smokes. When his eye lights upon the stranger sitting near the billiard table, he says to himself with a smile, 'That man's nothing if not a shoemaker', and shouts out, 'Hey there, snake in the grass!' in stentorian tones. The man gives a start, but looks straight ahead. 'Yes, you! The cobbler!' Now the stranger turns his head; he is livid. 'Who is this barfly?' he says slowly. 'Who is this drunk?' And he spits at Klikeš's feet. 'What? You dare to spit at me?' Klikeš cries in a rage. 'A Prague burgher?' He tries to stand, but the innkeeper shoves him back into his chair and makes for the stranger. Klikeš pounds on the table, saying that nobody has ever seen him drunk and if some great misfortune does cause him to take an occasional drop too many it is nobody's business but his own. In the meantime the innkeeper has smuggled out the stranger (who is only too happy for the assistance) by way of the kitchen. Klikeš goes on fulminating.

Suddenly the sound of a struggle comes from without. After a moment the innkeeper returns and says, 'He changed his mind, wanted to come back. But I tossed him into the street, tossed him into the street like a bundle into a pawnshop.'

Soon things are in full swing again, and someone at the opposite table starts to clap. 'Bravo! Bravo! Löfler's going to do the fly for us. Come on, Löfler! Do the fly!' Now everyone is clapping. Klikeš asks me whether I've ever seen anyone 'do the fly'. I say I haven't. He tells me it's great fun; I'll split my sides laughing. In fact, I've seen it a thousand times – every Prague tavern has someone who does it – and dislike it intensely. Löfler, who is sitting with his back to me, protests. It isn't quiet enough. 'Quiet! Quiet! Shhh!' Finally Löfler starts buzzing. First, like a fly flitting around a room, then banging at a window, and finally caught in a glass, thumping up and down in a panic. Applause. I join in. All eyes turn to see how I've enjoyed it. 'A real devil of a chap,' says Klikeš. 'There's no one like him anywhere. We could die laughing sometimes.' He empties glass after glass, evidently still fired up about the incident. From time to time he taps his stomach and says by way of apology, 'Ten inches below normal, heh heh heh!'

'You don't know what you're doing!' rings out all at once from the billiard table, and all heads turn instantly in that direction. Poor Ignác! The player he had been cheering on has failed him, and he is unable to contain his displeasure. General uproar. The player smacks the table with his cue. The lieutenant shouts, 'This time he's gone too far! Throw him out!' The innkeeper swears to throw Ignác out on his ear as soon as the accounts are done in the morning. Klikeš grins at me and says, 'Yet again.'

And yet again the waves subside. A pedlar has come in, a thin, dirty, unshaven specimen in a shiny, soiled suit. He says not a word but holds out his wares: a comb, a purse, a cigarholder. Nothing but refusals, shakes of the head. He makes the rounds of the tables in silence, then closes his box, straps it up and leaves.

Applause followed by 'Shhh! Shhh! Quiet!' This time Löfler does sausages sizzling and sputtering over a fire. Applause and laughter. Only Ignác – crushed, blinking timidly off to the side – is silent.

Löfler goes on to do a goitrous Tyrolean yodeller. It's repulsive, but I clap. The lieutenant is now all but shouting stories of a kind which would make me – were I a father flanked by wife and daughters – throw him out. Perhaps they've known him for a long time, but then they should have thrown him out long ago.

I say my goodbyes and take my leave.

An enjoyable evening on the whole. One must give these people their due.

★

I wake up late. When I go to a tavern of an evening, I sleep late. Actually, I always sleep late, though I hear there are those who fairly jump out of bed. Never mind: sleep well, study well.

A glorious day! I can't resist keeping the windows wide open. Of course sounds from all over the house waft through, but if I think of them as the distant murmur of a weir, they don't bother me much; on the contrary, it's a welcome change from the monotony of the closed rooms. Someone is singing in the flat above me, probably one of Semper's journeymen. He has a simple, artless voice, and the song is humorous:

The cause of her disgrace is
She lacks all social graces.

Heh heh heh.

Pepík has wandered into my room. He mustn't get into the habit, but I mustn't hurt his feelings. 'Come over here, Pepík. Tell me, do you know any songs?' 'Course I do.' 'Then sing one for me, a nice one, all right?' The boy launches into 'I Had a Little Dove', but when he comes to 'green oak' he blithely sings 'green yolk'. What can a Prague child know of oaks, after all? 'Time for you to go. I've got to be by myself now. You can't come and see me any more.' He's gone. A fine boy.

I'm doing Currency Regulations, but throwing in a bit of Commercial Law for good measure.

A terrible row at the Augustas'. Pepík's getting it again. The painter sees me going to shut the window and calls out across the yard, 'Damn that child! He never stops!' 'What's he done now?' 'Chewed up a letter from my brother the priest. How can I write back?' I shut the window anyway: 'She lacks all social graces' is still coming down from the tailor's.

I go downstairs for dinner with Semper. Ignác is still around, I notice. What a farce. For a while he and the innkeeper work on the accounts at the next table, Ignác squinting at the master in dumb horror, expecting yesterday's threat of dismissal to be carried out at any moment, the master blinking idly, his frayed features showing no awareness whatever of the affair. Ignác scuttles off the moment they finish.

The innkeeper sits down with us. 'Good soup,' I remark. 'All my soup is good,' he replies. 'What do you recommend with the meat, Ignác?' 'Whatever you like.' 'Some beets, then.' 'No.' 'No? It's right here on the menu.' Ignác holds his tongue; the innkeeper holds his sides. 'I'll bring it myself. He can't . . . He can't . . .' I stare at him in astonishment. 'He can't stand the sight of beets. They make him faint; they remind him of dry blood.' *Bon appétit!*

No decent conversation to spice up the meal. Our host is useless. 'What's in the papers today?' I ask. 'I don't read them; I go across to the shopkeeper now and then to find out what's going on.' I notice that the walls are scuffed with what looks like kick marks. 'How did they get there?' 'This used to be a dance hall.' 'And how long have you been here?' 'Me? Getting on for twelve years now.' Semper says even less, and what he does say consists mainly of 'Oh' and 'Hm'.

I go out into the garden towards evening. Half the household is there. By now I've met all the tenants except the young couple on the second floor and my railway man. It makes me dizzy to think of them all.

Mr Provazník, who lives above the painter – well, I don't know quite what to make of him. The few glimpses I'd caught of him at his window made his face seem long and yellow, like a noodle. Now I know why: he has a short black beard, but his lips and chin are clean-shaven. He is almost grey – he must be fifty – and walks with a marked stoop.

As I mount the steps to the garden, I notice Provazník walking about in the background. In the arbour in the right corner I see the landlord, his daughter, the painter and his wife, and Pepík. The landlord's feverish black eyes gaze upon me as if I were a total stranger. 'It's Dr Krumlovský, Father,' a mellow alto rings out. 'Oh, yes, Dr Krumlovský. I'd quite forgotten.' He offers me a thin, hot hand. 'With your kind permission I should like to unbend a bit here in the garden.' 'By all means,' he says, giving a cough and sputtering all over my shoe. We sit. I have no idea what to say. Perhaps the others don't mind the lull, but it's agony for me. I feel certain they are waiting to see how clever the new tenant will be at amusing them.

Pepík is my only hope. 'Come here, Pepík. How are you?' Pepík nestles up to me and props an elbow on my knee. 'Tell me a story.' 'Tell you a story, eh? The little rascal remembers the riddle I told him the other day, heh heh.' 'Tell me a fairy story.' 'But I don't know any fairy stories. No, wait. I do remember *one*.' And I intone, 'Once upon a time there was a king. Right. And this king had no children. Right. And it so happened that his eldest son went off on a journey.' General mirth. 'You're the rascal, not Pepík,' said the painter, wiping away two large tears from his watery eyes. An intelligent man, the painter. I'm flattered by his recognition. It never hurts to be thought witty. 'Go on, go on,' he says. 'This is a fairy story for grown-up children too.' I'm back where I started from. There *is* no more to the story. The last line is the whole point of it, but these good people don't see that. I pride myself on my ability to improvise, though; perhaps I can carry it off. I spin a long, long tale, but it doesn't work. I suddenly feel it's just so much drivel. People stop paying attention and start talking among themselves, thank goodness; only Pepík is still listening. It has to end somehow, though, and I'm beginning to falter. A happy thought! I pick up Pepík's hands as though I'd just noticed them and say, 'What dirty hands you have!' He looks. 'Bend down. I have a secret to tell you.' I bend down. 'Give me twelve kreutzers and I'll wash them.' I dig two six-kreutzer pieces out of my pocket and slip them to him, and he skips over to Semper's seven-year-old daughter, who has just come into the garden.

I look at the landlord's daughter, who is sitting next to me. How like her father she is! The thin face, the slender, transparent hand, the small chin and that tiny nose – is it even big enough to tweak? Not that it mars her face in any way; in fact, her face is rather pleasant with its black eyes. I must say I'm partial to black eyes; women with blue eyes always look blind to me.

'Are you musical, Dr . . .'

'Krumlovský,' she interjected. Her alto voice too is quite engaging.

'Yes, Otylka, I know. Dr Krumlovský.'

'We spoke of that when you were so kind as to visit me. I once played the violin, but that was long ago.' I don't even know how to hold a violin, but I can tell his mind has begun to wander. His daughter leans over to me and whispers sadly, 'Father tends to lose his memory in the afternoon.' But then the landlord pulls himself together and says in a croak, 'Come, Otylka. I should like to take a little walk. Oh, doctor. May I give you this?' He hands me a long white card that says, 'I apologise for speaking so softly. My throat is bothering me today.'

At this point Provazník comes up. He smiles at me, but his smile strikes me as ironic. He offers me his hand.

'How do you do, Dr Kratochvíl.'

'My name is Krumlovský.'

'That's odd. I know a Dr Kratochvíl, so I assumed all doctors were Kratochvíl, heh heh heh.'

His laughter is half wheeze, half sneer. I respond with a blank stare.

'What were you talking about, gentlemen? Oh, Mr Augusta. How is business?'

'Not very good. Rather slow.'

'Yet whenever I meet you on the stairs, you've got at least one wet canvas under your arm. You must find it child's play to turn out two a day.'

The painter smiles smugly and says, 'You can be sure none of those "professors" would be up to it.'

'Why not paint your portraits ahead of time and keep a supply on hand, heh heh heh! Though portrait painters must be the most superfluous people on earth. If not one of them existed, every one of the faces they paint would look just the same. Why not paint something else?'

I'd have laughed – Provazník's satire is much to my taste – but I see the poor painter is confused. Why torment him so?

'I started out with historical canvases,' he stammers, 'but they didn't bring in much. People don't understand history. A priest once commissioned a painting of the Capuchin sermon in the Wallenstein camp, and I did it up fine, if I may say so myself. But when it was finished, he refused it! He wanted the Capuchin sermon minus the Capuchin! That's right, a priest! And then I was supposed to do a painting of Žižka for the Kuckov Town Hall. The torture I went through! I sent them a sketch. They didn't like the boots. Would I please ask Mr Palacký if they were historically accurate.[3] Well, Mr Palacký gave me a favourable report, but Kuckov had its own expert, Malina by name, and this Malina decided my Žižka wasn't up to military snuff. I wrangled with them for ages, but in the end they wrote and told me I was being pilloried by the local press. No, history is dangerous.'

'Then try genre painting. A tinker mending a drunken musician's flute. Or *A Mouse in the Girls' School*.

You don't show the mouse; you show the young ladies and the schoolmistress perched on their desks. Think of the variations of terror on their faces!'

'Well, I've done that too, heh heh. I even had one exhibited. Everything was still in German at the time, and my piece was called *Häusliche Arznei, Home Medicine*. There's a man lying in bed and a woman taking him a pot of – '

'Ugh!'

'It wasn't so bad. You couldn't see the food. The pot was wrapped in a cloth to keep it warm . . .'

At a loss to help Augusta out of his predicament, I ask Provazník rather awkwardly, 'What day is today?'

'Just take a gander at our landlord's shirt collar, Dr Kratochvíl,' Provazník says with a smirk. 'He changes only once a week. By the looks of it, today is Thursday.'

The nerve of the man!

'Don't you feel sorry for him, though? It must be terrible, having your memory fail every afternoon.'

'Well, I imagine he sold straw hats at one time or another. Everyone who sells straw hats ends up batty, you know. It's the sulphur. Especially Tyroleans. They can't even add a column of numbers at the end.'

'But he's a good man, a worthy man.'

'Worthy, but as stupid as the day is long. I've known him for more than twenty years.'

'His daughter, poor girl, takes good care of him, doesn't she? She seems a pleasant sort, though not so young as she used to be.'

'It's all curiosity on her part. Female curiosity brought her into the world twenty years too soon, and now she regrets it. She's honest, though: she's told me off many times over.'

Provazník's effronteries make me uneasy.

'Let's go and chat with the landlord for a while,' I suggest.

'Yes, let's,' Augusta agrees and gives Provazník some thumps on the back. Provazník quakes skittishly at each one, but quickly recovers.

They both rise, their move wrenching Mrs Augusta out of a deep reverie that has kept her leaning motionless against the arbour for some time. 'You know what, darling? I think I'll make scrambled eggs for supper.' 'Good,' says the painter, continuing on his way. Then she takes the opportunity to remind me, in a strong lisp, that she had plenty of admirers and all the men were wild about her. To flatter her, I say, 'You can still see it.' You can still see what, she wants to know. I realise I've put my foot in my mouth, but can find no way out. 'That you were once beautiful,' I say. She turns up her nose and says she's not so old as all that and when she gets dressed up – and suddenly she's talking a mile a minute: why, only the other day a man walking behind her said, 'She looks good enough to eat', yes, and he'd have said the same if he'd been coming in the other direction, and . . . By the time I stammer a reply, she has run off.

I join the others in the garden. The landlord smiles at me as if he knew who I was, but then hands me another of his 'throat' cards. The conversation has turned to sugar refineries. Feeling I need to redeem my reputation as a wit, I say, 'So the young lady is an expert on sugar refineries?' 'Oh no, not in the least.' 'Not even in the sugary fineries of the pastry shops?' I laugh long and loud on the principle that laughter provokes laughter. The principle doesn't work. They don't appear to have grasped the joke.

The landlord asks me whether I'm musical and steps on my foot. I answer a sullen 'No', but immediately repent and add, 'You must attend the opera regularly?' 'No, I don't, actually. I hear a half-tone sharp with my right ear, so it's not worth it.' A remarkable man, this: in the afternoon he loses his memory, and he hears half a tone sharp with his right ear! 'I'd rather stay at home with my piano and work.' 'So you compose.' 'Not at present. For some years now I've been involved in rewriting Mozart. Wait till you hear Mozart when I'm through.' This time he sputters over Provazník's shoe. Wiping his shoe off on the lawn, Provazník says, 'I haven't been to the opera for many years either, and if I did go I'd go only to *Martha*.'

The landlord clasps me by the hand and takes me off to the side. He wants to tell me something, but he can't quite spit it out. All I can catch is a hissing sound, like steam escaping from a kettle. Three times round the garden and all I get is 'sss'. Then he comes up with 'There is no phosphorus in cabbage', and hands me another card.

At this point the painter grabs me away from him

and takes me off to a corner. Did I notice how he thumped Provazník on the back? Well, if Provazník ever got my goat I should do the same. I didn't even need to be rough about it; it would do the trick. An evil man, that Provazník, he says.

Then Provazník takes me off into another corner. What do I think of the idea of starting a company for making islands in the Vltava? He has a triumphant gleam in his eye. I say it sounds like a brilliant idea. 'Well, I've got any number of them. But people don't go for ideas nowadays. I wouldn't dream of even mentioning it to those fools.'

'How about that game of twenty-six?' the painter suggests. Very well, why not, just an hour. The painter has a pack of cards in a drawer in his arbour. We sit at a small table and choose partners. I'll be playing with the landlord against the painter and Provazník.

A fine game! After every trick the landlord inquires what trumps are. Since he can't remember what colour I've led, he fails to follow suit. I'm ready to wager he has picture cards, but he never declares them. When I ask him a question, he hands me another of his 'throat' cards. Provazník and Augusta are naturally way ahead of us and are whinnying with delight. I might as well simply throw down my cards and shovel out my coins. If Otylie didn't pay for her father, we'd never make it through a game: he keeps claiming he's paid. And to make matters worse, he tramps on my feet under the table. I pull them back and enjoy watching him searching feverishly for something to tread on.

All of a sudden he lets fly at me, accuses me of poor strategy: I should have played my king to his ace of spades. But the fact is we're not playing spades and *he* hasn't got the ace, *I* have it. But on he goes, his voice blaring like a trombone – and I have fifteen of his 'I apologise for speaking so softly' cards in my pocket! Otylie throws me a painful, pleading glance; I understand, I bite my tongue.

By the end of the hour I've lost more than sixty kreutzers.

The landlord has gone home with Otylie: the cool of the evening 'is bad for his throat'. Provazník's gone too. The Augustas' maidservant has brought the family their supper. I ask her to bring me a beer and something to eat from the tavern.

Now I've eaten and am talking to the painter. He tells me he's never been properly recognised: even at the Academy they tried to get rid of him early – he knew more than his professors, don't you see.

Home again. My head is reeling.

*

Never again will I leave the window open at night, not in the most sultry weather. At about two o'clock there was another row at the Augustas'. Mrs Augusta did a solo, and she has a voice that could saw through a tree trunk. I soon made out what had happened. The painter came home half-crazed with drink. As he was aware of it himself and feared knocking something over, he simply stood in the doorway and waited for his wife to light his way. As ill luck would have it, he fell asleep standing there and toppled with a crash.

The incident may explain why I don't hear the nightingale any more: since it doesn't give tongue until after midnight, it too may be coming from the tavern.

I see the landlord and his daughter in the garden. I go out, because I want a chance to talk to him when his memory is intact. Unfortunately I find Provazník with them. He wasn't visible from the window.

The landlord is sitting at the spinet, playing. 'Hello, Dr Krumlovský. Let me play you one of my old compositions, a song without words.' It's quite pretty, as far as I can tell, and even though the instrument is poor he plays with virtuosity and emotion. I applaud. 'And how did *you* like it, Mr Provazník?' 'Well, actually I prefer *Martha*, but it's nice enough – nice enough for the dunghill, that is. Look, why can't you write something to take care of bedbugs? I'd sing it night and day. They'll be the death of me, those bedbugs.' While Provazník turns away for a chuckle, the landlord gestures to me that he is not quite normal in the head. Then Provazník leans over and whispers, 'What I wouldn't give for a glimpse into the head of a musician. I bet what you'd find under that wild mane is a brain teeming with maggots.' Aware that he is the subject of our conversation, the landlord mutters, 'It takes more men to move a boulder than a match.' I try to save the day by asking Provazník whether he has ever studied music. 'Why, yes, actually, I have. I studied the violin, the flute and voice for three years – which makes nine altogether – and yet I have only the most rudimentary understanding of it.' I then turn to the landlord's daughter and ask politely how she slept. 'Very well, but this morning when I got up I was terribly depressed and couldn't stop weeping.' 'There must have been a reason for it. Someone as sensible as you . . .' 'So you think me sensible? Papa, Dr Krumlovský thinks I'm sensible!' and she laughed until she was nearly in tears again. I began to go on about how our tears in fact flow constantly throughout our lives, only we don't perceive it. I am convinced I'm being fascinating, but when I reach the part about the gleam in the human eye, that is, when I'm only half way through, the landlord suddenly stands and says, 'Come, Otylka, it's time to see about dinner', and off they go, leaving me in the clutches of Provazník.

I am terribly ill at ease in his presence, and that odd grin of his only makes matters worse. Yet I refuse to run away and finally venture to open the conversation. 'He's quite a fine musician, actually.' 'Yes, I hear he's particularly good at – what do you call it when you divide things up among the various clarinets?' 'Orchestration?' 'Yes, that's it. Though what's so hard about that? Put a hurdy-gurdy and a dog together and they don't sound so bad either.' I couldn't help laughing.

'You're looking rather poorly today, doctor.' 'Really, I can't imagine why . . .'

But suddenly Provazník rubbed his forehead, as though trying to remember something, then launched into the following monologue in a deep, deliberate, earnest voice: 'You're a reasonable man. I've no desire to make sport of you. You should know that I hate people. All my life I have been the butt of injustices, myriad injustices. For many years now I haven't so much as left the house. It began when I started turning grey. Everyone I met was sure to exclaim in wonder, "I do declare, you're almost grey!" The asses! Now I'm as grey as a mouse, but I've come up with a way to get back at them.' He smiled a blissful smile and went on. 'Before they can so much as open their mouths, I say to them with the gravest concern, "My God! What's wrong? You look terrible!" And all of them – every last one – take fright and start thinking something really is wrong with them. I know how to rile them! Over the years I've taken particular pleasure in noting everything, absolutely everything I've heard about everybody. I keep my material in strict alphabetical order. Come and see me some time, and I'll show you my complete file of Malá Strana notables. And whenever my gall runs over, I take out bundle after bundle and write anonymous letters. People must go out of their minds when they read about their secrets in the hand of a stranger. And no one has ever thought of me – no one! I should tell you, though, I've stopped lately. There's only one more I intend to write. That happy couple living next to me – I can't stand them. I must find some skeleton in their closet. I haven't had any luck thus far.'

I shuddered. Provazník went merrily on; he was speaking faster now. 'I was quite the rake, I was. Oh, the women I seduced when I was young! Don't worry. I won't seduce you. And don't worry about broken marriages either: I set my sights exclusively on the unattached. As a student I would go through the rolls of girls' schools, making lists of the worst scholars: they were always the loosest. I also kept track of all student love affairs, and the moment a couple quarrelled, there I was: an offended sweetheart is easy prey.'

I jumped up, unable to stand it any longer. 'I'm sorry. I've got to go.' And off I rushed.

As I fled I heard a loud guffaw. Had he been duping me all along?

Lately the guard's wife has been tidying up when I go down to dinner. The only time I see her is when I pass through the kitchen. Which is how it should be.

Yet another row at the Augustas' and another thrashing for Pepík. The cause: the kreutzers I gave him yesterday. He was brought home by a porter he had hired to hoist him on to his shoulders and be his 'horse', that is, carry him back and forth in front of our house.

As it turns out, Pepík had invited Semper's daughter, Márinka, to watch the spectacle from her window. First love, perhaps. I first fell in love when I was three, and I was thrashed for it too. But Pepík gets beaten far too often.

Evening in the tavern. The same people at the same tables. The conversation immediately turns to the Czech theatre. The fat lieutenant tells all and sundry that he has been to the Czech theatre and quite enjoyed the play. *Die Tochter des Bösewichts* it was, but he can't quite remember what it was called in Czech.[4] He asks. Nobody knows. The conversation goes on. What is the difference between comedy and a real play? With absolute authority the lieutenant asserts that a genuine play has five acts. It's just like a regiment, he says: four battalions in the field and one in reserve.

Then the conversation sinks to a virtual word-by-word repetition of what was said the day before yesterday: Klikeš goes on about breaded tripe, boiled chickens hatching from boiled eggs, and the two policemen who come once a year and drag the innkeeper off to the baths; the innkeeper counters with his bullet-hole pockmarks insult. The laughter is every bit as loud as it was then.

Again the younger daughter of the 'bottle' family stares at me, drinking me in as the sun drinks water; again the thin, dirty pedlar, saying nothing, selling nothing, and departing, so comic a figure that I could almost let him die of hunger out of a pure desire for amusement. Could he have taken a vow to walk for ever from one tavern to the next, always dirty, always silent, always luckless? Then Karel catches his flea for the spellbound audience, and Löfler garners applause for his buzzing fly and sizzling wurst. I must have witnessed the entire programme on my very first visit.

Ah, but there is something new, after all. Karel suddenly calls out to Löfler, 'How about the pigs?' Applause. They do the pigs. Sitting opposite each other, they wiggle their fists under the table-cloth as if they were pigs in a sack, and they squeal so naturally that the likeness is complete. I can see only Karel's face; his eyes are sparkling with joy.

I didn't get much studying done today.

★

We had a terrible storm in the night, but this morning the air is balmy. I run down to the garden with a book. No one is there.

Here comes somebody. It's only Pepík. I'll get rid of him somehow, and all will be well. 'So you lost those kreutzers, didn't you?' I say, patting him on the head. He looks up at me and says with a crafty smile, 'No, I didn't. I got them back from Papa.' 'You did? And what will you do with them now?' 'Promise not to tell?' 'You know I won't tell.' 'Bedříšek's going to give me the winning numbers!' 'Tell me, Pepík, who is this Bedříšek?' 'His mother's the lottery lady. He wouldn't tell me for a long, long time, but I've promised him half my money and now he says he will.' A child's naîvety is so touching. 'And what will you do with the money when you win?' 'Oh, lots of things. I'll buy Papa beer and Mama a gold brocade dress. I'll buy you something too.' He's a good-natured child, that Pepík.

He's a scoundrel, that Pepík. I'm trembling with rage.

The day grew hotter, so I went back to the flat. I was in a fine mood – the little devil! I sat down, and as I thought over what I'd been studying in the garden, my eye wandered about the room. It stopped short when it came to *Sunlit Sea*, my Navrátil gouache. The sunlight was all gone; it was all clouds. What I saw when I went up close was that the picture – plus a patch of the surrounding wall – was spattered with clay pellets. Evidently Pepík had used it for target practice.

I took down the painting and went to the painter to complain. He flew into a rage, and Pepík got a merciless thrashing before my eyes. I enjoyed every minute of it. My beautiful gouache!

Augusta says he can restore it for me.

Down with idleness! It was idleness pure and simple that made me order coffee with my dinner in the tavern: I couldn't be bothered making it myself. Now I've got to make another one to help me digest the first.

My studies are going badly again today. Suddenly I

hear a sabre clanking in the kitchen. Have our railway guards taken to wearing sabres?

I'm being called down to the garden for another game of twenty-six. I don't respond. They're arguing over whether I'm in. The painter claims I am. 'Let me serenade him,' Provazník says. 'That will bring him out, I promise.' And standing under my window, he sings in a hideous caterwaul:

> If you wonder why I'd plunder
> Town and country for a dumpling,
> I shall tell you, mademoiselle: you
> Ought to try one; it's really something.

Choking with laughter, he waits a few moments, then says, 'He can't be in. My voice would have drawn him out, like a cork from a bottle.'

I can't help myself. I do go down a little later.

They are discussing the storm. Mrs Augusta assures us ten times over and with great solemnity that no one would believe how frightened storms make her. 'It's true,' says her husband. 'She's terrified of them. Last night I had to go into the kitchen and wake up the maid and tell her to kneel down and pray. And that hussy falls asleep! I gave her the sack first thing this morning.' Provazník observes that praying can be harder than one thinks. 'I can recite the Ten Commandments only if I reel them off starting with the Lord's Prayer, and when I recite the Lord's Prayer I

always get mixed up at "in Heaven as it is on earth"
and have to start all over again.' Then Mrs Augusta
says the wind was so strong she knew someone must
have hanged himself and sure enough the milk-woman
told her in the morning that an ex-serviceman had
strung himself up in the Hvězda Preserve. 'A suicide!'
Provazník, whose mind was wandering, asks who was
killed by the suicide. 'Oh, of course. I know who.'

I turn to the landlord's daughter. Was she frightened, too? 'I didn't even know there was a storm. I
quite slept through it!' What a pleasant laugh she has!
She is putting together a large, freshly painted cage in
the form of a medieval castle replete with drawbridge,
turrets and oriels. Do I think it will do for a canary?
'Why, certainly!' I reply, and launch into an explanation of how canaries and castles . . . well, actually,
it was just one stupidity after another. Heaven knows
why I'm tongue-tied with this plain and simple
woman when I can twist the most sophisticated of
them round my little finger. I wonder how old she is.
When she laughs, she looks no more than nineteen;
when she's serious, she could be thirty. The tricks the
devil can play on a man!

Provazník exhorts the painter to try for at least a
modicum of fidelity – it is really of the utmost importance. Most people have no grasp of real art, he says,
and make the most ridiculous demands. And had the
painter heard that his Viennese colleagues were now
doing portraits with rollers? It was a great step forward: it takes them only fifteen minutes to roll one

out. Provazník doesn't stop his blather until Augusta
starts thumping him on the back.

Up comes the landlord, distributing his cards, his
voice a feeble croak.

Provazník takes me aside. Nobody does a thing for
the Prague poor, not a thing. People are always saying,
'The unfortunate creatures! There's no work for them!'
but nobody does a thing. He has an idea, though; it
may not be brilliant, but it could help any number of
the down-and-out. It doesn't even require a great
outlay: a small handcart with a kettle just large enough
to produce a steady supply of steam. A man could go
from house to house cleaning pipe stems. Considering
the number of smokers in Prague, it should be a most
profitable venture. What do I think of it? I marvel at
it.

Cards again. Why not keep the partners we had
yesterday? We're used to them. Everything, in fact, is
like yesterday, only today I lose seventy kreutzers.
The landlord fumes again towards the end. He and his
daughter leave. The painter and his wife are lost in
thought. 'Tomorrow's Sunday,' says the painter at
last. 'You know what? Buy a goose.'

Klikeš is terribly put out. He's a member of the municipal cavalry, their captain died today, and at the meeting about funeral arrangements Klikeš proposed that
they should telegraph to Vienna and request that the
captain be promoted to major posthumously, a
major's funeral being much more festive. But someone

a bit more sensible dissuaded them, and Klikeš is hopping mad.

Death continues to monopolise the conversation. One of the merchants on the square has had a death in the family. Who was it? 'Oh, his father,' says the innkeeper, 'and he was so old he was ashamed of living.' What did he die of? 'Consumption, like his father before him. That's what happens when it gets into the family.'

The pedlar. He really *must* have taken a vow!

★

It can't go on like this! This isn't studying – creeping along at a snail's pace, my thoughts anywhere but in my books. I can't say I'm distraught – that would be going too far – but I am distracted. My brain is full of figurines, my neighbours. I can feel them milling about – first one, then another taking over, turning a somersault before my eyes, saying its piece, flashing its own special grin. No, it can't go on like this! I didn't move to Malá Strana for these figures.

Eleven o'clock. I hear the sabre clanking in the kitchen again. Could he be a relative? Cavalry, perhaps.

Sobs and lamentations from the painter's wife; a painful yelp followed by whimpers and wails from the painter's dog. I piece together the dog's frightful offence: it has chewed up Mrs Augusta's purse with all the family mementos: a lock of her father's hair, the card from her wedding confession and God knows what else.

Half an hour of relative peace, then another racket at the painter's. The painter has returned, most likely from the wine shop. I can hear him talking loudly, then yelling at someone, and finally screaming, 'Well, let me tell you, you greedy pig, the liver goes to the head of the family! Everybody knows that, you witch!' He appears in the window. I duck. Then I hear, 'Tell me, Mr Semper, am I right or am I wrong? The liver of a goose – it goes to the head of the family, doesn't it?' I can't hear Semper's reply, but the painter shouts, 'There, you see?' Mrs Augusta must have cooked the liver in mourning for her heirlooms. The voices shout and wrangle on when suddenly the painter's rises up, saying, 'You mean it ate the two ten-guilder notes too? What are *we* going to eat?'

A beautiful, a tranquil afternoon. The kind of Sunday serenity that makes a man breathe free. How could I work? I had to go down to the garden. It was empty, possessed by a holy silence.

I walk at leisure, breathing in every bush, every plant. Everything is burnished with a special Sunday bloom. I am gradually overcome by an aching bliss; I would hop like a child, only I might be seen from a window. The air is silent, yet one listens and seems to hear the sounds of an infinitely distant and fabled land. I duck into an arbour and do in fact hop. Oh, how blissful it feels! I must do it again! There!

I walk from arbour to arbour, looking, thinking, imagining this family here, that one there, all their members, all their quirks. I feel myself smiling. I'm enjoying myself.

The spinet. The little old spinet with its feeble old tone. What would it tell us, could it but speak? The laughter it's witnessed, the sighs! The harmonies its spirit has soared in!

I sit down and open it. Five octaves – poor thing. It's so long since I last played! I had no desire to learn, and my teacher was neglectful. Yet oh, the golden days of youth! I fall into a deep reverie . . .

Surely I can still play something? Chords at least. C-sharp E A – there, that rings true. A D F-sharp – good! A little higher now: D F-sharp A, then F-sharp A D . . .

'So you play,' I hear the painter saying. 'How nice!'

I give a start. Behind me stands the entire citizenry of our garden republic. I freeze and therefore remain seated.

'Oh, do play something for us. Do!' the landlord's daughter chirps.

'But I can't. Really I can't. I've never in my life touched a piano. There *was* a time I played the violin, but . . .'

'That only makes it more interesting. I heard your chords. I'm sure you can do it. Please! Please!' When she clasps her hands beseechingly like that, she looks nineteen.

The devil knows why I don't take flight immediately. Man is a terribly complacent creature and therefore liable to make a fool of himself. 'I really can't, but well, if I convince you I can't, do you promise not to laugh at me?' I remember I used to know the march from *Norma* by heart; I'd even tried it once not so many years ago and seemed to make a go of it. Surely I can play it now. The first phrase is the same in the treble and bass: G B-flat D. I place my fingers on G B-flat D and off I go. But after the eighth bar I can go no farther . . .

'You really *don't* know how to play,' says Provazník with a snarl.

'Wood-chopping,' the landlord mutters.

I break out into the sweat of humiliation.

'Well, I think it's remarkable!' cries the landlord's daughter. 'He's never played the piano, yet look what he can do. You must have enormous talent, Dr Krumlovský!' I could hug her! What a heart! 'I've suspected it for a long time now. He whistles so well. What was it you were whistling this morning? *Traviata*, yes, I heard you.'

How observant! It's that womanly curiosity of hers. Or perhaps . . . Could it be? Blast it! No, why blast it? I can't quite say I desire her any more than, well, like her, but it would be a pity if . . .

'Let me play one of my songs without words,' says the landlord, who has taken my place at the spinet.

He starts to play, but after a few bars he too can go no farther. Of course. It's afternoon! I clap. Provazník sneers. 'A fine little ditty. Perfect for begging.'

Just then Mrs Augusta arrives. She has been searching for Pepík and finally found him at the skittle alley of a nearby garden restaurant. He had given two kreutzers to the boy who sets up the skittles, and instructed him to call out how many fell each time. For this Pepík gets his ears soundly boxed in front of all present and must sit through his mother's sermon. I notice she's stopped lisping. Ah, the curative powers of a hungry dog! 'You're to stay at home! You're not to budge! Now run and fetch me the baby!' Pepík shuffles off.

The next thing we know, a shrill scream fills the house. Pepík appears at the top of the steps clutching the baby by the scruff of the neck as if it were a puppy. The scream quickly subsides: the baby has turned blue. Mrs Augusta runs up to them, grabs the baby, and gives Pepík a few more slaps.

The painter too is in poor spirits, of course, moaning about how little his art brings in.

'Why not try woodcarving or sculpture?' Provazník suggests. 'You're still young enough to switch over.'

'Woodcarving! Why, woodcarvers are starving to death! Making monogrammed sausage skewers!'

I've invited the landlord's daughter to come and sit with me in an arbour. We're talking or, rather, as I notice, I'm talking. Today, unlike yesterday, I seem to have no trouble finding words. And if all my words are about me, myself, well, that's not so bad: at least when one speaks of oneself, one is passionate, well informed and specific. I can see she admires me. She keeps drawing my attention to talents or good qualities I exhibit. She has quite a lively mind. A pleasant creature!

Klikeš has a long and earnest chat with Semper at supper. Semper listens with what is for him unusually close attention. Klikeš, it is clear, wishes Semper to marry again and has even found him a bride. 'Twenty-six. Three thousand. A broad circle of gentlemen friends. Popular.' I may soon get an invitation.

The lieutenant keeps looking in my direction. I've caught his eyes on me twenty times at least. What's on his mind?

*

I am studying, but not very well. I'd rather be sitting down in the garden, either alone or with the others. My thoughts are off in the . . . (I can't remember where.)

Oh, dear! Today the painter's getting his row over with early. If I read things right, he's already managed to beat a) his wife, b) his boy, c) the dog. The dog is still whimpering.

Now he's come to see me. He wonders if I have a decent sheet of writing paper. He needs to write to his brother the priest and hasn't got anything of the sort at home. He hates writing; it's worse than death. But if he must write, he must have quiet or his thoughts aren't worth a damn. 'And quiet in that hellhole I live in is hard to come by. The only way I can create order is to give them a taste of my hand, and the moment there's a peep out of them I'll give them more. I've sacked the maid: she had a mouth like a millrace.' That's the fourth since I've come!

I've given him his paper and send him on his way. A red-eyed Pepík comes in shortly thereafter. Have I got a good pen I can lend his father? I give him a pen.

I hear the painter pacing the floor. He must be thinking hard.

I went down to the shop next door. When I need something now, I simply get it myself. As I was returning, I ran into a friend, Dr Jensen, the director of the insane asylum, taking a leisurely stroll near the house.

'Hello there, doctor. What brings you here?'

'Pure chance. I was taking a walk. I like walking through Malá Strana. And you?'

'I live here now.'

'Where?'

'In this house.'

'Would you mind if I came in and visited for a while?'

I like Dr Jensen. He's intelligent, sober, a good companion. He likes my flat. He looks things over and has something to say about everything. I press him to take a seat; he refuses, he'd rather stand: standing by the window is so pleasant at this time of day. He has his back to the garden and is facing the first-floor passageway. There is a mirror on the wall next to the window, and he keeps looking into it. Serious as he is, he must also be a bit vain about his person. How did I choose Malá Strana? I had hoped to find a peaceful place to study, but found my neighbours less than peaceful. Who are my neighbours? I start by describing Provazník, who will surely be of interest to him as a psychiatrist. I give a lively account, going into great detail, but I can see he's not interested and keeps looking into the mirror. Suddenly he gives a start and leans out of the window. Is that the landlord's daughter in the passageway? Amazed, I ask, does he know her, then? Oh, he's known the family for ever. The question that flashes into my mind as I recall the landlord's rather obvious eccentricities is slow to reach my lips, but I finally blurt it out. 'God forbid!' the doctor says with a smile. 'He's just a hypochondriac, though his imaginary illnesses cause him suffering enough. No, I've known them almost since childhood. They were friends of my mother's. I can't imagine why Otylie hasn't found a husband. She's good-looking, she's pleasant, she knows how to manage a household. What's more, she's got money: the house is free of debt and there's capital besides. It's a shame, really. Such a good match.' He leans out again, smiles and nods.

So that's what he means by pure chance. The only

accidental thing about his stroll is that I should have turned up. I suddenly feel less well disposed towards Dr Jensen.

He soon takes his leave, promising to call again should he happen this way. I have the feeling my response was less than gracious.

★

He's as much of a bachelor as I am. No, absolutely not – I'm not thinking of anything of the sort. But it is true that when a lawyer starts off with a bit of capital behind him . . . Heh heh. Heh heh heh. Why such stupid thoughts? And why now?

Neruda must be right when he claims that we men are jealous of every woman, even when we haven't the slightest interest in her ourselves.

The painter is pacing the floor. Still thinking.

A calamity at dinner: a family of flies in my soup. I was preoccupied enough to swallow papa and mama, but I drew the line at the floating embryo. Flies for me, letters for Pepík, heirlooms for the dog – what we don't manage to eat in this house!

Now I know who it is! I happened to be standing at the window when the sabre rattled again. I lean out, and whom do I see but the fat lieutenant from the tavern, the very one who figures so prominently in my notes. A relative of the guard's wife?

An evening chat in the garden. Provazník whispers to me with great glee that he's seen signs that the young wife who lives next door to him has been crying. I must say I find him disgusting. Then he asks the landlord whether he attended the funeral of the cavalry captain today. 'No, I didn't. I don't go to funerals. I haven't been to one since my father died. There was singing at the coffin, and someone sang off key. It was awful. That awful dissonance has haunted me all my days.' Poetic, isn't it?

Enter the painter. His ruddy face shows traces of anxious reflection. 'Finished the letter?' I ask. 'No. Tomorrow maybe. These things take time with me.' 'It takes time to persuade your brother the priest to send you a couple of hundred guilders.' 'A couple of hundred! That's mere chicken feed these days!' 'Says you!' Provazník counters indignantly. 'If only you had some imagination, you people! I could live easily on *one* hundred! It's child's play. I'd rent a field outside Prague and sow it – know what with? Thistles! A fowler would see it and rent it from me and catch goldfinches on it or I'd catch them myself.' 'Don't forget to fence it in.' 'Why?' 'To keep it draught-free. You wouldn't want the thistle getting rheumatism, would you?' The painter's becoming quite the wit.

The landlord is inordinately depressed today. He isn't handing out 'throat' cards, but he thinks his nose is about to fall off. An article he read this morning says it all begins with a cold, and as he's had a cold for some days now he's quite certain one of his nostrils 'is starting to dangle'. But it's afternoon now, and he can't remember which one it is.

Otylie looks on sadly and can scarcely hide her sighs. We've gone off on our own again and are sitting and chatting again, but today the proportion is reversed: she does most of the talking – grieving, pouring out her soul – and I listen, feeling rather low myself at the thought of what she's been through. I suspect my sympathy comforts her.

They've gone. I'm all alone in the garden. I can't go to the tavern today. I'm not up to mixing with people. It's not like me at all. I feel a combination of melancholy and bliss.

★

Yesterday and today I woke up early. Perhaps it's the heat. Rising early should be good for my studies, only – well, I *wake* up, I don't *get* up. Lying in bed is so pleasant and my thoughts come and go so freely that when a particularly agreeable one shimmers in my golden slumber I cling to it and dream on.

Truth to tell, the thoughts have only the most general connection to my studies. I'm doing Mining Law now, and the unfamiliar terminology makes its way into everything: my bed seems an open shaft where I prospect for golden visions. When I stand next to

Otylka, my thoughts describe a circle around us, protecting our excavation rights.

I see I've written the endearing 'Otylka' for 'Otylie'.
I must be thinking of her in new ways. Careful,
careful!

Things are unusually quiet at the painter's. Augusta is
sitting at the table, leaning his head on his hand and
gazing upward in meditation.

An afternoon call from – Dr Jensen! The man means
business!

I am scarcely more than civil to him, but he seems
not to notice; indeed, he ignores me almost completely.

Now he is back at the mirror by the window. There
is no sadder sight than – than a man in front of the
mirror.

He sees the landlord and his daughter passing
through the courtyard into the garden and calls to
them from the window, addressing them rather freely.
Some people abuse old friendships blatantly. They
invite him to join them in the garden, and he presses
me to go too. Come, let's see who . . . No, we shan't
see who anything, because I don't *want* anything, anything at all.

The garden has a different feel to it today. It feels alien
to me. The atmosphere is different, the people. But
the more I think about it, the more I see it's all Dr

Jensen. Jensen's a good talker in the sense that he's superficial enough to have something interesting to say about everything. Gradually everyone but Provazník has drifted in, and they're all hanging on his every word. I'm sure I shouldn't like to be 'interesting'.

I make a feeble attempt to appropriate the conversation by asking the painter, 'Finished the letter yet?' 'No, tomorrow. It has to brew a little.' Whereupon he turns to Jensen and says, 'You must lead an interesting life, doctor.' 'How so?' 'I mean, life in the asylum must be one laugh after another. Tell us about it.' Foiled again! Where is that Provazník when I need him? But Jensen seems put out. He discourses on the difference between mania and melancholy, but that's not what they had in mind; they want to hear about 'people who think they're somebody else', in other words, the man who claims to be king or the woman who believes she's the Virgin Mary. Jensen refuses to satisfy them, going on about clinical matters, until at one point he remarks that 'each and every one of us bears the germs of mental illness in our psyche'. Nearly all of them protest; only the landlord nods matter-of-factly and says, 'Many is the man who fails to realise what he has when he has his health.'

Jensen finally takes his leave, promising to call again soon. 'If you never call,' I say to myself, 'it will be too soon.'

Provazník has not put in an appearance.

People go on far too long about Jensen. 'He frightens me!' Otylie whispers in my ear. 'A modicum of tact can do wonders,' I reply.

Klikeš is constantly prodding Semper. The innkeeper keeps hovering in their vicinity, coughing and staring at Klikeš as if he wished to devour him.

★

Nine o'clock and Jensen is back, peering out into the garden and along the passageway, gazing at least three times into the mirror and for lengthy intervals. Does anyone take early walks in the garden? No, I reply monosyllabically. At last: I'm not bothering you, am I? Well, it's high time I got to work. Off he goes, offended. Serves him right.

Towards noon the painter sends his new maid to ask for an envelope. Now I watch him through the window. His wife and son stand beside the table, looking on as he writes the address.

The painter is pacing again, clutching the envelope. From time to time he stops and gazes pensively at the fruit of his mental labours. He must take a certain pride in it.

I am the first in the garden this afternoon. It seems an eternity before the others arrive. Otylie and the landlord do not appear for an hour. The landlord embarks on a political tirade which concludes that all the ills of the world stem from the fact 'kings are never satisfied with what they've got'. I nod vigorously. Out come one after another of his maxims; I admire them all. Then he takes to tying up vines, and Otylie and I slip off for an intimate chat. God only knows how it happens, but before long we're talking about my 'virtues'. Otylie praises them to the skies, stretching them as a cobbler stretches leather to get one more pair of shoes. Where could she have learned of my 'virtues'?

The painter and his wife, the former looking happy, all but triumphant, the latter wielding her tongue like a sword. 'Finished with the letter?' I ask. 'Of course!' he says, as if he could toss off the continent's correspondence in half a day. 'You should have told him about the guard's wife,' says Mrs Augusta. 'Priests love that sort of thing.' What should he have told him about the guard's wife? I wonder. 'I have one more letter to write. To my other brother in Tarnov. We've agreed to write twice a year.' Imperceptibly the conversation moves back to the guard's wife. Someone brings up the lieutenant and how the guard's wife pops out her head whenever he comes along. They keep glancing at me and laughing and suddenly it dawns on me: *that's* why I'm stupid! I'm so furious I can't remember what I said.

Then we have a threesome of twenty-six. All through the game I put up with the landlord's mistakes and agree with everything he says. I even stretch out my leg for him under the table; he stomps on it like an organist.

Provazník doesn't come down today either.

Never have I done anything so stupid in all my life!

I went to my friend Morousek's for supper. Since he lives on the far side of Smíchov, I took a cab at the gate. We talked well into the night; then I walked slowly home, my head racing with thoughts. It was a beautiful night, the streets all but empty, only a sleepy cabby urging his tired mare home, the mare dragging its feet, the vehicle barely trundling along. I found the monotonous rattle of its wheels almost pleasant. About two houses from my flat it caught up with me, and the cabby leaned down from his box and said, 'Wouldn't you like to have a seat, young man?' It was my own cab! I had forgotten to pay the man and discharge him, and he'd waited for me all that time. Three guilders I owed the villain!

There's no mistaking it – I'm in love!

This is how it might read, appearing out of nowhere among the notices in the newspaper: 'To Dr Krumlovský and his much esteemed bride Otylie . . .', though those fellows call all brides 'much esteemed'. No one must suspect a thing, even if . . . *We must clear things up between us!*

★

A fine spectacle! I'm shaking with rage! It's enough to make you sick!

The rattle of a sabre outside. A knock on the door. 'Come in!' In comes a sublieutenant (rather than the lieutenant I'd expected). I rise and give my visitor a curious glance. He is in full dress, complete with shako. He salutes.

'Are you Dr Krumlovský?'

I nod.

'I am here on behalf of Lieutenant Rubacký.' That is the name of the fat lieutenant from the tavern, the one who visits the guard's wife.

'And what does he want of me?'

'The lieutenant feels you insulted him by using certain expressions here in the garden yesterday, expressions having to do with himself and the guard's wife. He has sent me to demand satisfaction from you.'

I clapped my fist to my forehead and stared at him, trying to reconstruct what had gone on. Yes, the topic had come up and I had said something, but I couldn't for the life of me remember what it was.

The sublieutenant waited quietly for an answer. I could feel myself starting to tremble. 'I . . . It . . . There must be some mistake. Who told the lieutenant?'

'I don't know.'

A gossip? Or could the guard's wife have been listening from my window? With the lieutenant, perhaps?

'There *was* something said about them. I remember

that. But what could I possibly have said? I don't know the lieutenant, or know him only by sight.'

'That is none of my business, I'm sure. I am here to demand satisfaction.'

'But I assure you I have nothing against the lieutenant! On the contrary, I respect him, I . . .'

'As I've told you, I must have an answer.'

'Well, if on the basis of a piece of gossip the lieutenant believes I have insulted him – which, God knows, I never intended – then you may tell him I beg his pardon.'

'That is not enough.'

'But what does he want? Does he expect me to stand up in front of one and all and . . .'

'He expects you to fight.'

'Well, then he's mad! I've never fought in my life and I don't intend to start now!'

'I shall tell him so.'

And so saying, he saluted and slammed the door.

Good riddance!

I'm shaking with rage! A duel! I don't know which end of a sword is up. Besides, how can I, a doctor of law, a future lawyer, engage in an activity proscribed by § 57 of the Penal Code, especially given the consequences described in §§ 158–165? Lunatics! They're a pack of lunatics!

I hear the guard's wife bustling about in the kitchen and go to see her. I'd like to have it out with her, and do my best to broach the subject, but she responds with a truculent 'Go home and put some weight on' and turns her back on me. All right, then, I shall 'go home and put some weight on'. What an odd thing to say!

The garden seems quite strange today, and I'm very nervous. I can't do anything about it.

Provazník is back, staring at everyone like an owl and saying, 'My, my! You are looking poorly today!'

Sitting with Otylie in our arbour, I decide that today is the day for me to speak to her of love. Each time I try, however, the words seem to stick in my throat and I come out with pure drivel. I set it aside for today.

Provazník comes up, looks at us for a moment, then says, 'Do you intend to marry, doctor?'

How unpleasant! I swallow my embarrassment, force a smile to my lips, and reply, 'Why, yes, Mr Provazník, I do.'

'And right you are! It must be grand. And children are so amusing. Even more so than a butcher's dog.'

Damn him!

All the conversations seem to drag today. I don't say a word about my visitor.

★

This is awful! The devil lured me here to Malá Strana!

What can I do? It's my own fault. I could easily have said no. He probably wouldn't have made good on his threat. But even a lamb's blood can boil. He'll wound me – that's for certain. And I shan't do him a bit of harm. I'll take to my bed, fall behind in my studies; I may even miss the exam. Perhaps it would be better if he killed me!

The sabre-rattling again and the knock, followed by yesterday's sublieutenant, shako and all. He salutes and informs me that Lieutenant Rubacký has no intention of altering his demands. I respond, rather petulantly, that if yesterday I said no, today I say absolutely not. In that case, says the sublieutenant, he regrets to inform me that the lieutenant promises me a good whipping whenever he sees me. Furious, I leap to my feet and stand bristling before him. 'He'll use no whip on me, you have my word for it!' 'We'll see about that! Good day, sir.' 'Wait! What is his weapon?' 'The sabre.' 'Fine, I accept!' The sublieutenant stares at me in amazement. 'I accept!' I repeat, still bristling, 'but upon the following conditions: you must provide me with a weapon and a second, and you must give me your word – and the word of everyone else involved – that no one shall ever learn of the duel.'

'I give you my word of honour.' He takes his leave with great civility, exaggerated civility. He will return today or tomorrow to discuss the arrangements.

So I've done it! It may leak out somehow. The guard's wife may well have overheard our rather too vociferous dialogue – indeed, I'll wager she listened in: she's behind it all, in any case. From my present vantage point I can see I offended her female vanity from the start. But that didn't make me stupid. This does. And should she betray us, it's the end of my career! A clerk to the end of my days. True, I've got a bit of capital, and then there's Otylie – but would she even have me?

It goes without saying I've stopped studying. Oh, I have a book in front of me, but all I do is curse myself.

A letter has come in the post. It is postmarked Malá Strana, but is anonymous. Damn that Provazník!

> Dear Examination Candidate,
> You seem more of a candidate for matrimony than a candidate for the Bar. But your desire for matrimony is of the lowest order. You want a house, you want money; you don't want a wife. In any case, you can't want that withered old maid who, to make matters worse, is dead from the neck up ['dead from the neck up' – I've heard that several times from Provazník's lips]. Shame on you for selling yourself and your young life – and so cheaply too. Shame, shame, a hundred times shame!
> Signed: One Who Writes What Many Think

Just you wait! I may not get back at the lieutenant, but I'll get back at you. I've turned so belligerent I could take on the world!

I don't fear for my life; I don't fear being wounded. I'm still quite calm, in fact. Even though I've never seen a duel, never even imagined one, I know fear will come, and it's *fear* I'm afraid of. I'll be so wrought up my every nerve will tremble, my every muscle twitch; I'll shake with fever, yawn with fright. It will be horrible!

We're chatting in the garden, but what a trial! I'll make no declaration today. What good would it do? Have a kerchief ready, Otylie; find some gauze. If I die, it's all over; if I'm wounded, Otylka will nurse me – at least I think she will – and then the declaration will come of itself. As in novels.

Still, I have to talk about something. What? Finally I ask whether she is going to the Czech theatre tomorrow. What are they doing? she asks. Tyl's *Jan Hus*, I tell her. It's the sixth of July, the anniversary of his death at the stake.[5] 'I'd have liked to go, but I shan't go to *Hus*.' 'Why not? Surely not because he was a heretic?' 'No, because tomorrow is Friday, a fast day.' Provazník would see 'death from the neck up' in this; I see simplicity, and simplicity has its charms.

And here he comes, Provazník himself! I run up to him and drag him off to an arbour. 'How dare you, you villain, send me one of your anonymous letters? Well? Answer me.'

'Who told you about my anonymous letters?' he asks, white as chalk.

'You did, you blackguard!'

'I did?' he said with such imbecilic surprise in his face that I had to turn away to keep from laughing.

'And if you ever do anything like that again, I'll tear you limb from limb!'

I stalk off. At least I've learned something from the lieutenant.

Later we sit down to twenty-six, but when the painter takes the pack of cards from the drawer he immediately grabs Pepík by the scruff of the neck. Another hiding. Every heart has been cut out of the cards. He has pasted them on to white paper and given them to Semper's Márinka as a love token.

So we can't play, to my great relief.

We talk and talk, but nothing is said. Otylie and I go for a walk through the flowerbeds. Suddenly she turns to me, looks me in the eye, and asks whether anything's the matter. I'm speechless, but finally say, No, nothing, and force a laugh. She shakes her head and repeats several times that she's certain there's something troubling me.

She must feel a certain affection for me. Yes, she must.

I am at home, thinking. I'm amazingly calm. The fear has yet to come, but come it will.

Perhaps I can't quite believe the duel will take place.

But tomorrow . . .

★

There! Today I did get up early. I awoke before three and, instead of lolling in bed, got up at once. I feel terribly serious.

Now I don't know what to do with the time. I've been down to the garden twice, but came back up again immediately. I pick up one thing after another, but keep nothing for more than a moment.

When will the sublieutenant come?

Am I or am I not afraid? I'm nervous and shaking a bit, but that may just be feverish impatience.

He's been and gone. It will be tomorrow at six in the morning in the gardens of the Castle Barracks. They'll carry you out of the gardens, I thought, laughing to myself at what was not much of a joke.

He was the picture of courtesy. He even said something to the effect that 'he would be happy if the unfortunate incident could be settled somehow'. 'There's no need for that!' I blurted out. I could have kicked myself. But what of it?

I've gone to see my Smíchov friend Morousek. First, because I couldn't stand sitting at home, and second, because Morousek is a first-rate swordsman with a reputation for ruthlessness and I hope he can give me a few pointers.

Morousek is terribly unpleasant: I've told him everything – and he laughs. Some people can't take anything seriously. I ask him to show me a few tricks, anything he thinks might help. He says I can't learn a thing in so short a time. 'We'll see about that!' I say, nettled.

He takes out some combat foils, gives me a mask

and guard, and places me in position. First this then that! No, not like that! Watch out for the end of the foil! Good! Now my foil's on the ground. 'Keep a firmer grip on the weapon!' he says, laughing. 'But it's so heavy!' 'The sabre won't be much lighter. Come on! Try again!' After a while I'm as exhausted as if I were hoisting an anvil with one hand. To the tall, sinewy Morousek it's nothing at all. 'Take a rest,' he says, laughing again. Morousek was once a good deal more agreeable than he is now. I tell him so. 'That's your jitters talking.' 'No, it isn't. I'm not the least bit frightened. Really I'm not!' 'Well, then, let's try again.' Before long I'm exhausted again. 'We mustn't overdo it, or you won't be able so much as to lift an arm tomorrow morning. You'll stay for dinner and we'll practise on and off, but only for short intervals.' I had no intention of leaving, in any case. His wife thinks we're playing and laughs as she watches us. These people laugh at the drop of a hat.

Shortly before dinner Morousek asks whether Rubacký is a good swordsman. I don't know. 'Then there's nothing for it,' he says, bullying me back into the guard, 'but to learn the quick surprise attack. It's your only hope.'

It's a fine thing, the quick surprise attack, only I can't get the hang of it. I'm not quick enough to surprise anybody, Morousek tells me, but what can I do? 'Dinner's ready!' calls Mrs Morousek. I'm so glad!

But I can scarcely hold a spoon, and my hand shakes so that I spill my soup. Morousek laughs. 'Wait till you're standing over your chopped-up friend tomorrow!' I almost hope *I* get chopped up – if only to wipe the smile off Morousek's face.

Twice more he forces me to take up the sword. I slice away like a madman at the air and at Morousek, then collapse on the ground in mask and guard and refuse to get up. 'Upsy-daisy and rub yourself down with brandy.' I give myself a brandy rub until I smell so strong that Mrs Morousek picks up her embroidery and moves to the far end of the garden. I too should have liked to run away from myself!

I don't leave until late in the evening. My elbows and knees ache something awful. Have my legs been fencing too?

There's a letter waiting for me at home. From Otylie!

> Dear Dr Krumlovský,
> I must, I absolutely must speak to you some time today. Please go down to the garden the moment you return. You have only to whistle *Traviata* and I shall be with you. Forgive my scribble. I write out of sympathy for you.
>
> Otylie

The guard's wife has talked. There will be a scene!

I go down to the garden. The moon is shining, and I can see clearly through the courtyard and into the first-floor passageway. No one there.

I pace back and forth for a while. Someone has

appeared. A figure in white. I step out into the moonlight, then withdraw into the shadow. Time for *Traviata*. What in the world is the matter with me? I whistle
the trash all day long, and now I can't remember it
for the life of me. Still, she can't have missed me. I'll
just whistle something else. And since nothing but
'Pepík, Pepík, what's our little Káča up to?' comes to
mind, that's what I whistle.

'Is that you, Dr Krumlovský?' I hear from the
painter's window. 'What are you doing in the garden
so late?' The painter is hanging out of the window in a
shocking state of disarray. 'Though it's a lovely night,
isn't it? I have no desire to sleep either. Let's talk.'

The figure in the passageway has disappeared.

'I was just on my way home, actually,' I call out to
him in an intentionally louder than necessary voice.
That's all I need – to stand here and chat with the
painter! He'd probably keep me till morning.

I start off slowly across the courtyard, whistling
again. Believe it or not, *Traviata* has suddenly come
back to me. I pause, look one way, then the other.
There's no one on the stairs, no one in the passage.
Could Otylie have taken offence at my 'Pepík'?

Maybe it's better for us not to talk today. Yes,
definitely. But tomorrow?

The painter is still lolling at his window. I'd like to
look out at the passageway, but he would see me and
start a conversation. I draw the curtains.

Last will and testament. After all, I must put my

affairs in order. But it will be short, clear, no more than a line or two. I leave everything to my sister, and that's an end of it.

There. And now to sleep. I'm still calm, surprisingly so, but tomorrow I'll be trembling like a leaf, I'm certain.

I wind the alarm clock.

I see the painter at his window. Sleep tight, dilettante.

★

I've slept hardly two hours, yet feel rested. It's grey out – in July the day begins at three – grey and chilly. I give a great yawn. I'm shivering a little, though not actually trembling.

I don't know what to do with myself. I don't want to go down to the garden. To the street, then? No, in my feverish state I'd break into a run and tire myself out. Besides, my arms still ache from yesterday. Maybe I should go through my papers, straighten them up a bit.

Before I know it, it's half past five. I look about the room as though I'd forgotten something. What could I have forgotten?

Farewell, then.

I race down the steps into the courtyard, bound through the courtyard to the gate, and leap through

333

the gate into the street, practically weeping for joy –
yes, my eyes are moist. I'm like a prisoner emerging
from a vault into the light of day. I turn to the right,
to the left, I don't know which way to go.

'Krumlovský! Well?'

Morousek! Poor Morousek! I fall on his neck, the
tears running down my cheeks. I can't speak. 'Well?
Will there be a duel?' 'It's all over!' 'Thank God! But
let go of my arm, will you? You'll crush it to bits!' I
realise I'm clutching his arm like a vice.

'Here, hop in this cab. It's ours. Have you had
breakfast yet?' 'Breakfast? No.' 'Then let's go to a
wine shop.' 'Yes. No. Home first, then to the wine
shop.' Otylie must be anxious to hear how I've fared.

We climb into the cab. I laugh and prattle like a
child. Heaven knows what I'm saying. I don't even
notice we've arrived. I dance up the stairs, talking in
a loud, unseemly voice: I want everyone in the house
to hear.

The guard's wife flees from the kitchen to her room.
Surprised, aren't you? Well, this is only the beginning!

The familiar surroundings calm me down a little.
'Do you realise you haven't told me a thing?' says
Morousek, lighting a cigar and stretching out on the
couch.

Yes, right, I haven't said a word about it. I must
take hold of myself and gather my thoughts.

There were two of them at the entrance to the barracks. They took me across the courtyard, down the

steps and into the gardens, where the lieutenant and a doctor were waiting. One of the two officers who had met me at the gate introduced himself as my second. He told me that everything was as it should be, the weapons identical. I believe I bowed. Then Rubacký's sublieutenant and second came up to me and said, 'As the gentlemen harbour no particular personal animosity against each other, the duel will take place, but I propose it should be only to first blood. Is that acceptable to you, sir?' 'It is,' I replied. 'Agreed, then,' said the sublieutenant, and removed his overcoat. I did the same.

I was handed a sabre, and we took our stations and crossed swords, as you showed me yesterday. Suddenly, 'the surprise attack' invades my brain, waterfalls thunder, stars flash, and I hear both seconds crying 'Stop!' and leaping between us with their swords. Stepping back instinctively, I see a stream of blood trickling down my opponent's face. I think I saluted with my sabre as an officer should – yes, I'm sure I did, and presented it with a bow to my second. Then I pulled on my overcoat with great dignity and, hearing the doctor say, 'It's only a light wound,' took my leave. As I withdrew, someone muttered, 'A devilishly fierce fellow, that!' I could take on the whole world now. And nothing, absolutely nothing has leaked out. It's only a light wound, word of honour, so no one need know. And I have you to thank for it, dear friend!

Morousek laughs. 'Well, either he's a miserable

swordsman or you really did take him by surprise. In any case, you do me credit – and on your first try!'

I feel like a hero. I prance about the room, pause in front of the mirror, gaze at myself and essay a smile, but it looks silly on me.

Morousek stands. 'I'm starving. Let's go to that wine shop, shall we?' Oddly enough, I'm not hungry. 'So you haven't had breakfast yet, either?' 'When would I have had time?'

For the first time I realise how noble Morousek has been. 'Where did you find a cab so early?' 'I ordered it yesterday at noon, when you were visiting us.' 'Dear old Morousek!' I fling my arms around his neck. It's all he can do to shake me off. I can be incredibly strong at times.

A small wine shop. Two acquaintances: the innkeeper and Semper the tailor. We shake hands. 'How's this? The innkeeper out and about?' 'My first time out in ten years.'

We sit at another table. We have something to eat and drink, and Morousek, keeping his voice down, tries to persuade me to move. It's urgent, he says: the guard's wife is up to no good; besides, I'm unable to concentrate on my studies and time is of the essence. He's absolutely right. Where might I go? I'd prefer my former flat. 'Fine, then let's take a cab there and see if you can get it back.' What a friend! A splendid chap in every way. I'm terribly fond of him and can't for the life of me remember why I should ever have thought him the least bit disagreeable.

The innkeeper is hot under the collar; he raises his voice more and more, urging Semper not to marry, not on any account. Klikeš is the root of all evil. Women are contemptible. When Semper leaves to buy cigars, I go over and ask the innkeeper, 'Why do you so want to dissuade him?' 'I'm an innkeeper, aren't I? I've got a limited number of regulars and I've got to keep them.' 'But he needs a good housekeeper; he needs a mother for his daughter.' 'No, he's a good customer. He takes two meals a day and drinks more than his share . . .' But Semper is back.

The flat is unoccupied; they're only too glad to give it to me. I'll be moving back the day after tomorrow, Monday. What will Otylie say? She'll take it in her stride, I expect, especially as it will be both explanation and declaration. Besides, I can visit her every other day or even every day if she likes. Were the news of the duel to get about, they'd admire me – but my career comes first.

Morousek takes me home for dinner. We go through the duel again over the table. Morousek is in a jolly mood. I think he's making fun of me. That, to put it mildly, is both thoughtless and uncalled for.

I hurry home in the evening and head immediately for the garden.

Otylie is definitely angry. She won't answer my

questions, even tries to avoid me. I should have thought she'd be overjoyed to see me.

A woman's whims can be less than pleasant.

I go off to my former Old Town tavern and have a fine old time. I'm the soul of wit, if I do say so myself. They are surprised at how cheerful I am and how well I look. Yes, and only a few hours before I might have been laid out on my bier!

Tonight, I hope, I shall sleep soundly!

★

I awake very early – a result of yesterday's sleep – but am quite serene, as serene as a newborn babe in a nice warm bath, and after stretching my little arms and legs I return to the Land of Nod, where I lie blissfully until nine.

Dr Jensen is here. *Le pourquoi?* You're in for a surprise. Yes, this very day.

He presses my hand with unusual warmth and makes several attempts to light his cigar. He feels he must tell me what brings him here so that I shan't think it odd. He walks over to the table for matches. Tell me what brings him here? Does he think I'm blind? Now he's back at the mirror – a regular Narcissus!

'Just opposite you here on the second floor,' he begins, 'lives a man named Provazník. Oh, I forgot. You've spoken of him several times. In any case, ten years ago and again eight years ago he was a patient of ours at the asylum. At various intervals I have kept an eye on him at the request of his wealthy relatives, and they have recently asked me to resume. I was delighted to find you living in his house and especially in this flat, because I could be as inconspicuous as possible: he knows me and avoids me; he never goes into the garden when I'm there, though otherwise, as you tell me, he is there every day. I can see him perfectly here in your mirror: he is standing behind the curtains with only his head protruding slightly. I should mention that from all I've observed there is no need to fear a new breakdown.'

Both my mouth and eyes open wide. What? Was that all?

Admittedly, I feel a certain relief, though a certain disappointment as well.

The doctor has gone. I feel I ought to have called after him, 'If only you'd . . . because I . . . what I mean is, I'd never have . . .' And suddenly I can't imagine how the idea of rivalry ever entered my mind. I feel I . . . A man is a strange creature!

I have just informed the guard's wife in a few dry words that I shall be vacating the premises tomorrow evening. She heard me out with her eyes on the ground and never said a word. She always lowers her eyes now in my presence. I've tamed you!

Oddly enough, never once in all my time here did

I catch a glimpse of the guard. He always seemed to be . . . Well, maybe it's better this way. I suspect I'd only have felt sorry for him.

Otylie is still angry. To be honest, I am not particularly concerned. If anything, I feel slightly offended. When I announced to everyone in the garden that I was moving, she received the news coolly, even coldly, as though I'd told her I'd dropped a spoon. A woman is a strange creature!
Thank God I never declared my 'love' to her.

I've been back to my Old Town tavern. I am invigorated by those people and leave them feeling fitter for work. To work, yes, to work! Once I have done with this examination, I shall never need to take another!

★

I'm in the throes of moving.

Another thrashing at the painter's, another row: it's time for another letter. He's sent to me for paper again. I ask the maid to tell him I've finished packing and have no idea where it is.

The landlord's daughter is slicing lettuce in the garden. I watch her coolly. She's past her prime.

No more Malá Strana tales from Neruda, please!

Notes

This volume collects stories written in the decade 1867 to 1877 and published in 1878 as *Povídky malostranské* (Tales of Malá Strana).

INTRODUCTION

1 There are, for example, instances of anti-semitism in some stories – in particular 'A Week in a Quiet House' – which appear to reflect the cultural prejudices and racial stereotypes of the time and place he describes rather than Neruda's personal feelings.

HOW IT CAME TO PASS

1 These men, rebels all, were heroes of the fifteenth-century Hussite Wars. They belonged to the radical wing, known as the Taborites, which called for the abolition of feudalism in addition to communion in both kinds and related Church reforms. Especially in the period after the failure of the 1848 Revolution, when this story takes place, Czech patriots saw them as forerunners of their national movement. Žižka, their first and most prominent leader, had the reputation of being particularly uncompromising.

2 Each of these has Hussite overtones. The chalice sym-

bolises communion in both kinds and thus represents the Hussite call for democratisation within the Church; the halberd, a forerunner of the bayonet, was a common weapon in the fifteenth century and therefore among Hussite warriors; the flail was transformed from an agricultural implement to a weapon by the Hussites, who used it together with farmers' carts to form easily movable barricades.

3 Žižka defeated Emperor Sigismund at Německý Brod in southern Bohemia. Přemysl Otakar I ruled Bohemia between 1197 and 1230.

THE WATER SPRITE
1 In the Czech folk tradition the water sprite (*hastrman*) usually has a pigtail and wears breeches and a green frock-coat. The name Rybář means 'Fisher'.

FIGURES
1 Karel Hynek Mácha (1810–36) is the foremost Czech Romantic poet. See also the 'Introduction' to the present volume.

2 Czech cities had undergone forced Germanisation as a result of the Thirty Years' War. National reformers 'reintroduced' Czech to the urban populace during the nineteenth century as an integral part of their patriotic programme.

3 František Palacký (1798–1876) was the father of modern Czech historiography and a powerful figure in the Czech national movement. Albrecht von Wallenstein or Waldstein (Valdštejn in Czech), an important general in the Thirty

Years' War, made his fortune at the expense of the Czech anti-Catholic nobility. The scene with the Capuchin friar, however, comes more from Schiller's *Wallenstein* trilogy than from history. Jan Žižka was the military and ideological leader of the early fifteenth-century Taborite movement described in Note 1 to 'How It Came to Pass . . .'

4 The play in question is by Josef Kajetán Tyl (1808–56), the foremost playwright of the national movement. The situation reflects the primacy of German mentioned in Note 2 above. Even though the lieutenant has seen the play in Czech, he remembers the title in his own – faulty – German translation.

5 Like the play mentioned in the previous note, *Jan Hus* is by Josef Kajetán Tyl. It represents an appreciation of its eponymous hero, the great Czech priest who devoted his life to exposing the injustices of the clergy and laid the foundation for Luther's Protestant reforms. He was burned at the stake as a heretic at the Council of Constance in 1415.

Central European Classics

This series presents nineteenth- and twentieth-century fiction from Central Europe. Introductions by leading contemporary Central European writers explain why the chosen titles have become classics in their own countries. New or newly revised English translations ensure that the writing can be appreciated by readers here and now.

The selection of titles is the result of extensive discussion with critics, writers and scholars in the field. However, it can not and does not aim to be comprehensive. Many books highly prized in their own countries are too difficult, specific or allusive to work in translation. Much good modern Central European fiction is already available. Thus, for example, the contemporary Czech novelists Kundera, Hrabal, Klíma and Škvorecký can all be read in English. Could one as easily name four well-known and well-translated contemporary French, Dutch or Spanish novelists?

Yet, if one reaches back a little further into the past, one finds that it is the Central European literature written in German which has been most translated –

whether Kafka, Musil or Joseph Roth. We therefore start this series with books originally written in Czech, Hungarian and Polish.

The Central European Classics have been conceived and sponsored by the Central and East European Publishing Project. A charity based in Oxford, the Project has since 1986 worked to reduce the cultural and intellectual division of Europe by supporting independent, quality publishing of both books and journals in Central and Eastern Europe, and translations from, into and between the languages of Central and Eastern Europe. The Project's Chairman is Sir Ralf Dahrendorf, and its Board of Trustees comprises, beside the General Editor of this series, György Bence, François Furet, Raymond Georis, Jerzy Jedlicki, Jane Kramer, Laurens van Krevelen, Eda Kriseová, Per Wästberg and Elizabeth Winter. Sally Laird was Project Director at the inception of the series, and contributed much to its design.

We hope each book can be enjoyed in its own right, as literature in English. But we also hope the series may contribute to a deeper understanding of the culture and history of countries which, since the opening of the iron curtain, have been coming closer to us in many other ways.

Timothy Garton Ash